A LIFE

GUY DE MAUPASSANT was born of upper-middle-class parents in Normandy in 1850. After the failure of his parents' marriage he lived with his mother at Étretat, a newly fashionable seaside resort. Having enrolled as a law student in 1869, he was called up after the outbreak of the Franco-Prussian War in 1870 and served as a quartermaster's clerk in Rouen. Following the war he left the army and eventually secured a post as a minor civil servant. His favourite pastimes were womanizing and boating, especially at Argenteuil on the Seine, which was also a favourite haunt of the Impressionists. Flaubert, whom he knew through his mother, encouraged his literary activities and shaped both his style and his pessimistic outlook on life. Through Flaubert he came to know the leading figures in Parisian cultural life, notably Émile Zola, who recruited him to his new 'Naturalist' school of writing. *Boule de Suif*, his short story about a prostitute during the Franco-Prussian War, was hailed as a masterpiece by both Flaubert and the reading public. A leading figure in fashionable society and artistic circles, Maupassant wrote prolifically and was soon the bestselling author in France after Zola. During the following decade he wrote nearly 300 stories, 200 newspaper articles, six novels, and three travel books. He earned substantial sums of money, which he spent on yachts, women, travel, and houses, and on his mother, and his younger brother Hervé, who eventually died insane in an asylum in Lyons in 1889. Despite his enthusiasm for sex and outdoor pursuits, Maupassant's own health had never been good. A nervous disorder possibly inherited from his mother was compounded by syphilis, contracted in 1876, and he consulted numerous doctors in the course of his short life. On New Year's Day 1892 he attempted suicide with a paper-knife and was removed to the clinic of Dr Blanche at Passy, suffering from the syphilitic paresis, or general paralysis, which had driven him mad. He died on 6 July 1893 at the age of 42.

ROGER PEARSON is Professor of French in the University of Oxford and Fellow and Praelector in French at The Queen's College, Oxford. He is the author of *Stendhal's Violin: A Novelist and His Reader* (Oxford, 1988), *The Fables of Reason: A Study of Voltaire's 'contes philosophiques'* (Oxford, 1993), and *Unfolding Mallarmé: The Development of a Poetic Art* (Oxford, 1996). For Oxford World's Classics he has translated and edited Voltaire, *Candide and Other Stories* (1990) and Zola, *La Bête humaine* (1996), and revised and edited Thomas Walton's translation of Zola, *The Masterpiece* (1993).

OXFORD WORLD'S CLASSICS

*For over 100 years Oxford World's Classics have brought
readers closer to the world's great literature. Now with over 700
titles—from the 4,000-year-old myths of Mesopotamia to the
twentieth century's greatest novels—the series makes available
lesser-known as well as celebrated writing.*

*The pocket-sized hardbacks of the early years contained
introductions by Virginia Woolf, T. S. Eliot, Graham Greene,
and other literary figures which enriched the experience of reading.
Today the series is recognized for its fine scholarship and
reliability in texts that span world literature, drama and poetry,
religion, philosophy and politics. Each edition includes perceptive
commentary and essential background information to meet the
changing needs of readers.*

OXFORD WORLD'S CLASSICS

GUY DE MAUPASSANT

A Life
The Humble Truth

Translated with an Introduction and Notes by
ROGER PEARSON

OXFORD
UNIVERSITY PRESS

OXFORD

UNIVERSITY PRESS

Great Clarendon Street, Oxford OX2 6DP

Oxford University Press is a department of the University of Oxford.
It furthers the University's objective of excellence in research, scholarship,
and education by publishing worldwide in

Oxford New York

Auckland Cape Town Dar es Salaam Hong Kong Karachi Kuala Lumpur
Madrid Melbourne Mexico City Nairobi New Delhi Shanghai
Taipei Toronto

With offices in

Argentina Austria Brazil Chile Czech Republic France Greece
Guatemala Hungary Italy Japan South Korea Poland Portugal
Singapore Switzerland Thailand Turkey Ukraine Vietnam

Oxford is a registered trade mark of Oxford University Press
in the UK and in certain other countries .

Published in the United States
by Oxford University Press Inc., New York

Translated with an Introduction and Notes © Roger Pearson 1999

First published as a World's Classics paperback 1999
Reissued 2009

British Library Cataloguing in Publication Data

Data available

Library of Congress Cataloging in Publication Data

Maupassant, Guy de, 1850–1893
[Vie English]
A life/Guy de Maupassant; translated with an introduction and notes by Roger Pearson.
(Oxford world's classics)
Includes bibliographical references.
I. Pearson, Roger. II. Title. III. Series: Oxford world's classics (Oxford University Press)
PQ2349.V4E6 1999 843'.8—dc21 98-32139

ISBN 978-0-19-955551-2

Typeset by RefineCatch Limited, Bungay, Suffolk
Printed in Great Britain by
Clays Ltd, Elcograf S.p.A

CONTENTS

CONTENTS

INTRODUCTION

> A work of art is superior only if it is at once
> a symbol and the accurate expression of a
> particular reality.
>
> (Maupassant, *La Vie errante*)

*Readers who do not wish to learn details of the plot will prefer
to treat the Introduction as an Epilogue.*

Guy de Maupassant and *A Life*

What is a life? A biological blip or a subtle construct of will and
circumstance? A measured progress through time and space,
from the spasm of departure to a mortal terminus, or an eddy in
the swirling current of eternity? And how shall a storyteller con-
ceive a life? As a causal chain in which the child is truly father to
the man, or as some contingent and promiscuous sequence of
accident and ephemeral impulse? As a plotted adventure of
exploit, place, and character, or a grey tedium punctuated by
non-events and peopled with faceless non-entities? What if art
means pattern and life has none? How, then, can any story be true
to life? These are some of the questions which inform *A Life*
(1883), the first of Guy de Maupassant's six novels.

His own life did not lack for event or entity. Born in Normandy
in 1850, he was the elder son of Gustave de Maupassant, a man of
some means but little resolve, who squandered the means and
lavished such determination as he possessed upon the pursuit of
women. Guy's mother, Laure Le Poittevin, a cultivated but
febrile woman, had been a friend since childhood of Gustave
Flaubert (1821–80), author of *Madame Bovary* (1857) and later
the literary mentor and 'departed friend' to whose memory *A Life*
is dedicated. Maupassant's parents separated formally in 1863
(divorce, briefly legalized between 1792 and 1816, did not become
lawful again in France until 1884), and the young Guy went to

live with his mother and younger brother Hervé at Étretat on the coast of Normandy. In 1867 the two boys began to go to school in Rouen. Thus some of the 'exploit, place, and character' of his first novel is clearly drawn from life.

The Franco-Prussian War (1870–1) changed everything. The family finances were ruined, Maupassant had to abandon his studies, and after the war, the would-be lawyer became a minor civil servant, first in the department of the Minister for the Navy (1873–8), later in the Ministry of Education (1878–80). Meanwhile, under the tutelage of Flaubert and in the glamorous slipstream of Émile Zola (1840–1902), Maupassant embarked upon his career as a writer; the publication of his short story *Boule de Suif* in Zola's anthology *Les Soirées de Médan* (1880) constituted something of an arrival—and the beginning of a period of quite extraordinary creativity. In 1882 he not only completed *A Life* but published sixty-four short stories and thirty-five newspaper articles; in 1883 sixty-two short stories and twenty-six articles; in 1884 fifty-nine stories and twenty-four articles. No wonder that the former pen-pusher in the Naval Ministry could now afford his first (small) yacht. He bought *La Louisette* early in 1883, the year in which *A Life* was published, first in serialized form in the *Gil Blas* (27 February–6 April) and then in book form by Havard. Temporarily withheld from station bookstalls by Hachette, the franchise-holder, on account of at least one 'explicit' scene, it quickly became a bestseller and had soon sold more than 25,000 copies.

But the author of *A Life* was suffering from syphilis. He had contracted the disease most probably in 1876, and in a letter written to his friend Robert Pinchon in March 1877 he diagnosed himself with a considerable degree of bravado. But medical understanding of the disease was far from complete at that time, and the fact that Maupassant had already been—and continued to be—subject to nervous disorders meant that a number of his symptoms were susceptible of varying interpretations both by specialists and by the sufferer himself. By 1883, however, the effects of syphilis were increasingly taking their toll, and the ophthalmologist consulted by Maupassant explicitly addressed the possibility that his symptoms (hair-loss, headaches, eye problems) were directly attributable to the disease. Though syphilis was not necessarily fatal, it is likely that the patient confronted the reality of his premature demise; in the event, the 32-year-old novelist now had only ten years to live, ten years of physical and mental decline which culminated in his attempted suicide at the beginning of 1892 (when he slit his throat with a paper-knife on the night of 1 January) and his death in a psychiatric clinic on 6 July 1893. Not that syphilis alone may have been responsible for his torment: his brother Hervé, six years his junior, had earlier lost his reason and died in an asylum in 1889. By the time of Guy de Maupassant's death he had published over 300 short stories, 200 articles, six novels, two plays, and three travel books. In 1888 he was earning some 120,000 francs a year (the equivalent then of £4,800, and now, most approximately, of some £275,000–£300,000); in December 1891 he estimated his sales over the previous ten years at nearly 350,000 copies. The number of his mistresses is said to have exceeded that of his short stories. Few lives, perhaps, have demonstrated such an extraordinary combination of creative vitality and doomed mortality.

Maupassant began work on *A Life* at the age of 27. On 10 December 1877 he gave notice of his intentions to Flaubert, who responded enthusiastically to the projected story-line. Early in 1878 Maupassant envisaged completing the novel by the beginning of the following year, but after a productive spring he became bogged down during the summer in a plethora of incidental characters (and an excess of work at the Ministry). In the autumn he managed to draft Chapter VII, which set up the plot for the remainder of the novel; but he then left the novel to one side until the spring of 1881, preferring to advance his literary career via the theatre and achieving notoriety through the publication of some risqué verse and the story of the eponymous prostitute in *Boule de Suif*. Having now made a name for himself, he could spare the time to continue work on his novel, and Flaubert's death (on 8 May 1880), while causing Maupassant much immediate distress, perhaps also made it easier for him to attempt a genre in which his late mentor was the acknowledged master. Following a long visit to Algeria in the summer and autumn of 1881, Maupassant resumed work on *A Life* in November and completed a first draft by the spring of the following year, which he then continued to revise before submitting a final version for publication one year later.

Flaubert and Naturalism

Although Flaubert was not, as baseless rumour sometimes had it, Maupassant's biological father, the author of *A Life* was certainly heir to the Master's literary preoccupations. At the level of plot, Jeanne de Lamare's disappointments are reminiscent of Emma Bovary's discovery that life is not at all like a novel by Sir Walter Scott. Similarly, the comparative brevity with which a human life is summarized and the presentation of this life as a process of gradual and relentless dispossession owe something to *Un cœur simple* (1877), Flaubert's brief and poignant tale of a servant woman in Rouen. At the level of style, the influence is plain in the (almost) impersonal narrative voice, the intricate network of parallels and oppositions which underlies the action, the use of short paragraphs and laconic sentence rhythms, and above all the quest for 'fine writing', the ambition to bring to narrative a concerted orchestration of sound and sense more traditionally associated with poetry. Whereas, among his subsequent novels, *Bel-Ami* (1885) would offer a broad panorama of Parisian society reminiscent of Balzac, and *Pierre et Jean* (1888) would present a psychological study of marital infidelity and its consequences in a manner which situates the novel in a French tradition stretching back to Madame de Lafayette's *La Princesse de Clèves* (1678), Maupassant's first novel is most evidently 'the homage of a devoted friend' in memory of one who had once proclaimed his intention to write 'a book about nothing'[1]—by which Flaubert meant predominantly a novel in which the representation of the external world would count much less towards the overall

---

[1] Letter to Louise Colet, 16 Jan. 1852.

aesthetic effect than the 'inner force' with which, stylistically, the novelist shaped and presented his subject.

For both Flaubert and Maupassant, indeed, such a distinction between style and subject was scarcely tenable: a life *is* the construction we place upon it. Nowhere is this more manifest than in Flaubert's novel *L'Éducation sentimentale* (1869), the account of the amiable but feckless young Frédéric Moreau who meanders through life with no more urgency or direction than the Seine itself. The representative of a generation which had been fired with revolutionary ardour only to see the 1848 Revolution lead on to Louis-Napoléon's Second Empire and the triumph of bourgeois materialism, Frédéric spends most of his time falling in and out of love (if love it be) with a small number of women of varying class and shadowy moral character. Just as (famously) the colour of Emma Bovary's eyes changes according to which character in the novel is looking at her, so too the principal (and never-attained) object of Frédéric's erotic fantasies, Madame Arnoux, would appear to have at least three different Christian names and be simultaneously a Madonna of moral perfection, a nondescript and stereotypically bored housewife, and a woman whose sense of conjugal loyalty is no stronger than her husband's and who is to be espied all alone with an unknown gentleman in his carriage while attending the races at Longchamp. In other words, an age-old tradition of plot and character (heroic, handsome boy meets perfect, pretty girl and something happens—usually marriage or death) is replaced by a more 'naturalistic' structure (ineffectual chump happens to meet unremarkable females, and not much happens, repeatedly). But, as Flaubert recognized, shapelessness is not conducive to great art, and he wrote ten years later about the possible reasons for the lack of both critical and popular success which *L'Éducation sentimentale* had met upon publication: 'It is too true and, aesthetically speaking, it lacks *the distortion of perspective*. Having been so well put together, the structure [of the novel] disappears from view. Every work of art must have a high point, a summit, like a pyramid, or else the light must strike one point on the sphere. Now life is not like that. But Art is not inherent in Nature! No matter! I believe that no one has taken honesty further.'[2]

Maupassant was clearly influenced by Flaubert's attempts to write a different kind of novel, one which calls into question the philosophical assumptions about causality and identity implicit in traditional narrative procedures; and in his short essay 'Le Roman' (The Novel), published with *Pierre et Jean* in 1888, it is evident that he shares Flaubert's anxieties about the tension between the contingency of reality and the need for the novelist to present a concerted 'vision' (or perspective): if he is an artist, he will 'endeavour not to present us with a banal photograph of life but to provide us with a vision that is at once more complete, more startling, and more convincing than reality itself'. Life is full of surprises and contrasts, it can be brutal, 'full of inexplicable, illogical, and contradictory catastrophes'; whereas art 'consists in taking precautions and preparing for things in advance, in orchestrating clever, unseen transitions, and, by the sole skill of composition, in placing the essential events under the spotlight and lending the remainder a sufficient degree of relief, according to their relative importance, in order to convey a profound sense of the special truth one wishes to display'. All of us have our own way of seeing the world; the great artists are those who succeed in making us see the world through their own particular eyes.

Maupassant's own particular 'vision' has usually been described as 'naturalist'. In his excellent study of the naturalist novel, David Baguley has identified five main characteristics of the genre and divided it into two fundamental types. The first of the characteristics is that 'there will appear a scientific or sociological theme, posited and developed as the guiding principle of the novel, turning on a preoccupation with neurotic, pathological states or on the unmasking of the seamy side of life'. Secondly, 'the naturalist novel will admit a more poetic, decorative kind of discourse, which aestheticises the often sordid and banal reality that is being represented'. Thirdly, the plot will manifest itself 'as the reversal or parody of a "romanesque" [meaning 'romantic' or even 'novelettish'] or heroic action, subjecting man—or, more

[2] Letter to Mme Roger des Genettes, Oct. 1879.

frequently, woman—to some ironic or degrading fate, displaying the emptiness of human existence, disclosing the veiled depravities of bourgeois life' (Baguley sees *A Life* as exemplary under this heading). Fourthly, 'the action will take place within the detailed, thoroughly documented representation of a particular milieu'. Finally, there is 'an often ferocious and uncompromising element of satire of bourgeois manners'.

Of the two fundamental types, one 'takes up the tragic model of the fall, presenting it as a process of deterioration, prolonged in time and deriving its causality from particular determining factors (hereditary taints, neurotic dispositions, adverse social conditions)'; while in the other 'the determining factor is more generalised, a fundamental inadequacy of the human condition which traps the individual in the inextricable dilemmas, frustrations and disillusionment of daily existence'. 'The process of disillusionment', Baguley continues, 'becomes the only dynamic element in these works, which seem plotless like *L'Éducation sentimentale*, following the repetitive course of biological needs and constant deceptions in which life is frittered away before its inevitable extinction.'[3] In short, the 'characteristic movement' of the naturalist novel—of both types—is 'in the direction of disintegration and confusion.' It depicts the human individual 'being subjected to a *natural* condition' and as such therefore subject to an inevitable process of entropy.[4]

Does *A Life* display these characteristics? To which fundamental type of the naturalist novel does it correspond? While there is no dominant scientific theme, a clear sociological thread can be seen running through the novel. Such an assertion may seem surprising in view of the eminent Marxist critic Georg Lukács's well-known comment that 'the purely private character of the action [of *A Life*] deprives it of an historical character'. For Lukács, 'the essential action of the novel [which is set in the period 1819–*c*.1848] is quite "timeless"; the Restoration, the July Revolution, the July Monarchy, etc., events which objectively must make an extremely deep impression upon the daily life of an

---

[3] David Baguley, *Naturalist Fiction: The Entropic Vision* (Cambridge, 1990), 94–6.
[4] Ibid. 208, 215.

aristocratic *milieu*, play practically no part'.[5] This is true, yet the process of disintegration which takes place within the novel would seem to include a gradual decline in wealth and influence which is characteristic of the aristocracy as a whole. Jeanne's family, the Le Perthuis des Vauds, are seen—like the de Lamare family before them—to fall on hard times: poor estate management, well-bred munificence, and a waster of a grandson are sufficient to reduce a potential annual income of 30,000 francs to some 8,000. The Fourvilles have no heir; the elderly Brisevilles are like 'conserved specimens of the nobility', buried away in their dusty chateau, seeing no one but 'writing frequently to their noble relations scattered throughout France' (p. 87) in a frenzy of sterile caste solidarity; and the Cortuliers are so insufferably condescending and wedded to the past that even Julien de Lamare, despite his snobbery, cannot countenance another visit.

A Life presents a world in which the members of the aristocracy seem like dinosaurs; where Jeanne must sell her house to a man who has made his fortune out of sugar-refining; where it is now money, not 'breeding', that counts ('without money we're all just ignorant country folk': p. 204); where her own maid, thanks to the Baron's generosity but also to Rosalie's husband's hard work, has achieved her 'place in the sun' (p. 204) and has almost as much money as her former employer (p. 204); where Jeanne's son squanders a fortune in speculative investments and ends up so destitute that he and his mistress are obliged to flee their creditors. A quiet revolution had taken place, ostensibly set in the first half of the century but still proceeding in the second. It was a shift in social relations which Maupassant had experienced at first hand, both in the loss of his family's wealth and in his own attainment of riches through becoming a bestselling author.

As to 'neurotic, pathological states' and the 'unmasking of the seamy side of life', it is evident that Baguley's criteria are of more immediate relevance to Zola's *Thérèse Raquin* (1867) and *L'Assommoir* (1877). But there is clearly something pathological about this decline of the aristocracy, if only at a symbolic level. The monstrous physique of the Comte de Fourville, his avid

[5] Georg Lukács, *The Historical Novel* (Harmondsworth, 1969), 237.

enthusiasm for hunting, shooting, and fishing, and his violent murder of his wife and her lover foreshadow the atavistic figure of Jacques Lantier in Zola's *La Bête humaine* (1890); while the Baroness's 'hypertrophy' seems to bespeak a distortion of affectivity, a swollen sentimentality born of inaction and the determination to live resolutely in the past—the past of her own extra-marital fling, but a past also in which the only tree that truly mattered was genealogical. And Jeanne's own emotional make-up likewise betrays considerable instability. As a 17-year-old just out of the convent she is filled with 'unruly joy' (p. 19) which has her racing along the clifftops or swimming (quite implausibly for a young girl of her time and social rank) far out to sea, where she would 'let out piercing shrieks of sudden, frantic joy, and slap the surface of the sea' (p. 20). In Corsica the sight of a particularly beautiful bay has tears welling from her eyes, the evidence (at least in the opinion of her callous husband and quite probably also in that of the sexist Maupassant) of 'women's "nerves"', these emotional disturbances to which the sensitive creatures [are] subject, becoming overwrought at a mere trifle, as easily agitated by some fond enthusiasm as by total disaster, and capable of being thoroughly upset, of being driven wild with joy or despair, by the least identifiable of sensations' (p. 67). Not that Rosalie ever seems to suffer from such 'nerves'... Perhaps it is only well-born ladies, like Jeanne, or Gilberte de Fourville, or indeed Maupassant's own mother, who betray this pathological pattern of the *grande hystérique*.

And what of the other characteristics of the naturalist novel? Clearly the pupil of Flaubert has aimed at 'a poetic, decorative discourse', as any page will demonstrate; and equally clearly the landscape and customs of Normandy are the subject of a 'detailed, thoroughly documented representation of a particular milieu'. Is the plot based on 'a reversal or parody of a "romanesque" or heroic action, subjecting man—or, more frequently, woman—to some ironic or degrading fate, displaying the emptiness of human existence, disclosing the veiled depravities of bourgeois life'? If one substitutes 'aristocratic' (and 'ecclesiastical') for 'bourgeois', then *A Life* displays all of this. The

conventions of romance dictate that the nubile Jeanne, freshly
released from her convent incarceration, shall meet '*Him!*': 'All
she knew was that she would adore him with her heart and soul
and that he would cherish her with all his might.' Mr Right shall
appear and they shall have two children, 'a son for him and a
daughter for her' (pp. 14–15). Why should there be any delay?
Perhaps this person she hears walking along the road on her very
first night at Les Peuples is indeed 'Him'... The tale of Pyramus
and Thisbe which adorns her bedroom will prove wide of the
mark as she later experiences marital rape and then her husband's
infidelities; and the dream of idyllic parenthood will be replaced
by the bitter experience of an unloving son and a stillborn daughter. Instead of a world of conjugal loyalty unto death, she discovers that her father and mother have both been unfaithful to
their marriage vows, and that her only friend, Gilberte, is deceiv-
ing her doting husband, the Comte de Fourville, and sleeping
with Julien. By the time she does encounter the spectacle of true
devotion (ironically, in the relationship between her son and his
supposedly unsuitable mistress), her maternal love has become so
bitterly possessive that she fails to see through her prejudice and
jealousy to perceive its reality. She discovers the 'depravities' taking place behind the imposing façades of chateau and manor-
house, and eventually sees the irony whereby Rosalie's arranged
marriage with the splendidly named Désiré Lecoq has provided
her maid with more affection and security than her own 'love-
match' with a callous and avaricious hypocrite. She is degraded
materially by the loss of her house and fortune, socially by the
humiliation of her final visit to Paris, and sexually by the horror
of her wedding-night, by her priest's approval of masturbation as
the antidote to an inattentive husband, by the necessity of intercourse with a husband she loathes in order to bear a child, and by
an ultimate 'unsexing' as she comes to abhor sensuality with the
vehemence of the fanatical Abbé Tolbiac, who stones courting
couples and excludes the 'fallen' from communion. For Jeanne, a
life is one in which the illusions of romance are replaced by the
bleak vista of hopeless despair: 'She believed herself to be so
directly the target of unrelenting misfortune that she became as

fatalistic as an Oriental; and the habitual experience of seeing all her hopes and dreams crumble and vanish meant that she shrank from all further endeavour' (p. 231).

Human Destiny and the Seasons

It is true, then, that *A Life* presents the story of a seemingly inevitable process of degradation and disintegration, an 'entropic' vision which combines elements from both of Baguley's 'fundamental types' of naturalist novel. It is also true that this process is very emphatically seen as corresponding to some essential rhythm of nature. Just as the novel replaces the illusions of romance with some of the realities of adult sexuality, so too it substitutes for Rousseauistic idealism (as espoused by the Baron at the beginning of the novel) a view of nature in which the differences between human beings, animals, and plants become imperceptible within the broader context of immutable and irresistible cycles of nature. For one of the most prominent features of *A Life* is the way in which human destiny is interwoven with the pattern of the changing seasons and the vagaries of the weather. The novel opens on 3 May as the budding school-leaver contemplates her future and stands 'ready to reach out for all the good things in life of which she had so long been dreaming' (p. 3). Spring gives way to summer, and her courtship with Julien de Lamare leads to marriage—on 15 August, as though the Feast of the Assumption were to mark the miraculous accession of the virginal Jeanne to a heaven of marital bliss. Following her first orgasm under the burning skies of Corsica, the return to Normandy and a drab life of routine is marked by autumnal melancholy; and her youthful dreams of romance and excitement are replaced by a winter of discontent in which the frozen landscape of late January becomes the scene of suicidal despair. But the seed of the future, of her son Paul, is stirring within her, and with pregnancy comes the following spring and a period of parturition prematurely ended in late July. So the cycle continues until the final pages of the novel when, on an evening in spring, 'an infinite peace lay upon the tranquil earth and the seed that lay germinating within': and as Jeanne cradles her unnamed grand-daughter in her lap, 'a feeling of soft, gentle warmth, the warmth of life, touched her legs and entered her flesh' (p. 239).

The relationship between human destiny and the cycles of nature is at the very least symbolic and quite frequently causal. A cold wind is blowing on the day of Jeanne's summer wedding, and there is a smell of autumn in the air. Another cold wind, the Mistral, marks the end of her honeymoon. A violent storm accompanies the tumultuous murder of Julien and Gilberte. Mama dies at haymaking time. But these details seem like mere vestiges of the pathetic fallacy when compared with the occasions on which human beings appear to respond instinctively to the promptings of nature. As the sap rises, the physical relationship between Julien and Gilberte blossoms, and even Jeanne herself feels 'vaguely unsettled by this fermenting of life around her' (p. 139). Later, at the end of the novel, when she spends day after day sitting in front of the fire, the arrival of spring fills her with 'a restless excitement' (p. 233), and soon she is roaming the coun-tryside once more as though filled with the 'unruly joy' of earlier days. The universe is governed by the rhythm of creation—germination, gestation, decay, death—and human beings are no less subject to its irresistible force than animals, or insects, or plants. Such is the view of Creation which, later in the novel, the Baron is said to hold:

a fateful, limitless, all-powerful force . . . simultaneously life, light, earth, thought, plant, rock, man, beast, star, God, insect; which cre-ated precisely because it *was* Creation, stronger than any individual will, vaster than any capacity to reason, and productive for no purpose, without cause or temporal limit, in all directions and in all shapes and dimensions, across the infinite reaches of space, as chance and the proximity of world-warming suns dictated. (p. 170)

The passage of the seasons is profoundly sexual and the setting of the sun is a diurnal act of copulation, which Jeanne witnesses during her boat trip at Étretat: 'the sea arched its gleaming, liquid belly beneath the sky and waited, like some monstrous bride, upon the arrival of the fiery lover descending towards her'

(p. 35). The Baron is thus perhaps justified in his ambition to let Jeanne learn the facts of life from 'the spectacle of natural love, of the simple courtship of animals' (p. 4). But of course the irony will be that she learns about sexual intercourse at the hands of an animal-like Julien, who 'grabbed her in his arms, rabidly, as though filled with a ravenous hunger for her' (p. 56); and when she does chance to observe two birds mating (p. 141), it serves only to make her realize why Julien and Gilberte are taking so long to return to their horses.

This equation between human beings, animals, insects, and inanimate objects is constantly demonstrated. The equivalence is no longer one of straightforward and comfortable allegory, as in the La Fontaine fables of which Jeanne is so fond ('the fox and the stork, the fox and the crow, the cicada and the ant, and the melancholy heron': p. 210), but rather an implicit devaluation of human dignity. Aunt Lison's attempted suicide is an 'episode' on a par with the death of Coco the horse, and Lison herself is of so little human consequence that mention of her name inspires no more affection than the words 'sugar-bowl' or 'coffee-pot' (p. 44). For Jeanne, newly married, two ladybirds sheltering under a leaf provide an image of domestic harmony (p. 49), while on her way to Corsica her heart leaps with the dolphins (p. 60). Slaughter the dog—for the novel is the story of his life too—is born during a murderous assault by the Abbé Tolbiac (which prefigures the Comte de Fourville's destruction of the 'love nest' shared by Julien and Gilberte), is given a 'wet-nurse' (a cat: even the boundaries of species disintegrate), lives most of his life alone and chained to a barrel, and dies after a period of howling agitation which Jeanne later sees as analogous with her own restless anguish (p. 234).

In the end, human activity has as little importance as the ceaseless flitting of the pendulum bee in Jeanne's clock, itself a beehive in which the only honey is life's monotony. This timepiece (like Mama's watch, still ticking after her death) comes to symbolize the patterns of repetition and circularity which characterize our clockwork existence—and with which Maupassant has shaped the 'subject' of his novel. For 'a life' is, if nothing else, a passage

of time, at once a journey into the unknown and a round-trip
from infancy to dotage. Hence the emblematic importance of the
calendar which Jeanne packs into her travelling-bag on the first
page, and of the calendars which, in the final chapter, she salvages
from the attic and pins onto the tapestries downstairs before circling the sitting-room 'as though it had been hung with prints
depicting the Stations of the Cross' (p. 232). For Jeanne, life—all
life—is much less a 'progress', more a circuit, a reliving of other
people's lives, of her own past life. The young girl who started
out with such hopes for the future and convinced of her own
unique individuality (for all the stereotypical character of her
romantic ambitions) turns out to be no more than a sad amalgam
of her mother and aunt. Already, as she listens to Mama's remin-
iscences during their first days together at Les Peuples, Jeanne
'could see herself in these stories of former days, and was startled
by the similarity of their thoughts, by the kinship of their desires;
for every heart imagines itself the first to thrill to a myriad sensations which once stirred the hearts of the earliest creatures and
which will again stir the hearts of the last men and women to walk
the earth' (p. 23). But by the end of the novel she has still failed
to realize how much life has repeated itself. Just as her own
mother inhabits a world of romantic fantasy (p. 22) and lives in
the past, periodically consulting her 'relics' (p. 22; p. 145), so
Jeanne has her own repertoire of fantasies (pp. 93–4) and
comes to live almost exclusively in the past (through her calendars). While she escapes her mother's 'hypertrophy', Jeanne
nonetheless ends up 'frail and dragging her feet now, as Mama
used to' (p. 206), feeling 'as though she were no longer able to
breathe properly' (p. 216), and obliged like her mother to take
exercise with the aid of the ever-mobile Rosalie (p. 230). Just as
Mama had wept when Jeanne was sent away to school (p. 4), so
Jeanne weeps when the time comes to send her son to college in
Le Havre (pp. 189–90). For mother as for daughter, endless
walks up and down the avenue at Les Peuples are the symbol of
a monotonous and repetitive existence (pp. 21, 76, 118, 144–5).
Yet at least her mother knew the thrill of true love in her adulterous affair with Paul d'Ennemare, whereas Jeanne's response to

Julien's treacheries is not to repeat the betrayal of her friend Gilberte and seek consolation in the arms of the Comte de Fourville, but rather to become 'dead to all carnal need' (p. 143) in the manner of her maiden aunt. For both women compulsive embroidery provides a channel for displaced desire; each attempts or at least contemplates suicide; and, like Lison, Jeanne eventually comes to feel all alone in the world, at her small house at Batteville, where 'no one paid her any attention' (p. 218). The metamorphosis is complete when, during Jeanne's trip to Paris, the 'rapid, timorous steps' (p. 226) with which she walks up and down the gardens of the Palais-Royal recall the 'short, rapid, silent steps' (p. 44) with which Lison flits unremarked hither and thither at Les Peuples.

Not only does Jeanne's life repeat that of others, it repeats itself. Sometimes she intends the repetition, as when she revisits the wood near Étretat, only to find that the place of her first sexual stirrings has now become the scene of a double treachery (p. 141). At other times the parallels are implicit. Thus her oblivious rapture at the lunch party following the 'baptism' of the new boat ('She saw nothing, thought nothing, said nothing, as her head swam with joy': p. 40) finds a tragic echo in her crazed absence of mind during the lunch following her final visit to Les Peuples and the mad vision of her deceased parents sitting by the fireside ('She ate what was put in front of her, she heard people talking but had no idea what they were talking about': p. 237). 'I'm going to die . . . I *am* dying' (p. 102), she thinks to herself, one bitterly cold night before discovering Julien in bed with Rosalie; 'I'm going to die. I *am* dying', she thinks, in the midst of her labour pains before giving birth to her son (p. 122).

And if the climactic moments in her life can be so repetitious, what of the long days, and months, and years which elapse between 3 May 1819 and the end of the novel, nearly twenty-nine years later in the spring of 1848? As monotonous, presumably, as the cold, autumnal days that follow her return from honeymoon: 'And the remaining days in the week were like the first two; and every week in the month was like the first' (p. 79). Part of Maupassant's intention here is no doubt to achieve 'the effect of dreariness' which Henry James considered to be the essential 'subject' of the novel.[6] But there are more surreptitious patterns of repetition, which suggest that the author of *A Life* wished to instil a strong sense of cyclicity in his reader. Our final view of Jeanne at the end of the novel is of her being driven off to a new life, cradling a baby in her arms; and we may be reminded of the first journey in the novel when, as the Le Perthuis des Vauds set off for their new life at Les Peuples, 'Jeanne felt as though she were coming back to life', while beside her sits Rosalie, 'nursing a parcel on her knees' (p. 7). The conveyance has changed from an expensive private carriage to a peasant's cart, and the identity of the person in the driving seat has changed (with the sociological significance noted above), but the message remains the same: 'plus ça change, plus c'est la même chose.' Superficial mutations serve to throw into relief the fundamental constants of universal experience.

Narrative and the Novel

This tension between sameness and difference, between stasis and change, is central to *A Life*, and not least because this is the first novel of a writer whose narrative skills were particularly suited to the form of the short story. It has traditionally been held that the distinguishing feature of a novel is its capacity to follow the evolution of an individual, or a group of individuals, or even a society, through time: to account for change, to chart a sequence of cause and effect, whether psychological or socio-historical, to document a process. In the short story, on the other hand, the focus is more usually—for reasons of brevity—on a single event, on some unique moment upon which a human destiny may depend (which is why the genre of the short story has sometimes been compared to drama). The difference in length can therefore be seen to entail two potentially quite different moral universes: briefly stated, in the novel people do things, in the short story things happen to people. In these terms one might argue that while *A Life* has the appearance of being a novel, both its

---

[6] Henry James, 'Guy de Maupassant' (1888), in *Selected Literary Criticism*, ed. Morris Shapira (London, 1963), 106.

narrative structure and its moral universe owe more to the short story.

As regards narrative structure, it is plain that the novel is constructed predominantly as a series of quasi-theatrical scenes interspersed with succinctly summarized and for the most part indeterminate blanks of time. Homecoming—visit to Yport—boat-trip—'baptism' of new boat—wedding-night—honeymoon in Corsica—Rosalie in childbirth—Jeanne's discovery of Julien and Rosalie—suicidal dash through the snow—fishing by torchlight—death of Mama—slaughter of litter—slaughter of Julien and Gilberte—return of Rosalie—moving house—trip to Paris—last visit to Les Peuples... Each episode is narrated with a minimum of secondary detail and a maximum of dialogue and 'visual aids', permitting the reader to experience each 'hammer-blow' of fate with the immediacy of Jeanne herself. Indeed, such is the discrete status of each episode that several had already served—or were later reworked—as short stories in their own right (*An Evening in Spring*, *The Bed*, *The Vigil*, *Old Things*, *A Tale of Corsica*, *Shepherd's Leap*, *A Meeting*, *A Humble Drama*). Time slows or accelerates as the subject demands: moments of high drama occupy several pages while for the transformation of Paul from infant into ungrateful son (so that the hammer-blows can continue) over some twenty-two years are covered in a single chapter (Ch. XI).

As to moral universe, is this the story of a free agent or of a series of events passively undergone? On the one hand, this is assuredly the story of a life, of Jeanne de Lamare, who leaves school, falls in love, marries, is deceived by her husband, has a son who abandons her, and is finally saddled—and blessed—with a grandchild to raise. But, as we have seen, this seeming onward march of events is characterized by repetition and circularity. Such alterations as occur in Jeanne's circumstances constitute an unrelenting series of dispossessions, both of her property and of the persons she loves or cares for: her husband, her parents, her only woman friend, her son. Jeanne begins the novel as a stereotype and ends it as a nonentity. By the same token, while the novel abounds symbolically in journeys and excursions, these changes of location prove most usually to be mere forays into sameness. The first journey of all apparently represents a liberation (from convent education) and a new beginning; but this new beginning takes place in an old chateau that has been restored (some critics have seen it as symbolizing the Restoration of the French Monarchy in 1815, shortly before the period in which the opening of the novel is set), and the liberation proves to be merely the substitution of one form of incarceration for another (a loveless marriage and 'a quotidian reality', in which there is 'nothing left to do, today, tomorrow, ever again': p. 75). Certainly the honeymoon in Corsica provides a different landscape—and serves to recall the Napoleonic excitement and 'liberation' which preceded the Restoration—but the statutory account of the maquis and the depredations of Corsican jealousy (in the story related by Paoli Palabretti) will prove to be no more 'exotic' than the Comte de Fourville's violent murder of his wife and Julien de Lamare upon the cliffs of Normandy. The various calls paid on fellow aristocrats are but pointless journeys into the mothballed irrelevance of the *ancien régime*, while Jeanne's final expedition to Paris brings her not a reunion with her son but the most desolate sense of isolation: 'And she felt more entirely alone in this bustling crowd, more wretched and lost, than if she had been standing in the middle of an empty field' (p. 227). For these reasons, Mama's daily exercise up and down her avenue epitomizes the novel's presentation of time and place: ever on the move, departing and returning, desperately trying to breathe yet dead to any enthusiasm other than her genealogical and amatory past, this Baroness who had 'waltzed in the arms of every man in uniform under the Empire' (p. 22) is always going nowhere. Like the long, straight wake behind the steamer taking the newlyweds to Corsica, or the long, straight railway line stretching to the horizon in the final chapter, the trail of grassless dust left by Mama's dragging foot symbolizes the unswerving rut of purposeless time.

Towards a Conclusion

For Jeanne herself life is not an active journey into the future but a passive disintegration beneath the weight of a cruel destiny. Already we have seen how at the end of the novel 'she believed herself to be so directly the target of unrelenting misfortune that she became as fatalistic as an Oriental' (p. 231); and part of this passivity derives from her role as a subordinated woman. Having been told by her father on her wedding-night to 'remember this, and only this, that you belong totally to your husband' (p. 52), she becomes the victim of her husband's despotism. Physically his slave and economically his dependant, she is powerless to protest at his infidelity as the Abbé Picot forces a conjugal reconciliation on her in the name of Christian forgiveness, and her husband and father leave her bedroom to patch up their quarrel over a manly cigar. And whereas on this occasion she wants to leave Julien but is prevented by the Church, later the fanatical Abbé Tolbiac calls on her to reject her adulterous husband when she is financially and legally unable to do so (p. 172). But from Julien's sexual oppression she learns what Maupassant believes to be a universal lesson: 'that two people are never completely one in their heart of hearts, in their deepest thoughts, that they walk side by side, entwined sometimes but never completely united, and that in our moral being we each of us remain forever alone throughout our lives' (p. 64). Likewise later in the novel, when Jeanne is returning from Yport with her father and observes the lights in the scattered farmhouses, she is filled with 'an acute sense of the isolation in which all creatures live, of how everything conspires to separate them and keep them apart, to remove them far away from that which otherwise they might love' (p. 91).

She who had looked forward to a perfect union with 'Him' comes to have a deeply pessimistic outlook on the world which owes much to her creator's nihilism and the philosophy of Schopenhauer (1788–1860), whose recently translated writings had struck such a chord in him. Keeping vigil over her mother's corpse, Jeanne reflects on the meaning of life and the conundrum that is death:

So there was nothing, then, but sorrow, grief, misfortune, and death. It was all just deceit and lies, things to make one suffer and weep. Where was there a little respite and joy to be found? In another life no doubt! When the soul had been delivered from its ordeal upon earth! The soul! She began to reflect on this unfathomable mystery . . . Where, then, was her mother's soul at this precise moment . . .? Far, far away, perhaps. Somewhere in space? But where? . . . Recalled to God? Or scattered, randomly assumed into the process of new creation, mingling with the seeds that were about to spring into life? (p. 152)

Compare Maupassant's remarks in a letter to Flaubert on 5 July 1878: 'From time to time I have such a clear perception of the pointlessness of everything, of the unthinking malice of creation, of the emptiness that lies ahead (whatever form the future may take) that I am filled with a sad indifference towards all things and I just want to sit in a corner and stay there, devoid of hope and free from all vexation.'

Some such thoughts appear to be going through Jeanne's mind at the end of the novel, as she remains for days on end seated by the fire in her sitting-room, 'not moving, her eyes fixed on the flames, letting her sorry thoughts wander where they pleased and observing the sad procession of her miseries' (p. 229). Desperately she tries to make sense of what has gone before, and her obsessive attempts to spell the name of her son in the air suggest that writing may be the means to such an understanding—as if she were anticipating the task of Maupassant himself. For as she wanders down the *via dolorosa* that is memory lane, circling round the calendars in her living-room as if they were prints representing the (fourteen) Stations of the Cross, so here, in the fourteenth and final chapter, the novelist brings his story full circle and may seem to offer both hope and meaning in his ending. Jeanne has reached her Calvary in the house at Batteville, forsaken not by God but by the son whose birth had been her heart's salvation ('she realized that she had been saved, secured against all despair, that she now held in her arms something she could love to the ultimate exclusion of all else': p. 123). But Rosalie departs for Paris and returns—on the third day (p. 238)—with the means of her heart's resurrection, the unnamed baby girl whose warmth penetrates her flesh. For *A Life* is thus entitled not so much because it recounts the life of Jeanne de Lamare (since her life, far from ending with the novel, is seen to begin anew), but because the one ray of hope in the midst of despair is provided by 'a life'—that simple, biological cog in the great wheel of Creation, to which human beings may respond with a sense of purpose and the instinct to protect. A life becomes a reason for living.

The banality of Rosalie's closing remark: 'You see, life's never as good or as bad as we think'—which is no less banal for having been proclaimed to Maupassant by Flaubert in a letter at the end of December 1878—recalls the banality of the exchange between Jeanne and her father as they return home from Yport: ' "Life is not all fun" [Jeanne observes.] The Baron sighed: "I'm afraid not, my child, and there's nothing we can do about it" ' (p. 92). In a novel which claims in its subtitle to be presenting 'the humble truth', the homespun character of these observations is perhaps appropriate; and of course in the case of Rosalie the comment is entirely in keeping with her resilient practicality, which has seen her through a life of wildly fluctuating fortunes. But does her remark constitute a 'message'? Is this Maupassant's final word?

For all its mediocrity it does underscore the suggestion of a 'resurrection' at the end of the novel, and yet perhaps it is only Jeanne and Rosalie who see things in such a light. A more sceptical reader might interpret this moment (and several critics have) as merely the first stage in a further cycle of failure and disillusionment. On the other hand, the generality of the remark may remind us that while Jeanne's life has been almost unrelievedly grim, hers has not been the only life on display; and thus it may encourage us to look back on the narrative and realize that the almost exclusive focus on Jeanne's point of view may have obscured the degree to which fortunes have indeed been mixed. For this is a novel which opens with a picture of joy marred by rain and ends with a portrait of despair illuminated by sunshine and hope (represented not only by the baby but by the possibility that Paul, despite all previous evidence to the contrary, might actually arrive by the same train on the following day). Through-

out the novel we see that sexual desire, while it may be an instinctive urge which makes human beings no different from dolphins
or ladybirds, is indeed *natural*. Chastity is a perversion and
breeds prurience (the Abbé Picot), pathological violence and fanaticism (the Abbé Tolbiac), or lonely misery (Lison). The sexual
appetites of the young men and women of Normandy are part of
life; and the sexual act, like nature, can be variously good or bad,
both a source of joy—to Jeanne (briefly), to her parents (whether
maritally or extra-maritally), to Julien and Gilberte—and yet also
a brutal act of rape. Love does exist: Mama has known it, perhaps
her husband too, Jeanne knows it (briefly), the Comte de Fourville knows it (illusorily and unrequitedly), Paul and his mistress
know it (unto death). But hatred too exists, and the hurt that
comes with betrayal. For all 'the sad procession of her miseries'
(p. 229) Jeanne should at least count herself fortunate to have
known the joy of parenthood when she can see how both her aunt
and the Comte de Fourville are conscious of having missed out.
They have been prevented from engendering and nurturing a life.

As one who learned many lessons from Flaubert, Maupassant
will not have failed to be aware of the Master's favourite dictum:
'Human stupidity lies in wanting to conclude'; and the author of
A Life would seem to have concluded his first novel with the most
ambivalent and inconclusive of aphorisms. Yet if there is one
unambiguous villain in Maupassant's first novel, it must surely be
the Abbé Tolbiac, because people of his sort, as the Baron puts it,
'hate the physical': 'Such people must be resisted, it is our right
and duty to do so. They're inhuman' (p. 170). Life is for living;
Jeanne needs something to live for; the warm, living flesh of a
baby brings her back to life. What a terrible and poignant irony it
must, therefore, have been for Maupassant himself that his first
(and illegitimate) child should have been born on the very day
that the first instalment of his first novel was published, and that
midway through its publication he should have been told by an
eye specialist, Dr Landolt, what he had already suspected: that he
had syphilis, a disease contracted—and passed on—in the very
act of creating a life. Or perhaps it was not an irony. He first
mentions his syphilis (in the letter to Pinchon) nine months

before he tells Flaubert of his plans for his first novel. Was it perhaps the prospect of his own mortality that made him start *A Life*? And was it the prospect of his first-born that made him end the novel as he did? 'In the midst of life we are in death,' and *vice versa*; or as Norbert de Varenne, the nihilistic poet in Maupassant's second novel *Bel-Ami*, puts it: 'to live is to die': 'Life is a hill. For as long as we're climbing, we have our eyes on the summit and we feel happy; but as soon as we arrive at the top, we suddenly see the way down and the end, which is death. It's slow going on the way up, but fast on the way down.'[7] In *A Life* the ascent is brief the descent protracted and unflinchingly, compellingly, told.

[7] *Romans*, ed. Louis Forestier (Paris, 1987), 299.

NOTE ON THE TRANSLATION

This translation is based on the text of *Une vie* edited by Louis Forestier in the Pléiade edition of the *Romans* (Paris, 1987). First published in 1883, *Une vie* was published in a revised edition by Ollendorff in 1893. Forestier follows the latter text in the belief that Maupassant himself made the corrections to his 1883 text; Antonia Fonyi (GF-Flammarion, 1993) argues that Maupassant was too ill by this time to do so, and that even when he was well, he was not much given to the revision of his previously published work. While Fonyi's arguments have some force, the matter remains uncertain; and it has seemed best to follow what is still regarded as the standard edition. The variants between the 1883 and 1893 editions are in any case not of major consequence.

Une vie was first published in English (in an anonymous translation) by Henry Vizetelly in 1888 as no. 8 in his series of 'Boulevard Novels', and bore the title *A Woman's Life*. A subsequent (bowdlerized) translation, by Henry Blanchamp, preferred *A Woman's Soul* (London, 1907), but thereafter *A Woman's Life* was thought to be the appropriate title by Bree Narran (London, 1920) and Antonia White (London, 1949). Katharine Vivian's translation for the Folio Society in 1981 retains the French title. To date there have been thirteen translations of the novel into English, of which only one (by Marjorie Laurie in the 1920s) has been entitled *A Life*.

The most widely available translation of *Une vie* has been the version by H. N. P. Sloman in Penguin Classics (1965), who retains the unsatisfactory title of *A Woman's Life*. Sloman's practice of running Maupassant's short paragraphs together has not been followed in the present translation on the ground that Maupassant's practice in this respect is an intentional stylistic device and one which he owed in large measure to Flaubert.

In the preparation of this translation I am once more deeply indebted both to my wife Vivienne for her encouragement and

patient reading of the typescript and to I. P. Foote for his pains-
taking and invariably well-judged advice on how inaccuracy,
infelicity, and anachronism might be avoided.

SELECT BIBLIOGRAPHY

IN ENGLISH

Maupassant in Translation

Novels

Bel-Ami, trans. Douglas Parmée (Harmondsworth, 1975).
Pierre et Jean, trans. Leonard Tancock (Harmondsworth, 1979).

Short Stories

A Day in the Country and Other Stories, trans. and ed. David Coward (Oxford, 1990).
Mademoiselle Fifi and Other Stories, trans. and ed. David Coward (Oxford, 1993).
A Parisian Bourgeois' Sundays and Other Stories, trans. Marlo Johnston (London and Chester Springs, Pa., 1997).

Biographies

Francis Steegmuller, *Maupassant. A Lion in the Path* (NewYork, 1949; repr. London, 1950; 1972).
Paul Ignotus, *The Paradox of Maupassant* (London, 1966).
Michael Lerner, *Maupassant* (London, 1975).
Roger L. Williams, *The Horror of Life* (London, 1980); pp. 217–72 provide a judicious and well-informed account of Maupassant's medical history.

Critical Studies

Edward D. Sullivan, *Maupassant the Novelist* (Princeton and Oxford, 1954).
—— *Maupassant: The Short Stories* (London, 1962).
Richard B. Grant, 'Imagery as a Means of Psychological Revelation in Maupassant's *Une vie*', *Studies in Philology*, 60 (1963), 669–84.
Albert H. Wallace, *Maupassant* (New York, 1973).
Naomi Schor, '*Une vie* or the Name of the Mother', in her *Breaking the Chain: Women, Theory and French Realist Fiction* (New York,

1985), 48–77. A translation of '*Une vie*/Des Vides ou le nom de la mère', *Littérature*, 26 (May 1977), 51–71.

Mary Donaldson-Evans, *A Woman's Revenge: The Chronology of Dispossession in Maupassant's Fiction* (Lexington, Ky., 1986). Of particular relevance to *A Life*.

IN FRENCH

Standard Editions of Maupassant

Collected Works

Romans, ed. Louis Forestier, Bibliothèque de la Pléiade (Paris, 1987).

Contes et nouvelles, ed. Louis Forestier, 2 vols., Bibliothèque de la Pléiade (Paris, 1974–9).

Œuvres complètes, ed. Gilbert Sigaux and Pascal Pia, 17 vols., Cercle du Bibliophile (Evreux, 1969–71).

Chroniques, ed. Hubert Juin, 3 vols. (Paris, 1980). Brings together over 200 texts published between 1876 and 1891.

Editions of Une vie

Une vie, ed. André Fermigier, Folio Classique (Paris, 1974).

Une vie, ed. Antonia Fonyi, GF-Flammarion (Paris, 1993).

Biographies

Armand Lanoux, *Maupassant le Bel-Ami* (repr. Paris, 1983).

Henri Troyat, *Maupassant* (Paris, 1989).

All biographies of Maupassant are subject to caution: solid biographical evidence is in short supply, many myths are perpetuated from one biography to the next, and undue reliance is frequently placed on Maupassant's fictions as sources of biographical information. A valuable discussion of these issues is provided by Jacques Lacarme, 'Le *Maupassant* de Morand ou la biographie impossible', in *Maupassant et l'écriture*, ed. Louis Forestier (Paris, 1993), 271–83.

Critical Studies

General

Pierre Cogny, *Maupassant, l'homme sans Dieu* (Brussels, 1968). A valuable overview.

Mariane Bury, *La Poétique de Maupassant* (Paris, 1994). An analysis of Maupassant's literary art.

André Vial, *Guy de Maupassant et l'art du roman* (Paris, 1954). Still the standard work.

On Une vie

André Vial, *La Genèse d'"Une vie', premier roman de Guy de Maupassant* (Paris, 1954).

Marcel Desportes *et al.*, *Analyses et réflexions sur 'Une vie' de Guy de Maupassant et le pessimisme* (Paris, 1979).

François Bessire *et al.* (eds.), *Lectures de 'Une vie' de Maupassant. Le Thème du pessimisme* (Paris, 1979).

Henri Mitterand, 'Clinique du mariage: *Une vie*', in his *Le Regard et le signe. Poétique du roman réaliste et naturaliste* (Paris, 1987), 159–67.

Bernard Valette, *Guy de Maupassant. 'Une vie'* (Paris, 1993).

Jean-Louis Cabanès, '*Une vie* ou le temps perdu', in Yves Reboul (ed.), *Maupassant multiple. Actes du colloque de Toulouse 13–15 décembre 1993* (Toulouse, 1995), 79–86.

Mariane Bury, *'Une vie' de Guy de Maupassant*, Collection Foliothèque (Paris, 1995). The most useful introductory guide to the novel.

FURTHER READING IN OXFORD WORLD'S CLASSICS

Honoré de Balzac, *Eugénie Grandet*, trans. Sylvia Raphael, introduction by Christopher Prendergast.

Gustave Flaubert, *Madame Bovary*, trans. Gerard Hopkins, ed. Terence Cave.

A CHRONOLOGY OF
GUY DE MAUPASSANT

1850   5 August: Birth of Henry René Albert Guy de Maupassant,
        probably at Fécamp on the coast of Normandy, the first
        child of Gustave de Maupassant and Laure Le Poittevin.

1851–4 Comfortably off, the Maupassants live in a number of places
        in the Normandy area (Rouen, Fécamp, Étretat) before
        moving into the Château de Grainville-Ymauville near
        Goderville in the vicinity of Le Havre.

1856   Birth of Guy's brother, Hervé.

1859   Financial problems lead Gustave de Maupassant to enter
        employment with the Banque Stolz in Paris. Family move to
        Passy. October: Guy enters the Lycée Napoléon (now the
        Lycée Henri IV), where he remains for the academic year.

1860   Failure of the marriage between Gustave and Laure. Gustave
        remains in Paris, where he works for the Banque Évrard for
        the next twenty-five years. Laure and her two sons move to
        Étretat, where Laure has bought a house, Les Verguies.

1863   Legal separation of Gustave and Laure (divorce not being
        legalized until 1884). October: Guy becomes boarder at a
        Catholic school in Yvetot. Begins writing verse.

1863–8 Schooling at Yvetot, holidays swimming and boating at
        Étretat. On one occasion swims to the assistance of the poet
        Swinburne, who has got into difficulties. Following expul-
        sion from school for some lewd verse, Maupassant is sent as
        a boarder to the Lycée Corneille in Rouen. His *correspondant*
        (a friend of the family chosen by parents of boarders to act
        as guardian) was Louis Bouilhet (b. 1821), the writer, city
        librarian, and close friend of Flaubert. Bouilhet and
        Flaubert encourage and advise him in his writing.

1869   18 July: death of Louis Bouilhet. 27 July: passes his
        baccalaureate ('mention passable'). August: meets the

---

This Chronology is based on that provided by Louis Forestier in his edition of
Maupassant's *Contes et nouvelles* in the Bibliothèque de la Pléiade.

painter Gustave Courbet (1819–77). October: enrols as a law-student in Paris, and lives in the same apartment block as his father.

1870   15 July: France declares war on Germany. Maupassant is called up and, after training, posted as a clerk to Rouen. 1 September: French defeat at Sedan.

1871   28 January: Armistice signed. September: leaves the army.

1872   Applies to join the Ministry for the Navy and the Colonies as a civil servant. Application refused, then Maupassant offered an unpaid position pending a vacancy. Begins to be a frequent summer visitor to Argenteuil on the Seine, where boating and female company occupy his time.

1873   1 February: appointed to a position on a monthly salary of 125 francs, plus an annual bonus of 150 francs. Continues to spend time at Argenteuil when he can.

1874   25 March: confirmed in his post at the Ministry and salary increased. Continues to enjoy life at Argenteuil, and to write verse, stories, and plays.

1875   February: his first short story to be published, *La Main d'écorché*, appears under the pseudonym Joseph Prunier.

1876   Now fully involved in Parisian literary life (Flaubert, Mallarmé, Zola, Huysmans, Mendès, Turgenev). Consults doctor about chest pains.

1877   2 March: aware of having contracted syphilis. August: obtains two months' sick leave. Suffering from hair-loss, headaches, eye problems, stomach pains. December: tells Flaubert of his plans for a novel (*A Life*).

1878   Transfers to the Ministry of Education. Working on *A Life*. Leaves it to one side to concentrate on a long poem (*La Vénus rustique*) and some short stories. 10–13 October: invites Flaubert to his mother's house at Étretat and shows him his unfinished novel. Maupassant is now earning 2,000 francs a year, and receiving an annual allowance from his father of 600 francs.

1879   19 February: first night of his play *L'Histoire du vieux temps*, which is well received.

1880   January–February: accused of publishing an obscene poem (*Une fille*). A letter in his defence from Flaubert contributes to the case being dropped. Further health problems, including an eye lesion and renewed hair-loss. 16 April: Zola publishes the anthology of Naturalist writing *Les Soirées de Médan*, stories about the Franco-Prussian War including Maupassant's *Boule de Suif*, which Flaubert hails as a masterpiece. 8 May: sudden death of Flaubert. 1 June: obtains first of several periods of sick leave until he ceases work in 1882. September–October: visits Corsica with his mother.

1881   May: publication of *La Maison Tellier*, the first of his many collections of short stories. Resumes work on *A Life*. July–August: visits Algeria and writes commissioned newspaper articles. On his return continues work on *A Life*.

1882   1 October: a fragment from the beginning of *A Life* published in the review *Panurge*.

1883   27 February: birth of Lucien Litzelmann, son of Josephine Liztelmann and thought to be Maupassant's child. (This traditional attribution of paternity has recently been questioned by Jacques Lacarme: see Select Bibliography.) On the same day *A Life* begins to appear in serialized form in the magazine *Gil Blas*. The last instalment appears on 6 April. Maupassant's first novel is then published by Havard. Health problems continue, which his eye specialist relates to syphilis. Hachette refuses to sell *A Life* in its station bookstalls but reverses its decision after Maupassant appeals in June to the government.

1884   January: publication of *Au soleil*, his first travel book.

1885   6 April–30 May: *Bel-Ami*, his second novel, appears in *Gil Blas* and is then published by Havard.

1886   19 January: marriage of Hervé. 1–15 August: visit to England. Stays with Baron Ferdinand de Rothschild at Waddesdon Manor, near Oxford. Visits Oxford, then London. 23 December: first instalment of *Mont-Oriol*, his third novel, appears in *Gil Blas*.

1887   January: *Mont-Oriol* published in book form.

1888   9 January: publication of *Pierre et Jean*, his fourth novel, together with an essay, 'Le Roman', by way of a preface. June: publication of *Sur l'eau*, his second travel book.

1889   May: publication by Ollendorff of *Fort comme la mort*, his fifth novel. August: takes brother to an asylum in Lyons. 13 November: death of Hervé.

1890   6–24 January: publication of *La Vie errante*, his third travel book, in series of articles in *L'Écho de Paris*, before its publication in book form in March. 15 May: his final completed novel, *Notre cœur*, begins to appear in the *Revue des deux mondes*: published in book form in June. His health is now giving serious cause for concern.

1891   January–March: begins another novel, *L'Angélus*. 4 March: first performance of his play *Musotte*.

1892   After visiting his mother on New Year's Day, he returns home (at Cannes); tries to kill himself that night by slitting his throat with a paper-knife. 8 January: taken to the clinic of Dr Blanche in Passy (now part of Paris) and diagnosed as suffering from paresis (or general paralysis), the tertiary stage of syphilis.

1893   6 July: death of Maupassant. 8 July: burial in the cemetery of Montparnasse. Zola gives the funeral oration.

1903   8 December: death of Laure de Maupassant in Nice at the age of 82.

A LIFE

For Mme Brainne

The homage of a devoted friend,
in memory of a departed friend.*

GUY DE MAUPASSANT

I

Her trunks packed, Jeanne walked over to the window, but it had not stopped raining.

All night long the downpour had rattled on the rooftiles and against the window-panes. The lowering, water-laden sky seemed to have burst asunder and to be emptying itself onto the land, thinning the soil to a pap and dissolving it like sugar. Squalls of warm, heavy air gusted intermittently. The sluicing gurgle of overflowing drains filled the deserted streets, where the houses stood, like sponges, soaking up the penetrating moisture that made their walls sweat with damp from cellar to attic.

Jeanne, having left the convent on the previous day and being now at last forever free, ready to reach out for all the good things in life of which she had so long been dreaming, was afraid that her father might hesitate to set out if the weather did not clear; and for the hundredth time that morning she scanned the horizon.

Then she noticed that she had forgotten to pack her calendar in her travelling-bag. She took it down from the wall, a small piece of card divided into months and bearing the date of the current year 1819 in gilt numbering surrounded by an intricate pattern, and proceeded to cross out the first four columns with a pencil, putting a line through each saint's name as far as 2 May, the day she had left the convent.

A voice outside the door called:

'Jeannette!'

'Come in, Papa,' Jeanne answered.

And her father appeared.

Baron Simon-Jacques Le Perthuis des Vauds was a gentleman out of the previous century, at once an eccentric and a kindly soul. As an enthusiastic disciple of Jean-Jacques Rousseau* he loved nature with a lover's passion, its fields, its woods, its animals.

As an aristocrat by birth, he instinctively abhorred what had happened in '93;* but being philosophical by temperament and liberal by education, he denounced tyranny with a mild and vociferous hatred.

His great strength, and also his great weakness, was his kindliness, a kindliness that had not arms enough to caress or to give or to embrace, the kindliness of a creator, undiscriminating, unresisting, as though some sinew of his will were paralysed, as though his motor-force lacked some essential element. It was almost a vice.

Being of a theoretical cast of mind, he had planned his daughter's education in every particular, with the intention of rendering her at once happy, good-natured, honest, and loving.

She had remained at home until the age of twelve, and then, despite her mother's tears, she had been sent to the Convent of the Sacred Heart.

There he had kept her firmly shut away, cloistered, unknown and unknowing, ignorant of human things. It was his wish that she should be returned to him a virgin at the age of seventeen so that he himself might imbue her with a kind of poetry of reason and thereby, out in the countryside, in the midst of the fecundated land, unlock her soul and dispel her ignorance with the spectacle of natural love, of the simple courtship of animals, of the serene laws of existence.

And now she was leaving the convent, radiant, full of youthful sap and a hunger for happiness, primed for all the joyful experiences, all the charming chance occurrences, that she had already mentally rehearsed in solitary anticipation throughout her idle daylight moments and the long hours of the night.

She resembled a portrait by Veronese,* with hair so blonde that its sheen seemed to have been transferred to her skin, an aristocrat's skin barely tinged with pink and dappled with the faintest down, a sort of pale velvet that became just perceptible when caressed by the rays of the sun. And her eyes were blue, of that opaque blue to be found on Delft figurines.

She had a mole on the left side of her nose, and another to the right, on her chin, which bore one or two curly hairs of such a colour as to be scarcely distinguishable from her skin. She was tall, with a well-developed bosom and a shapely figure. Her clear voice seemed at times too shrill; but her generous laugh made those around her feel joyful. Frequently, in a familiar gesture, she would raise her two hands to her temples as though to smooth her hair.

She ran to her father and gave him a hug as she kissed him:

'Well, are we leaving?'

He smiled, shaking his head covered in hair that was already white and which he wore rather long; and he gestured towards the window:

'How do you expect us to travel in such weather?'

But she implored him with playful, wheedling affection:

'Oh please, Papa, do let's be off. It will be fine by the afternoon.'

'But your mother will never agree to it.'

'Yes, she will. I'll see that she does.'

'Well, if you can manage to persuade your mother, I shall have no objection myself.'

And away she hurried to the Baroness's room. For she had awaited this day of departure with growing impatience.

Since her arrival at the Convent of the Sacred Heart she had never been out of Rouen, her father having forbidden all such diversions before she should reach the age upon which he had fixed. Twice, only, she had been taken to spend a fortnight in Paris, but that too was a city, and she dreamt only of the country.

Now she was going to spend the summer at their property at Les Peuples, an old family chateau perched on the cliffs near Yport;* and she was eagerly looking forward to this joyous life of freedom beside the sea. Moreover it had been agreed that she was to be made a present of this manor-house and that she would live there permanently after she was married.

And this rain, which had fallen without respite since the previous evening, was the first great sorrow of her life.

But three minutes later she came running out of her mother's room, screaming the house down:

'Papa, Papa, Mother's agreed! Have the horses harnessed!'

The deluge did not abate; indeed it seemed to fall even more heavily as the berline drew up at the door.*

Jeanne stood ready to climb into the carriage as the Baroness
came down the stairs, supported on one side by her husband
and on the other by a tall housemaid as strong and strapping as a
lad. She was a Norman girl from the Pays de Caux,* who looked
at least twenty though she was eighteen at most. The family
treated her rather as a second daughter, for her mother
had suckled Jeanne* at the same time as her. She was called
Rosalie.

It was in fact her principal function to help her mistress as she
walked, for the Baroness had grown enormously fat in recent
years as the result of cardiac hypertrophy, which ailed her
constantly.

Breathing heavily, the Baroness reached the front steps of the
old town-house, saw the courtyard streaming with water, and
muttered:

'Really, this is not very sensible.'

Her husband replied with his usual smile:

'The decision was yours, Madame Adélaïde.'

Because she bore the sonorous name of Adélaïde, he always
prefaced it with a 'Madame' which he uttered with a certain air of
faintly mocking respect.

Thereupon she continued her progress and struggled into the
carriage, whose springs sagged. The Baron sat down by her side,
while Jeanne and Rosalie took their places with their backs to the
horses.

Ludivine, the cook, brought piles of cloaks which they spread
over their knees, as well as two baskets which they tucked away
under their legs. Then she climbed up beside Père Simon and
wrapped herself in a large rug, which covered her head completely. The caretaker and his wife came to say goodbye and shut
the carriage-door. They listened to the final instructions about
the trunks, which were to follow in a cart; and away the travellers
went.

Père Simon, the coachman, sat with his head bowed and his
shoulders hunched beneath the rain, disappearing under the
triple cape of his box-coat. Howling gusts of wind and rain beat
against the carriage-windows and flooded the roadway.

Drawn by two horses at a brisk trot, the berline proceeded rapidly down towards the quayside and along the line of tall ships whose masts, yards, and rigging rose forlornly into the teeming sky like trees stripped bare of their leaves. Then it turned into the long Boulevard du Mont Riboudet.

Soon they were crossing open countryside; and from time to time the blurred outline of a rain-drenched willow could be seen through the watery murk, its branches dangling like the limbs of a corpse. The horses' hooves splashed through the puddles as the four wheels span sunbursts of mud.

No one spoke; their spirits seemed as thoroughly dampened as the waterlogged earth. Mama leant her head back and closed her eyes. The Baron gazed out gloomily at the unchanging, sodden landscape. Rosalie, nursing a parcel on her knees, was sunk in the animal-like rumination of common folk. But beneath this warm, streaming rain, Jeanne felt as though she were coming back to life, like some indoor plant which has been returned out of doors; and the fullness of her joy sheltered her, like foliage, from despondency. Although she said nothing, she felt like singing, like putting her hand out of the window to fill it with water and drink; and she delighted to be thus borne away at the trot, to see the desolation of the countryside and to feel surrounded and protected in the midst of this deluge.

And beneath the relentless rain a cloud of steam rose from the gleaming hindquarters of the two horses.

Gradually the Baroness dropped off to sleep. Her face, framed by six dangling corkscrew curls of hair, grew progressively slack, gently propped upon the three great billows of her neck whose nethermost ripples merged into the broad ocean of her bosom. Her head rose and sagged with each breath; the cheeks filled, and then a rasping snore would issue from between her parted lips. Her husband leaned towards her and gently placed a small leather wallet in her hands where they lay crossed upon the amplitude of her stomach.

This contact woke her; and she considered the object with a misty gaze, in the dazed stupor that follows upon the interruption of sleep. The wallet fell to the floor and came open.

Banknotes and gold coins scattered through the carriage. She awoke completely; and her daughter's gaiety exploded in a burst of laughter.

The Baron picked up the money and placed it on her lap:

'There, my dear, that's all that's left of my farm at Életot.* I sold it to pay for the repairs at Les Peuples. We'll be spending a good deal of time there from now on.'

She counted out six thousand four hundred francs* and calmly put them in her pocket.

This was the ninth farm sold out of the thirty-one which they had been left by their parents. Nevertheless they still owned enough land to bring in twenty thousand francs a year, and which could easily have brought in thirty thousand if it had been well managed.

As they lived simply, this income would have sufficed if their household had not contained a bottomless well upon which they never ceased to draw: generosity. It made the money evaporate off the palm of their hands as surely as the sun removes the water from a marsh. It simply flowed away, leaked from them, vanished. How? Nobody quite knew. Time and again one or other of them would say: 'I just don't know how it's happened. I've spent a hundred francs today, just on little things.'

Moreover, this readiness to give was one of the great joys of their life; and they were magnificently, touchingly, of one mind on the subject.

'And is my house beautiful now?' asked Jeanne.

'You'll soon see, my child', replied the Baron cheerfully.

Slowly, however, the violence of the downpour began to abate; and eventually it was no more than a sort of misty drizzle, the finest spray of rain dancing in the air. The vault of cloud seemed to be lifting and paling; and suddenly, through some invisible gap, a long, slanting ray of sunlight fell upon the pastures.

The clouds having now parted, the azure reaches of the sky appeared. The gap grew bigger, like a veil being rent in two, and a beautiful, pure sky of clear, deep blue covered the world.

A cool, gentle breeze wafted by, like a happy sigh from off the land; and whenever they drove along the edge of a garden or a wood, they could hear the brisk song of a bird drying its feathers.

Evening was approaching. Everyone in the carriage was asleep now, except Jeanne. Twice they stopped at wayside inns to allow the horses to rest and be given some oats and water.

The sun had set; church bells tolled in the distance. In one little village they were lighting the lamps; and the sky began to shine with a swarm of stars. Here and there the lights from a house would pierce the darkness like pinpricks of fire; and all at once, from behind a hillside, through branches of fir, the moon rose, red and huge, like a bleary eye roused from sleep.

It was so mild that they had left the carriage-windows down. Jeanne was dozing now, exhausted by her fantasies and replete with visions of happiness. Occasionally, when the numbness that came from adopting one position for too long caused her to open her eyes, Jeanne would look out and see the trees of a farmstead passing in the luminous darkness, or even a few cows lying here and there in a field, who raised their heads. Then she would shift in her seat and try to recover the thread of some dream; but the constant rumble of the carriage filled her ears and defeated her thoughts, and she would close her eyes again, feeling as though her mind were as stiff as her cramped body.

But stop they did. Men and women were standing by the carriage-doors bearing lanterns. They had arrived. Jeanne, suddenly awake, leapt down from the carriage. Father and Rosalie, their path lighted by a farmer, almost had to carry the Baroness, who was exhausted and groaning in distress, constantly repeating in a low, weak voice: 'Oh, good heavens! My poor dears!' She did not want anything to drink or eat, but went to bed and at once fell asleep.

Jeanne and the Baron had supper alone.

They smiled at each other and clasped one another's hands across the table; and then, both of them filled with childish excitement, they began to tour the refurbished manor-house.

It was one of those vast, tall Norman residences, half farmhouse, half chateau, built of white stone that had turned grey, and spacious enough to accommodate an entire clan.

A huge hall ran right through the house, dividing it in two, with large doors that opened to front and back. A double staircase seemed to bestride the entrance, leaving the centre empty, with its two flights joining at the first floor like a bridge.

On the ground floor, to the right, stood the door into the enormous drawing-room, which was hung with tapestries on which birds strutted against leafy backgrounds. All the furniture was upholstered in petit point and depicted scenes from the fables of La Fontaine;* and Jeanne gave a start of delight to see a chair she had loved as a small child, which showed the story of the Fox and the Stork.

The drawing-room gave onto the library, which was full of old books, and onto two further rooms, which were unused. To the left was the dining-room with its new wooden panelling, then the laundry room, pantry, and kitchen, and a small closet containing a bath.

A corridor ran lengthwise along the middle of the first floor. The ten doors of the ten bedrooms were lined up along the passage. At the far end, on the right, was Jeanne's bedroom. They went in. The Baron had had it entirely redecorated, simply using draperies and furniture which had been lying untouched in the attic.

Tapestries of Flemish origin and some considerable antiquity filled the room with strange figures.

But on catching sight of her bed, Jeanne shrieked with delight. At its corners four large birds carved in oak, all black and shining with polish, served as the bed's supports and seemed to be its guardians. The sides bore two broad garlands of carved fruits and flowers; and four delicately fluted columns, surmounted by Corinthian capitals, supported a cornice of roses and cupids entwined.

There it stood, at once monumental and yet thoroughly graceful, despite the severity of the wood which had darkened with age.

The counterpane and the bed's canopy sparkled like two starry firmaments. Made of antique silk, they were dark blue in colour and studded with large fleur-de-lis embroidered in gold.

Having admired the bed at length, Jeanne lifted her lamp to examine the tapestries and discover their subject.

A young nobleman and a young lady both dressed in green, red, and yellow, and in the strangest garb, were conversing beneath a blue tree on which some white fruits were ripening. A large rabbit of the same colour was nibbling at a tuft of grey grass.

Just above these figures, and supposedly in the distance, could be seen five little round houses, with pointed roofs; and above them, almost in the sky, a bright red windmill.

Large floral patterns swirled through the scene.

The other two panels were very similar to the first, except that four little men in Flemish costume were to be seen coming out of the houses and raising their arms to the sky in utter consternation and fury.

But the last tapestry depicted a moment of drama. Beside the rabbit, which was still nibbling away, the young man lay stretched out on the ground and appeared to be dead. The young lady, her eyes on the young man, was driving a sword into her breast, and the fruits on the tree had turned black.

Jeanne was about to give up trying to make sense of the story when in one corner she spotted a tiny little animal which in real life the rabbit could have eaten as easily as a blade of grass. But it was a lion.

Then she recognized the sorry tale of Pyramus and Thisbe;* and although she smiled at the crudity of the drawings, she felt happy at the thought of being enclosed within the confines of this love story which would forever speak to her of the hopes she had nurtured, and that each night this ancient legend of tender devotion would look down upon her as she slept.

The rest of the furnishings brought together the most disparate of styles. There were items of furniture such as each succeeding generation keeps in the family and which make old houses rather resemble museums by containing a selection of everything. A superb Louis XIV commode, plated with dazzling brass, was flanked by two Louis XV chairs which still had their original upholstery of floral silk. A rosewood writing-table stood opposite the fireplace, while on the mantelpiece was an Empire clock beneath a glass globe.

It was a bronze beehive, suspended by four marble columns

over a garden of gilt flowers. A thin pendulum protruded from the hive through a wide slit and transported a tiny bee with enamel wings endlessly to and fro above the flower-bed.

The clock face, of painted porcelain, was set into the side of the beehive.

It began to chime eleven o'clock. The Baron kissed his daughter goodnight and retired to his room.

Then, reluctantly, Jeanne went to bed.

After one last look round her room, she extinguished the candle. But to the left of her bed, of which only the head was placed against the wall, there was a window, and through it the moonlight flooded in, casting a pool of brilliance across the floor.

This light was reflected back onto the walls, where pale gleams played wanly over the motionless romance of Pyramus and Thisbe.

Through the other window, opposite the end of the bed, Jeanne could see a tall tree suffused in soft light. She turned on her side and closed her eyes, but then, after a while, opened them again.

She felt as though she were still being jolted by the carriage, and its rumbling seemed to be continuing inside her head. At first she lay there without moving, hoping that repose would eventually make her go to sleep; but the restlessness of her mind soon communicated itself to her whole body.

She could feel the muscles twitching in her legs, and she was beginning to grow feverish. So she got out of bed and, with feet and arms bare, looking like a ghost in her long nightdress, she crossed the patch of moonlight that lay across the floor, opened the window, and looked out.

It was such a bright night that she could see as clearly as though it were daylight; and Jeanne recognized the countryside she had once loved so dearly during her early childhood.

Immediately facing her was a large lawn, as yellow as butter in the nocturnal light. Two huge trees stood in front of the house like ballet-dancers on their points, a plane-tree to the north and a lime to the south.

On the far side of this great expanse of grass, a small copse of trees marked the boundary of the area sheltered from the sea gales by five rows of ancient elms: gnarled, stripped bare, and half eaten away, they had been shaped into a roof-like slope by the ceaseless action of the wind from the sea.

What thus constituted a kind of park was bounded to right and left by two long avenues of enormously tall poplars, called *peuples* in Normandy, which separated the landlord's residence from the two dependent farms which abutted it, one of which was lived in by the Couillard family, the other by the Martins.

These *peuples* had given their name to the chateau. Beyond this enclosed space stretched a vast, uncultivated plain, dotted with gorse-bushes, where the wind whistled and chased throughout the day and night. Then the land came to a sudden halt at a sheer, white cliff which dropped a hundred metres to the waves breaking at its foot.

In the distance Jeanne gazed at the broad expanse of the sea, rippled like moiré silk and seemingly asleep beneath the stars.

In the stillness left by the departed sun, all the different smells of the land filled the air. A jasmine clambering round the ground-floor windows gave off its steady, pungent scent that mingled with the fainter perfume of its newly unfolded leaves. Slow eddies of breeze brought with them the reek of the salty sea-air and the oozing slime of seaweed.

At first Jeanne simply yielded to the pleasure of breathing in the air: and the peace of the countryside soothed her like a cool bath.

All the animals that bestir themselves at dusk to carry on their obscure existence under cover of the tranquil night filled the semi-darkness with their silent bustle. Large birds flitted past, without a cry, mere blotches, shadows; the murmur of invisible insects barely caught the ear; while noiseless errands were accomplished across the dewy grass or the sand along the deserted paths.

Alone, one or two melancholy toads sounded their short, monotonous croak at the moon.

Jeanne felt as though her heart were swelling, filled like this clear night with silent susurrations and all at once teeming with a thousand roving desires like these nocturnal creatures whose rustling was all around her. By some affinity she felt at one with this living poetry; and in the soft, pale brilliance of the night she sensed a preternatural stirring, the tremor of impossible hopes, as though bliss were on the breeze.

And she began to dream of love.

Love! For the past two years it had filled her with growing anxiety at its approach. She was now free to love; all that remained was for her to meet him. Him!

What would he be like? She did not quite know, did not even speculate in the matter. Quite simply, he would be *him*.

All she knew was that she would adore him with her heart and soul and that he would cherish her with all his might. They would walk together on evenings such as this, beneath the ashen gleam of the stars. On they would go, hand in hand, cleaving tightly to one another, listening to each other's heart beat, feeling the warmth of the other's shoulder, mingling their love with the balm of a limpid summer's night, so completely at one that by the simple power of their tender devotion they would be able to penetrate each other's innermost thoughts.

And things would always be thus, in the serenity of an indestructible affection.

And all at once it seemed to her that she could feel him there now, beside her; and a sudden quivering of indeterminate sensual longing ran through her from head to toe. She hugged herself, unconsciously, as though to embrace her dream; and as her lips reached out towards the unknown, there passed over them something to make her almost faint, as if the breath of spring had kissed her with a lover's kiss.

Suddenly, over there behind the house, coming from the road, she could hear footsteps in the night. And as her startled soul thrilled in a transport of belief in the impossible, in providential accidents, in divine presentiments and romantic combinations of circumstance, she thought: 'And if that were he!' She listened nervously to the rhythmic footfall of the walker, convinced that he was about to stop at the front gate and ask for shelter.

When he had passed by, she felt the sadness of a disappointment. But she realized how she had been carried away by her hopes, and she smiled at her folly.

Then, feeling a little calmer, she allowed her mind to wander along more sensible paths, trying to peer into the future, arranging her life in advance.

She would live here with him, in this peaceful chateau overlooking the sea. She would doubtless have two children, a son for him, a daughter for her. And she could see them running across the grass between the plane-tree and the lime, while father and mother looked on with delight, exchanging loving glances over their heads.

And she remained there for a long, long time, dreaming in this fashion, while the moon completed its passage across the sky and vanished beneath the sea. The air was turning cooler. In the east the horizon was brightening. A cock crowed in the farm on the right; others answered from the farm on the left. Through the walls of the hen-houses their raucous voices seemed to come from very far away; while up in the immense vault of the sky, now imperceptibly turning whiter and whiter, the stars vanished from view.

Somewhere a bird awoke and gave a tiny cry. Twittering began, timid at first, coming from amidst the foliage; then it grew bolder, turning vibrant and joyful, and was taken up from branch to branch and from tree to tree.

Suddenly Jeanne could feel brightness upon her; and raising her head which she had buried in her hands she closed her eyes, dazzled by the radiance of the dawn.

A mountainous bank of crimson clouds, partly hidden behind the great avenue of poplars, cast glimmers of blood-red light upon the wakened earth.

And slowly, piercing the brilliance of the mists, darting fire upon the trees, and the plain, and the ocean, and across the whole horizon, the huge, blazing globe shone forth.

And Jeanne began to feel a wild happiness. A sense of delirious joy, an infinite tenderness at the splendour of things, filled her heart to bursting. This was her sun! her dawn! the beginning of

her life! the daybreak of her aspirations! She stretched out her
arms towards the radiant space, desirous of embracing the sun
itself; she wanted to speak out, to proclaim a message as holy as
the birth of this day; but she remained dumbstruck in her impo-
tent enthusiasm. Then, placing her forehead in her hands, she felt
her eyes fill with tears; and she wept, deliciously.

When she looked up again, the magnificent display of the new
dawn had already vanished. She, too, felt spent and a little weary,
as though her fires had cooled. Leaving the window open she
went and lay on the bed, turning things over in her mind for a few
minutes longer before falling into such a deep sleep that at eight
o'clock she failed to hear her father calling her and woke only
when he came into her room.

He wanted to show her all the things that had been done to the
house, to *her* house.

The front of the house faced inland and was separated from
the road by a vast courtyard planted with apple-trees. This
road—a so-called parish way—ran between the peasants' small-
holdings and joined the main highway from Le Havre to Fécamp
some half a league hence.

A straight avenue led from the wooden entrance-gate to the
front steps. The outhouses—low buildings rendered with shingle
and topped with thatch—extended on either side of the courtyard, along the length of the ditches separating it from the two
farms.

The roofing on the old manor-house had been replaced; all the
woodwork had been restored, the walls repaired, the rooms
repapered, and the whole of the interior repainted. And against
its weathered exterior the new shutters, painted a silvery white,
looked like stains, as did the patches of fresh plaster against the
broad, grey surface of the front façade.

The other side of the house, in which one of Jeanne's bedroom
windows was situated, afforded a distant view of the sea, over the
copse and the screen of elms gnawed away by the wind.

Arm in arm, Jeanne and the Baron inspected everything, each
little nook and cranny; and then they strolled along the long
avenues of poplars which formed the boundary of what was called

the park. The grass had grown long beneath the trees, spreading out in a carpet of green. The copse, at the far end, was an enchanting spot with its muddle of tiny, twisting paths separated by leafy partitions. A hare started up suddenly, alarming Jeanne, and then leapt over the bank and made off through the gorse towards the cliff

After lunch Madame Adélaïde, who was still exhausted, announced that she was retiring to rest, and the Baron suggested that they went down to Yport.

Off they went, passing first through the hamlet of Étouvent, in which Les Peuples was located.* Three farmhands greeted them as if they had known them all their lives.

They entered the woodland that slopes down a twisting valley towards the sea.

Presently the village of Yport came into sight. Women, sitting on their front steps mending clothes, watched them as they passed by. The main street ran downhill, with a gutter in the middle and piles of rubbish standing by the doorways, and it gave off a strong smell of pickling brine. Brown fishing-nets, with gleaming scales sticking to them here and there like tiny silver coins, were hanging out to dry against the cottage-doors, while from inside came the various aromas generated by these large families, each one crowded together into a single room.

One or two pigeons were walking along the edge of the gutter in search of sustenance.

Jeanne took in the scene, which for her had the interest and novelty of a stage set.

But suddenly, rounding the end of a wall, she caught sight of the sea, a smooth, dark expanse of blue stretching away as far as the eye could see.

They stopped, opposite the beach, and gazed. Out at sea sails were passing, white as birds' wings. To right and left loomed the towering cliff. A headland of sorts interrupted the view in one direction, while in the other the coastline extended indefinitely until it was no more than a faint smudge.

A harbour and some houses could be seen in one of its nearer

indentations; and tiny little waves, edging the sea with a frill of
foam, plashed gently onto the shingle.

The local fishing-boats had been hauled up the sloping beach
over the smooth pebbles and lay on their sides, proffering their
shiny, plump, pitch-coated cheeks to the sun. A few fishermen
were getting them ready for the evening tide.

A sailor came up selling fish, and Jeanne bought a brill, which
she insisted on carrying back to Les Peuples herself.

Then the man offered his services for boat-trips, repeating his
name in emphatic sequence to impress it on the memory: 'Lastique, Joséphin Lastique.'

The Baron promised not to forget it.

They turned and headed back towards the chateau.

As Jeanne found the fish tiring to carry, she poked her father's
walking-stick through its gills, and each took one end; and mer-
rily they climbed back up the hill again, chatting away like two
children, faces to the wind and eyes shining, while the brill,
which felt heavier and heavier, swept the grass with its oily tail.

II

For Jeanne a charming life of freedom now began. She read, she
daydreamed, she wandered about by herself in the surrounding
countryside. She ambled aimlessly along the roads, her thoughts
far away; or else she scampered down the little winding valleys
where, like golden copes, a shock of flowering gorse topped the
ridges on either side. Its sweet, pungent smell, intensified by the
heat, turned her head like fragrant wine; and the distant sound of
waves breaking on a beach bore her spirits up on a swell of peace.

Sometimes she would have to lie down on a bank of thick grass,
overcome by lassitude; while at other moments she would suddenly, at a bend in the valley or through a gap in the grass, catch
sight of a corner of blue sea sparkling in the sunshine, with a sail
visible in the distance, and she would be filled with unruly joy as
though at the mysterious approach of imminent felicities.

In the fresh and gentle air of this place and amid the calm
serenity of its smoothly curved horizons, she grew to love the
solitude; and she would remain sitting on the hilltops for so long
that little wild rabbits would come bounding past her feet.

Often she would start running along the clifftop, exhilarated by
the lightness of the air and tremulous with the exquisite delight
of being able to move about as effortlessly as the fishes in the
water or the swallows in the sky.

She made memories wherever she went, like a sower casting
seed upon the soil, memories of the kind so deep-rooted that they
remain unto death. She felt as though she were strewing her heart
amidst all the clefts and folds of these valleys.

She developed a passion for bathing. She would swim off into
the distance, strong and bold, oblivious to the danger. It felt good
to be in this cold, clear, blue water that lifted her up and rocked
her to and fro. When she was far from the shore, she would lie on
her back, her arms folded across her chest, and gaze into the deep
blue of the sky broken only by the sudden flight of a swallow or
the white silhouette of a seabird. From here nothing could be

heard but the distant murmur of the waves breaking on the shingle and faint, indeterminate sounds coming off the land, which barely carried to her across the undulations of the waves. Then Jeanne would sit up in the water, let out piercing shrieks of sudden, frantic joy, and slap the surface of the sea with the palms of her hands.

Sometimes, when she ventured out too far, a fishing-boat would come and fetch her.

She would return to the house, pale from hunger but with a spring in her step, invigorated, a smile playing on her lips and eyes brimming with happiness.

The Baron, meanwhile, was planning great agricultural schemes. He wanted to experiment, to introduce reforms, to try out new equipment and acclimatize new breeds; and he spent part of his day in conversation with the farmers, who would shake their heads in sceptical distrust at his initiatives.

Frequently he would accompany the fishermen of Yport out to sea. Once he had visited all the caves and springs and rock pinnacles in the area, he wanted to fish as though he were just a simple fisherman like them.

On the days when there was a good breeze, when the plump hull rides the crest of the waves under a filling sail and from each side of the boat the long fishing-line stretches away down into the sea, pursued by shoals of mackerel, he would be there, his hand trembling with anxiety, holding the thin string that quivers as soon as a fish is hooked and begins to struggle.

He would go out by moonlight to lift the nets which had been laid the night before. He loved to hear the creaking of the mast and to breathe in the sharp gusts of cool night air; and having tacked about in search of his buoys, taking his bearings from the jagged outline of a rock, the roof of a churchtower, or the light-house at Fécamp, he loved just to drift quietly in the first rays of the rising sun, which glistened on the slimy backs of the large, fan-shaped skate and on the fat bellies of the turbot lying on the boat-deck.

At each mealtime he would regale them with enthusiastic accounts of his excursions; and in turn Mama would tell him how many times she had walked up and down the great avenue of poplars, the one on the right by the Couillards' farm, the other being insufficiently in the sun.

Ever since she had been advised to 'exercise', she had become a determined walker. As soon as the dampness of early morning was gone, she would come downstairs on Rosalie's arm, wrapped in a cloak and two shawls, with a black hooded bonnet pulled down over her head, itself further covered by a red knitted scarf.

Then, dragging her left foot, which was slightly heavier and which had already traced two dusty furrows all the way up and down the path where the grass had been worn away, she set off once more on the endless journey which brought her in a straight line from the corner of the house to the first shrubs on the edge of the copse. She had had a bench placed at each end of this itinerary; and every five minutes she would stop and say to the poor, long-suffering maid supporting her:

'Let's sit down, my dear. I am a little tired.'

And with each rest she would leave an article of clothing behind on the bench, first the scarf from round her head, then a shawl, and then the other shawl, the bonnet, and finally the cloak. This resulted in two large piles of clothing at each end of the avenue, which Rosalie would carry back on her free arm when they went in for lunch.

And in the afternoon the Baroness would begin again at a more leisurely pace, taking longer rests and sometimes dozing off for as much as an hour on a chaise-longue which had been wheeled outside for her.

She called this taking 'her' exercise, just as she used to refer to 'my' hypertrophy.

A doctor she had consulted ten years earlier about her short-ness of breath had talked of hypertrophy. Since then this word, the meaning of which she barely understood, had remained fixed in her mind. She would insist on the Baron, and Jeanne, and Rosalie each feeling her heart, though they no longer could, buried as it now was beneath the bloated mass of her chest. But she energetically refused to allow herself to be examined by any new doctor in case further ailments were discovered; and she

would talk of 'her' hypertrophy at every opportunity and with
such frequency that it appeared as though this condition were
peculiar to her, as if it belonged to her as something unique over
which other people had no rights.

The Baron would talk of 'my wife's hypertrophy' and Jeanne
of 'Mummy's hypertrophy' the way one referred to her dress, or
her hat, or her umbrella.

She had been very pretty in her youth and pencil thin. Having
waltzed in the arms of every man in uniform under the Empire,
she had read *Corinne*,* which made her cry; and this novel had, as
it were, left its mark on her ever since.

As her figure had grown stouter, so her soul had taken wing on
more poetic flights of fancy; and when corpulence at length con-
fined her to an armchair, her thoughts began to rove through a
series of amorous fantasies of which she imagined herself the
heroine. Among these she had her favourites, which she would
actively recall to mind in the course of her dreaming, like a music
box being constantly rewound and playing the same tune over and
over again. All those langorous romances about swallows and
captive maidens* never failed to bring a tear to her eye; and she
was even quite fond of some bawdy songs by Béranger* on account
of their wistful sentiments.

Often she would sit motionless, for hours on end, lost in
her dream world; and living at Les Peuples gave her enormous
pleasure because it provided the scenery for her soul's imagin-
ings. The surrounding woods, the deserted heath, the vicinity of
the sea, all of it reminded her of the novels by Walter Scott*
which she had been reading for the past few months.

On rainy days she would remain closeted in her bedroom,
going through what she called her 'relics'. These were all the old
letters she had kept, from her father and mother, from the Baron
during their engagement, and from others besides.

She kept them locked away in a mahogany writing-desk surmounted at each corner by brass sphinxes; and in a special voice
she would say: 'Rosalie, my dear, bring me my memory drawer.'

The maid would open the desk, take out the drawer, and place
it on a chair beside her mistress, who then slowly began to read

the letters, one by one, occasionally shedding a tear over them.

From time to time Jeanne would take Rosalie's place and accompany Mama on her walk, listening as she reminisced about her childhood. The young girl could see herself in these stories of former days, and was startled by the similarity of their thoughts, by the kinship of their desires; for every heart imagines itself the first to thrill to a myriad sensations which once stirred the hearts of the earliest creatures and which will again stir the hearts of the last men and women to walk the earth.

Their slow progress matched the slow pace of the narrative, which was sometimes interrupted for a few moments by bouts of breathlessness; and then Jeanne's thoughts would race ahead of the stories newly begun, towards a future filled with joyful events, and she would revel in her happy expectations.

One afternoon, as they were resting on the far bench, she suddenly caught sight of a fat priest coming towards them from the other end of the avenue.

He greeted them from a distance, assumed a smiling expression, and then greeted them again when he was three paces away, enquiring loudly:

'Well now, your ladyship, and how are we today?'

It was the local priest.

Having been born in the days of the Enlightenment thinkers* and then brought up during the Revolutionary period by a father who was a non-believer, Mama seldom went to church, although some manner of female religious instinct made her fond of clerics.

She had quite forgotten about the Abbé Picot, her priest, and blushed on seeing him. She apologized for not having spared him the obligation of paying a call on them. But the fellow did not seem to have taken umbrage; he looked at Jeanne and complimented her on her healthy appearance, then sat down, placed his priest's three-cornered hat on his knees, and mopped his brow. He was extremely fat and extremely red in the face, and he was sweating profusely. He kept removing from his pocket an enormous check handkerchief which was drenched in perspiration, and wiping it across his face and neck; but hardly had this damp piece of cloth been returned to the black depths of his clerical habit than new beads of sweat formed on his skin and dripped onto the bulge of his cassock-clad stomach, fixing the errant particles of road dust into little round stains.

He was a cheerful sort, the typical country priest, tolerant, garrulous, and altogether a good fellow. He told them stories, talked about the local people, and seemed not to have noticed that his two female parishioners had not yet been to church, the Baroness having been as remiss in this respect as she was uncertain in her faith, and Jeanne having been only too happy to be released from the convent where she had tasted her fill of religious ceremonies.

The Baron appeared. His pantheistic beliefs made him indifferent to all dogma. He was amiably civil towards the Abbé, whom he knew slightly, and invited him to stay for dinner.

The priest knew how to make himself welcome thanks to that intuitive skill which the cure of souls gives to even the most ordinary of men who are called by the chance of events to exercise power over their fellows.

The Baroness made a fuss of him, perhaps drawn to him by the kind of affinity which brings people of a similar nature together, since the ruddy face and breathlessness of this portly man appealed to her in her wheezing obesity.

By the time they had reached dessert, his good spirits were quite those of the feasting curate, that relaxed familiarity which comes with the end of a convivial meal.

And all at once, as though struck by a sudden, happy thought, he exclaimed:

'But wait, I have a new parishioner I must introduce to you, Monsieur le Vicomte de Lamare!'

The Baroness, who had the entire armorial of the province at her fingertips, enquired:

'Is he one of the Lamares de l'Eure?'

The priest bowed:

'Yes, Madame, he is the son of the Vicomte Jean de Lamare, who died last year.'

Then Madame Adélaïde, who treasured the nobility above all

else, asked a whole series of questions and learnt that the young man, having paid his father's debts and sold the family mansion, had found himself a small hunting-lodge on one of the three farms which he owned in the commune of Étouvent. These estates brought in some five to six thousand a year in total; but the Vicomte, being of a thrifty and sober disposition, intended to spend the next two or three years living simply in this modest *pied-à-terre* in order to accumulate sufficient funds to cut a figure in the world and marry well without incurring debts or mortgaging his farms.

The priest added:

'He's such a charming fellow, so sensible and mild-mannered. But he doesn't find much to amuse him round here.'

The Baron answered:

'Then bring him to see us, Monsieur l'Abbé. Perhaps that may offer him some distraction from time to time.'

And they began to talk of other things.

When they went into the drawing-room after coffee, the priest asked if he might take a turn round the garden, being accustomed to a little exercise after his meals. The Baron accompanied him. Slowly they walked the length of the white-fronted chateau before retracing their steps. Their shadows, the one thin, the other round and wearing a mushroom on its head, came and went, now before them, now behind, depending on whether they were walking towards the moon or away from it. The priest was chewing a kind of cigarette which he had taken out of his pocket. He explained its use with a countryman's frankness:

'It helps me belch. My digestion's not very good.'

Then, promptly looking up at the bright moon riding in the sky, he declared:

'Ah, there's a sight one never tires of.'

And he went in to take his leave of the ladies.

III

On the following Sunday the Baroness and Jeanne went to Mass, out of tactful deference towards their priest.

They waited for him after the service in order to invite him to lunch on Thursday. He came out of the vestry arm-in-arm with a tall, elegant young man. On catching sight of the two ladies, he gestured in delighted surprise and exclaimed:

'How opportune! Allow me, your ladyship, Mademoiselle Jeanne, to introduce to you your neighbour, Monsieur le Vicomte de Lamare'.

The Vicomte bowed, said how he had long wished to make the ladies' acquaintance, and began to converse with the easy, well-bred assurance of a man who has lived. He had one of those fortunate faces which women dream about and all men find disagreeable. His black, curly hair cast a shadow over his smooth, tanned forehead; and two large eyebrows, as regular in shape as though they had been artificially drawn, lent depth and tenderness to his dark eyes, the whites of which seemed faintly tinged with blue.

His long, thick eyelashes lent his expression the passionate eloquence that unnerves the grand lady in her drawing-room and makes the young lass in a bonnet turn to look as she carries her basket through the streets.

The languid charm of this look suggested a profundity of thought and made his slightest remark seem important.

The beard, thick, glossy, and finely combed, concealed a slightly too prominent jaw.

They parted after many civilities.

Two days later Monsieur de Lamare paid his first visit.

He arrived as they were trying out a garden bench which had just been installed that very morning beneath the tall plane-tree opposite the drawing-room windows. The Baron wanted another placed beneath the lime-tree to balance it: Mama, an enemy of symmetry, did not. The Vicomte, on being consulted, was of the same view as the Baroness.

Then he spoke of the region, which he declared to be very 'picturesque', having chanced in the course of his solitary walks upon many ravishing 'beauty spots'. From time to time his eyes would, as though by chance, encounter Jeanne's; and she was left with a singular sensation by this sudden, rapidly averted gaze in which there appeared appreciative admiration and the beginnings of an instinctive compatibility.

As it turned out, Monsieur de Lamare senior, who had died the previous year, had known an intimate friend of Monsieur des Cultaux, Mama's father; and the discovery of this acquaintance-ship occasioned an endless conversation about marriages, dates, and relations. The Baroness performed progidious feats of memory as she traced the ascendants and descendants of other family trees, never losing track as she circulated in the complex labyrinth of genealogies.

'Tell me, Vicomte, have you heard mention of the Saunoys de Varfleur? The eldest son, Gontran, married a Coursil girl, one of the Coursil-Courvilles, and the youngest married one of my cousins, Mademoiselle de la Roche-Aubert, who was related by marriage to the Crisange family. Well, Monsieur de Crisange was a close friend of my father's and must have known your father also.'

'Yes, Madame. Wasn't that the Monsieur de Crisange who emigrated and whose son lost all his money?'

'The very same. He asked for my aunt's hand in marriage, after the death of her husband, the Comte d'Éretry; but she wouldn't have him on account of the fact that he took snuff. By the way, do you know what became of the Viloises? They left the Touraine around 1813, after a number of reverses, and went to live in the Auvergne, and I've not heard of them since.'

'I think, Madame, that the old Marquis died after falling off his horse, and left one daughter married to an Englishman and the other to somebody called Basolle, a tradesman, and a rich one by all accounts, who had seduced her.'

Names heard and recalled since childhood from the conversations of elderly relatives now came back to them. And the marriages which had taken place within these families of equivalent rank assumed the importance of major public events in their eyes. They spoke of people they had never met as though they knew them well; while these same people, in other parts of the country, spoke of them in the same manner; and across the distances they felt intimately connected, almost by friendship, by marriage even, in virtue of this simple fact of belonging to the same class, the same caste, of being of equal blood.

The Baron, by nature somewhat antisocial and by education out of sympathy with the beliefs and prejudices of the people of his own set, hardly knew the local families at all, and so questioned the Vicomte about them.

Monsieur de Lamare replied: 'Oh, there's not much in the way of nobility round here,' rather in the tone of one declaring that there were very few rabbits along this part of the coast. And he gave details. Only three families were to be found within a relatively short distance: the Marquis de Coutulier, who was, in a manner of speaking, the head of the Norman nobility; the Vicomte and Vicomtesse de Briseville, persons of excellent breeding but who lived rather cut off from the world; and finally the Comte de Fourville, a sort of monstrous bogeyman who was said to make life mortally wretched for his wife and who lived the life of a huntsman in his manor-house at La Vrillette, which had been built in the middle of a lake.

One or two parvenus had bought property here and there and hobnobbed with each other. The Vicomte did not know them.

He took his leave; and his final glance was directed towards Jeanne, as though he were addressing a special goodbye to her of a more cordial, warmer kind.

The Baroness found him charming and, above all, very much the perfect gentleman: 'Yes, indeed, a most well-mannered young man.'

They invited him to dinner the following week. He became a regular visitor.

He would most often arrive towards four o'clock in the afternoon, join Mama in 'her' avenue, and offer his arm while she took 'her' exercise. When Jeanne had not gone out, she would support the Baroness on the other side, and the three of them would slowly walk up and down the broad, straight path, endlessly to and fro. He barely spoke to Jeanne. But his eye often caught hers, his own having the appearance of black velvet while hers seemed to be made of blue agate.

On several occasions they both accompanied the Baron down to Yport.

When they happened to be on the beach one evening, Père Lastique approached and, without removing his pipe—the absence of which would have been even more surprising perhaps than if his nose were missing—declared:

'With that there wind, yer lordship, 'e could get as far as Étretat tomorrow, and back again, no bother at all.'

Jeanne clasped her hands.

'Oh, Papa, wouldn't you like to?'

The Baron turned towards Monsieur de Lamare:

'Would you join us, sir? We could go for lunch.'

And the expedition was decided upon there and then.

Jeanne was up at dawn. She waited for her father, who took longer to dress, and they set off through the dew, first across open country, then through the wood, which was alive with birdsong. They found the Vicomte and Père Lastique sitting on a capstan.

Two other sailors helped them to launch the boat. Their shoulders against the side of the hull, the men pushed with all their might. Progress was slow across the level part of the beach. Lastique slipped greased wooden logs beneath the keel and then, on resuming his place, drawled out his never-ending 'aaaay hup' by way of regulating the communal effort.

But when they reached the slope, the boat suddenly took off and careered down the smooth pebbles with a great racket, like the sound of rending cloth. It came to an abrupt halt in the shallow foam at the water's edge, and everyone took their seat on the benches; then the two fishermen who remained behind on land pushed them off.

A steady light breeze, coming in off the sea, skimmed the water, wrinkling its surface. They hoisted the sail, which filled a little, and quietly the boat departed, barely rocked by the waves.

First they sailed directly away from the shore. Out towards the horizon the dipping sky merged with the sea. On the landward side, the tall, sheer cliff, indented here and there with sloping, sunlit grass, cast a thick shadow at its foot. Far astern brown sails could be seen coming out from the white jetty at Fécamp, while ahead stood a strangely shaped rock, which bulged out, pierced by a hole, and looked rather like an enormous elephant plunging its trunk into the sea. It was the small Porte at Étretat.*

Jeanne, gripping the side of the boat with one hand and feeling slightly dizzy from the motion of the waves, was gazing into the distance; and it seemed to her that only three things were truly beautiful in the whole of creation: light, space, and water.

No one spoke. Père Lastique, who was holding the tiller and the sheet, would occasionally take a swig from a bottle hidden under his seat; and he went on smoking his stump of a pipe, which seemed to be inextinguishable. A thin wisp of blue smoke rose steadily from it, while another exactly similar issued from the corner of his mouth. No one ever saw the man relight the clay bowl, which was blacker than ebony, or fill it with tobacco. Sometimes he would take hold of it in one hand, remove it from between his lips, and from the same corner of his mouth from which the smoke emerged, would squirt a long jet of brown saliva into the sea.

The Baron, seated aft, was keeping an eye on the sail in his capacity as crew. Jeanne and the Vicomte found themselves sitting side by side, which each found a little disturbing. Some unknown force caused their eyes to meet each time they raised them, simultaneously, as though a secret affinity had alerted them; for there already existed between them that intangible and indeterminate attraction which arises so quickly between two young people, when the fellow is not unhandsome and the girl is pretty. It made them feel happy to be seated next to each other, perhaps because their thoughts were indeed about each other.

The sun was climbing in the sky, as if to have better sight of the vast sea stretched out beneath; but then, in a moment of apparent coquettishness, it wrapped itself in a thin haze that veiled it from its own rays. The mist hung low, transparent and golden, obscur-

ing nothing from view but softening the distance. The astral body
darted forth its flames and began to melt this dazzling cloud:
when it had reached its full strength, the haze evaporated, vanished away; and the sea, mirror-smooth, began to shimmer in its
light.

Jeanne, quite overcome, murmured:

'How beautiful it is!'

The Vicomte replied:

'Oh yes, indeed!'

The serenity of this clear, bright morning seemed to find an
echo in their hearts.

And all at once they caught sight of the great arches of Étretat,
where it seemed as though the cliff were walking out to sea on
two legs, while yet remaining high enough to serve as archways
for ships to pass beneath. In front of the nearest of them there
rose a needle of pointed white rock.

They touched land, and while the Baron, as the first to alight,
held the boat fast by a rope, the Vicomte took Jeanne in his arms
to set her ashore without her feet getting wet; then they walked
up the steep bank of stony beach, side by side, both stirred by this
brief moment of embrace, and all at once heard Père Lastique
saying to the Baron:

'They'd make a fine couple, I'll be bound.'

In a little inn next to the beach they enjoyed a delightful lunch.
The ocean, dulling mind and speech alike, had left them taciturn;
the table made them talkative, like children on their holidays.

The simplest things became a source of endless merriment.

As he sat down to table, Père Lastique carefully hid his pipe,
which was still smoking, in his beret; and they laughed. A fly, no
doubt attracted by his red nose, came and landed on it several
times; and when he chased it away with a flick of his hand that
was too slow to swat it, the fly flew off and settled on a muslin
curtain, already stained by many others of its kind, where it
seemed to be keeping an eye on the sailor's gleaming proboscis,
for it would resume its flight anew and return once more to settle
thereupon.

With each journey the insect made, helpless laughter ensued;

and when the old man, irritated by its tickling, murmured 'Obstinate bugger,' Jeanne and the Vicomte began to weep with mirth, writhing in their seats, desperately trying not to laugh and pressing their napkins to their mouths in an effort to remain silent.

After coffee, Jeanne said: 'Shall we walk?' The Vicomte rose from the table; but the Baron preferred to sun himself on the beach:

'Off you go, children, you can come back for me in a hour.'

They set off in a straight line between the few cottages in the locality; and having passed a small chateau which was more like a large farmhouse, they found themselves in an open valley that stretched away in front of them.

The motion of the sea had sapped their energy and disturbed their normal sense of balance; the fresh, salty air had made them hungry, then lunch had left them dazed; and the merriment had drained them. Now they felt slightly wild and wanted to run about madly in the fields. Jeanne could hear a buzzing in her ears, stirred as she was by new and sudden sensations.

A pitiless sun shone down on them. On each side of the road fields of ripe corn drooped in the heat. All about them the grasshoppers chattered raucously, as numerous as blades of grass, scattering their shrill, deafening cry amidst the wheat and rye and the gorse covering the hillsides.

No other sound rose beneath the torrid sky, whose shimmering, yellowed blue seemed to be on the point of turning red, like metal too close to a brazier.

Spotting a small wood some way off on the right, they made towards it.

Sunk between two banks a narrow path led in under tall trees that blocked out the sun. A kind of mouldy chill greeted them as they entered, the dampness that makes the skin shiver and penetrates the lungs. The grass had withered, for lack of light and freshly circulating air; but the ground was covered in moss.

On they went.

'Look, we can sit down a while over there,' she said.

Two old trees had died and left a gap in the green canopy

overhead, through which light was streaming down and warming the earth. It had stirred the seeds of grass, dandelion, and creeper into life, and started small white flowers into bloom like a mist, and foxgloves that looked like rockets. Butterflies, bees, stocky hornets, huge gnats that looked like the skeletons of flies, a thousand winged insects, ladybirds that were pink and spotted, devil's coach-horses, some with a greenish gleam, others black and horned, all thronged this warm well-hole of light as it bored into the chilly shade cast by the dense foliage.

They sat down, their heads out of the sun but their feet still in the warmth. They observed all these tiny, teeming lives, born of a single sunbeam; and, moved by the spectacle, Jeanne kept saying:

'Oh, how good it feels. How wonderful the countryside is! There are moments when I'd like to be a fly or a butterfly and hide among the flowers.'

They talked about themselves, about their habits and tastes, in the low, intimate voice of persons confiding. He said how tired he was, already, of life in society, how weary of his futile existence; just more and more of the same; one never encountered anything genuine, or sincere.

Life in society! She would have liked to experience it; but she was convinced in advance that it could not compare with life in the country.

And the closer their hearts became, the more punctiliously they called each other 'Monsieur' and 'Mademoiselle', and the more also their eyes shone and their gazes met; and it seemed to them both as though some new goodness of soul were entering into them, a more general and widespread fondness, a concern for a whole host of things about which they had not previously cared.

They made their way back; but the Baron had set off on foot for the Chambre aux Demoiselles, a cave suspended beneath the ridge of a cliff and they waited for him at the inn.

He did not reappear until five in the afternoon, having been for a long walk along the coast.

They climbed back into the boat. Gently it left the shore under a following wind, smoothly, without appearing to move forward. The breeze came in warm, lazy gusts, momentarily filling the sail

and then letting it fall, limp, against the mast. The sea was
opaque, stagnant-looking; and the sun, drained of its fires and
pursuing its curving path, was gently sinking towards it.

Again the torpor of the sea made everyone fall silent.

At length Jeanne said:

'Oh, how I would love to travel.'

'Yes,' replied the Vicomte, 'but there is no joy in travelling
alone. There have to be two of you, at least, so that one can share
one's impressions.'

She pondered this:

'That's true... I like going for walks on my own, though...; and
it's so nice, just dreaming away all by myself.'

He looked at her for a long moment:

'But two people can also dream together.'

She lowered her eyes. Was this a hint? Perhaps. She studied the
horizon as though trying to see beyond it; then, slowly, she said:

'I would like to go to Italy...; and Greece... oh, yes, Greece...
and Corsica! It must be so wild and beautiful there!'

He preferred Switzerland, for its chalets and lakes.

She said:

'No, I'd prefer places that are quite unspoilt, like Corsica, or
else very old and full of memories, like Greece. It must be so
comforting to rediscover the traces of peoples and nations whose
history we've known about since childhood, to see the sites where
the great events occurred.'

The Vicomte, less extravagantly, declared:

'England attracts me greatly. It is a most instructive part of the
world.'

Then they began to tour the globe, discussing the delights of
each country, from pole to equator, enthusing about imagined
landscapes and the improbable customs of certain nationalities
like the Chinese or the Lapps; but in the end they came to the
conclusion that the most beautiful country in the world was
France, with its temperate climate that was cool in summer and
mild in winter, its richly fertile countryside, its green forests, its
great, placid rivers, and its cultivation of the fine arts to a degree
unparalleled anywhere since the great age of Athens.

Then they fell silent.

The sun, having sunk lower in the sky, seemed to be oozing blood; and a broad streak of light ran like a dazzling highway across the water from the edge of the ocean right up to the wake of the boat.

The last puff of wind died away; every ripple vanished; and the sail hung motionless, scarlet red. It was as though a boundless peace had numbed all space, creating silence for this elemental encounter; while the sea arched its gleaming, liquid belly beneath the sky and waited, like some monstrous bride, upon the arrival of the fiery lover descending towards her. He was hastening on his downward course, crimson, as though flushed with desire for their embrace. He joined with her; and, little by little, she consumed him.

Then, from the horizon, a cool air came; a shiver rippled across the heaving breast of the water as if the sun, engulfed, had breathed a sigh of satisfaction upon the entire world.

Dusk was brief; the night unfurled, studded with stars. Père Lastique took hold of the oars; and they noticed that the sea was phosphorescent. Jeanne and the Vicomte, sitting side by side, watched the shifting glints of light moving about in the boat's wake. They had almost ceased from thought and were lost in indeterminate contemplation, breathing in the night with a delicious sense of well-being; and as Jeanne's hand was resting on the bench, her neighbour's finger placed itself, as though by accident, against her skin; she did not move, surprised, happy, disturbed by this merest of contacts.

Later that evening, at home once more and back in her bedroom, she felt strangely agitated and so filled with emotion that the slightest thing moved her to tears. Seeing her clock, she thought that the little bee was beating like a heart, the heart of a friend; that it would be the witness to her entire life, that she would live out her joys and sorrows to the sound of its brisk, regular tick-tock; and she stopped the gilded insect in its flight to plant a kiss upon its wings. At that moment she could have kissed anything. She remembered having hidden an old doll from her childhood at the back of a drawer; she looked for it, found it again with the joy of one reunited with a much-loved friend, and, hugging it to her chest, covered the toy's painted cheeks and curly flax with burning kisses.

And, still holding it in her arms, she reflected.

Was this *him*, the husband promised by a thousand secret voices, placed in her path by a supremely benevolent Providence? Was this the being created especially for her, to whom she would devote her life? Were they the two predestined persons whose affections would unite and hold fast to one another, merging indissolubly, engendering *love*?

She did not yet feel all the tumultuous surges of her whole being, the wild ecstasies, the profound upheavals of self in which she believed passion to consist. It seemed to her nevertheless that she was beginning to love him, for she sometimes felt quite faint at the thought of him; and she did think of him, all the time. His presence caused her pulse to race; she blushed or turned pale each time she caught his gaze, and she trembled at the sound of his voice.

She hardly slept that night.

Then, day by day, the unsettling desire to love took hold of her more and more. She kept consulting her feelings, just as she consulted daisies, clouds, coins tossed in the air.

And then, one evening, her father said to her:

'Tomorrow morning you must make yourself beautiful.'

'Why, Papa?' she enquired.

'It's a secret,' he replied.

And when she came downstairs the next morning, all fresh looking in a brightly coloured dress, she found the drawing-room table covered in boxes of confectionery; and, on a chair, an enormous bouquet of flowers.

A carriage entered the courtyard. On it was marked: 'Lerat—Confectioner—Fécamp. Wedding Breakfasts'; and Ludivine, with the help of a pantry-boy, was removing a succession of large flat baskets through a flap-door at the back of the carriage. They smelled good.

The Vicomte de Lamare appeared. His trousers were tight-fitting and strapped down inside dainty polished boots which showed off the smallness of his feet. The lace of his shirt-frill tumbled from the opening of his long, waisted morning-coat, while a finely-woven cravat wound several times round the neck obliged him to carry his head high—a dark-haired, handsome head that bore the mark of grave distinction. He seemed different from usual, with that particular appearance which grooming sud-denly lends to even the most familiar of faces. Jeanne observed him in astonishment as if she had never seen him before; he looked every inch the gentleman, she thought, a great nobleman from head to toe.

He bowed with a smile:

'So, my dear companion before God,* are you ready?'

'But for what?' she stammered. 'What's happening?'

'You'll find out all in good time,' said the Baron.

The horse and carriage advanced to the door; Madame Adélaïde, in her best finery, came down from her room supported by Rosalie, who seemed so impressed by the elegant appearance of Monsieur de Lamare that Papa muttered:

'I say, Vicomte, I do believe that our maid finds you to her liking.'

He blushed to the roots of his hair and pretended not to have heard; picking up the large bouquet of flowers, he presented it to Jeanne. She accepted it, even more astonished than before. The four of them climbed into the barouche; and Ludivine the cook, who was bringing the Baroness some cold broth to sustain her on the journey, declared:

'It's just like a wedding, Madame, and no mistake.'

On reaching Yport they alighted from the carriage; and as they walked through the village, the fishermen came out of their houses, dressed in their new clothes (the creases were still vis-ible), greeted them, shook hands with the Baron, and fell in behind as though this were a procession.

The Vicomte had offered Jeanne his arm, and together they walked in front.

When they reached the church, they stopped; and the great silver cross appeared, held aloft by a choirboy walking in front of another young lad, dressed in red and white, who was carrying the stoup of holy water in which the sprinkler was dipped.

Behind them came three elderly cantors, one of whom had a limp, then the serpent-player,* and then the priest, whose stomach bulged out beneath the gold-embroidered stole overlapped across it. He bid them good day with a smile and a nod; then, with eyes half-closed, lips moving in prayer, and biretta pulled well down over his forehead, he followed his surplice-clad attendants in the direction of the sea.

On the beach a crowd was waiting round a new boat draped with garlands. Its mast, sail, and rigging were covered in long ribbons which fluttered in the breeze, and its name *Jeanne* could be seen in gold letters on the stern.

Père Lastique, who had been charged with looking after this boat which the Baron had bought, stepped forward to meet the cortège. The men all doffed their hats in unison; and a line of pious women, wearing huge, black cloaks that fell in great folds from their shoulders, knelt down in a circle before the cross.

The priest, flanked by two choirboys, came and stood at one end of the boat, while at the other end the three elderly cantors— grubby-looking in their white habits, chins unshaven, with a solemn expression on their faces and eyes firmly fixed on their book of plainsong—sang loud and flat in the clear morning air.

Each time they drew breath, the serpent-player continued with his solitary bellowing; and his little grey eyes vanished behind his bulging, breath-filled cheeks. The skin on his neck, and even on his forehead, seemed to be coming away from his flesh, so hugely did he swell as he blew.

The calm, limpid sea looked as though it were attending the baptism of one of its skiffs in a mood of quiet contemplation, barely breaking on the shore in wavelets no larger than a finger, with the faint sound of a rake scraping the shingle. And the great white seagulls, their wings outstretched, wheeled past in the blue sky, soaring away and returning in long, curved flight above the kneeling crowd, as if they too wanted to see what was going on.

But the singing drew to a close after a rousing amen that lasted fully five minutes; and the priest, in a thick voice, gurgled a few words in Latin of which only the sonorous endings were audible.

Then he walked round the boat sprinkling it with holy-water and began to murmur prayers, having now taken up a position beside the hull and facing the 'godfather' and 'godmother' who stood quite still, hand in hand.

The young man retained the serious expression of a handsome swain, but the young lady, suddenly overcome with emotion and feeling faint, began to tremble so violently that her teeth were chattering. The dream which had been haunting her for some time had just assumed, all at once and somewhat in the manner of a hallucination, the appearance of reality. There had been talk of weddings, and here was a priest, who was giving his blessing, with people in surplices chanting prayers. Was she not the bride?

Had her fingers twitched nervously? Had her own heart's obsession coursed through her veins and communicated itself to the heart of the man standing next to her? Did he understand? Did he guess? Had he, too, been overwhelmed by this seeming intoxication of love? Or was it rather that he simply knew from experience that no one could resist him? She suddenly realized that he was squeezing her hand, gently at first, then firmly, and more firmly still, almost crushing it. And without any change of expression or anyone noticing, he said, oh yes, most certainly, he quite distinctly said:

'Oh, Jeanne, if you wished it, this might be the moment of our betrothal.'

She bent her head very slowly, which perhaps meant 'yes'. And the priest, who was still sprinkling holy-water, cast a few drops on their fingers.

It was over. The women stood up. The return journey was a rout. The cross, still in the choirboy's hands, had lost its dignity; away it flew, swaying to right and left, or pitching forwards as if it were about to land flat on the ground. The priest, his praying at an end, was trotting along behind; the cantors and the serpent-player had disappeared up a side-street, in a hurry to get changed, and the fishermen hastened along in groups. As though kitchen smells were wafting through their brains, one single thought was causing them to lengthen their stride and their mouths to water, reaching down to the pit of their stomach and setting their stomachs rumbling.

A good lunch was waiting for them at Les Peuples.

The big table had been laid in the courtyard beneath the apple-trees. Sixty persons took their place; fishermen and farmworkers. The Baroness, in the middle, had the two priests on either side, the one from Yport and the one from Les Peuples. The Baron, opposite her, was flanked by the mayor and his wife, a thin and already elderly woman of peasant stock, who kept acknowledging people with little waves of the hand to right and left. Her narrow face was tightly framed in her large Norman bonnet, just like the head of a white-crested hen, and her eyes were round and permanently astonished; she ate in short, rapid bursts as if she were pecking at her plate with her nose.

Jeanne, seated beside the 'godfather', was afloat with happiness. She saw nothing, thought nothing, said nothing, as her head swam with joy.

'But what is your Christian name?', she asked.

'Julien,' he replied. 'Didn't you know?'

But she did not answer, thinking:

'How often I shall be saying that name in future!'

When the meal was over, they left the courtyard to the fishermen and went to the other side of the house. The Baroness began to take her exercise, supported by the Baron and escorted by her two priests. Jeanne and Julien walked towards the copse and entered its narrow, overgrown paths; and suddenly he took hold of her hands:

'Tell me now, will you be my wife?'

Again she bent her head; and as he stammered: 'Please tell me, I beg you!', she lifted her eyes towards his, quite gently, and in the look she gave him he read her reply.

IV

One morning the Baron entered Jeanne's bedroom before she had risen, and sat down at the foot of her bed:

'Monsieur le Vicomte de Lamare has asked us for your hand in marriage.'

She felt like hiding her face under the sheets.

Her father went on:

'We have postponed making our reply.'

She was gasping for breath, choking with emotion. Presently the Baron added with a smile:

'We didn't want to do anything without asking you. Your mother and I are not opposed to such a marriage, but we have no wish to force you into it. You are much wealthier than he is, but when a whole life's happiness is at stake, it doesn't do to become preoccupied with money. He has no surviving relatives; so if you were to marry him, it would be like a son joining our family, whereas with someone else it is you, our daughter, who would be going off to be with strangers. We like the boy. Do you... like him?'

'I accept, Papa,' she stammered, blushing to the roots of her hair.

And Papa, gazing deep into her eyes and still smiling, muttered:

'I thought as much, young lady.'

She spent the rest of the day as though in a state of inebriation, not knowing what she was doing, absent-mindedly picking up the wrong thing by mistake, and her legs felt limp with fatigue although she had walked nowhere.

Towards six o'clock, as she was sitting with Mama beneath the plane-tree, the Vicomte appeared.

Jeanne's heart began to beat wildly. The young man came towards them without apparent emotion. When he reached them, he took the Baroness's hand and kissed her fingers; and then, lifting the young lady's quivering hand in its turn, he placed upon it a long, full kiss of tenderness and gratitude.

And so began the blissful period of engagement. They would converse alone in the corner of the drawing-room or else seated on the bank at the far side of the copse overlooking the wild heathland. Sometimes they would stroll along Mama's avenue, he talking of the future, she staring at the dusty trail left by the Baroness's foot.

The matter being now decided, there was a general desire to hasten its conclusion; and so it was agreed that the ceremony should take place in six weeks' time, on the fifteenth of August; and that the young couple would depart immediately on their honeymoon. Asked which country she would like to visit, Jeanne decided on Corsica, where they would be more on their own together than in the cities of Italy.

They awaited the moment appointed for their union without undue impatience, but suffused, wrapped all about in a delicious tenderness of feeling, savouring the exquisite charm of inconsequential caresses, of squeezed fingers, of passionate gazes so protracted that their very souls seemed to merge, and all the while dimly aware of a vague longing for more substantial embraces.

It was decided to invite no one to the wedding apart from Aunt Lison, the Baroness's sister, who lived as a paying guest in a convent at Versailles.

After their father's death, the Baroness had wanted to keep her sister by her; but the old maid, convinced that she was a burden to everyone, no better than a useless nuisance, withdrew into one of those religious houses that rent out apartments to persons having the misfortune to be all alone in the world.

From time to time she would come and spend a month or two with her family.

She was a small woman of few words, who faded into the background and appeared only at mealtimes before then retiring once more to her room where she would remain closeted for hours on end.

She had the kind face of a little, old lady, even though she was only forty-two, and a gentle, sad look in her eyes; she had never counted for anything in her family. As a small child, hardly anyone had ever kissed her, seeing that she was neither pretty nor boisterous; and she used to sit sweetly and quietly in the corner. Ever since then she had always been the one to be sacrificed. As a young girl, nobody had taken the slightest interest in her.

She was rather like a shadow or a familiar object, like a living piece of furniture one is used to seeing every day but without giving it a moment's notice.

Her sister, from habit acquired in the parental home, looked on her as a failure, as someone of absolutely no consequence. Everyone treated her with a casual familiarity which masked a kind of well-meaning disdain. She was called Lise, and seemed to be embarrassed by this smart, youthful name. When it became evident that she was not getting married, and doubtless never would, Lise had turned into Lison. Since the arrival of Jeanne she had become known as 'Aunt Lison', a humble relation, all prim and proper and dreadfully shy, even with her sister and brother-in-law, who nevertheless felt a certain fondness for her, but a fondness that was a mixture of undiscriminating kind-heartedness, instinctive compassion, and natural generosity.

Sometimes, when the Baroness talked about her distant childhood, she would date things by referring to the 'time of Lison's little episode'.

Nothing further would be said; and this 'little episode' remained as though shrouded in mist.

One evening Lise, then aged twenty, had tried to drown herself, no one knew why. Nothing in her previous life, or in her behaviour, could have led one to anticipate such an act of madness. She had been dragged out of the water, half dead; and her parents, raising their arms in indignation rather than trying to ascertain the mysterious cause of this act, had been content to refer to her 'episode', rather as they spoke of the accident which had befallen Coco the horse, who had broken its leg shortly before that on stumbling in a rut and had had to be put down.

Since then Lise, soon to be Lison, had been considered weak in the head. The mild contempt which she inspired in her kin gradually communicated itself to everybody else in the vicinity. Even little Jeanne, with her child's intuitive understanding, never bothered with her, never went upstairs to give her a kiss in bed, and never even went into her room. Indeed, only Rosalie the maid, who performed the few necessary chores in this room, seemed to know where it was.

When Lison came into the dining-room for lunch, the 'Little One' would routinely go up to her and proffer her forehead to be kissed; but that was that.

If anyone wanted to speak to her, a servant was sent to fetch her; and if she was not there, no one was concerned, no one gave her a thought: it would never have occurred to any of them to worry about her or say: 'But wait, I haven't seen Lison this morning.'

She took up no space; she was one of those creatures who remain strangers, even to their own family, like unexplored lands, and whose death leaves no gap, no empty place in a household, one of those people who are incapable of entering into the lives and loves and everyday routines of those around them.

When someone said 'Aunt Lison', those two words stirred almost no affection in anyone. It was as if they had said 'the coffee-pot' or 'the sugar-bowl'.

She always walked with short, rapid, silent steps; never making a noise or bumping into anything, seemingly able to communicate to objects themselves this capacity to make not a sound. Her hands appeared to be made of some sort of wadding, so lightly and delicately did she handle everything she touched.

She arrived toward the middle of July, in a great state of excitement at the prospect of this marriage. She brought a pile of presents, which, since they were from her, passed almost unnoticed.

The day after she came, no one noticed she was there any more.

But extraordinary emotion was brewing within her, and her eyes never left the betrothed couple. She busied herself making the trousseau with singular energy, feverishly working away like a simple seamstress in her room where no one came to see her.

She kept presenting the Baroness with handkerchiefs which she had hemmed herself, and table napkins on which she had embroidered their initials, asking her:

'Will this be all right, Adélaïde?'

And Mama would casually examine the object in question before replying:

'My poor Lison, you really must not go to so much trouble.'

One evening, towards the end of the month, after a day of oppressive heat, the moon rose on one of those clear, warm nights which are so unsettling, which melt and uplift the heart, and seem to stir all the hidden poetic impulses of the soul. Gentle breezes wafted into the drawing-room from the surrounding fields. The Baroness and her husband were playing a languid game of cards in the pool of light cast by the lampshade; Aunt Lison was seated between them, knitting; and the young couple leaning on the sill of the open window were gazing out at the garden filled with moonlight.

The lime and the plane-tree cast their shadows over the great lawn that stretched away, pallid and gleaming, as far as the copse, which was in total darkness.

Irresistibly drawn by the tender charm of the night, and by the soft glow of light suffusing the trees and shrubbery, Jeanne turned to her parents:

'Papa, we're just going out for a walk, across the grass in front of the house.'

The Baron did not look up from his cards, but said: 'Off you go then, children,' and continued to play the hand.

They went outside and began to walk slowly across the expanse of white lawn in the direction of the little wood on the far side.

It was getting late, but they had no thought of returning to the house. The Baroness was tired and wanted to go up to her bedroom:

'We must call the lovers in,' she said.

The Baron glanced across the vast, luminous garden, where the two shadowy figures were slowly wandering about.

'Let's leave them,' he replied, 'it's so pleasant outside. Lison will wait for them, won't you, Lison?'

The old maid looked up nervously and replied in her timid voice:

'But of course I'll wait for them.'

Papa helped the Baroness up from her chair and, tired himself after the heat of the day, said:

'I shall retire also.'

And he departed with his wife.

Then Aunt Lison in turn stood up and, leaving her knitting on the arm of the chair, the wool and the large needle, she came over to lean on the windowsill and gazed out at the enchanting night.

The betrothed were walking back and forth, across the lawn, from the copse to the front steps and back again. Their fingers entwined, they were no longer talking, as though they had taken leave of themselves and had now merged with the poetic ambiance visibly emanating from the earth.

Suddenly, in the frame of the window, Jeanne caught sight of the old maid outlined against the bright light of the lamp.

'Look,' she said, 'Aunt Lison's watching us.'

The Vicomte lifted his head and said, in the unheeding tone of someone speaking without thinking:

'Yes, so she is.'

And they continued to dream, to stroll, to be in love.

But dew was falling on the grass, and they both shivered slightly in the cool air.

'Let's go in,' she said.

And they returned indoors.

When they entered the drawing-room, Aunt Lison had resumed her knitting; she was bent over her work, and her thin fingers were trembling a little, as though they were very tired.

Jeanne walked over to her.

'Aunt, we're going up now.'

The old maid turned her eyes towards her; they were red, as though she had been crying. The lovers paid no attention; but the young man suddenly noticed that the young lady's delicate shoes were all wet. He was immediately concerned and enquired tenderly:

'But your dear little feet, aren't they cold?'

And at once the aunt's fingers began to tremble so violently that she dropped her knitting; the ball of wool rolled away across the floor; and, quickly hiding her face in her hands, she began to weep in great, convulsive sobs.

The young couple just stood there, watching her in astonishment. Jeanne fell to her knees and spread her arms wide, quite overcome, and kept repeating:

'But what's the matter, Aunt Lison, what's the matter?'

Then the poor woman stammered her reply, in a voice thick with tears, her body stiff with misery:

'It was when he asked you... about your dear little feet... aren't they cold?... no one has ever said anything like that to me... never, not once.'

Taken by surprise, and filled with pity towards her, Jeanne nevertheless felt like laughing at the thought of a lover lavishing words of tenderness on Lison; and the Vicomte had turned away to hide his amusement.

But all at once the aunt got up, left her wool on the floor and her knitting on the armchair, and disappeared without a light into the darkness of the staircase, groping her way towards her bedroom.

Left on their own, the two young people looked at each other, at once entertained and moved. Jeanne murmured:

'Poor Aunt!...'

Julien continued:

'She must be a little off her head this evening.'

They were holding hands, reluctant to part for the night, and gently, very gently, they exchanged their first kiss standing in front of the empty chair recently vacated by Aunt Lison.

The next day they scarcely had a thought for the old maid's tears.

By the end of the fortnight which preceded the wedding Jeanne was in a moderately calm and tranquil state, as though she had been wearied by sweet feelings.

During the morning of the great day, moreover, she was left with no time to reflect. All she felt was a huge sense of emptiness throughout her body, as if her flesh and blood and bones had all dissolved beneath her skin; and each time she touched something she noticed that her fingers were markedly trembling.

She did not recover possession of herself until she was

standing in the chancel of the church and the service was already
under way.

Married! Here she was, married! The whole sequence of
events, all the comings and goings, all the things that had taken
place that day since dawn seemed like a dream now, a complete
and utter dream. There are moments like this when everything
around us appears to have changed—even gestures take on a new
meaning—right down to the hours of the day, which no longer
seem to occupy their appointed place.

She felt dazed, above all astonished. Even as recently as the
previous evening nothing in her life had yet changed; it had simply been that her life's constant goal was coming closer, almost
close enough to touch. She had gone to sleep a girl; and now she
was a woman.

So she had passed beyond the barrier which seems to conceal
the future with all its joys and dreamt-of happiness. It was as
though a door had opened before her: she was about to enter in
upon the Anticipated.

The ceremony was coming to an end. They passed into the
vestry, which was almost empty; for they had invited no one; and
then out they came again.

When they appeared at the door of the church, a loud bang
made the bride jump and the Baroness let out a great cry: it was a
salvo of gunshots, fired by the villagers; and the shooting continued all the way back to Les Peuples.

Light refreshments were served to the family, their own priest
and the priest from Yport, the mayor, and the witnesses chosen
from among the principal farmers of the region.

Then they took a stroll in the garden as they waited for the
wedding breakfast. The Baron, the Baroness, Aunt Lison, the
mayor, and the Abbé Picot began to walk up and down Mama's
avenue; while in the avenue opposite the other priest was striding
up and down reading from his breviary.

From the far side of the house one could hear the noisy merriment of the farmworkers drinking cider beneath the apple-trees.
The whole district, decked out in its Sunday best, filled the courtyard. The boys and girls were chasing each other about the place.

Jeanne and Julien walked through the copse, then climbed the bank and, without exchanging a word, began to gaze at the sea. It was a little chilly, even though this was the middle of August; the wind was coming from the north, and the great sun gleamed harshly in the clear blue sky.

In search of shelter the young couple crossed the heath and headed off towards the right in the direction of the wooded valley that winds its way down to Yport. As soon as they reached the woods, they were out of the wind, and they left the main track on a narrow path which led in beneath the branches. There was scarcely room for them to walk side by side; then she felt an arm sliding slowly round her waist.

She did not speak, panting, almost unable to breathe, her pulse racing. Low branches stroked their hair; frequently they had to stoop in order to get past. She picked a leaf; two ladybirds, like two delicate red shells, were huddled together beneath it.

So, innocently and a little comforted, she said:

'Look, a happy couple.'

Julien's mouth brushed across her ear:

'Tonight you will become my wife.'

Although she had learned many things during her days roaming the countryside, she still thought only of the romance of love, and was surprised. His wife? Was she not that already?

Then he began to kiss her with little rapid kisses on her temple and on her neck, just where the curls of her hair began. Repeatedly startled by these male kisses to which she was unaccustomed, she instinctively averted her head to elude such attentions even as, at the same time, she thrilled to his touch.

But suddenly they found themselves at the edge of the wood. She stopped, disconcerted at being so far from home. What would people think?

'Let's go back.'

He removed his arm from her waist and, as each turned, they found themselves face to face, so close that they could feel one another's breath on their faces; and they gazed at each other. They gazed at each other with one of those long, hard, penetrating looks when two souls think they are merging into one. They sought each other out in their gaze, behind their gaze, in that impenetrable unknown of their being; they took each other's measure in one silent, stubborn interrogation. What would they be to each other? What would this life be like that they were about to lead together? What did they have in store for each other, what joys, what moments of happiness or disappointment, during the long, indissoluble tête-à-tête that is marriage. And it seemed to both of them that they had never truly seen each other before.

And all at once Julien placed both hands on his wife's shoulders and planted a full, deep kiss on her mouth such as she had never before experienced. Down the kiss went, down into her veins and into her very marrow; and she felt such a strong, mysterious jolt that she pushed Julien blindly away with both arms and almost fell backwards.

'Let's go, let's go,' she stammered.

He said nothing, but took hold of her hands and held them in his.

They said nothing on their way back to the house. The remainder of the afternoon seemed long.

They all sat down to table at dusk.

The meal was simple and quite short, contrary to Norman custom. A kind of embarrassment inhibited the guests. Only the two priests, the mayor, and the four farmers who had been invited displayed some of the coarse merriment that is traditional at wedding feasts.

If the laughter seemed to be fading, a quip from the mayor was enough to set it off again. It was getting on for nine; they would soon be having coffee. Outside, beneath the apple-trees in the front courtyard, the country dancing was beginning. Through the open window one could see the whole festive scene. Candle-lanterns hanging from the branches turned the leaves the colour of verdigris. Young rustics and their wenches cavorted in a circle singing a dancing song at the tops of their voices, thinly accompanied by two violins and a clarinet perched on a large kitchen-table which had been set out by way of a stage. At times the noisy singing of the farmworkers would blot out the sound of the instruments; and their frail harmonies seemed to be torn into shreds by the wild, unruly voices, falling from the air in tatters, in tiny fragments of a few scattered notes.

Refreshments were being served to the crowd from two large barrels surrounded by blazing torches. Two serving-girls were kept constantly busy rinsing the glasses and bowls in a tub and then holding them still dripping beneath the taps from which flowed either a red stream of wine or a golden stream of clear cider. And men thirsty from dancing, or placid old men, or young girls wet with perspiration all pressed forward, reaching out their arms to grab in their turn whatever receptacle came to hand before tilting their head back and downing great quantities of their chosen liquid.

Bread, butter, cheese, and sausage had been laid out on a table. People would come and grab a mouthful from time to time, and this wholesome and exuberant celebration under the canopy of candlelit branches made the dreary guests indoors feel like joining in the dancing and long to drink from the belly of these fat casks and eat bread and butter and raw onion.

The mayor, who was keeping time to the music with his knife, cried out:

'Bless my soul but this is good. It's like being at the Marriage at Cannes.'*

There was a ripple of stifled laughter at this. But the Abbé Picot, being a born enemy of secular authority, retorted:

'At Cana, you mean.'

The gentleman would not be told:

'No, monsieur le curé, I know what I meant. When I say Cannes, I mean Cannes.'

They rose from the table and proceeded into the drawing-room. Then they went outside to mingle with the country folk in their merrymaking. After which the guests left.

The Baron and Baroness were having some sort of whispered quarrel. Madame Adélaïde, more out of breath than ever, seemed to be refusing to do as her husband asked. Eventually she said, almost out loud:

'No, dearest, I just can't, I simply wouldn't know how to go about it.'

Then Papa abruptly left her side and walked over to Jeanne.

'Shall we take a stroll, my child?'

Thoroughly agitated, she replied:

'Just as you wish, Papa.'

They went out.

The moment they stepped beyond the door, on the side of the house that faced towards the sea, they were met by a sharp gust of wind—one of those chilly summer breezes that already bear the scent of autumn.

Clouds were racing across the sky, now obscuring, now once more revealing the stars.

The Baron pressed his daughter's arm to his as he tenderly squeezed her hand. They walked along for a few minutes. He seemed hesitant, troubled. Finally he made up his mind.

'My darling child, I am about to fulfil a rather difficult role which really ought to fall to your mother; but as she refused to do it, there is nothing for it but for me to take her place. I'm not sure how much you know about the facts of life. There are mysteries which one carefully conceals from children, and from girls especially, girls whose thoughts must remain pure, irreproachably pure, until we entrust them to the arms of the man who will see to their happiness. It falls to him to remove the veil from the sweet secret of existence. But if they have not hitherto had the slightest suspicion of it, then often they take exception to the somewhat brutal reality that underlies their dreams. Wounded in their soul, and even in their bodies, they refuse to grant their husband that which the law, the law of humans and the law of nature, accords him as an absolute right. I cannot say more, my darling; but remember this, and only this, that you belong totally to your husband.'

What in fact did she know? What did she surmise? She had begun to tremble now, her heart cast down, as if in premonition, by a painful and overwhelming melancholy.

They returned indoors. A surprising spectacle brought them up short at the door to the drawing-room: Madame Adélaïde was sobbing on Julien's chest. Her tears, great noisy tears which sounded as though they were coming from the bellows in a forge, seemed to issue simultaneously from her nose, her mouth, and her eyes; while the young man stood there in embarrassed silence endeavouring to hold up this large woman who had collapsed into his arms as she sought to commend her sweet, beloved, darling daughter to his care.

The Baron rushed forward.

'Come, come, no tearful scenes, please, I beg you'; and taking hold of his wife, he sat her down in a chair while she wiped the tears from her face. Then he turned towards Jeanne:

'Quickly now, my child, kiss your mother goodnight and off to bed.'

On the verge of tears herself also, she quickly embraced her parents and fled from the room.

Aunt Lison had already retired to her bedroom. The Baron and his wife remained alone with Julien. And the three of them felt so awkward that no one could think what to say, with the two men just standing there, in evening dress, gazing into space, and Madame Adélaïde slumped in her chair and still emitting the occasional sob. Their embarrassment was becoming intolerable, so the Baron began to talk of the journey upon which the young couple were to embark in a few days' time.

Up in her bedroom Jeanne was being helped out of her clothes by Rosalie, who was in floods of tears. All fingers and thumbs, she could find neither pin nor ribbon, and appeared decidedly more upset than her mistress. But Jeanne paid little heed to her maid's tears: it seemed to her as though she had entered another world, or departed for another planet, leaving behind all she had ever known, all she had ever held dear. Everything in her life and her way of looking at things seemed to have been turned upside-down; it even occurred to her to wonder, bizarrely, 'did she love her husband?' Suddenly he now seemed like a stranger whom she hardly knew. Three months earlier she hadn't even known of his existence, and now she was his wife. Why was it so? Why fall into marriage so quickly, as though into a gaping pit that opens in your path?

When she had put on her nightclothes, she slipped into bed; and the cool sheets made her shiver, adding to the feeling of coldness and sad loneliness which had made her heart heavy for the last two hours.

Rosalie fled from the room, still sobbing; and Jeanne waited. She waited, tense with anxiety, for this dimly perceived something which had been obscurely announced by her father's words, this mysterious revelation of the great secret of love.

Without her having heard anyone climb the stairs, there came three gentle knocks on the door. She trembled horribly and made no reply. Again there was a knock, and the door-handle grated. She hid her head beneath the bedclothes, as if a burglar had entered the room. Boots creaked faintly on the parquet floor; and suddenly someone touched her bed.

She started nervously and gave a little cry; and taking her head out from under the covers, she saw Julien standing in front of her, gazing at her with a smile.

'Oh, you did give me a fright!' she said.

'Weren't you expecting me?' he rejoined.

She did not reply. He was still in full evening dress, wearing the serious expression of the handsome young man; and she felt dreadfully ashamed to be lying in bed like this in front of one so proper and correct.

They were both at a loss as to what to say or do next, not even daring to look at each other at this solemn and decisive moment upon which the intimate happiness of their whole lives depended.

He had a vague sense perhaps of the dangers attendant upon this encounter, of the ready self-control and artful tenderness that is required if no offence is to be given to the subtle reticence and infinite delicacy of feeling of a virginal soul raised on dream and fantasy.

So, gently, he took her hand and kissed it, and then, kneeling by the bed as though at an altar, he murmured in a voice as soft as a gentle breeze:

'Will you love me?'

At once reassured, she raised her head from the pillow in a cloud of lace and smiled:

'I already do, my dearest.'

He placed his wife's small, slender fingers in his mouth and, in a voice muffled by this fleshy obstruction, said:

'Will you show me that you love me?'

She replied, troubled once more and not quite understanding what she was saying, acting on the memory of what her father had said:

'I am yours, my dearest.'

He covered her wrist with moist kisses and, rising slowly from the floor, began to bring his face close to hers even as she began once more to hide it.

Suddenly, throwing one arm across the bed, he took hold of his wife through the sheets while slipping his other arm beneath the pillow and raising her head upon it: and in a soft, soft whisper he asked:

'So, then, will you make a little space for me, beside you?'

She took fright, instinctively, and stammered:

'Oh, please, not yet.'

He seemed disappointed, a little piqued, and he continued in a tone of voice that was still cajoling but now a little more brusque.

'Why not yet, since we shall eventually?'

She resented this remark; but, submissive and resigned, she said for the second time:

'I am yours, my dearest.'

Then he disappeared very rapidly into the dressing-room; and she could hear his movements quite clearly, the rustle of clothing as he undressed, the clink of money in his pocket, the successive clatter of boots being removed.

And all at once, dressed only in underwear and socks, he darted across the room to place his watch on the mantelpiece. Then he hurried back into the little room that adjoined her bedroom, where he busied himself a while longer, and quickly Jeanne turned over on her side and shut her eyes as she sensed his approach.

She almost jumped out of bed when she felt a cold, hairy leg slide in roughly beside her; and, burying her face in her hands, distraught, on the point of crying out in fear and alarm, she huddled at the far edge of the bed.

At once he took her in his arms, though she still had her back to him, and he kissed her voraciously, on the neck, on the errant lace of her nightcap, on the embroidered collar of her nightdress.

She lay quite still, stiff with dreadful anxiety as she felt a strong hand seeking out her breasts which she had sought to conceal between her elbows. The shock of this brutal contact left her gasping for breath; and more than anything she wanted to escape, to run to the other end of the house and lock herself away, far from this man.

He had stopped. She could feel the warmth of him on her back. Then her terror began to abate, and suddenly it occurred to her that she had only to turn over and kiss him.

In the end he seemed to lose patience and said in an unhappy voice:

'So you don't want to be my little wife, then?'

She muttered through her fingers:

'Am I not that already?'

He replied with a touch of ill humour:

'No, my dear, you are not. Come now, stop making fun of me.'

His cross tone affected her deeply, and all of a sudden she turned towards him to say she was sorry.

He grabbed her in his arms, rabidly, as though filled with a ravenous hunger for her; and he covered her face and neck with rapid kisses, biting kisses, frenzied kisses, dazing her with his caresses. She had parted her hands and lay motionless beneath his striving, no longer conscious of what she was doing, of what he was doing, lost in a mental confusion which prevented her from understanding what was happening. But suddenly she was torn by a sharp pain; and she began to groan, writhing in his arms as he possessed her violently.

What happened next? She could scarcely remember, for she had lost all power of thought; she had the impression somehow that he was showering her lips with a hail of tiny, grateful kisses.

Then he must have said something, and she must have replied. Thereupon he made further advances, which she rejected with horror; and as she fought him off, she felt the same thick hair on his chest as she had previously felt on his leg, and she recoiled in shock.

Eventually tiring of his fruitless solicitations, he lay back on the bed and was still.

Then she began to reflect; and, filled with despair to the depths of her soul, disillusioned in her dreams of a quite different kind of intoxication, in cherished expectations which had now been destroyed, in a dream of happiness which had burst like a bubble, she said to herself:

'So that's what he calls being his wife! That! That!'

And she lay thus for a long while, desolated, her eyes wandering over the tapestries on the walls, along the ancient love story that ran round her room.

But since Julien was now silent and lying still, she slowly turned her head to look at him, and she saw that he was asleep! Asleep, with his mouth open and an untroubled expression on his face! He was asleep!

She could not believe it, and was filled with indignation, feeling more outraged by his sleep than by his brutality, as though she had been treated as a mere convenience. How could he sleep on such a night as this? Did what had happened between them seem perfectly normal to him? Oh! She would rather have been beaten, violated again, and bruised with odious caresses till she had lost all consciousness.

She lay there without moving, propped on one elbow and leaning towards him, listening to the gentle sound of breathing coming from his lips, which at times was almost a snore.

Day broke, faintly at first, then lighter, then pink, then dazzling bright. Julien opened his eyes, yawned, stretched, looked at his wife, smiled, and enquired:

'Did you sleep well, my darling?'

She noticed that he now said 'tu' to her,* and she replied in astonishment:

'Of course. And you?'

'Oh, me, yes, very well.'

And turning on his side, he kissed her and began calmly to converse. He told her of his plans for the future, and how they might make savings; and this word, which featured on several occasions, surprised Jeanne. She listened to him without really taking in what he was saying, and gazed at him as meanwhile all manner of thoughts flitted through her mind, barely leaving an impression.

Eight o'clock struck.

'Come, it's time we were up,' he said. 'We shall look ridiculous if we lie in.' And he got out of bed first. When he had finished getting ready, he was kindness itself as he assisted his wife in all the intricate details of her toilette, refusing to allow Rosalie to be summoned.

Just before he left the room, he stopped her:

'By the way, it's all right to call each other "tu" now when we're on our own, but in front of your parents it might be better to wait a little. It will seem perfectly normal once we are back from our honeymoon.'

She did not make an appearance until lunchtime. And the day passed in its usual manner, just as if nothing had happened. It was simply that there was another man in the house.

V

Four days later the coach arrived to take them to Marseilles.

After the anguish of the first night, Jeanne had already grown used to contact with Julien, to his kisses and loving caresses, although her repugnance at their more intimate relations had not diminished.

She found him handsome, she loved him; and she felt once more happy and light of heart.

The farewells were brief and without sadness. Only the Baroness seemed upset; and just as the coach was leaving, she placed a large purse, as heavy as lead, in her daughter's hand:

'This is for your minor expenses, for the things a young wife needs,' she said.

Jeanne quickly put it in her pocket; and away the horses went.

Towards evening Julien asked her:

'How much money did your mother give you in the purse?'

She had forgotten all about it, and emptied the purse out onto her lap. A stream of gold poured forth: two thousand francs. She clapped her hands.

'Oh, I *shall* be able to spoil myself,' she said, gathering the money up again.

After a week's travelling, in stifling heat, they reached Marseilles.

And the next day the *Roi-Louis*, a small steamer bound for Naples via Ajaccio, bore them off to Corsica.

Corsica! The maquis! Bandits! Mountains! Napoleon's birthplace! Jeanne felt as though she were leaving reality behind and entering into a waking dream.

Standing side by side on the deck, they watched as the cliffs of Provence slipped past. The sea, calm and intensely blue, as though it had congealed, solidified, under the fierce glare of the sun, stretched away beneath a boundless sky, itself almost excessively blue.

'Do you remember our boat trip with Père Lastique?' she said.

By way of reply he gave her a darting kiss on the ear.

The steamer's paddle-wheels slapped the sea, disturbing its deep slumber; and behind them, in one long trail of spume, in a broad, pale streak of churning water, foaming like champagne, the wake of the boat stretched away, undeviating, as far as the eye could see.

Suddenly, no more than a few yards ahead of them, an enormous fish, a dolphin, leapt out of the water, then dived back in again head-first and disappeared. Startled and afraid, Jeanne shrieked and threw herself against Julien's chest. Then she began to laugh at her fright and watched anxiously to see if the creature would reappear. A few moments later it rose up again like a large mechanical toy. Presently it fell back, only to reappear once more; and then there were two of them, then three, then six, frolicking, it seemed, around the ponderous ship, escorting this monstrous brother of theirs, this wooden fish with fins of iron. They would pass to port only to return again on the starboard side, and then, as though they were playing a game, or taking part in some mad chase, they would leap up into the air in one great curve, first one at a time, then all together, before plunging back into the sea in single file.

Jeanne clapped her hands, quivering with delight each time these enormous, effortless swimmers rose into view. Her heart leapt like them in wild, innocent joy.

Suddenly they were gone. They surfaced one more time, far across the sea; then they vanished from sight, and for a few moments Jeanne felt a pang of sadness at their departure.

Evening came, a calm, gentle, radiant evening, full of light and peace and contentment. Not a breath of air, not a ripple on the water; and this limitless repose of the sea and the sky merged with the smooth tranquillity of their slumbrous souls.

The great disc of the sun was gently sinking in the sky, far away in the distance towards invisible Africa—Africa, that blazing land whose scorching heat seemed almost to have reached them already; but a kind of cool caress, quite unlike a breeze, played across their faces as soon as the sun went down.

They did not want to return to their cabin which reeked of all the dreadful smells of steamships; and they both stretched out on the deck, side by side, wrapped in their coats. Julien fell asleep at once; but Jeanne lay there with her eyes open, stirred by the newness of it all. The steady thrash of the paddles soothed her; and she gazed above her at the legions of stars, so piercingly bright, that twinkled as though at anchor in this limpid, southern sky.

Towards morning, however, she dozed off. Sounds, voices, woke her. The sailors were singing as they cleaned the ship. She shook her husband, who lay fast asleep, and they got to their feet.

She took deep, exhilarating draughts of the salty mist, and it coursed through her to the very tips of her fingers. Everywhere, nothing but sea. Ahead of them, however, something grey and as yet blurred in the nascent dawn, a kind of piled mass of strange, pointed, indented clouds seemed to have been laid upon the waves.

Then it appeared more distinctly: the shapes etched themselves more sharply on the lightening sky, and a long line of strange-looking, horn-tipped mountains emerged into view. It was Corsica, swathed in a kind of delicate veil.

The sun rose behind it, bringing the definition of dark shadows to the mountain-ridges and their jagged outcrops; and then each peak caught the light while the rest of the island remained bathed in mist.

The captain of the ship appeared on the deck, a short, elderly man, who had been simultaneously tanned, dried, stunted, wizened, and shrunk by the harsh, salty winds; and in a voice grown hoarse from thirty years of giving orders and worn out by shouting above all the gales, he said to Jeanne:

'Ah, the hussy! Can't you just smell her?'

And indeed she could smell a strong and singular scent of plants, of wild aromas.

The captain went on:

'That's the smell of Corsica, Madame, her special perfume, like a pretty woman's. Even if I'd been away twenty years, I would recognize it five miles out to sea. I come from here. And apparently the great man, away over there on Saint Helena,* is always talking about the smell of home. We're from the same family.'

And, removing his hat, the captain saluted Corsica and bowed to the distance, to the great Emperor imprisoned far across the ocean, who was one of his family.

Jeanne was so moved that she nearly wept.

Then the mariner pointed to the horizon:

'The Sanguinaires.'

Julien was standing beside his wife, with his arm round her waist, and they both peered into the distance trying to make out the place he had indicated.

Eventually they noticed a number of rocks shaped like pyramids. Presently the ship rounded them and entered a huge, sheltered bay girded by an array of tall mountains, the lower slopes of which seemed to be all covered in moss.

The captain drew their attention to this vegetation:

'The maquis.'

The circle of mountains seemed to close behind the ship as it moved slowly forward across an expanse of blue water which was so clear that in places it was possible to see right to the bottom.

And suddenly the town appeared, at the far end of the inlet, all white, nestling by the water's edge at the foot of the mountains.

There were some small Italian boats lying at anchor in the harbour. Four or five rowing-boats came out to hover round the *Roi-Louis*, ready to take off its passengers.

Julien, who was collecting together their luggage, whispered to his wife:

'If I give the cabin steward twenty sous, that should be enough, shouldn't it?'

For a week now he had been continually asking the same question, and each time it pained her. She replied, with slight impatience:

'When one's not sure how much to give, one always ends up giving too much.'

He was for ever haggling with waiters and maîtres d'hôtel, with coach-drivers and hawkers of every kind, and when, after much discussion, he had finally succeeded in beating them down, he would rub his hands and say to Jeanne:

'I just don't like being robbed.'

She would be filled with trepidation whenever a bill arrived, already knowing full well what remarks he would make about every item, humiliated by his bartering, blushing to the roots of her hair at the look of disdain on the face of the servants whose eyes followed him as they clutched his inadequate tip in their hand.

He had another such exchange with the boatman who set them ashore.

The first tree she saw was a palm!

They registered at a large, deserted hotel in the corner of a huge square and ordered lunch.

When they had finished dessert, and just as Jeanne was rising from table ready to stroll round the town, Julien took her in his arms and murmured lovingly in her ear:

'Perhaps, my sweet, we might go and lie down for a little while.'

She was taken aback.

'Lie down? But I'm not tired.'

He clasped her to him.

'I want you. You know... It's been two days now!...'

She turned crimson, deeply embarrassed, and stammered:

'What, now? But what would people say? What would people think? How could you possibly dare ask for a room in the middle of the day? Oh, Julien, please, I beg you, no.'

But he cut her short:

'I really don't care a fig what hotel staff may say or think. Just see if I do.'

And he rang the bell.

She said nothing more, her eyes fixed on the floor, rebelling in her flesh and soul against this incessant desire of her husband's, obeying only with disgust, resigned yet humiliated, seeing in this wanting something bestial, degrading, in a word, something dirty.

Her senses had not yet been awakened, and her husband was treating her now as if she shared his burning need.

When the porter arrived, Julien asked him to show them to their room. The man—the true Corsican type covered in hair

almost to his eyeballs—did not understand and assured them that
their accommodation would be got ready by the evening.

Julien explained impatiently:

'No, now. We are tired after the journey, and we would like to
rest.'

Then a smile crept through the servant's beard, and Jeanne felt
like running away.

When they came down an hour later, she dared not walk past
the people they encountered, persuaded that they were going to
laugh and whisper behind her back. In her heart she felt resentful
towards Julien for not understanding as much, for lacking this
finer sense of modesty, this instinctive delicacy of feeling; and she
felt as though there were a veil between them, a barrier, and
realized for the first time that two people are never completely
one in their heart of hearts, in their deepest thoughts, that they
walk side by side, entwined sometimes but never completely
united, and that in our moral being we each of us remain forever
alone throughout our lives.

They spent three days in this little town hidden away at the
end of its blue gulf, as hot as a furnace behind the wall of mountains that prevented the wind from reaching it.

Then an itinerary was fixed upon for their onward journey, and
so that they should find no route barred, they decided to hire
horses. Accordingly they chose two little, wild-eyed Corsican
stallions, scrawny-looking but full of stamina, and set out one
morning at daybreak. A guide accompanied them on a mule and
carried provisions, for inns are unknown in this wild place.

At first the road ran along the edge of the gulf before leading
off quite soon into a shallow valley that ran in the direction of the
great peaks. Often they would cross watercourses that were
almost dry, but where the last vestige of a mountain torrent still
trickled beneath the stones, like an animal in hiding, gurgling
warily.

The wild terrain seemed thoroughly bare. The hillsides were
covered in tall grass, parched yellow by the burning heat of the
season. Sometimes they would pass mountain-dwellers, either on
foot, or riding a small horse, or sitting astride a donkey no bigger

than a dog. And all of them had a loaded rifle slung over their shoulders, ancient rusty weapons that were fearsome instruments in their hands.

The pungent scent of the aromatic plants which cover the island seemed to clog the air; and on the track climbed, gently upwards through the long folds of the mountains.

The granite peaks, variously pink or blue, lent a fairy-tale appearance to the landscape, while on the lower slopes green forests of towering chestnut seemed like mere shrubbery, so vast are the undulations of the land in this region.

Occasionally the guide would stretch out a hand in the direction of the tall escarpments and say a name. Jeanne and Julien would look, see nothing, and then finally make out something grey that looked like a pile of stones that had fallen from the summit. It was a village, a little granite hamlet hanging there, clinging to the rock-face, just like a bird's nest, and almost invisible against the immense backdrop of the mountain.

This long journey at a walk was beginning to irritate Jeanne. 'Let's canter,' she said. And she spurred her horse forward. Then, not hearing her husband cantering along beside her, she turned round and began to laugh wildly as she saw him coming towards her, white as a sheet, holding on to the horse's mane and bouncing up and down in the strangest manner. His good looks and general demeanour as the 'parfit knight' only made his clumsy panic seem all the more comic.

They slowed to a trot. The road now stretched ahead between two limitless thickets which cloaked the entire hillside.

This was the maquis, the impenetrable maquis, a mixture of holm oak, juniper, arbutus, gum, buckthorn, heather, laurustinus, myrtle, and box all bound together as though by twining strands of hair, with scrambling clematis and monstrous ferns, with honeysuckle, cistus, rosemary, lavender, and bramble, a tangled fleece laid across the backbone of the mountain-ridges.

They were both hungry. The guide caught up with them and led them to one of those delightful springs which are so common in mountainous terrain, a thin, rounded trickle of ice-cold water coming from a small hole in the rock and running down a chestnut leaf which had been left there by some passer-by as a means of delivering the tiny rivulet of water safely into his mouth.

Jeanne felt so elated that it was with some difficulty that she refrained from shrieking with joy.

They set off again and the road began to descend, along the edge of the gulf of Sagone.* Towards evening they passed through Cargèse,* the Greek town founded there in former times by a colony of refugees who had been driven out of their own country. A group of tall, beautiful girls were standing beside a fountain, looking strikingly graceful with their slender hips, and long hands, and trim waists. When Julien shouted a greeting, they replied with lilting voices in the mellifluous language of their abandoned homeland.

On arriving in Piana they were obliged to ask for hospitality, according to the custom of ancient times and remote regions. Jeanne was trembling with excitement as they waited outside the door at which Julien had knocked. Oh, this was what you called a real journey, with all the unexpectedness of untrodden paths.

They so happened to have called on another young couple. They were received much as the messenger sent from God must have been received by the early fathers, and they slept upon a mattress of maize, in an old tumbledown house where every roof-timber—perforated by woodworm and crawling with those long ship-worms that eat their way through beams—creaked, and seemed to breathe and sigh.

They departed at sunrise, and presently they stopped opposite what seemed like a veritable forest of crimson granite. There were pinnacles, and columns, and turrets, astonishing shapes wrought by the elements, by the biting wind and the sea-fret.

Rising to a height of some three hundred metres, these extraordinary rocks—slender, round, twisted, hooked, grotesque, unplanned, fantastical—bore the likenesses of trees, plants, animals, monuments, human beings, robe-clad monks, horned devils, huge birds, of a whole monstrous multitude, a nightmare menagerie turned to stone at the behest of some whimsical deity.

Jeanne fell silent, gripped by the spectacle, and she took hold of Julien's hand and squeezed it, overcome by the need to love as she stood face to face with the beauty of things.

And suddenly, emerging from this vision of chaos, they came upon another bay, entirely surrounded by a blood-red wall of granite. And in the blue sea lay the reflections of these scarlet rocks.

Jeanne stammered: 'Oh, Julien,' but could find no other words, overcome with wonder, as a lump formed in her throat. Two tears welled from her eyes. He looked at her in amazement and asked:

'What's wrong, my sweet?'

She wiped her cheeks, smiled, and in a rather unsteady voice said:

'Oh, nothing... It's just my nerves... I don't know... It took me by surprise. I feel so happy that I get quite overcome at the slightest thing.'

He did not understand women's 'nerves', these emotional disturbances to which the sensitive creatures were subject, becoming overwrought at a mere trifle, as easily agitated by some fond enthusiasm as by total disaster, and capable of being thoroughly upset, of being driven wild with joy or despair, by the least identifiable of sensations.

These tears seemed ridiculous to him and, in his preoccupation with the poor surface of the path along which they were riding, he said:

'You'd do better to pay attention to your horse.'

They made their way down an almost impassable track to the bottom of this gulf, and then turned to the right with the intention of riding up through the dark shadows of the Val d'Ota.

But the way ahead looked particularly treacherous.

'How about going up on foot?' Julien suggested.

She wanted nothing better, delighted to walk and be alone with him after her recent excitement.

The guide went on in front with the mule and the horses, and they followed slowly behind.

The mountain, riven from top to bottom, gaped before them. The path leads into the cleft at this point and runs along the bottom between two enormous walls of rock; and a substantial torrent flows through the crevasse. The air is icy cold, the granite looks black, and what blue sky is visible far above seems strangely surprising, dizzying.

A sudden noise made Jeanne jump. She looked up; an enormous bird had flown out of a hole, an eagle. Its outspread wings seemed to touch the two walls of the chasm, and it soared into the blue where it disappeared from sight.

Further on, the cleft in the mountain divides; and the path climbs in sharp zigzags between the two ravines. With nimble, reckless steps Jeanne went first, dislodging the pebbles as she climbed, and peering fearlessly over the edge. He followed her, a little out of breath, his eyes fixed on the ground to prevent vertigo.

Suddenly sunlight poured down on them; it was like emerging from hell. They were thirsty, and a trail of dampness led them through a jumble of rocks towards a tiny spring which had been channelled along a hollowed-out stick for the use of goatherds. A carpet of moss covered the ground round about. Jeanne knelt down to drink; and Julien followed her example.

And as she was savouring the coolness of the water, he grabbed her by the waist and tried to steal her place at the end of the wooden conduit. She resisted; and they tussled with their lips, pressing against the other's and trying to push them out of the way. As fortunes fluctuated in the struggle, each would grip the tiny end of the pipe and try to hang on to it; and the trickle of cold water, alternately consumed and released, would vanish and reappear, splashing their faces, their necks, their clothes, their hands. Little drops of water, like pearls, gleamed in their hair. And kisses mingled with the current.

Suddenly, in a moment of amorous inspiration, Jeanne filled her mouth with the clear liquid and, with cheeks bulging like water-skins, made to offer Julien some mouth-to-mouth refreshment.

He proffered his lips, smiling, head back and arms spread wide; and he drank in a single draught from this spring of living flesh as it decanted a stream of burning desire down into his innermost core.

Jeanne was pressing against him with unusual warmth; her pulse was racing, her bosom swelling, and her eyes seemed moist and soft. She murmured gently: 'Oh, Julien... I love you!', and now she in her turn pulled him towards her, falling back on the ground and bringing her hands up to a face crimson with shame.

He fell upon on her, embracing her wildly. She panted in excited anticipation; and suddenly she cried out, struck as though by lightning by the sensation which this anticipation had itself called forth.

They were a long time in reaching the top of the path, for she was trembling and aching all over, and it was evening by the time they reached Evisa where they were to stay with one of their guide's relatives, Paolo Palabretti.

He was a very tall, slightly stooped man, with the gloomy air of a consumptive. He took them to their room, a sorry bedroom of bare stone but handsome by the standards of this country where fine living is still unknown; and he was busy telling them—in his own language, the Corsican patois that is a mishmash of French and Italian—how pleased he was to receive them, when he was interrupted by the bright sound of a voice; and a short, dark woman, with large black eyes, a skin warmed by the sun, a narrow waist, and teeth continually bared in endless laughter, rushed forward: she embraced Jeanne, shook hands with Julien, and kept saying: 'Good-day, Madame, good-day, Monsieur, is everything all right?'

She took their hats and shawls, bearing them all away on a single arm for she wore the other in a sling, and then bid them all go out, having told her husband:

'Take them for a walk until dinner-time.'

Obeying at once, Monsieur Palabretti placed himself between the young couple and began to show them round the village. He drawled away as he shuffled along, coughing repeatedly and commenting with each bout:

'It's the cold air from the valley, it's got to my chest.'

He led them along a remote path beneath some huge chestnut trees. Suddenly he stopped and said in his expressionless voice:

'This is where my cousin Jean Rinaldi was killed by Mathieu

Lori. Look, I was standing there, right beside Jean, when Mathieu appeared ten paces away. "Jean," he shouted, "don't go to Albertacce, don't go, Jean, or I'll kill you, I will." I took Jean by the arm: "Don't go, Jean, he will, you know." It was all about a girl they were both chasing after, called Paulina Sinacoupi. But Jean began to shout: "I'm going, Mathieu, and you're not going to stop me." Then Mathieu aimed his gun, before I could even lower my own, and fired. Jean rose two feet into the air, like a child skipping, honestly, Monsieur, and he fell back on top of me, so that I dropped my gun and it ended up under that big chestnut-tree over there. Jean's mouth was wide open, but he never uttered another word, he was dead.'

The young couple gazed in amazement at the tranquil witness to this crime.

'And the murderer?' Jeanne enquired.

Paoli Palabretti coughed for a long time and then continued:

'He escaped into the mountains. It was my brother who got him, killed him the following year. You know, my brother Philippi Palabretti, the bandit.'

Jeanne shivered:

'Your brother? A bandit?'

A flash of pride shone in the placid Corsican's eye:

'Oh, yes, Madame, he was famous, he was. Felled six gendarmes. He died with Nicolas Morali when they were cornered in the Niolo, after putting up a fight for six whole days, and already near dead from starvation.'

Then he added with an air of resignation: 'That's the way it has to be round here,' in exactly the same tone of voice as he kept saying: 'It's the cold air from the valley.'

Then they went back for dinner, and the little Corsican woman treated them both as though she had known them for twenty years.

But Jeanne was anxious. Would she again experience in Julien's arms that strange, urgent jolt to the senses that she had felt as she lay on the moss by the spring?

When they were alone together in their bedroom, she was worried that once more she would remain unmoved by his kisses. But she was soon reassured; and that was her first night of love.

The next day, when it was time to depart, she could not bear to leave this humble dwelling where it seemed as though a new form of happiness had begun for her.

She inveigled the Corsican's little wife into her bedroom and, having made it quite clear that she was not trying to give her a present in return for her hospitality, she insisted, crossly even, that she wanted to send her a memento from Paris once she had returned home, a memento to which she seemed to attach an almost superstitious significance.

The young Corsican woman refused for a long time. Finally she consented:

'Very well, then,' she said. 'Send me a little pistol, a small, tiny one.'

Jeanne stared at her. The woman added, whispering it in her ear as though she were sharing some sweet, intimate confidence:

'So I can kill my brother-in-law.'

And with a smile she quickly unravelled the bandages round her bad arm, and then, displaying her plump, white flesh and the scar which had almost healed where the arm had been stabbed right through by a dagger, she said:

'If I hadn't been as strong as him, he'd have killed me. My husband is not a jealous man, he knows he can trust me; and of course he's not in good health, you know, and that cools his blood. In any case, I'm an honest woman, Madame, I am; but my brother-in-law believes anything anybody tells him. He gets jealous on my husband's account; and he'll be at it again, I know he will. Then I'd have a little pistol, and I wouldn't need to worry, I'd be sure of getting my revenge.'

Jeanne promised to send the weapon, and embraced her new friend tenderly before departing on her way.

The remainder of her journey was like a dream, just one long embrace, a wild intoxication of caresses. She saw nothing, neither the landscape nor the people nor the places where they stayed. She had eyes only for Julien.

There then began a period of intimacy at once childish and full of charm, as they whispered sweet nothings, and left silly, delightful messages for each other, and gave pretty little names to every highway and byway of their bodies, each nook and cranny, where it pleased their mouths to roam.

As Jeanne slept on the right, her left nipple was often exposed when they awoke. Julien noticed the fact and christened it 'the Outdoor Type', while the other one became 'Lover Boy' because the pink flower at its summit seemed more responsive to kisses.

The deep track between the two became known as 'Mama's Avenue' because he often passed up and down it; and another, more intimate route was dubbed the 'Road to Damascus' in memory of the Val d'Ota.

When they arrived in Bastia, they had to pay the guide. Julien rummaged in his pockets. Not finding the necessary, he said to Jeanne:

'Since you're not using the two thousand francs your mother gave you, why not let me carry them? They'll be safer in my money-belt; and it'll save me having to get change.'

And she handed him her purse.

They reached Leghorn, visited Florence, Genoa, the whole of the Corniche.

One morning, when the mistral was blowing, they found themselves back in Marseilles.

Two months had passed since their departure from Les Peuples. It was now the fifteenth of October.

Chilled by the great cold wind which seemed to be coming all the way from Normandy, Jeanne felt sad. For some time Julien had seemed changed, tired, indifferent; and she was afraid, though she knew not of what.

She postponed their journey home for four days, unable to bring herself to leave this pleasant sunny region. It seemed to her that her tour of happiness was at an end.

Finally they left.

They were to go shopping in Paris for all the things they would need in setting up home at Les Peuples; and Jeanne was looking forward to bringing home some treasures, thanks to Mama's present. But the first thing she thought of was the pistol which she had promised to the young Corsican woman at Evisa.

The day after they arrived she said to Julien:

'Darling, could I have Mummy's money back? I want to do my shopping.'

He turned towards her with a look of annoyance on his face.

'How much do you need?'

She was taken aback and stammered:

'Well... whatever you think.'

He replied:

'You can have a hundred francs, but whatever you do, don't squander them.'

She did not know what to say, feeling embarrassed and at a loss.

Finally she said haltingly:

'But I gave you the money to...'

He did not let her finish.

'Yes, quite so. But since we share the same purse, what does it matter if it's in your pocket or mine? It's not as if I'm refusing to let you have any, after all, since I'm actually giving you a hundred francs.'

She took the five gold coins without a further word; but she dared not ask for more, and bought only the pistol.

A week later they set off on their way back to Les Peuples.

VI

In front of the white gate and its two brick pillars, the family and servants stood waiting. The post-chaise drew up, and long embraces ensued. Mama was crying; Jeanne, deeply affected, wiped away a tear; Father paced nervously up and down.

Then, while the luggage was being unloaded, an account of the journey was delivered beside the drawing-room fire. Words poured in abundance from Jeanne's lips; and within half an hour the story was told, all of it, except perhaps for one or two details forgotten in the haste of narrative.

Then the young woman went to unpack: Rosalie, who was also in a particularly emotional state, helped her. When they had finished, and all the linen and dresses and toilet articles had been put away in their usual place, the maid left her mistress; and Jeanne, feeling rather weary, sat down.

She wondered what to do next and tried to think of some occupation for her mind, some task for her hands. She had no wish to go back down to the drawing-room where her mother was dozing; she thought of going for a walk, but the countryside seemed so dreary that just looking at it out of the window made her heart sink with melancholy gloom.

Then she realized that there was nothing left for her to do, ever. Her whole childhood at the convent had been taken up with the future, and she had busied herself with fantasies. In those days the continual excitement provided by her hopes and aspirations had filled her hours so that she never noticed their passing. Then, hardly had she stepped outside the austere walls within which her illusions had taken shape, when her expectation of love had been immediately fulfilled. The man she had hoped for, and met, and loved, and married in a matter of weeks—as one does marry when one is suddenly certain—had carried her off in his arms without allowing her a single moment's pause for reflection.

But the sweet reality of their first days together was now to become the everyday reality that closed the door on indeterminate hopes, on the charming, anxious uncertainties of the unknown. Yes indeed, the waiting was over.

And so there was nothing left to do, today, tomorrow, ever again. And she sensed all this in some way as a kind of disillusion, as the collapse of her dreams.

She stood up and went to press her forehead against the cold window-pane. Then, having gazed for some time at the dark clouds rolling across the sky, she decided to go out.

Was this still the same countryside, the same grass, the same trees as she had known in May? What had become of the sunlit merriment of the leaves and the verdant poetry of the lawn with its blazing dandelions and blood-red poppies, where daisies shone like stars and yellow butterflies quivered whimsically as though pulled by invisible strings? And that heady air laden with life, and smells, and tiny atoms of fertility, was gone.

The avenues, drenched by continual autumn showers and thickly carpeted in fallen leaves, stretched away under thin, shivering poplars that were now almost bare. Their slender branches trembled in the wind, trying to shake off some last leaf that was ready to drop into the space below. And all day long, like a steady, lugubrious downpour, these final leaves, now all yellow, like large gold coins, endlessly detached themselves, spiralled in the air, fluttered, and fell.

She walked as far as the copse. It had a mournful air, like a room where a person lies dying. The towering walls of greenery that separated the lovely little winding paths and gave them their secret intimacy had been scattered to the four winds. Spindly branches jostled one another amidst the delicate lattice-work of intermingled shrubs; and as the wind swept the fallen leaves along, stirring them and piling them periodically into heaps, their dry rustle sounded like the rasping sigh of a mortal agony.

Tiny birds were hopping about in search of shelter, twittering as though they felt the cold.

The lime and the plane-tree, however, being protected by the thick screen of elders which had been deployed as a first line of defence against the sea gales, still wore their summer finery, and seemed to be dressed, the one in red velvet and the other in orange silk, tinted thus by the first cold days according to the nature of their sap.

Jeanne walked slowly up and down Mama's avenue, beside the Couillards' farm. Something weighed upon her, like a foreboding of the long periods of boredom to come during the life of monotony and routine that was now commencing.

Then she sat down on the bank where Julien had spoken to her of love for the first time; and she remained there, daydreaming, her mind almost vacant, her heart quite numb, wanting to lie down, to sleep and thereby escape the sadness of this day.

Suddenly she caught sight of a seagull being carried across the sky by a gust of wind; and she recalled the eagle that she had seen, back there, in Corsica, in the darkness of the Val d'Ota. Her heart registered the sharp pang which comes with the memory of something good that is now over; and all at once she saw again the radiant island with its wild perfume, its sun that can ripen orange and citron, its mountains with their rosy peaks, its blue bays, its ravines where torrents race.

And then the bleak, damp countryside around her, the baleful falling of the leaves, and the grey clouds chased along by the wind, enveloped her in such a thick pall of desolation that she returned to the house simply in order not to burst out sobbing.

Mama, slumped in front of the fireplace, was dozing, being accustomed to the melancholy of the days and no longer conscious of it. Papa and Julien had gone off for a walk, deep in discussion about their affairs. And night fell, strewing gloomy shadow through the vast drawing-room which gleamed fitfully in the light from the fire.

Through the windows, a last vestige of daylight was sufficient to reveal the grubby spectacle of nature at year's end, and a grey sky which looked as though it, too, had been smeared with dirt.

Presently the Baron appeared, followed by Julien; and as soon as he entered the room, which was plunged in darkness, he rang the bell and called out:

'Come on, quickly, some light! It's miserable in here.'

And he sat down by the fireplace. As his wet feet steamed

beside the flame and the mud dropped from the soles of his shoes, dried by the heat, he rubbed his hands cheerfully:

'I'm sure there's going to be a frost,' he said. 'The sky's clearing to the north and there's a full moon tonight. It's sure to be a hard one.'

Then, turning towards his daughter:

'So, my little one, are you glad to be back home, back in your own house with your old parents?'

This simple question quite demolished Jeanne. She flung herself into her father's arms, eyes brimming with tears, and kissed him urgently as though asking to be forgiven; for despite her heart's efforts to be cheerful, she felt unutterably sad. And yet she remembered how much she had looked forward to the joy of seeing her parents again; and she was astonished to sense this distance from them and how it paralysed her affection: it was as though, after long thinking from far away about those one loves and having grown unaccustomed to seeing them at every hour of the day, one then felt, on being reunited with them, a kind of pause in one's affection until such time as the bonds of communal living should be retied.

Dinner lasted a long time, and there was little conversation. Julien appeared to have forgotten all about his wife.

In the drawing-room afterwards she dozed by the fire, opposite Mama who was fast asleep; and on being momentarily roused by the voices of the two men arguing, she asked herself in an attempt to stir her brain to action whether she, too, was going to be overtaken by this same dreary lethargy that comes from unbroken routine.

The fire in the hearth, a gentle, reddish glow throughout the daytime, was now coming to life, all bright and crackling. It darted long gleams of light onto the faded upholstery of the armchairs, onto the fox and the stork, and the melancholy heron, and the ant and the cicada.

The Baron came up to the fire and stretched his hands out towards the blazing logs with a smile:

'Ah, it's drawing well this evening. There's a frost, my dears, there's a frost.'

Then he placed his hand on Jeanne's shoulder and said, point-
ing to the fire:

'There you are, my sweet, the best place in all the world: the
fireside—the fireside with one's nearest and dearest sitting round
it. Nothing to match it. But still, it's bedtime. You young things
must both be exhausted?'

Having gone upstairs to her bedroom Jeanne wondered how
she could twice return to the same place—a place she thought she
loved—and yet find it so different on each occasion. Why did she
now feel in some way bruised? Why did this house, this whole
beloved countryside, everything for which till then her heart had
danced, now seem to her so utterly depressing?

But suddenly her eye fell on the clock. The little bee was still
flitting from left to right, from right to left, with the same rapid,
constant movement, above the vermilion flowers. Then all at once
Jeanne felt a surge of affection and was moved to tears at the sight
of this little mechanical object that seemed to be alive, chiming
the hours for her and ticking away like a heartbeat.

Certainly she had not been so affected when she embraced her
father and mother. The heart has its mysteries whereof reason
naught doth know.

For the first time since her marriage she found herself sleeping
alone in her own bed, Julien having gone to another room on the
grounds that he was tired. Indeed it had been agreed that from
now on they would each have a separate bedroom.

She took a long time to go to sleep: she found it strange not to
feel another body next to hers, having got out of the habit of
sleeping alone, and she was kept awake by the nagging wind that
was tearing at the roof.

In the morning she was woken by a great gleam of light, and
her bed was tinged the colour of blood; and the window-panes, all
spattered with hoar-frost, were coloured a flaming red as though
the whole sky were on fire.

Wrapping herself in a long dressing-gown, she ran to the
window and opened it.

A sharp, invigorating blast of icy wind rushed into the room, a
biting cold that stung her skin and brought tears to her eyes; and

there in the middle of a crimson sky a large, round sun, bloated and rheumy like a drunkard's face, was rising behind the trees. The ground, covered in white frost, was now hard and dry, and it rang under the feet of the farm-people. In this one night the branches of the poplars had all been stripped bare of their remaining leaves; and beyond the heath could be seen the long, greenish line of the sea, flecked with streaks of white.

The plane and the lime-tree were rapidly shedding their foliage in the squalling wind. With each gust of icy air, swirls of leaves loosened by the sudden frost would scatter into the wind like a flock of birds taking off. Jeanne dressed, went outside, and for something to do, set off to visit the farmers.

Up went the Martins' arms in greeting, and the farmer's wife kissed her on both cheeks; then they pressed her to a glass of noyau. She went across to the other farm. Up went the Couillards' arms; the farmer's wife pecked her on both ears, and she had to partake of a small glass of cassis.

After this she returned home for lunch.

And the day passed like the one before it, only cold rather than wet. And the remaining days in the week were like the first two; and every week in the month was like the first.

Little by little, however, her yearning for far-off lands began to fade. Habit placed a coating of resigned acceptance over her existence rather like the scale deposit left behind by certain types of water. She began once more to take some slight interest in the hundred-and-one little things which make up everyday life, to have a care for its simple, nondescript, routine activities. And she developed a kind of reflective melancholy, an unspecific disenchantment with living. For what did she want? What did she desire? She did not know. She felt no worldly need, no longing for pleasure, no desire even for the delights that were to hand. What delights, indeed? Like the old armchairs in the drawing-room that were dulled with age, everything was gradually losing its colour in her eyes, everything was fading, and taking on a drab and pallid hue.

Her relationship with Julien had changed completely. He seemed quite different since their return from honeymoon, like an actor who has finished playing a role and reverted to his normal self. He scarcely paid her any attention, or even spoke to her; all trace of love had abruptly disappeared; and few were the nights when he came to her bedroom.

He had taken charge of the household and its estates, renegotiating leases, hounding the tenants, cutting back on expenditure; and having now assumed the air of a gentleman-farmer himself, he had lost all the polish and elegance of the suitor.

Though it was streaked with stains, he never changed out of an old velvet hunting-jacket, with brass buttons, a leftover from his younger days which he had found lying in his wardrobe; and having fallen into the neglectful ways of one who no longer needs to make himself presentable, he had stopped shaving, and his long, ill-kempt beard detracted startlingly from his good looks. His hands were no longer manicured; and at the end of every meal he would drink four or five little glasses of cognac.

When Jeanne had tried gently to reproach him, he had replied with such a curt 'leave me be' that she no longer dared offer him advice.

She had reconciled herself to these changes in a way which surprised even herself. He had become a stranger to her, a stranger whose heart and soul were a closed book. She thought about the matter a great deal, and wondered how it was that having met, fallen in love, and married in such a sudden rush of intimate affection, they should now suddenly find themselves as distant from each other as if they had never shared a bed.

And how was it that she did not find this abandonment more hurtful? Was this what life was like? Had they made a mistake? Did the future hold nothing more for her?

If Julien had remained handsome, well-groomed, elegant, attractive, would she perhaps have minded more?

It had been agreed that in the New Year the newlyweds should be left on their own, and that Father and Mama would return for a few months to their house at Rouen. The young pair were not to leave Les Peuples this particular winter, but rather complete the process of settling in by getting to know and find pleasure in the place where they were to spend the rest of their lives. They had a number of neighbours, moreover, to whom Julien would present his wife. These were the Brisevilles, the Couteliers, and the Fourvilles.

But the young couple could not begin their visits yet because it had so far proved impossible to get the painter to come and change the family coat-of-arms on the carriage.

For indeed the Baron had ceded the old family carriage to his son-in-law; and Julien would on no account have consented to present himself at the chateaux in the vicinity until the shield of the de Lamare family had been quartered with that of the Le Perthuis des Vauds.

Now there was only one man thereabouts who still had an expert knowledge of heraldic ornament, and this was a painter from Bolbec, called Bataille, who was summoned in turn to all the manor-houses in Normandy to affix these precious decorations to their carriage-doors.

Finally, one December day just as they were finishing lunch, a man appeared at the gate, opened it, and began to walk up the main avenue. He was carrying a box on his back. It was Bataille.

He was ushered into the dining-room and waited on like a gentleman; for his specialist trade, his constant dealings with the entire aristocracy of the region, and his knowledge of heraldry, its emblems and time-honoured terminology, had turned him into a kind of living blazon whose hand all gentlemen were prepared to shake.

Pen and paper were sent for at once and, while he ate, the Baron and Julien sketched out the quartering of their escutcheons. The Baroness, always in a froth when such issues were at stake, offered advice; and Jeanne herself took part in the discussion as though some mysterious interest had suddenly stirred within her.

Bataille, while continuing with his lunch, would give his opinion, occasionally grabbing a pencil to illustrate a possible design; he cited examples and described all the seigneurial carriages in the area. In his thinking and even in his voice he seemed to carry an aura of nobility.

He was a short man, with grey, close-cropped hair, and his hands, which reeked of turpentine, were stained with various colours of paint. It was said that he had once been involved in some unsavoury scandal; but the general consideration in which he was held by all the titled families had long since erased this blot on his name.

When he had finished his coffee he was conducted to the coach-house, where the wax-cloth was taken off the carriage. Having examined the vehicle, Bataille solemnly pronounced his verdict as to the dimensions which he thought necessary for his chosen design; and then, after some further discussion, he began his task.

Despite the cold, the Baroness had a chair brought so that she could observe the work in progress. Then she asked for a foot-warmer, as her feet were frozen: and she began to chat quietly with the painter, asking him about certain marriages of which she had not previously had news, and about a number of recent births and deaths, using this information to complete the family trees which she carried around in her head.

Julien had remained beside his mother-in-law, sitting astride a chair. He smoked his pipe, spat on the ground, listened, and continued to watch as his nobility was translated into colour.

Presently Père Simon, who was on his way to the kitchen-garden with his spade over his shoulder, stopped to consider the work; and once the news of Bataille's arrival had reached the two farms, it was not long before both farmer's wives appeared on the scene. Standing on either side of the Baroness, they went into ecstasies, and kept saying:

'Finicky work, mind, getting things just right on them machines.'

It did not prove possible to complete the escutcheons on the two doors until the next day, when they were ready towards eleven. Everyone was there in a trice; and the carriage was hauled out so that they could all have a better look.

It was perfect. They complimented Bataille on his work, and off he went with his box on his back. And the Baron, his wife, Jeanne, and Julien were all agreed that the painter was a fellow of considerable talent who, if circumstances had allowed, could most certainly have become an artist.

However, further changes were required on account of various reforms which Julien had instituted as economy measures.

The old coachman had been made a gardener: the Vicomte himself had assumed responsibility for driving the carriage, and he had sold off the coach-horses in order to save on their feed.

Next, he had appointed a young cowherd called Marius as groom, since there had to be someone to hold the animals once the masters and mistresses had stepped down from the carriage.

And finally, in order to have horses for the carriage, he had added a special clause to the Couillards' and Martins' leases which required each farmer to supply one horse on one day per month and on a date of the Vicomte's own choosing, in return for which they were dispensed from providing fowl for the Baron's table.

So it was that, the Couillards having brought along a huge great nag with a yellow coat and the Martins a small beast that was shaggy and white, the two animals were put to harness side by side; and Marius, completely swamped inside one of Père Simon's old livery uniforms, led up this equipage to the foot of the front steps.

Julien, groomed and erect, had recovered some of his former elegance; but despite his efforts his long beard still lent him a common air.

He inspected the harness, the carriage, and the little groom and deemed them satisfactory, the only really important thing in his eyes being the newly painted armorial bearings.

The Baroness, who had been helped down from her room by her husband, struggled into the carriage and sat down, propping herself against some cushions. Jeanne appeared in her turn. At first she laughed at the pairing of the two horses, and commented that the white one was actually the grandson of the yellow. Then she caught sight of Marius: his face was almost entirely invisible beneath his top-hat and rosette, which only his nose prevented from falling further; his hands had vanished up his sleeves; and his legs were swathed in the skirts of his uniform, from under which his feet protruded strangely at the bottom, shod in enormous pumps; and when she saw him tilt his head back to see, and lift his knee at every step as if he were about to bestride a river, and grope about like a blind man as he tried to do as he was bidden, completely engulfed and lost to view inside these ample clothes, she was seized with uncontrollable mirth, and simply could not stop laughing.

The Baron turned round, observed the little fellow in disbelief, and then, yielding to the infectious merriment, burst out laughing, calling on his wife to look, himself barely able to speak:

'L-l-look at Ma-Ma-Marius! Wh-what a sight! My goodness me, what a ri-ridiculous sight!'

Then the Baroness, having leaned out of the carriage door to take a look, was overcome by such a fit of mirth that the whole carriage danced on its springs, as though it were jolting along a road.

But Julien enquired, ashen-faced:

'What on earth are you all laughing at? Have you gone mad?'

Jeanne, convulsed with helpless laughter and quite unable to recover herself, sat down on a step. The Baron did likewise; and in the carriage similarly convulsive sneezing, together with a kind of rhythmic clucking, suggested that the Baroness for her part was choking. And suddenly Marius's frock-coat began to heave. He must have seen the joke, because deep under his hat he too was in a fit of laughter.

Thereupon Julien leapt forward in exasperation. With one blow he parted the boy from his gigantic hat, and away it flew onto the lawn. Then, rounding on his father-in-law, he blurted out in a voice trembling with anger:

'You have no right to laugh like this. We wouldn't be in this situation if you hadn't wasted your fortune and frittered away your estates. Whose fault is it if you're ruined?'

All the laughter ceased at once, frozen. And nobody said a word. Jeanne, now on the verge of tears, climbed in beside her mother. The Baron, nonplussed and silent, sat down opposite the two women; and Julien took his place on the box, having pulled the boy up beside him. The latter was crying, and his cheek was swelling up.

It was an unhappy drive and seemed to last for ever. In the carriage no one said anything. Being all three of them downcast and embarrassed, they did not want to admit what burdened their hearts. They realized that they could not have talked about anything else, so preoccupied were they by this one painful thought, and so they preferred to remain in gloomy silence rather than broach such an unpleasant subject.

Proceeding at the unequal trot of the two horses, the carriage skirted the edge of the farmyards along the way, scattering black hens who made off in long, panic-stricken strides and dived into the hedges, where they disappeared from view. From time to time they were chased by an angry Alsatian, who would then return home, the hairs still up on his back, and turn round to bark at the carriage one last time. A gangling lad in muddy clogs, ambling along with his hands in his pockets, his blue shirt billowing behind him in the wind, would stand aside to let the horses and carriage past, awkwardly doffing his cap and revealing his hair that was plastered to his skull.

And between each farm it was open country again, where other farms could be seen dotted here and there in the distance.

At length they entered a great avenue of firs leading off the main road. The deep, muddy ruts made the carriage lurch from side to side, and caused Mama to cry out. At the end of the avenue there was a white gate which was shut; Marius ran to open it, and they drove round an enormous lawn until the curve in the drive brought them to the front of a huge, tall, gloomy building with closed shutters.

The door in the middle opened suddenly; and a doddery old servant, dressed in a red-and-black striped waistcoat partly covered by an apron, came slowly down towards them with short, sideways steps. He asked for the name of the visitors and ushered them into a spacious drawing-room where, with some difficulty, he opened the shutters. The furniture was shrouded in dust-sheets, and the clock and candelabras were wrapped in white linen; a musty air, the cold, damp atmosphere of yester-year, seemed to pierce their flesh and lungs and hearts with sadness.

They all sat down and waited. A few steps heard in the corridor above suggested unaccustomed haste. The residents of the house, having been taken by surprise, were changing as quickly as they could. This took a long while. A bell rang several times. Other steps could be heard coming down a staircase, then going up again.

The Baroness felt the penetrating cold keenly and kept sneezing. Julien paced up and down. Jeanne sat glumly beside her mother. And the Baron leant against the marble mantelpiece, and stared at the floor.

Finally one of the tall doors swung open to reveal the Vicomte and Vicomtesse de Briseville. They were both short, skinny, sprightly figures, of no readily identifiable age, at once formal and ill at ease. The wife, wearing a floral silk dress and a small widow's cap with ribbons, spoke rapidly in a high-pitched voice. The husband, dressed in a rather grand, close-fitting frock-coat, greeted them with a bend of the knees. His nose, his eyes, his long, exposed teeth, his hair which seemed coated with wax, and his fine, full-dress attire all gleamed with the gleam of objects of which much care is taken.

After the initial words of welcome and the exchange of neighbourly pleasantries, no one could think of anything else to say. Mutual satisfaction was expressed, albeit without evident reason. Each party did so hope that they might continue to maintain such excellent and cordial relations. It was such a blessing to be able to meet like this when one lived in the country the whole year round.

And they could feel the glacial atmosphere of the drawing-room entering their bones, and their throats became hoarse. The Baroness was now coughing without having quite stopped sneezing. Then the Baron gave the signal for departure. The Brisevilles would not hear of it:

'What? So soon? Do please stay a little longer.'

But Jeanne had already risen to her feet, despite signs from Julien who considered the visit too short.

They wanted to ring for the servant to call the carriage to the front. The bell no longer worked. The master of the house rushed out, and returned to inform them that the horses had been stabled.

They would have to wait. Each of them tried to think of something, anything, to say. They talked about how rainy the winter had been. Jeanne, trembling involuntarily with nervousness, enquired what her hosts could possibly find to do all year long, living entirely on their own together as they did. But the Brisevilles were astonished at the question; for they were constantly kept busy, writing frequently to their noble relations scattered throughout France, spending their days engaged upon minuscule matters, as formal with each other as with perfect strangers, and conversing majestically about the most trivial of concerns.

And beneath the high, blackened ceiling of this vast, unlived-in drawing-room, all wrapped in dust-sheets, this man and this woman—so tiny, and neat, and proper—seemed to Jeanne like conserved specimens of the nobility.

At last the carriage came past the windows drawn by its pair of ill-matched nags. But Marius was nowhere to be found. Thinking he was free until the evening, he had doubtless disappeared off into the countryside.

Furious, Julien requested that he be sent home on foot; and after much bowing and salutation on all sides, they set off back to Les Peuples.

As soon as they were safely ensconced in the carriage, Jeanne and her father—though still borne down by the memory of Julien's brutal remarks—began to laugh again as they mimicked the gestures and speech of the Brisevilles. The Baron imitated the husband, and Jeanne the wife, but this touched the Baroness's aristocratic nerve and she said to them:

'You're quite wrong to mock like that. They are thoroughly *comme il faut* and belong to excellent families.'

The pair of them fell silent so as not to upset Mama, but from time to time they just could not help it: Papa and Jeanne would catch each other's eye and begin again. He would bow ceremoniously and enquire in a solemn voice:

'Your chateau at Les Peuples must be very cold, Madame, exposed as it is every day to the full force of the wind from the sea?'

And she would assume a pinched expression and reply in a simpering tone, with a tremulous little toss of the head like a duck bathing:

'Oh, my dear sir, there is always something to keep me busy here, you know, the whole year round. And then, of course, we have so many relations to write to. And Monsieur de Briseville leaves everything to me. He is engaged upon learned research with Monsieur Shovel, the abbé. They are writing the religious history of Normandy together.'

Then it was the Baroness's turn to smile, in tolerant vexation, as she reminded them:

'It's not right to laugh at people of our own class like that.'

But suddenly the carriage stopped; and Julien was shouting out to someone behind. Then Jeanne and the Baron leaned out of the windows and saw a singular creature apparently rolling towards them. Legs entangled in the swirling skirt of his livery coat, blinded by his headgear as it teetered now to one side, now to the other, flapping his sleeves like the sails of a windmill, floundering wildly through the large puddles, tripping on every stone along the road, jigging and leaping about, all covered in mud, it was Marius running after the carriage as fast as his legs would carry him.

When he had caught up, Julien leaned down, grabbed him by the collar, and hoisted him up beside him; then, letting go of the reins, he began to rain blows down upon the hat, shoving it right down onto the lad's shoulders as it echoed like a drum. The boy was screaming inside it, trying to get away and jump off the seat, while his master held him with one hand and kept hitting him with the other.

Distraught, Jeanne stammered: 'Papa... Oh Papa!', and the Baroness, filled with indignation, grabbed her husband's arm and said:

'Jacques, for goodness sake, make him stop.'

Then in a flash the Baron lowered the front window, grabbed his son-in-law by the sleeve, and shouted in a shaking voice:

'Have you quite finished hitting that child?'

Julien turned round in astonishment:

'Can't you see what the little blighter's done to his uniform?'

But the Baron thrust his head out between the pair of them and replied:

'What does it matter? That's not a reason to be so hard on him.'

Julien grew angry once more:

'Please, let me be, it's none of your business,' and he raised his hand again. But his father-in-law seized it in a trice and brought it down with such force that he banged it against the wood of the seat; and he shouted, 'If you don't stop now, I shall get out and make damn sure you do!' so violently that the Vicomte calmed down at once, and, shrugging his shoulders without further reply, he cracked the whip and the horses set off at a canter.

Ashen-faced, the two women sat quite still, and the pounding heartbeats of the Baroness could distinctly be heard.

At dinner Julien was more charming than usual, and behaved as if nothing had happened. Jeanne, her father, and Madame Adélaïde, calm, affable people unaccustomed to bearing grudges and mollified at seeing him be so pleasant, now relaxed into merriment with a convalescent's sense of well-being; and when Jeanne mentioned the Brisevilles again, her husband joined in the fun, though he added at once:

'All the same, they do have the grand manner.'

No further visits were undertaken, each of them being afraid to broach the question of Marius again. They decided simply to send their neighbours a card at New Year, and then to await the first mild days of spring before going to call on them.

Christmas came. The priest and the mayor and his wife came to dinner. They were invited again for New Year's Day. These occasions provided the sole distractions to break the monotonous chain of passing days.

Papa and Mama were to leave Les Peuples on the ninth of January. Jeanne wanted them to stay on, but Julien was far from enthusiastic; and the Baron, in the face of his son-in-law's increasing coldness, ordered a post-chaise to come from Rouen.

On the eve of their departure, when everything was packed,

and as it was a clear, frosty night, Jeanne and her father decided to go down to Yport, which they had not visited since her return from Corsica.

They went through the wood where she had walked on her wedding-day, then completely at one with the person whose life-long companion she was in the process of becoming—this wood where she had received her first caress, and quivered with her first, trembling foretaste of that sensual love which she would come finally to know only in the wild setting of the Val d'Ota, beside the spring where they had drunk, mingling their kisses with the water.

The leaves were gone, and the climbing vegetation too, leaving only the sound of the branches, and the dry rustle of denuded thickets in winter.

They entered the little village. The empty, silent streets reeked of the sea, of fish and kelp. The huge, brown nets were still there, hung up to dry outside the doors or else spread out on the shingle. The cold, grey sea, and its unceasing rumble of breaking surf, was beginning to recede with the ebbing tide and to uncover the greenish rocks beneath the cliffs that ran towards Fécamp. And all along the beach the large fishing-boats lay heeled over on their sides like huge, dead fishes. Night was falling, and the fishermen were arriving in small groups on the upper part of the beach;* trudging along in their great sea-boots, their necks wrapped in woollens, a litre of spirits in one hand and a ship's lantern in the other. For a long time they moved about among the tilting craft; with Norman deliberation they loaded their nets, their buoys, a large loaf of bread, a pot of butter, a glass and their bottle of *trois-six*.* Then, having righted the boat, they gave it a shove towards the water's edge, and it would begin to career noisily down the shingle before breasting the foam and rising on the waves, where it hovered for a few seconds and then unfurled its brown wings before disappearing into the night, its tiny lamp glowing at the top of the mast.

And the tall figures of the fishermen's wives, their bony frames protruding under their thin dresses, stayed until the last fisher-man had left and then made their way back to the sleeping village, their raucous voices disturbing the deep slumber of its dark streets.

The Baron and Jeanne stood there watching these men vanish into the distance, departing as they did each night to risk their lives in order to avoid starvation, and yet still so poor that they never ate meat.

The Baron, exalted by the spectacle of the ocean, murmured: .

'What a terrible beauty it has. How magnificent the sea is, with darkness falling and all those lives in peril upon its waters? Don't you think, Jeannette?'

She forced a smile:

'Nothing like the Mediterranean, though.'

But her father was indignant:

'The Mediterranean! Pah! It's like oil, like a glass of cordial, and blue like the water you wash clothes in. But look how fearsome this sea is, and how rough the waves are. And think of all those men who've set sail on it, and already they're out of sight.'

Jeanne conceded with a sigh:

'Well, perhaps you're right.'

But the word 'Mediterranean' which had sprung to her lips had caused a further pang, casting her mind back to those far-off lands, where her dreams lay buried.

Instead of returning through the woods, father and daughter now made for the road and climbed the hill at a steady pace. They said little, saddened by the imminent departure.

From time to time, as they walked beside a farm ditch, they would be assailed by the smell of crushed apples, that aroma of fresh cider which seems to hang over the entire Norman countryside at this time of year, or else by the rich scent of cowsheds, the good, warm stench of manure. A small, lighted window at the far end of the yard would indicate the presence of the farmhouse.

And Jeanne had the feeling that somehow her soul was expanding and could grasp invisible things; and these little glimmers of light scattered through the fields suddenly gave her an acute sense of the isolation in which all creatures live, of how everything conspires to separate them and keep them apart, to remove them far away from that which otherwise they might love.

Then, in a tone of resignation, she said:

'Life is not all fun.'

The Baron sighed:

'I'm afraid not, my child, and there's nothing we can do about it.'

And the next day, after Papa and Mama had gone, Jeanne and Julien were left alone together.

VII

Card-playing now entered the lives of the young couple. Each day after lunch Julien would play several games of bezique with his wife, while he smoked a pipe and washed his meal down with cognac, of which he was soon drinking six to eight glasses. Afterwards she would go up to her bedroom, sit by the window, and as the wind rattled the frame or the rain beat against the panes, doggedly embroider a petticoat frill. Sometimes, when she grew weary, she would look up and gaze into the distance at the dark sea and its foaming waves. Then, after a few minutes of blank contemplation, she would resume her work.

Indeed there was nothing else for her to do, since Julien had taken complete charge of the household by way of satisfying to the full his need to rule and his taste for thrift. He displayed ferocious meanness, never tipping the servants and reducing expenditure on food to the strict minimum. Ever since she had come to live at Les Peuples, Jeanne had been in the habit of ordering a small Norman pastry from the baker each morning, but Julien put a stop to this particular outgoing and condemned her to toast.

She said nothing, in order to avoid all the remonstrations and discussions and quarrelling; but each new manifestation of her husband's avarice was like the prick of a needle. To her, who had been brought up in a family where money counted for nothing, it all seemed unworthy and hateful. How often had she heard Mama say: 'But money's there to be spent!' Now Julien was always saying to her: 'Will you never learn to stop throwing money away?' And each time he had managed to reduce a bill or someone's wages by a few pence, he would slip the change into his pocket and proclaim with a smile: 'Little streams make big rivers.'

Meanwhile, on certain days, Jeanne began once more to dream. She would gently lay down her needlework, and with her hands limp and her eyes vacant, she would reconstruct one of her girlhood fantasies and duly embark upon a sequence of charming adventures. But all of a sudden the sound of Julien's voice giving Père Simon an order would snatch her from her soothing reverie; and as she resumed her patient work, she would say to herself: 'Ah, that's all over now,' and a tear would drop onto her fingers as they pushed the needle forward.

Rosalie too, once so cheerful and always singing, was a changed person. Her plump cheeks had lost their rosy sheen and, nearly hollow now, sometimes almost looked as though they had been smeared with mud.

'Are you feeling unwell, my dear?' Jeanne would often ask her, but the maid always replied: 'No, my lady.' Her cheeks would colour slightly, and then she would quickly make her escape.

Where once she had raced about the place, she now walked with difficulty, dragging her feet; she seemed to have lost interest in her appearance and had stopped buying things from the pedlars, who now showed her their silk ribbons and their bodices and their various bottles of scent all in vain.

And the great house seemed to echo emptily, sunk in gloom, its front stained with long grey streaks by the rain.

At the end of January the snow came. Far away to the north the thick cloud could be seen arriving across the dark sea; and the white flakes began to fall. In the course of a single night the whole plain was buried, and the trees appeared next morning draped in what seemed like frozen spume.

Wearing high boots and looking particularly hirsute, Julien spent his time at the far end of the copse, hidden just behind the ditch separating it from the heath and on the look-out for migrating birds. From time to time a shot would shatter the frozen silence of the fields; and wheeling flocks of black crows would take off from the tall trees.

Occasionally, out of boredom, Jeanne came downstairs and stood on the front steps. Sounds of life could be heard in the far distance, echoing across the slumbering tranquillity of the bleak, ghostly expanse.

Soon all she could hear was the dull boom of the waves in the distance and the faint, steady whisper of the icy powder falling softly, ceaselessly, to earth.

And the level of the snow rose inexorably beneath the endless cascade of this thick, feather-light foam.

On one such pale morning, Jeanne was warming her feet at the bedroom fire while Rosalie, who seemed more changed with every day that passed, was slowly making the bed. Suddenly Jeanne heard a whimper of pain behind her. Without turning her head, she asked:

'What's wrong?'

The maid replied as usual: 'Nothing, my lady,' but her voice sounded exhausted, almost on the point of extinction.

Jeanne's mind was already on something else when she realized that she could no longer hear the girl moving about:

'Rosalie!' she called.

Nothing stirred. Then, thinking that she had quietly left the room, she called out 'Rosalie!' more loudly and was about to reach for the bell when a deep groan, close by, startled her, making her shiver in sudden apprehension.

The servant-girl, her face completely white and with a wild look in her eyes, was sitting on the floor, leaning against the wooden bedstead with her legs stretched out in front of her.

Jeanne rushed towards her:

'What is it? What is it?'

The girl said nothing, made no gesture of reply, but simply stared at her mistress with a crazed expression, gasping as though she were riven by some dreadful pain. Then suddenly she arched her entire body and slid down onto her back, biting back a cry of distress behind clenched teeth.

Then, beneath her dress, which was stretched tight across her parted thighs, something moved. And all at once there came a strange noise, like lapping, a strangled, choking sound. Then suddenly there was a long, cat-like mewling, a frail lament already charged with suffering, the first cry of pain of a child entering upon life.

Jeanne understood in a flash and rushed blindly to the staircase shouting:

'Julien! Julien!'

He answered from below:

'What is it?'

She had great difficulty in getting the words out:

'It's... it's Rosalie. She's...'

Julien dashed up the stairs, two at a time, and burst into the room, where he lifted the girl's dress in a trice and revealed a hideous little lump of crumpled, fretful flesh, a slimy, huddled thing writhing about between two bare legs.

He straightened up with an evil look on his face and began to hustle his distraught wife out of the room:

'This is none of your concern. Away. Fetch Ludivine and Père Simon for me.'

Trembling all over, Jeanne went down to the kitchen and then, not daring to return upstairs, proceeded into the drawing-room, where no fire had been lit since the departure of her parents; and waited there anxiously for news.

Soon she saw the pantry-boy running out of the house. Five minutes later he came back with the widow Dentu, the local midwife.

Presently there was a great commotion on the staircase, as though an injured person were being carried somewhere; and then Julien came to tell Jeanne that she could go back up to her room.

She was shaking as though she had just witnessed a fatal accident. She sat down once more in front of the fire in her room and asked:

'How is she?'

Preoccupied and tense, Julien was pacing up and down the room: he appeared to be seething with anger. He did not reply at first. Then, after a few moments, he stopped:

'What are you going to do with the girl?'

She did not understand and looked at her husband:

'What? How do you mean? I've no idea.'

And suddenly he shouted, as though he had lost his temper:

'But we can't keep a bastard in the house.'

Jeanne was thoroughly nonplussed for a moment. Then, after a long silence, she said:

'Well, in that case, dearest, perhaps it could be sent out to a wet-nurse?'

He did not let her finish:

'And who's going to pay? You, I suppose?'

Again she thought for a long while, trying to find a solution, till finally she said:

'But the father will take responsibility, for the child I mean; and if he marries Rosalie, then the problem is solved.'

Julien, furious, as though he had lost all patience, retorted:

'The father!... the father!... And do you know who he is, this father of yours?... No, you don't, do you? Well, do you?...'

Jeanne, upset, was roused:

'But he simply won't abandon the girl like this. He'd be a coward! We'll ask his name, we'll go and see him, and then he'll have to explain himself.'

Julien had calmed down and begun to walk about again:

'My dear, she refuses to give the man's name. And she's no more likely to tell you than she is me... And then, what if he wants to have nothing to do with her?... We cannot keep an unmarried mother and her bastard under our roof, do you hear me?'

Jeanne refused to give in and repeated:

'Well, he's a miserable wretch then, whoever he is. But we're bound to find out one day who it is, and then he'll have us to reckon with.'

Julien, now red in the face, was becoming angry again:

'But what happens in the meantime?'

She could not think what was best, and so asked him:

'Well, what do *you* suggest then?'

At once he gave his opinion:

'Oh, as far as I'm concerned, it's perfectly simple. I'd give her some money and send her and her brat packing.'

But his young wife was indignant and would have none of it:

'No, never. That girl and I shared the same wet-nurse when we were babies, we grew up together. She has done wrong, I accept that, but that's not a reason for me to throw her out. And if necessary I'll bring the child up myself.'

At this Julien let fly:

'Oh, and some reputation we'll have then, won't we, us with our name to think about and our relations! Everyone will go round saying that we harbour vice, that we give shelter to sluts, and no respectable person will want to set foot here again. But really, what are you thinking of? You must be off your head.'

She had remained calm:

'I shall never allow Rosalie to be turned out. And if you don't wish to keep her, then my mother will take her back. Anyway, we're bound to discover sooner or later who the father of her child is.'

Thereupon he left the room in exasperation, slamming the door and shouting:

'Women and their daft ideas!'

That afternoon Jeanne went upstairs to visit the new mother. The maid, watched over by the widow Dentu, was lying quite still in bed, with her eyes open, while the nurse rocked the newborn child in her arms.

As soon as she saw her mistress, Rosalie began to sob, hiding her face under the sheets and shuddering with despair. Jeanne wanted to embrace her, but Rosalie would not let her, and continued to hide herself. Then the nurse intervened and uncovered her face; and she stopped resisting, still weeping, but more gently now.

A meagre fire was burning in the hearth; it was cold, and the child was crying. Jeanne did not dare mention the little thing in case she brought on a further outburst. She had taken her maid's hand, and kept repeating in a mechanical tone:

'Everything will be all right, everything will be all right.'

The poor girl was watching the nurse out of the corner of her eye, and gave a start every time the infant cried; and as each wave of unhappiness swept over her, temporarily choking her and erupting in a convulsive sob, the tears she was trying so hard to restrain gurgled in her throat.

Jeanne kissed her again and whispered softly in her ear:

'We'll take good care of it, my dear, you'll see.'

Then, as a new bout of crying began, she promptly made her escape.

Each day she returned, and each day Rosalie would burst into tears at the sight of her mistress.

The child was sent out to a wet-nurse nearby.

Meanwhile Julien scarcely spoke to his wife, as if he were still very angry with her over her refusal to dismiss the maid. One day he returned to the subject, but Jeanne took from her pocket a letter in which the Baroness asked for the girl to be sent to her immediately if they decided not to keep her on at Les Peuples. Furious, Julien exclaimed:

'Your mother's as mad as you are.'

But he stopped insisting.

A fortnight later the young mother was able to get up and resume her duties.

Then Jeanne sat her down one morning, took hold of her hands, and said with a penetrating look:

'Now then, my dear, tell me the whole story.'

Rosalie began to tremble, and stammered:

'What, Madame?'

'Whose child is it?'

Then the maid was once more overcome with terrible misery, and tried desperately to free her hands so that she could cover her face.

But Jeanne embraced her against her will and tried to console her:

'Yes, of course, it's all very unfortunate, my dear. You had a moment's weakness, but it happens to lots of people. If the father marries you, that will be that, and we'll be able to take him into service with you.'

Rosalie continued to groan as if she were being tortured, and from time to time she would try to tug herself free and run off.

Jeanne went on:

'I realize that you're ashamed; but you can see that I'm not angry, that I'm speaking quite calmly to you. If I ask you to tell me the father's name, it's for your own good, because I can see from your unhappiness that he's abandoned you and I want to prevent that. Julien will go and find him, you see, and we'll force him to marry you. And since we'll have both of you here, we shall soon see to it that he makes you happy as well.'

This time Rosalie gave such a sudden tug that she managed to withdraw her hands from her mistress's and ran off like a wild thing.

That evening, at dinner, Jeanne said to Julien:

'I tried to get Rosalie to tell me the name of her seducer, but I had no success. Why don't you have a try, so that we can force the miserable wretch to marry her?'

But immediately Julien grew angry:

'Look here, I don't want to listen to another word about this business. You were the one who wanted to keep her, so keep her, but stop pestering *me* about it.'

He seemed to have become even more irritable since the birth; and he had developed this habit of always shouting at his wife when he spoke to her, as though he were in a permanent temper, while she, on the contrary, lowered her voice and tried to be gentle and conciliatory in order to avoid argument. And often she cried, at night, in her bed.

Despite his constant irritation her husband had resumed his amorous ways, having neglected them since their return from honeymoon, and it was rare for him to go three nights in succession without crossing the conjugal threshold.

Rosalie was soon entirely better and became less miserable, although she remained in a state of nervous alarm, as though haunted by some unidentified menace.

And twice more she escaped when Jeanne tried to question her again.

Julien, too, seemed suddenly more agreeable; and his young wife once again began to entertain some vague hopes for the future, and to find amusement in things, although she occasionally felt unwell and experienced peculiar, unpleasant sensations which she mentioned to no one. The thaw had still not set in; and, for nearly five weeks now, stretching over the uniform blanket of hard, gleaming snow, the sky had remained as clear as blue crystal by day, and by night strewn with stars which looked like hoar-frost, so sharp and bitter chill was the air in the vast reaches of space.

The farms, each one isolated in its square of yard behind screens of tall, rime-powdered trees, seemed to be lying asleep in their white nightshirts. Neither man nor beast ventured forth; only the cottage chimneys provided signs of hidden life, as slender threads of smoke rose straight up into the ice-cold atmosphere.

The heath, the hedgerows, and the boundaries of elm all seemed dead, as though they had been killed off by the cold. From time to time a cracking sound could be heard coming from the trees as if their wooden limbs had snapped beneath the bark; and occasionally a large branch would come away and fall to the ground. The relentless frost was turning the sap rock-hard and splintering the grain.

Jeanne waited anxiously for the mild winds to return, attributing to the terrible rigours of the weather all the ill-defined ailments that were now afflicting her.

Sometimes she could not eat, and felt nauseated by the sight of food; sometimes her pulse raced wildly; sometimes her meagre repasts made her feel sick with indigestion; and her nerves, always tense and on edge, made her life one of constant and intolerable restlessness.

One evening the thermometer fell yet further, and Julien, who was shivering with cold as they left the dinner-table (for the dining-room was never properly heated on account of his constant endeavour to save on firewood), rubbed his hands together and whispered:

'It'll be good to share a bed tonight... What do you say, my sweet?'

He laughed in his good-natured way of old, and Jeanne threw her arms round his neck; but she did in fact feel so out of sorts that evening, beset with such pains and so strangely on edge, that she asked him softly, kissing him on the lips as she did so, to allow her to sleep alone. She told him briefly what ailed her:

'If you don't mind, darling. To be quite honest, I'm not feeling very well. I'm sure I'll be better by tomorrow.'

He did not insist:

'As you wish, my dear. If you're ill, you must take care of yourself.'

And they changed the subject.

She went to bed early. Julien, for once, had the fire lit in his bedroom. When he was told that it was 'burning nicely', he kissed his wife on the forehead and departed.

It was as though the entire house were being kneaded by the frost; as it penetrated the walls, they gave off little sounds as though they too were shivering; and Jeanne lay in bed shaking with the cold.

Twice she got up to put more logs on the fire and to fetch skirts, dresses, and old clothes to pile on her bed. She could not get warm; her feet were turning numb, and tremors ran up and down her calves and even her thighs, making her toss and turn without respite, leaving her excessively restless and unsettled.

Soon her teeth began to chatter; her hands trembled; her chest grew tight; her heart was pounding in slow, dull thumps and even seemed occasionally to miss a beat altogether; and she was gasping for air as though it could no longer find a way through to her throat.

A terrible sense of panic took hold of her entire being as the implacable cold chilled her to the marrow. Never before had she felt like this, never had she felt so evidently as though life were departing from her body and she was on the point of breathing her last.

She thought:

'I'm going to die... I *am* dying...'

And in sheer terror she jumped out of bed, rang for Rosalie, waited, rang again, waited again, shuddering, frozen to the bone.

The maid did not come. No doubt she was in that first, deep sleep from which nothing would rouse her; and so, not knowing what she was doing, Jeanne rushed barefoot out onto the landing. Silently she groped her way up the stairs, found the door, opened it, called out 'Rosalie!', continued forward, bumped into the bed, ran her hands across it, and then realized it was empty. It was empty and completely cold, as though no one had slept in it.

Surprised, she thought to herself:

'What! But she can't have gone running off again in weather like this!'

But with her heart now suddenly in a tumult, beating wildly and making her gasp for breath, she went downstairs again, her legs almost giving way beneath her, to wake Julien.

She burst into his room, driven by the conviction that she was going to die and wanting to see him before she lost consciousness.

In the light of the dying embers, she saw, beside her husband's, the head of Rosalie resting on the pillow.

On hearing her scream, they both shot up in bed. She remained standing there for an instant, motionless with the shock of this discovery. Then she fled back to her room; and hearing Julien desperately calling her name, a horrible dread took hold of her that she would have to see him, to hear his voice, to listen to his excuses, his lies, to look him in the face; and once more she dashed out onto the landing and ran downstairs.

She was now rushing headlong through the darkness, in danger of tumbling down the stairs and breaking her limbs on the stone. She just kept going, impelled by an overwhelming need to get away, to make no further discoveries, to see no one ever again.

When she reached the bottom, she sat down on a step, still in her bare feet and dressed only in her nightdress; and there she remained, at her wits' end.

Julien had jumped out of bed and was quickly getting dressed. She could hear his movements, the sound of his footsteps. She stood up again, determined to flee him. Already he, too, was coming down the stairs, and shouting: 'Jeanne, listen!'

No, she didn't want to listen, didn't want him to come anywhere near her; and she rushed into the dining-room as though she were being pursued by a murderer. She looked for a means of escape, somewhere to hide, a dark corner, any means of avoiding him. She huddled beneath the table. But already he was opening the door, a lamp in his hand, still calling 'Jeanne' over and over again, and she darted away once more, like a hare, rushed into the kitchen and ran round it twice like a cornered animal; and when he caught up with her again, she immediately tore open the door that led into the garden and rushed outside.

All at once the icy contact of the snow into which she sank, sometimes up to her knees, lent her a desperate energy. She was not cold, although she was scarcely dressed; she could feel nothing, so numbed had she been by the shock to her soul, and on she ran, as white as the ground itself.

Down the main avenue she went, then through the copse and over the ditch, before heading off across the heath.

There was no moon, and the stars gleamed like a scattering of fiery seed over the blackness of the sky; but there was sufficient light to see the dull, white expanse of the plain, a frozen stillness amidst an infinity of silence.

Jeanne moved quickly, effortlessly, not knowing where she was going, not thinking of anything at all. And suddenly she found herself at the edge of the cliff. She came to a sudden, instinctive halt and crouched down on her haunches, devoid of all intention and all will.

In the dark hole before her, the mute, invisible sea gave off the salty reek of its seaweed at low tide.

She remained like this for a long time, her mind as calmly passive as her body; then, all at once, she began to tremble, and to tremble wildly, like a sail flapping in the wind. Her arms and hands and feet began, as though set in motion by some irresistible force, to quiver, to vibrate in a series of rapid jerks; and suddenly she became, once more, acutely and painfully conscious.

Scenes from the past now flashed before her eyes; that trip with him in Père Lastique's fishing-smack, their conversation, her incipient love, the christening of the boat; and then she cast her mind even further back to that night of fond dreams when she had first arrived at Les Peuples. And now! Now! Oh, her life lay in pieces, all joy had gone, all hope for the future was henceforth doomed; and that terrible future, full of torment and betrayal and despair, loomed before her. She might as well die; that way it would all be over and done with in a twinkling.

But a voice was shouting in the distance:

'This way, I've found her footprints. Quick, quick, this way!' It was Julien out searching for her.

Oh, she did so not want to see him again. From the abyss,

right there in front of her, she could hear the faint sound of the sea now gently washing over the rocks.

She stood up, already poised to throw herself forward, and then, by way of a final, desperate farewell to life, she groaned the last word of the dying, the last word uttered by young soldiers eviscerated in battle:

'Mother!'

All at once she was transfixed by the thought of Mama; she saw her sobbing; she saw her father kneeling by her crumpled body, and in that single moment she felt the full force of their grief and their despair.

And so she subsided onto the snow, and made no further attempt to escape when Julien and Père Simon, with Marius behind them holding a lantern, grabbed her by the arms to pull her back, so close was she to the edge.

She offered them no resistance, for she could no longer move. She was aware of being carried off; put to bed, and rubbed with scalding cloths. After that all memory faded, all conscious thought disappeared.

Then a nightmare—if it was a nightmare—took possession of her. She was lying in bed in her room. It was daylight, but she could not get up. Why? She had no idea. Then she could hear a faint noise on the floor, a sort of scraping or rustling sound, and suddenly a mouse, a tiny grey mouse, was darting across her bedclothes. Another one followed immediately, then a third, which came scampering up towards her chest with quick, tiny steps. Jeanne was not afraid; yet she wanted to catch the beast and stretched out her hand, but to no avail.

Then more mice, ten, twenty, hundreds, thousands of them, appeared from all sides. They were climbing up the bedposts, running along the draperies, crawling all over the bed. And soon they got in beneath the covers; Jeanne could feel them against her skin, tickling her legs, running up and down the entire length of her body. She could see them coming up from the foot of the bed and wriggling under the sheets right beneath her chin; and she tried to fight them off, making sudden grabs to try and catch one but finding herself clutching thin air.

She became frantic and tried to get away, screaming, but it was if she were being held fast, as though powerful arms were twined around her and preventing her from moving; but she saw no one.

She had lost any sense of time. It must all have lasted a long while, a very long while.

Then she awoke, feeling tired and bruised, but calm. She felt weak, so weak. She opened her eyes, and was not at all surprised to find Mama sitting in the room, with some large man she did not know.

What age was she? She had no idea, and thought that she was still a little girl. In fact she could remember nothing.

The large man said:

'Look, she's coming round.'

And Mama began to cry. Then the large man said:

'Come, come, calm yourself, my lady. She will be fine now, I promise you. But don't say anything to her, not a single word. You must let her sleep.'

And it seemed to Jeanne as though she remained in this drowsy state for a long time, overtaken by a deep, heavy sleep whenever she tried to think; and indeed she made no effort to remember the slightest thing, as though she were dimly afraid of the reality that had begun to make its reappearance inside her head.

But once, as she was waking, she caught sight of Julien, alone next to her; and immediately it all came flooding back to her, as if a curtain had suddenly gone up on the whole of her past life.

She felt a horrible anguish in her heart and wanted to run away again. She threw back the sheets, jumped out of bed, and fell to the floor, her legs unable to support her.

Julien rushed towards her; and she began to scream that he wasn't to touch her. She twisted and rolled about on the floor. The door opened. Aunt Lison came running in with the widow Dentu, followed by the Baron, and then finally Mama, who arrived panting and distraught.

They helped her back into bed; and at once she closed her eyes again, slyly, so as not to have to speak, so that she could reflect in peace.

Her mother and her aunt were tending her, and enquiring anxiously:

'Can you hear us, Jeanne? My dear little Jeanne?'

She pretended not to hear and made no reply; and she saw quite distinctly that the day was drawing to a close. Night came. The nurse took up position by her bed and made her drink a little from time to time.

She drank without a word, but she could no longer sleep; she was painfully trying to piece things together again, trying to remember, as though there were holes in her memory, great blank empty spaces where events had left no mark.

Little by little, with sustained effort, she recalled all the facts.

And then she reflected upon them with unwavering persistence.

Mama, Aunt Lison, and the Baron were there, so she had been very ill. But Julien? What had he told them? Did her parents know? And Rosalie? Where was she? And then, what should she do? What should she do? An idea struck her—she would go back to Rouen, with Papa and Mama, just like before. She would be a widow; that was all.

Then she waited, listening to what was being said around her, understanding perfectly but without letting on, relishing the return of her reason, at once patient and cunning.

Finally, that evening, she found herself alone with the Baroness, and she called to her softly:

'Mama!'

She was astonished at the sound of her own voice: it seemed quite changed. The Baroness clasped her by the hands:

'Jeanne, my dearest, my darling Jeanne! Do you recognize me, my dear?'

'Yes, Mama, but please don't cry. We have a lot to talk about. Did Julien say why I ran off into the snow?'

'Yes, my sweet, you had a very high fever, and you were in great danger.'

'No, that's not it, mother. The fever came afterwards. But did he tell you how I caught the fever, and why I ran off?'

'No, my dear.'

'It was because I found Rosalie in bed with him.'

The Baroness thought that she was still delirious, and stroked her:

'Sleep now, my darling. Calm yourself. Try and get some sleep.'

But stubbornly Jeanne insisted:

'I am completely lucid now, Mama. This isn't more of the nonsense I must have been talking the last few days. I felt unwell one night, so I went to find Julien. Rosalie was in bed with him. I was so upset I just lost my head, and I ran off into the snow to go and throw myself over the cliff.'

But the Baroness kept saying:

'Yes, my darling, you have been very ill, very ill.'

'No, mother, I really did, I found Rosalie in Julien's bed, and I want to leave him. I want you to take me back to Rouen, like before.'

The Baroness, whom the doctor had advised to humour Jeanne, replied:

'Yes, dear.'

But Jeanne was losing patience:

'I can see you don't believe me. Go and fetch Papa. At least I'll make him understand.'

So Mama struggled to her feet, took hold of her two sticks, and shuffled out of the room, returning some minutes later on the Baron's arm.

They sat down by the bed, and Jeanne began at once. She told them everything, precisely, in a low, faltering voice: about Julien's strange character, his rough ways, his avarice, and lastly about his infidelity.

By the time she had finished, the Baron could see that she was not raving, but he did not know what to think, or say, or do.

He took her hand, tenderly, like in the old days when he used to tell her stories to send her to sleep:

'Listen, my darling we must go carefully. We mustn't rush things. You must try and put up with your husband until we've decided what to do... Will you promise me that?'

'Very well,' she murmured, 'but I shan't stay here any longer once I'm better.'

Then she added in a whisper:

'Where is Rosalie now?'

The Baron answered:

'You won't see her again.'

But she insisted:

'Where is she? I want to know.'

Then he admitted that she was still with them; but he assured her that she would soon be packing her bags.

On leaving the sick girl's room, the Baron, beside himself with anger and wounded in his father's love, went to find Julien.

'Sir,' he said sharply, 'I have come to ask for an explanation for your conduct towards my daughter. You have been unfaithful to her with your maid. That is doubly shameful.'

But Julien played the innocent, and denied it hotly, on oath, as God was his witness. In any case, what proof had they? Was Jeanne not off her head? Hadn't she just suffered brain fever? Hadn't she run off into the snow one night, in a moment of delirium, at the start of her illness? And it had been precisely when she was in the middle of one of those fever fits and running round the house almost stark naked, that she claimed to have seen the maid in her husband's bed!

He lost his temper, and talked of instituting proceedings; he took vehement exception. The Baron, nonplussed, apologized, and asked his pardon, offering to shake hands on the matter, but Julien refused.

When Jeanne heard of her husband's response, she was not angry but replied:

'He's lying, Papa, but we'll prove him guilty in the end.'

And for two days she said nothing more, quietly turning the matter over in her mind.

Then, on the third morning, she demanded to see Rosalie. The Baron refused to summon the maid, saying that she had left. Jeanne would not give in, and kept insisting:

'Well, have someone go and fetch her then.'

She was already in a state of irritation when the doctor walked in. They told him everything so that he might be the judge. But suddenly Jeanne burst into tears, agitated beyond measure, and almost shouted:

'I want to see Rosalie! I want to see her!'

Then the doctor took her hand and said softly:

'Calm yourself, Madame, any undue excitement could have serious consequences. You see, you are pregnant.'

She was shocked, dumbstruck, and it seemed to her at once that she could feel something stirring within her. Then she fell silent, not even listening to what was said to her, withdrawing deep into her own thoughts. She could not sleep that night, kept awake by the novel and singular idea that a child was alive, there, in her womb; she felt sadness, for she was pained by the thought that it should be Julien's son; and she felt anxious too, worrying that he might resemble his father. The next morning she asked to see the Baron:

'Papa, my mind is made up. I want to know everything, especially now. Do you understand me, I want the whole story. And you know you're not to upset me in my present condition. So listen. Go and fetch the priest. I need him here to make sure that Rosalie tells the truth. Then, as soon as he's come, have her sent up to me, and you and Mama must stay here in the room. And above all, see that Julien suspects nothing.'

An hour later the priest walked in, fatter than ever and as breathless as Mama. He sat down next to her in an armchair, his stomach tipping forward between his splayed legs; and, mopping his brow as usual with a check handkerchief, he began with a jocular remark:

'Well, your ladyship, we're neither of us getting any thinner, are we? A fine pair we make!'

Then, turning towards the sickbed:

'And what's this I hear, my young lady? Another christening on the way, eh? Ha, ha, and not just a boat this time either!'

And then he added in a solemn voice:

'One more to fight for king and country.'

Then, after a moment's reflexion:

'Unless it's to be a fine mother... like you, my lady', he said, bowing in her direction.

But at that moment the far door opened. Rosalie, tearful and distraught, clung to the door frame, refusing to enter, while the

Baron urged her forward. Losing patience, he grabbed hold of her and pushed her into the room. Then she put her hands over her face and stood there, sobbing.

As soon as Jeanne saw her, she sat up in bed at once, looking whiter than her own sheets; and the thin nightshirt clinging to her chest rose and fell with the wild pounding of her heart. She was choking for air, unable to speak and barely able to breathe. Finally, in a voice breaking with emotion, she said:

'I don't need... to ask you... Just seeing you... standing there... your shame before me.'

After pausing to catch her breath, she went on:

'But I want to know everything, everything... every last detail. I've asked the priest to come so that it will be like confession. Do you understand?'

Standing quite still, Rosalie was almost shrieking between her clenched hands.

The Baron, who was becoming increasingly angry, grabbed hold of her arms and pulled them apart, and then forced her down onto her knees by the bed:

'Come, speak up, you must answer.'

She remained kneeling on the floor, in the posture traditionally attributed to Mary Magdalene, her bonnet at an angle, her apron on the floor, and her face once more covered with her hands that had been set free again.

Then the priest said to her:

'Now, my child, listen carefully to what is said to you and give your answer. We wish you no harm, but we must know what happened.'

Leaning out over the side of her bed, Jeanne watched her.

'It's perfectly true, isn't it,' she said, 'that you were in Julien's bed when I walked in on you both?'

Rosalie groaned through her hands:

'Yes, Madame.'

Then at once the Baroness began to cry too, with a great choking sound, and her convulsive sobs joined with those of Rosalie.

Looking straight at the maid, Jeanne asked:

'How long had it been going on?'

Rosalie stammered:

'Since 'e came.'

Jeanne did not understand. 'Since he came... So... since... since the spring?'

'Yes, Madame.'

'Since the moment he entered this house?'

'Yes, Madame.'

And Jeanne, as though desperate to unburden herself of her questions, interrogated her rapidly:

'But how did it happen? How did he ask you? How did he get round you? What did he say? When, and how, did you agree? How could you possibly have given yourself to him?'

And this time Rosalie parted her hands, seized with a no less desperate desire to speak, a burning need to reply:

'I dunno. It was the day 'e first come to dinner 'ere, 'e came to me room. 'e'd 'idden in the attic, like. I didn't dare scream, or there'd 've been trouble. 'e got into bed wi' me, I didn't know wot I was doing, and 'e did, like, w'at 'e wanted wi' me. I didn't say nothing coz, well, I thought 'e were nice.'

Then Jeanne, with a shriek:

'But... your... your child... it's his?'

Rosalie sobbed:

'Yes, Madame.'

Then they both fell silent.

All that could be heard was the sound of Rosalie and the Baroness weeping.

Jeanne, quite overcome, could feel her own eyes fill; and the tears coursed silently down her cheeks.

Her maid's child had the same father as her own! Her anger had abated now, and all she could feel within her was the gradual onset of a deep, dismal, and boundless despair.

At length she went on, but in a different voice, the choked voice of a woman crying:

'When we came back from... overseas... from our honeymoon... when did he start again?'

The maid, who was now completely slumped on the floor, stammered:

'The first night... 'e came the first night.'

Each word twisted the knife in Jeanne's heart. So, the first night, the night they returned to Les Peuples, he had left her for this girl. That's why he let her sleep alone!

She had heard enough now, she didn't want to listen to any more.

'Get out,' she shouted, 'get out.' And when Rosalie continued to lie there, in a state of collapse, Jeanne called on her father:

'Take her out, take her away!'

But the priest, who had said nothing until now, judged that the moment had come for a little sermon.

'What you have done, my girl, is very wrong, very wrong; and the good Lord will not find it easy to forgive you. Think of the hellfire that awaits you if you do not behave yourself from this day forth. Now that you have a child of your own, you must mend your ways. Her Ladyship will help you, I am sure, and we shall soon find you a husband...'

He would have gone on at length, but the Baron, having once more grabbed Rosalie by the shoulders, now hauled her to her feet, dragged her as far as the door, and then threw her out into the corridor as if she were a parcel.

When he returned, looking even paler than his daughter, the priest continued:

'Well, there you are. They're all the same in the country. It's terrible, but there's nothing you can do about it, and one just has to show some tolerance for natural weakness. They never get married until they're pregnant, Madame.'

And he added with a smile:

'It's almost a local custom.'

Then he added indignantly:

'Even the children are at it. Last year, for example, in the cemetery, didn't I catch a boy and a girl out of the confirmation class! I told their parents, and do you know what they said to me? "But what can we do, Father? It's not us wot taught 'em them dirty things, we can't stop 'em."—So there you are, Monsieur, your maid is just like all the others...'

But the Baron, who was shaking with anger, broke in:

'Her? What do I care about her? It's Julien I find outrageous. It's appalling what he's done, and I shall take my daughter away.'

And he paced up and down, working himself into a lather:

'It's appalling the way he's betrayed my daughter, absolutely appalling. He's a scoundrel, that man, a miserable, good-for-nothing blackguard, and I'll tell him so, I'll slap his face, I'll beat him to death with my stick!'

But the priest, slowly taking a pinch of snuff as he remained seated beside the weeping Baroness, was endeavouring to fulfil his mission of bringing peace and light to all, and said:

'Come now, Monsieur, if we're honest about it, he's only done what everybody does. How many husbands do you know who have remained faithful to their wives?'

And, with good-natured malice, he added:

'What about you, for example? I bet even you have had your piece of fun. Come now, hand on heart, it's true, isn't it?'

Completely taken aback, the Baron had stopped dead in front of the priest.

'Oh yes, you're just like all the others. Who knows, maybe you even helped yourself to a pretty maid like her. I tell you, everybody does the same. Your wife hasn't been any the less happy on that account, has she? You've loved her just as much, haven't you?'

The Baron stood stock-still, completely at a loss.

It was true, by God, that he had done exactly the same, and lots of times, what's more, whenever he'd had the opportunity; and he hadn't even drawn the line at doing it under the conjugal roof. And when they were pretty, he hadn't let the fact that they were his wife's maids stop him either! Did that make him a good-for-nothing wretch? Why did he take such a stern view of Julien's conduct when it had never even occurred to him that his own was in any way to blame?

And the Baroness, still quite breathless from her sobbing, had the shadow of a smile on her lips as she remembered her husband's philandering, for she was the sentimental type, quick to soften and to look on things with a kindly eye, the kind of person for whom amorous adventures are simply part of life.

Jeanne lay prostrated and motionless on the bed, staring into the distance and reflecting bitterly. Something Rosalie had said kept coming back, wounding her in her soul, drilling its way into her heart: 'I didn't say nothing coz well, I thought 'e were nice.'

She, too, had thought he was nice; and it was solely for that reason that she had given herself, bound herself for life, renounced all other aspirations, all the plans she had had, all those things waiting to be discovered. She had fallen into this marriage, into this gaping pit, only to climb back to the surface again and find herself surrounded by this wretchedness and misery and despair, and all because, like Rosalie, she had thought he was nice!

The door burst open. Julien appeared with a furious look on his face. He had seen Rosalie wailing on the staircase and had come to discover what was going on, realizing that something was afoot and that no doubt the maid had talked. The sight of the priest rooted him to the spot.

In a trembling but even voice, he asked:

'What's up? What's happening?'

The Baron, who had felt so violent a moment or two earlier, did not dare say anything, fearing that his son-in-law might use the priest's own argument and cite him as an example. Mama was weeping even more profusely; but Jeanne had propped herself up on her fists and was staring, panting, at this man who had brought her so much cruel suffering. She stammered:

'What's happening is that we know everything now, that we know all about your despicable behaviour ever since... ever since the very first day you set foot in this house. What's happening is that the maid's child is yours... yours... as mine is... they'll be brothers...' A wave of unbearable pain swept over her at this thought, and she fell back on the bed, weeping uncontrollably.

He stood there open-mouthed, not knowing what to say or do. The priest intervened once again:

'Come, come, my young lady, we mustn't get ourselves into such a state. You must be reasonable.'

He stood up, approached the bed, and placed his warm hand on the forehead of the despairing woman. This simple contact soothed her strangely; she relaxed at once, as if this strong, coarse hand that was used to making gestures of absolution and offering comforting caresses had brought her a mysterious peace in its touch.

Still standing there, the kindly soul continued:

'Madame, one must always forgive. You have suffered a great misfortune, but God, in his mercy, has compensated you for it, since you are to bear a child. This child will be your consolation. And it is in this child's name that I beg you, that I call on you, to forgive Monsieur Julien the error of his ways. It will provide a new bond between you, an earnest of his faithfulness in the future. Can you remain separated in your heart from him whose flesh you bear within your body?'

She offered no reply, crushed, aching, exhausted now, with no strength left either for anger or resentment. Her nerves seemed to have gone slack, to have been gently severed, as though she were scarcely any longer alive.

The Baroness, who found it quite impossible to understand how people could harbour grudges, and who was in any case temperamentally incapable of prolonged effort, murmured:

'Come now, Jeanne.'

So the priest took the young man's hand and, drawing him towards the bed, placed it in that of his wife. He tapped the two hands gently as though to unite them once and for all; and then, abandoning the professional tones of a sermonizer, he said contentedly:

'There, that's done. Believe me, it's better this way.'

Then the two hands which had briefly come together parted at once. Julien, not daring to kiss Jeanne, kissed his mother-in-law on the forehead, turned round, and took the Baron's arm. The latter offered no resistance, on the whole glad that the matter had been settled in this way; and off they went to smoke a cigar.

Presently the exhausted patient dozed off to sleep as the priest and Mama talked quietly together.

The Abbé would say something, explaining and expanding on his suggestions; and each time the Baroness would nod in agreement. At length he said, by way of conclusion:

'So, that's agreed then. You shall let the girl have the farm at Barville, and I shall be responsible for finding her a husband, some decent, sensible lad. Oh, with a property worth twenty thousand francs, there'll be plenty of takers all right. We'll be spoilt for choice.'

And the Baroness was smiling happily now, as two tears hovered on her cheeks, the moist traces of their descent already dried.

'Yes, that's agreed,' she said, wishing to make sure of the detail. 'Barville is worth at least twenty thousand francs. But we'll register it in the child's name, and the parents can have the benefit of the income during their lifetime.'

And the priest rose to his feet and shook hands with Mama:

'Don't get up, my lady, don't get up. I know what one step costs!'

As he was leaving the room, he encountered Aunt Lison coming to visit the patient. She did not notice anything; no one told her anything; and she never knew anything, as usual.

VIII

Rosalie had left the house, and Jeanne was approaching the term of her difficult pregnancy. She felt no pleasure in her heart at the prospect of becoming a mother, for she had suffered too much unhappiness. She awaited the arrival of her child without curiosity, burdened rather by apprehension and the thought of nameless misfortunes yet to come.

Spring had arrived very gradually. The bare trees shook gently in a breeze that was still cool, but in the wet grass along the ditches, where autumn leaves lay rotting, the yellow primroses were beginning to show themselves. The entire plain, the farm-yards and the waterlogged fields, gave off a damp smell, like the aroma of something fermenting. And a host of tiny green shoots were emerging from the brown soil and gleaming brightly in the sunshine.

A large woman, as stout as a castle keep, had taken Rosalie's place and supported the Baroness on her monotonous walks up and down the avenue, where the trail left by her dragging foot remained constantly muddy and wet.

Papa gave his arm to Jeanne, who had grown heavy herself now and was still not well; and Aunt Lison, anxiously preoccupied by the coming event, took her hand on the other side, deeply per-turbed by this mysterious process that she herself would never experience.

They walked along together like this for hours on end, scarcely exchanging a word, while Julien went out riding all over the coun-tryside, having suddenly acquired a taste for this pursuit.

Nothing further happened to interrupt their drab routine. The Baron, his wife, and the Vicomte paid a visit to the Fourvilles, with whom Julien already seemed very well acquainted, though no one quite knew how. Another formal visit was exchanged with the Brisevilles, still buried away in their sleepy manor.

One afternoon, about four o'clock, as two people on horseback, a man and a woman, came trotting into the courtyard at the front of the house, Julien entered Jeanne's bedroom in a great state of excitement.

'Quick, quick, you must go down. It's the Fourvilles. It's only a casual visit, nothing more, on account of your condition. Tell them I've gone out but that I'll be back presently. I'm just going to smarten up.'

Surprised, Jeanne went downstairs. A pale, pretty young woman, with an unhappy face, blazing eyes, and lustreless fair hair that looked as if not a single ray of sunlight had ever touched it, calmly introduced her giant of a husband, a sort of bogeyman with a huge, red moustache. Then she continued:

'We have had the opportunity of meeting Monsieur de Lamare on several occasions. He has told us how unwell you are, and we did not wish to wait a moment longer before paying you a simple neighbourly visit, without any fuss or formality. Indeed, as you see, we have come on horseback. The other day, moreover, I had the pleasure of receiving a visit from Madame, your mother, and the Baron.'

She spoke with complete assurance, in a tone at once intimate and well bred. Jeanne was captivated and adored her at once. 'Here is a friend,' she thought to herself.

The Comte de Fourville, on the other hand, seemed like a bear who had strayed into a drawing-room. When he sat down, he placed his hat on the chair next to him, hesitated for a moment as he wondered what to do with his hands, placed them on his knees and then on the arms of the chair, and eventually clasped them together as if he were about to pray.

Suddenly Julien walked in. Jeanne was astonished and barely recognized him. He had shaved. He was handsome, elegant, attractive, just as he had been at the time of their engagement. He shook the hairy paw of the Comte, who seemed to have woken up at his arrival, and kissed the hand of the Comtesse, whose ivory cheeks turned slightly pink while her eyelids fluttered briefly.

And he talked. He was his old, charming self. His large eyes, filled once again with tender solicitude, were like mirrors for love's reflection; and his hair, dull and coarse but a moment ago, had been restored by brush and scented oil to its former condition as a mass of soft, gleaming waves.

As the Fourvilles were leaving, the Comtesse turned to him and said:

'I wonder, my dear Vicomte, whether you would care to go riding next Thursday?'

Then, as he was bowing to her and softly answering: 'But gladly, Madame,' she held Jeanne's hand and said in a clear, affectionate tone, smiling warmly:

'Ah, when you're well again, the three of us will be able to go galloping all over the countryside. It will be marvellous. Would you like that?'

With one easy sweep of her arm she gathered the train of her riding-habit, and the next moment she had sprung into the saddle with the lightness of a bird. Her husband, meanwhile, awkwardly bowed farewell and bestrode his large Norman mount, upon which he sat bolt upright like a centaur.

When they had disappeared round the bend by the gate, Julien, who seemed spellbound, burst out:

'What thoroughly charming people! They will certainly be worth knowing.'

Jeanne, happy also but not quite sure why, replied:

'The little Comtesse is delightful, I think I shall like her. But the husband looks rather a brute. Where did you meet them?'

He was rubbing his hands together cheerfully:

'I met them by chance at the Brisevilles'. The husband does seem a bit of a rough sort. He's mad about shooting, but he's a nobleman through and through, no question of that.'

And dinner that evening was almost merry, as if some secret source of happiness had entered the house.

After that nothing out of the ordinary occurred until the end of July.

One Tuesday evening, as they were sitting under the plane-tree by a wooden table on which stood two little glasses and a small carafe of brandy, Jeanne suddenly let out a sort of scream and, turning very pale, clutched both hands to her sides. A sudden, sharp pain had shot through her, and then vanished at once.

But ten minutes later she felt another pain, longer this time but less acute. She had great difficulty in returning indoors, having to be almost carried by her father and her husband. The short distance from the plane-tree to her bedroom seemed never-ending; she groaned involuntarily and kept asking to sit down, to stop for a moment, overcome by an unbearable sensation of heaviness in her stomach.

She had not reached her term, for the baby was not due until September; but since they were worried that something might have happened, a carriage was harnessed, and Père Simon left at the gallop to fetch the doctor.

He arrived about midnight, and immediately he recognized the symptoms of premature labour.

Once Jeanne was lying in bed the pains had eased a little, but she was seized with an appalling sense of dread, of desperation, like a faltering of her whole being, as though she had felt a mortal premonition, the mysterious touch of death. It was one of those moments when it passes so close that its breath chills our heart.

The bedroom was full of people. Mama sat slumped in a chair, sobbing. His hands shaking, the Baron rushed about, fetching things, asking the doctor's opinion, in a state of utter confusion. Julien was pacing up and down, with a look of concern on his face but otherwise quite calm; and the widow Dentu stood at the foot of the bed, wearing an expression suitable to the occasion, the air of a woman of experience for whom life holds no surprises. Midwife, tender of the sick, and guardian of the dead, she was used to receiving the new arrivals, registering their first cry, giving their newborn flesh its first wash and wrapping it in its first clothing, and then listening with the same imperturbable calm to the last words, the last gasp, the last little tremor of the departing, cleaning them too for the last time, sponging their worn-out bodies with vinegar and wrapping them in their last sheet. Thus had she developed an unshakeable indifference to every contingent feature of birth and death.

Ludivine the cook and Aunt Lison remained discreetly out of sight beside the door into the entrance-hall.

From time to time the patient would utter a faint groan of distress.

For two hours it looked as though they would have to wait a long while; but towards daybreak the pains suddenly came on again, strongly, and soon they were excruciating.

And as the involuntary cries of pain forced their way through her clenched teeth, Jeanne kept thinking of Rosalie, who had not suffered, who had scarcely even let out a moan, and whose child, the bastard child, had emerged without difficulty and without torment.

In her wretched, troubled soul she kept making comparisons between herself and Rosalie; and she cursed God, whom she had hitherto considered just. She railed against the culpable favouritism of destiny, and the criminal lies of those who preach goodness and the straight path of virtue.

Sometimes the agony became so acute that her mind went blank. Such remaining strength, and life, and consciousness as she possessed served only to make her feel the pain.

During the intervals of peace she could not stop looking at Julien; and a further agony, an agony of the soul, gripped her as she remembered the day when her maid had collapsed at the foot of this selfsame bed, with her child between her legs, the brother of the little creature that was now so cruelly tearing her own entrails apart. She recalled with absolute clarity her husband's every gesture, every look, every word, as he had caught sight of the girl stretched on the floor; and now she could read his thoughts as if they had been written in his very movements, the same boredom, the same indifference towards her as towards the maid, the same lack of concern felt by the selfish male, for whom fatherhood is simply a nuisance.

But a fierce contraction seized hold of her, a spasm of such severity that she thought:

'I'm going to die. I *am* dying!'

Then her inner being rose up in angry revolt, filled with a need to curse and furious with hatred for this man who had ruined her life and for this unknown child that was killing her.

She tensed herself in one supreme effort to expel the burden from her. Suddenly it seemed as though her belly all at once were emptying itself; and the pain began to ease.

The nurse and the doctor were leaning over her, handling her. They removed something; and soon she was startled to hear that muffled sound she had heard once before; and then the little cry of distress, the faint mewling of the newborn child, entered into her soul, her heart, her whole, wretched, exhausted body; and instinctively she wanted to reach out and hold it.

She felt a surge of joy flood through her, bearing her up towards the new happiness which had just come forth. In a single instant she found herself delivered, assuaged, happy, happy in a way she had never known before. Her heart and her flesh were coming back to life. She could feel it now: she was a mother!

And she wanted to see her child! He had no hair or nails, having arrived too soon; but when she saw the little mite move, when she saw him open his mouth and utter his little cries, when she touched this living, grimacing, wrinkled little object born before its time, she was overwhelmed with irresistible, rapturous delight, and she realized that she had been saved, secured against all despair, that she now held in her arms something she could love to the ultimate exclusion of all else.

From that moment on she had but one thought: her child. She immediately became the fanatical mother, and was all the more besotted for having been deceived in her passion and disappointed in her hopes. She had to have the cradle constantly by her bed; and then, when she could get up, she remained sitting by the window for days on end, rocking the little bed beside her.

She was jealous of the wet-nurse; and when the thirsty little creature stretched out his arms towards her plump breast with its bluish veins and took the button of brown, wrinkled flesh between its greedy lips, she would stare, pale and trembling, at the strong, placid peasant woman and want to snatch her son away from her, to beat and scratch this breast from which he was drinking so eagerly.

Then, for his adornment, she insisted on personally embroidering the finest linen with intricately elegant patterns. He was swathed in clouds of lace, and magnificent bonnets were set upon his head. It was all she talked about, interrupting conversations to show off a napkin or a bib or the especially fine work on some ribbon; and, quite oblivious to anything anyone else might be saying, she would go into ecstasies as she endlessly fingered pieces of cloth and held them aloft to see them better. Whereupon she would suddenly enquire:

'Do you think this will suit him?'

The Baron and Mama smiled at this frenzy of maternal affection; but Julien, aware of his routine being disrupted and his own overriding importance being diminished by the advent of this wailing and omnipotent tyrant, and also unconsciously jealous of the little male specimen that was usurping his position in the household, kept remarking in angry frustration:

'She's such a bore, it's always her and her little baby.'

Soon she was so obsessed by her devotion that she spent entire nights sitting next to the cradle watching the child sleep. Since she was wearing herself out with these avid and unnatural vigils, no longer taking any rest herself and growing gradually weaker and thinner and beginning to cough, the doctor gave orders that she should be separated from her son.

She became angry, and wept, and pleaded; but her entreaties fell on deaf ears. Each evening he was placed in the care of his nurse; and each night his mother would get up and go in her bare feet to press her ear to the keyhole to make sure that he was sleeping peacefully, that he had not woken up, that there was nothing he needed.

On one occasion Julien caught her doing this, having come home late after dining at the Fourvilles'; and thenceforward she was locked in her bedroom to oblige her to go to bed.

The christening took place towards the end of August. The Baron was godfather, and Aunt Lison godmother. The child was given the names Pierre-Simon-Paul, but Paul for short.

Early in September Aunt Lison quietly took her leave; and her absence went as unnoticed as formerly her presence had been.

One evening after dinner, the priest appeared. He looked awkward, as though he were the bearer of mysterious tidings, and after a series of inconsequential remarks he requested the Baroness and her husband to grant him a few moments in private.

The three of them departed and slowly made their way down to the far end of the main avenue, deep in animated conversation, while Julien, left alone with Jeanne, felt at once surprised, disconcerted, and irritated by this secrecy.

He insisted on accompanying the priest when the latter took his leave, and they disappeared together in the direction of the church, where the angelus was being rung.

The air was cool, almost chilly, and the others soon returned indoors to the drawing-room. They were beginning to doze off when suddenly Julien returned, red in the face and looking furious.

Standing in the doorway, and not caring that Jeanne was present, he screamed at his parents-in-law:

'Have you gone mad, for God's sake, throwing away twenty thousand francs on that girl!'

Everyone was so surprised that nobody said anything. He continued, bellowing with rage:

'How can anyone be so stupid? Do you want to leave us without a penny to our name?'

Then the Baron recovered himself and tried to interrupt:

'Be silent! Remember that your wife is present.'

But Julien was beside himself with anger and frustration:

'I'm damned if I care. Anyway, she can see perfectly well what's going on. This is money stolen from her.'

Shocked, Jeanne looked at him blankly and mumbled:

'What is this all about?'

Then Julien turned to her, calling her to witness as though she were some business partner being similarly denied some anticipated profit. He quickly told her about the plan to marry Rosalie, and about the gift of the land at Barville, which was worth at least twenty thousand francs.

'But your parents are mad, my dear,' he repeated, 'stark, raving mad! Twenty thousand francs! They're quite simply off their heads! Twenty thousand francs on a bastard!'

Jeanne listened, unmoved, without anger, astonished at her

own calm, and now indifferent to anything that did not concern her own child.

The Baron was choking with rage, and could think of no reply. Eventually he let fly, stamping his foot and shouting:

'You mind your tongue! Really, this is quite outrageous. Whose fault is it that we've had to provide a dowry for the maid now that she's a mother? And whose child is it? Yet now you say you'd rather have abandoned it.'

Astonished by the violence of the Baron's reaction, Julien stared at him. Then he resumed in a more measured tone:

'But fifteen hundred francs would have been quite enough. These girls all have children before they get married. And whose child it is doesn't really matter one way or the other. Whereas by giving away one of your farms worth twenty thousand francs, not only are you acting against our financial interests, you're also telling the whole world what happened. You might at least have spared a thought for *our* name, for *our* position.'

And he spoke sternly, as a man who knows the law and is confident of the strength of his own case. Confounded by this unexpected argument, the Baron stood there gaping. So Julien, sensing his advantage, proceeded to his summing-up:

'Fortunately nothing has been settled yet. I know the lad who's to marry her. He's a decent fellow, he'll not cause any trouble over this. I'll see to matters.'

And with that he left the room, no doubt afraid of prolonging the discussion and glad that everyone had remained silent, which he took to be a sign of their consent.

As soon as he had gone, the Baron, thoroughly nonplussed and shaking all over, exclaimed:

'Really, this is too much, too much.'

But as Jeanne looked up at her father's flustered expression, she suddenly burst out laughing, with that bright, cheerful laugh she used to have whenever she noticed something amusing.

'But Papa, Papa,' she said, 'did you hear how he said it: "twenty thousand francs!"?'

And Mama, as much given to mirth as she was to weeping, now remembered the furious expression on her son-in-law's face, his indignant outbursts, and his vehement refusal to allow a girl he had seduced to be offered money that was not even his; and, in her happiness also at finding Jeanne in such good humour, she began to shake with that wheezy laugh of hers, which brought tears to her eyes. The mirth proved infectious and set the Baron off in his turn; with the result that, as in happier days, they all three laughed and laughed until they hurt.

When they had recovered themselves a little, Jeanne said with surprise:

'It's odd, it doesn't affect me any more. He seems just like a stranger to me now. I cannot believe I am actually his wife. As you see, I can laugh at his... at his... want of delicacy.'

And without knowing quite why, they all kissed each other, still smiling fondly.

But two days later, after lunch, when Julien had just gone out riding, a tall lad somewhere between twenty-two and twenty-five and wearing a brand-new blue smock, with sharp creases and puffed sleeves buttoned at the wrist, sneaked in through the front gate, as if he had been lying in wait there since morning; he stole along the edge of the ditch next to the Couillards' farm, came round the corner of the house, and warily approached the Baron and the two women, who were still sitting under the plane-tree.

He had removed his cap on seeing them, and he now came forward, bowing and looking rather embarrassed.

As soon as he was close enough to be heard, he mumbled:

'Your 'umble servant, milord, ma'am, and company.'

Then, as no one spoke, he announced:

'Me name's Désiré Lecoq.'

Since this name meant nothing, the Baron asked him:

'What do you want?'

Whereupon the lad became completely unnerved at the prospect of having to explain himself. Continually looking down and up again, from the cap in his hands to the top of the chateau roof, he stammered:

'It's Father, like. 'e 'ad a word wi' me, 'e did, about this 'ere business...', and then he paused for fear of giving too much away and compromising his interests.

The Baron, at a loss, replied:

'What business? I've no idea what you're talking about.'

Making up his mind, the fellow then lowered his voice and said:

'This 'ere business wi' your maid, Rosalie.'

Having realized what he meant, Jeanne stood up and left, carrying her baby in her arms.

'Come and sit down,' said the Baron, indicating the chair which his daughter had just vacated.

The peasant sat down at once, muttering:

'Much obliged.'

Then he waited as though he had nothing more to say. Finally, after a rather long silence, he steeled himself, looked up at the blue sky, and said:

'Very fine weather, eh, for the time of year. Good for the land, like, for the seeds, as 'ave already been planted.'

And he fell silent again.

The Baron was growing impatient. He broached the matter abruptly, in a curt tone:

'So you're the one who's going to marry Rosalie?'

The fellow became nervous at once, as this went against the grain of his usual Norman caution. Having been put on his guard, he replied with more spirit:

'It all depends. Mebbe yes, mebbe no. It all depends.'

But the Baron was becoming irritated by these evasions:

'For God's sake, answer me straight. Is that why you've come or isn't it? Will you have her or won't you?'

Bewildered, the young lad now kept his eyes firmly on his feet:

'If it's as Father says, I'll 'ave 'er, but if it's as Monsieur Julien says, I won't.'

'And what did Monsieur Julien say?'

'Monsieur Julien says as how I'd get fifteen 'undred francs; Father says as how I'd get twenty thousand. I'll 'ave her for twenty thousand, but not for fifteen 'undred, I won't.'

At this the Baroness, ensconced in her chair and observing the worried expression on the face of this yokel, began to laugh in little short bursts. The peasant watched her out of the corner of his eye, not at all pleased and wondering what was so funny. He waited.

The Baron, embarrassed by this haggling, cut it short:

'I told the priest that you would have the farm at Barville, during your lifetime, after which it would pass to the child. It's worth twenty thousand francs. I am a man of my word. Is it a deal, yes or no?'

The young fellow smiled with an air of humble satisfaction, and his tongue was suddenly loosened:

'Oh, well, if that's 'ow it lies, I won't say no! That's all as was 'olding me back. When Father talked to me, I wanted to say yes straightaway like, honest I did, and then I thought, well, I'd be glad to 'elp his lordship out coz 'e'll see me right for it. It's true, ain't it? When people 'elp each other out, there always come a time, later on, when they see each other right. But Mister Julien, 'e came to see me, and then it were only fifteen 'undred. I said to myself: "Better find out, I 'ad," and 'ere I am. Not as I 'ad any doubt, mind, but I thought I'd better find out. 'onest dealings makes 'onest friends. Ain't that so, y'r lordship?'

This could not go on.

'When do you wish the marriage to take place?' the Baron enquired.

Then the lad at once became his timid self again, thoroughly ill at ease. At length he said hesitantly:

'But, well, shouldn't we like sign a bit o' paper or som'ing first?'

This time the Baron lost his temper:

'But damn it, you'll have the marriage contract. That's the best bit of paper you could possibly sign.'

The farmhand insisted:

'But till then, like, couldn't we just sign a bit o' paper? Never did anyone any 'arm, you know.'

The Baron stood up to bring matters to a close.

'Answer me yes or no. Now, this minute. If you've changed your mind, say so. I have someone else who's interested.'

Whereupon the fear of a rival panicked the wily Norman. He made up his mind and held out his hand as though he had just bought a cow:

'Shake on it, your lordship, it's a deal. And 'e be the bugger that breaks it.'

The Baron shook on it, and then shouted:

'Ludivine!'

The cook's head appeared at the window.

'Bring us a bottle of wine!'

They drank to the conclusion of the deal.—And the lad departed with a lighter step.

Julien was told nothing of this visit. The contract was drawn up in great secrecy, and then, after the banns had been published, the wedding took place one Monday morning.

A neighbour's wife carried the baby to church, behind the bridal couple, like an earnest of future good fortune. And nobody in the district thought anything of it; they simply envied Désiré Lecoq. He'd been born under a lucky star, they would say as they smiled knowingly but without the slightest trace of disapproval.

Julien made a terrible scene, which caused his parents-in-law to cut short their stay at Les Peuples. Jeanne watched them leave without undue sadness, for Paul had now become an inexhaustible source of happiness to her.

IX

Now that Jeanne was fully recovered after her confinement, it was decided to return the Fourvilles' visit and to call also on the Marquis de Coutelier.

Julien had recently bought a new carriage at auction, a phaeton requiring only one horse,* so that they could go out twice a month.

One clear December day it was harnessed, and after a two-hour journey across the Norman plains they began to descend between the wooded slopes of a small valley, at the bottom of which lay fields ploughed and sown for crops.

This cultivated land was soon replaced by meadows, and the meadows in turn gave way to a marsh full of tall reeds, now dry at this season, whose long leaves looked like yellow ribbons and rustled in the breeze.

All at once, after a sudden bend in the valley, the chateau of La Vrillette came into view. It had been built against the tree-covered slope on one side, while on the other the whole length of its wall rose from a large lake, which extended across to a wood of tall firs that stretched up the opposite side of the valley.

They had to pass over an ancient drawbridge and through a huge Louis XIII gateway before reaching the main courtyard, in front of an elegant manor-house of the same period with brick architraves and flanked by small round towers roofed in slate.

Julien gave Jeanne a detailed account of the different parts of the building, as though he were a regular visitor and had an intimate knowledge of the place. He did the honours of the house, enthusing over its beauty:

'But just look at that gateway! Isn't it all so grand, eh? The whole of the other elevation rises out of the lake, with a magnificent flight of steps leading down to the water's edge; and four boats are kept moored at the bottom, two for the Comte and two for the Comtesse. Over there to the right, where you can see the screen of poplars, that's where the lake ends and where the river begins and flows all the way down to Fécamp. The place is full of wildfowl. The Comte loves going shooting here. Ah, this is what you call a noble residence.'

The front door had opened, and the pale Comtesse emerged to extend a smiling welcome to her guests; she wore a dress with a train, which made her seem like a chatelaine from a bygone age. She looked exactly like the Lady of the Lake,* born to live in this fairy-tale castle.

The drawing-room had eight windows, four of which gave onto the lake and the dark fir-wood covering the hillside directly opposite.

The greenery with its dark tones made the lake appear deep, forbidding, and lugubrious; and when the wind blew, the moaning in the trees sounded like the voice of the marsh.

The Comtesse took Jeanne's hands in hers, as though they had been friends since childhood, and bid her sit down, before seating herself next to her on a low chair, while Julien, in whom the neglected refinements of gracious living had been reviving over the previous five months, chatted and smiled with a gentle, intimate air.

The Comtesse and he talked about their riding. She was poking mild fun at his style of horsemanship, calling him 'Sir Gallopbad', and he joined in her laughter, christening her the 'Queen of the Amazons'. The sound of a gun going off just beneath the windows made Jeanne give a little cry. The Comte had just shot a teal.

His wife called to him at once. They heard the sound of oars, the thud of boat against stone, and then he appeared, a towering figure in boots followed by two very wet dogs, red-haired like him, who lay down on the rug by the door.

He seemed more at ease in his own home, and delighted to see the visitors. He gave orders for more wood to be put on the fire, and for Madeira and biscuits to be brought. Suddenly he exclaimed:

'But stay and dine with us! You must!'

Jeanne, whose thoughts were never far from her child, declined the invitation; he insisted, and as she continued firmly to refuse, Julien gestured in sudden impatience. So, anxious that he should not revert to his ill-natured and quarrelsome self, and although she hated the idea of not seeing Paul again until the following day, she accepted.

The afternoon was delightful. They went to visit the springs first. These rose at the foot of a mossy rock in the middle of a clear pool, where the water was in constant motion, as though it were on the boil. After that they went out in a boat, along what seemed like channels purposely cut through the forest of dry reeds. The Comte rowed, seated between his two dogs who kept sniffing the wind; and with each pull of his oars he raised the large boat and drove it forward. From time to time Jeanne would trail her hand in the cold water and savour the icy chill as it coursed up her fingers and through her veins. Away in the stern of the boat sat the Comtesse wrapped in shawls, and Julien, both of them wearing the permanent smile of happy people whom happiness has left with nothing to say.

Evening came on in long, icy ripples of breeze, gusts of northerly air blowing through the withered rushes. The sun had sunk behind the fir-trees; and even the sight of the red sky, dotted with strange little scarlet clouds, was enough to make them feel cold.

They returned to the vast drawing-room, where a huge fire was blazing. A feeling of warmth and good cheer gladdened their hearts from the moment they walked in. Then the Comte, prompted to merriment, took hold of his wife in his muscular arms, lifted her up to his face like a child, and planted two smacking kisses on her cheeks, the very picture of a fine, contented man.

Smiling, Jeanne observed this friendly giant whom everyone referred to as the ogre simply on account of his moustache, and she thought to herself:

'How mistaken we are about people, every day of our lives.'

Looking over, almost involuntarily, towards Julien, she saw him standing in the doorway, desperately pale, staring at the Comte. Concerned, she walked over to her husband and whispered:

'Are you unwell? What's wrong?'

'Nothing, leave me alone,' he replied crossly. 'I was cold, that's all.'

When they passed into the dining-room, the Comte asked if he might allow his dogs to join them; and they came at once and sat on their haunches to left and right of their master. He kept giving them scraps to eat and stroked their long, silky ears. The animals stretched out their heads and wagged their tails, quivering with contentment.

After dinner, as Jeanne and Julien were preparing to leave, Monsieur de Fourville detained them further so that he could show them torchlight fishing.

He positioned them, and the Comtesse, on the steps which led down to the lake; and then he climbed into his boat with a servant who was carrying a cast-net and a lighted torch. It was a clear, sharp night, and the sky was sprinkled with gold.

The torch sent strange, flickering streaks of fire wriggling across the water: gleams of light danced over the reeds, and lit up the great screen of fir. Then suddenly, as the boat turned, the huge, fantastical shadow of a man stood out against the illumin-ated edge of the wood. The head rose higher than the trees, disappearing into the sky, while the feet sank into the waters of the lake. Presently this monstrous creature raised its arms as though to grab the stars. All at once the immense limbs straight-ened, then fell; and there was a faint sound of thrashing water.

The boat having now gently swung round once more, the pro-digious phantom seemed to be running along the edge of the wood, as this was illuminated by the turning light. Then it van-ished into the invisible distance; suddenly it reappeared again, not as tall but more distinct, its strange movements outlined on the wall of the chateau.

And the Comte's voice boomed out:

'Gilberte, I've caught eight.'

The oars beat the water. The enormous shadow was now motionless on the wall, but gradually shrinking in height and girth; its head seemed to be coming down, its body to grow thin-ner; and when Monsieur de Fourville came back up the steps, still followed by his servant carrying the torch, the shadow had been reduced to the proportions of his own person, and repeated his every gesture.

In his net eight large fish lay writhing.

When Jeanne and Julien were on their way home, all wrapped up in the cloaks and rugs which they had been lent, Jeanne said almost involuntarily:

'He's a fine man, the giant!'

And Julien, who was driving, answered:

'Yes, he is. But he should restrain himself more when he's in company.'

One week later they called on the Couteliers, who were thought to represent the highest nobility in the province. Their estate at Reminil adjoined the large town of Cany. The new chateau, built in the reign of Louis XIV, was hidden away in a magnificent park entirely surrounded by walls: the ruins of the old castle could still be seen in the grounds, perched on a rise. Liveried footmen ushered the visitors into a large, imposing room. Right in the centre stood a kind of column supporting a huge Sèvres bowl, and on the plinth, under a glass plaque, was a letter in the King's hand inviting the Marquis Léopold-Hervé-Joseph-Germer de Varneville, de Rollebosc de Coutelier, to accept this gift from the Sovereign.

Jeanne and Julien were admiring this royal offering when the Marquis and the Marquise entered. The lady wore powdered hair, displayed perfunctory charm, and seemed affected in her endeavour to appear gracious. The man, a stout personage with white hair swept up high on his head, invested his gestures, his voice, and his whole bearing with a haughtiness that proclaimed the importance of his position.

They belonged to that class of person for whom etiquette is all and whose every thought, or feeling, or word seems stilted.

They spoke for themselves alone, never waiting for a reply, smiling with an air of unconcern; and they gave the constant impression of being engaged in carrying out the duty, imposed by their birth, of receiving the minor nobles of the region with politeness.

Julien and Jeanne felt numbingly awkward and tried desperately to be agreeable, too embarrassed to stay longer and yet inexpert at finding a pretext to leave; but the Marquise herself brought the visit to a close, naturally, simply, stopping the conversation stone dead like a queen politely dismissing someone from her presence.

On their way home Julien said:

'If you have no objection, I think we might pay rather fewer visits. The Fourvilles are enough for me.'

And Jeanne agreed.

December passed slowly, that black month like a dark hole at year's end.

The period spent shut up indoors began again as it had the previous year. But Jeanne was not bored, for she was constantly busy with Paul, upon whom Julien looked askance with a nervous and unhappy eye.

Often, when his mother held him in her arms, caressing him with the frantic tenderness that mothers feel for their children, she would hold him out to his father and say:

'Come, do give him a kiss. Anyone would think you didn't love him.'

With an air of disgust he would brush his lips across the baby's smooth forehead, his whole body arched forward so that it should remain out of reach of the tiny, clenched hands that were never still. Then he would depart abruptly, as though driven away by some feeling of revulsion.

The mayor, the doctor, and the priest came to dinner from time to time; on other occasions it was the Fourvilles, with whom they were becoming more and more friendly.

The Comte appeared to adore Paul. He would hold him on his knees throughout their entire visit, for whole afternoons on end. He handled him gently, despite his great, giant's hands; he would tickle the end of his nose with the points of his long moustache, and then kiss him in affectionate bursts, like a mother. It pained him constantly that his own marriage had remained childless.

March was bright, dry, and almost mild. Comtesse Gilberte once more mentioned the possibility of the four of them going riding together. Jeanne, rather weary of the long evenings, the long nights, and the long, monotonous days, each one just like the last, accepted, thoroughly delighted by these plans; and for a week she enjoyed herself making a riding-habit.

So they began their excursions. They always rode in pairs, the Comtesse and Julien in front, the Comte and Jeanne a hundred paces behind. The latter chatted away quietly, like old friends, for friends they had become, brought together by integrity and simplicity of heart. The former were often whispering together, occasionally bursting into storms of laughter, or suddenly looking at each other as if their eyes had things to tell of which their mouths could never breathe a word; and all of a sudden they would go galloping off, prompted by an urge to flee, to ride further and further away.

Then Gilberte appeared to become irritable. Her shrill voice, borne on the breeze, would sometimes reach the ears of the two riders dawdling along behind. Then the Comte would smile and say to Jeanne:

'Some days my wife gets out of bed on the wrong side.'

One evening, on their way home, as the Comtesse was busy urging her mare on, spurring it and then repeatedly pulling on the reins, they could hear Julien saying to her several times:

'Take care, take care, for goodness' sake. She'll run away with you.'

'Too bad. It's none of your business,' she replied in such a harsh, clear tone that every word rang out across the countryside as if they were suspended in mid-air.

The horse reared and bucked, lashing out with its hooves, foaming at the mouth. Suddenly the Comte, now concerned himself, cried out at the top of his powerful lungs:

'Do be careful, Gilberte!'

Then, as though out of defiance, in one of those moments of impatience when a woman decides that nothing shall stop her, she struck the animal a cruel blow between the ears with her riding-crop, and it reared up, enraged, beating the air with its front legs. Whereupon, having lowered its feet to the ground, it took a formidable leap forward and tore off across the plain as fast as its legs would carry it.

It crossed a meadow first and then raced across some ploughed fields, kicking up the damp, heavy soil behind it and going so fast that it was difficult to distinguish horse and rider.

Astonished, Julien remained where he was, calling out in desperation:

'Madame! Madame!'

But the Comte let out a sort of grunt, bent over the neck of his heavy mount to urge it forward with the whole weight of his own body, and sent it galloping off at such a speed, goading it, dragging it forward, rousing it by voice, gesture, and spur, that the huge horseman seemed to be carrying the stout creature between his legs and lifting it into the air as though he were trying to take off. They raced along at unimaginable speed, without the slightest deviation to right or left; and in the distance Jeanne could see the two silhouettes of the man and woman receding further and further into the distance, getting smaller and smaller, fading away until they disappeared from sight, like two birds chasing each other that gradually pass from view and vanish beyond the horizon.

Then Julien came over, still at the walk, and muttering furiously beneath his breath:

'I think she's gone quite mad today.'

And they both set off in pursuit of their friends, who had now disappeared down into a dip in the plain.

A quarter of an hour later they caught sight of them coming back; and presently they met up with them.

The Comte, red in the face, sweating, laughing, happy, triumphant, was holding the reins of his wife's quivering mount in his iron grip. She was pale, her face tense and unhappy; and she was supporting herself with one hand on her husband's shoulder as if she were about to faint.

That day Jeanne understood how deeply the Comte was in love.

After that, during the following month, the Comtesse seemed more joyful than she had ever been. She came to Les Peuples more frequently, always laughing and throwing her arms round Jeanne in sudden rushes of affection. It was as though some mysterious delight had descended upon her life. Her husband, too, was a picture of happiness: he could not keep his eyes off her, and tried at every moment to touch her hand, her dress, in a redoubling of the passion he felt for her.

One evening he said to Jeanne:

'We are very happy at the moment. Gilberte has never been so loving as she is now. The bad moods have gone, the angriness. I feel that she loves me. Until now I was never quite sure.'

Julien, too, seemed changed, more cheerful, no longer so impatient, as if the friendship between the two families had brought peace and joy to each.

Spring was unusually early and warm.

From mild morning till warm, peaceful dusk, the sun was starting the whole surface of the earth into life. A process of sudden, powerful, simultaneous germination was under way, one of those unstoppable upsurges of sap, like a desperate longing to be reborn, that nature seems to display sometimes in exceptional years, and when it would appear as though the whole world itself were being rejuvenated.

Jeanne felt vaguely unsettled by this fermenting of life around her. She would grow suddenly faint at the sight of a tiny flower in the grass, experience moments of delicious melancholy, hours and hours of dreamy lassitude.

Then she was overtaken by fond memories of the early stages of her love; not that she felt any return of affection for Julien, all that was over, well and truly over; but her whole body, caressed by the breeze and penetrated by the smells of spring, grew restless, as though her flesh were responding to some invisible and tender appeal.

She took pleasure in being alone, abandoning herself to the sun's warmth, suffused through and through by indeterminate and serene sensations, a sensual satisfaction that left no room for thought.

One morning, while she was dozing in this state, she suddenly had a vision of that sunny gap in the dark foliage, in the little wood near Étretat. That was where, for the first time, she had felt her body thrill at the presence of the young man who then had loved her; that was where he had first given mumbled expression to the timid longings of his heart; and that was where, also, she had thought herself in sudden contact with the radiant future of her hopes.

And she wanted to see that wood again, to make a sort of sentimental, superstitious pilgrimage there, as if a return to that place should effect some change in the direction of her life.

Julien had departed at dawn, she knew not whither. So she had the Martins saddle up the little white horse which she sometimes rode now; and off she went.

It was one of those days that are so peaceful that nothing seems to stir, not a blade of glass, not a single leaf; everything seems to have come to rest for ever, as if the wind were dead, as if even the insects had vanished.

A supreme, burning stillness descended from the sun, imperceptibly, like a haze of gold; and Jeanne contentedly let her horse carry her along at a walk, soothed by its gait. From time to time she would look up to see a tiny little white cloud no bigger than a pinch of cotton wool, a wisp of vapour just hanging there, forgotten, left all alone up there in the midst of the blue sky.

She descended the valley that leads down to the sea through the great archways in the cliff known as the Portes d'Étretat, and slowly she came to the wood. Sunlight was flooding down through the green foliage that was still sparse. She looked in vain for the spot, wandering up and down the narrow paths.

Suddenly, as she was crossing a broad avenue, she caught sight of two saddled horses tethered to a tree at the far end, and recognized them at once; they belonged to Gilberte and Julien. Having begun to weary of being on her own, she was pleased at this unexpected meeting, and put her mount to the trot.

When she had reached the two horses, which were standing there patiently as though accustomed to these long waits, she called out. There was no reply.

A woman's glove and the two riding-crops were lying on the trampled grass. So they must have been sitting there and then gone off somewhere, leaving their horses behind.

She waited for a quarter of an hour, twenty minutes, puzzled, wondering what could be keeping them. As she had dismounted and was standing quite still, leaning against a tree trunk, two little birds, not seeing her, landed on the grass right next to her. One of them was hopping agitatedly round the other, its wings raised and quivering, chirping and bobbing its head; and suddenly they mated.

Jeanne was taken by surprise, as though she were ignorant of such things. Then she said to herself: 'But, of course, it's spring,' whereupon another thought occurred to her, a suspicion. She looked again at the glove, the crops, the two abandoned horses; and quickly she remounted her horse, filled with the irresistible desire to get away.

She was galloping now, as she made her way back to Les Peuples. Her mind was busy, working things out, assembling the facts, putting two and two together. How had she not guessed sooner? How had she not noticed? How had she not understood why Julien was absent so frequently, why he had become the elegant gentleman once more, why he had become less irritable? She remembered too how tense and abrupt Gilberte had been, her exaggerated playfulness, and, more recently, the kind of rapt ecstasy in which she had been living, and which had made the Comte so happy.

She put her horse to the walk, for it was time for some serious reflection and the rapid pace prevented her from thinking straight.

After the initial shock her heart had become almost calm again: she felt no jealousy or hatred, only contempt. She scarcely thought about Julien—nothing surprised her now where he was concerned; but the double betrayal by the Comtesse, by her friend, sickened her. So everybody, then, was perfidious, mendacious, insincere. And tears sprang to her eyes, for sometimes one weeps as bitterly over the passing of illusions as over the dead.

She resolved nevertheless to pretend that she knew nothing, to shut her heart to passing affections, and to love only Paul and her parents from now on; and to present a calm exterior in the presence of everyone else.

Immediately on returning home she rushed to her son, carried him off to her room, and kissed him madly for an hour without interval.

Julien returned home for dinner, charming and all smiles, full of goodwill and consideration.

'Are Papa and Mama not coming this year?' he asked.

She was so grateful to him for this kind thought that she almost forgave him her discovery in the wood; and filled all at once with the overwhelming desire to see, as soon as possible, the two people she loved most in the world after Paul, she spent the whole evening writing to them, to hasten their arrival.

They sent word that they would return on 20 May. It was now the 7th.

She awaited them with growing impatience, as though she felt, beyond even her daughterly affection, a new need to associate once more with honest souls; to be able to talk and lay bare her heart with people of wholesome character, untainted by infamy, whose whole life, in every action, thought, and wish, had been lived with decency.

Her feeling now was of a sort of isolation, the isolation of her own righteous conscience among all these people whose conscience was failing them; and although she had learnt instantly how to dissemble, and even though she welcomed the Comtesse with hand outstretched and a smile on her lips, she was aware that this sense of vacuity, this contempt for human beings, was growing within her and gradually taking her over; and every day the local gossip would fill her soul with yet more disgust, and lower still further her opinion of mankind.

The Couillards' daughter had just had a child, and the marriage was about to take place. The Martins' servant-girl, an orphan, was pregnant; a young girl who lived nearby, aged fifteen, was pregnant; and a woman whose husband had died, a poor, sordid woman with a limp and called the Muddy Widow because she was so revoltingly dirty, she too was pregnant.

One was forever hearing about yet another pregnancy, or about the amorous escapade of some girl, or some peasant wife and mother, or some rich, respectable farming gentleman.

The hot spring weather appeared to have caused the sap to rise as much in men as in plants.

And Jeanne, whose deadened senses had ceased to respond,

whose bruised heart and sentimental soul alone seemed to be
stirred by the warm and fecund breeze, who dreamed, exaltedly
but without desire, passionate in her dreams but dead to all carnal
need, was astounded by all this filth and bestiality, which filled
her with repugnance and which she was coming more and more
to despise.

The coupling of human beings now provoked her to outrage,
as though it were unnatural; and if she harboured a grudge
against Gilberte, it was not because she had stolen her husband,
but for the very fact that she too had sunk into this universal mire.

She, after all, was not of coarse peasant stock, at the mercy of
base instinct. How could she possibly have given herself in the
same way that these brutes did?

On the very day when her parents were due to arrive, Julien
stirred her feelings of revulsion anew by blithely telling her—as
though it were something funny and entirely natural—the story
of how the baker, having heard a noise in his oven the previous
day, which was not a baking day, had gone to catch what he
thought was a stray cat and found his wife: 'and it wasn't bread
she was putting in her oven.'

To which he added:

'The baker blocked up the opening; they nearly suffocated in
there. It was the small boy from the baker's who went and told the
neighbours, because he'd seen his mother go in there with the
blacksmith.'

And Julien kept repeating with a laugh:

'Ah, it's the food of love they're giving us, the rascals. It's like
something out of La Fontaine.'*

Jeanne did not dare touch another piece of bread.

When the post-chaise drew up at the bottom of the front steps
and the Baron's happy face appeared at the carriage window, the
young woman's heart and soul were filled with deep emotion, a
tumultuous upsurge of affection the like of which she had never
experienced before.

But she was shocked, indeed felt almost faint, when she caught
sight of Mama. Over the six winter months the Baroness had
aged ten years. Her huge, flabby, pendulous cheeks had turned

purple, as though swollen with blood; the light seemed to have gone from her eyes; and she could no longer move without supporting herself on both arms. Where previously she had simply had difficulty breathing, she now wheezed and found it so hard to catch her breath that it was painfully embarrassing to be near her.

Having seen her every day, the Baron had not noticed this deterioration in her condition; and when she complained of her constant breathlessness and her increasing weight, he would reply:

'Don't worry, my dear, I've never known you any different.'

Jeanne, having accompanied them up to their bedroom, withdrew to her own room to cry, deeply shocked and distraught. Then she went to find her father, threw herself into his arms, her eyes still full of tears, and said:

'Oh, how changed Mother is! What is it? What's wrong with her? Please tell me.'

He was very surprised, and replied:

'Do you think so? Really? But no, I've been with her all the time. I haven't noticed anything wrong with her, I promise you. She's just the same as she's always been.'

That evening Julien said to his wife:

'Your mother's in a bad way. I think it may be serious.'

And when Jeanne burst out sobbing, he said impatiently:

'Come, come, I'm not saying we've lost her. You always exaggerate things so. She's changed, that's all, it's only natural at her age.'

By the end of the first week Jeanne had stopped worrying, having grown used to her mother's altered appearance, and perhaps having suppressed her fears in the way people are always suppressing or refusing to acknowledge their qualms or besetting concerns out of a sort of selfish instinct, a natural desire for peace of mind.

The Baroness, unable to walk properly, now went out for no more than half an hour each day. When she managed one length of 'her' avenue, she could not move another inch and insisted on having a rest on 'her' bench. And when she felt incapable of even getting to the far end, she would say:

'That's enough. My hypertrophy has taken the legs from under me today.'

She rarely laughed now, simply smiling at the things which would have had her roaring with mirth the year before. But as her sight remained excellent, she spent whole days reading *Corinne* or Lamartine's *Méditations*.* Then she would ask for the 'memory drawer' to be brought to her. Presently, having emptied out onto her lap the old letters that were so dear to her heart, she would put the drawer down on a chair beside her and replace her 'relics' in it, one by one, having slowly reread each of them. And when she was quite, quite alone, she would kiss some of them, as in secret one kisses the locks of hair belonging to persons now dead and whom once one loved.

Sometimes when Jeanne entered the room unexpectedly, she would find her mother weeping tears of sadness.

'But Mama, what is it?' she would exclaim.

And the Baroness would heave a deep sigh and say:

'It's my relics that do it to me. You know, when you stir up memories of things that were once so good and that are now no more! And then there are the people you'd almost forgotten about, and suddenly you're reminded of them. It's as if you can see them and hear them again, and it has a dreadful effect on you. You'll discover what I mean, later on.'

When the Baron chanced by during these moments of melancholy, he would say under his breath:

'Jeanne, my dear, take my advice, burn your letters, all of them, from your mother, from me, all of them. There's nothing worse when you're old than going back over your youth.'

But Jeanne, too, kept her correspondence, and although she was quite different from her mother in every way, she was putting together her own 'box of relics', out of a kind of hereditary instinct for dreamy sentimentality.

A few days after their return the Baron had to absent himself to attend to some business, and he departed.

The season was magnificent. Mild nights, teeming with stars, followed upon calm evenings, serene dusks upon radiant days, and radiant days upon brilliant dawns. Mama soon began to feel better; and Jeanne, no longer mindful of Julien's affair and Gilberte's treachery, felt almost wholly content. The countryside was full of flowers and scents; and the wide sea, forever calm, shone in the sunlight from morning till evening.

One afternoon Jeanne took Paul in her arms and went for a walk across the fields. She looked down in turn at her son and at the flower-speckled grass along the way, overcome by warm, boundless happiness. Every few minutes she would kiss her child, hugging him passionately to her; and then as some new heady aroma from the countryside wafted over her, she would feel faint, overwhelmed by an infinite sense of well-being. She began to dream of his future. What would he become? One minute she wanted him to be a great man of position and renown, the next minute she preferred him to be quite ordinary, remaining by her side, devoted and loving, his arms ever opened wide to embrace his Mama. When she loved him with her selfish mother's heart, she wanted him to remain her son, nothing but her son; but when she loved him with her passionate reason, it was her ambition that he should become a somebody out in the world.

She sat down at the edge of a ditch, and began to gaze at him. It seemed to her as though she had never seen him before. And she was suddenly astonished at the thought that this little person would one day grow up, that he would walk with a steady gait and have a beard on his cheeks and speak in a deep voice.

In the distance someone was calling her. She looked up. It was Marius running towards her. She thought that someone had called to visit her, and she stood up, annoyed at being disturbed. But the lad was running towards her as fast as he could, and when he was close enough, he shouted:

'Madame, it's her ladyship, she's not well.'

It was as though she felt a drop of icy water run down her spine; and she set off at great speed, her thoughts in turmoil.

From some way off she caught sight of a crowd of people gathered under the plane-tree. She rushed forward, and as the group parted she saw her mother lying on the ground, with her head resting on two pillows. Her face was quite black, her eyes were closed, and her chest, which had been gasping for breath for the past twenty years, was now still. The wet-nurse took the child from the young woman's arms and bore him away.

'What's happened? How did she fall?' asked Jeanne, with a wild expression on her face. 'Fetch the doctor.'

And as she turned round, she caught sight of the priest, who somehow or other had received word. He offered to help and hastily pulled up the sleeves of his cassock. But neither the vinegar nor the eau de Cologne nor continual rubbing had any effect.

'She should be undressed and put to bed,' said the priest.

Joseph Couillard, the farmer, was there, as well as Père Simon and Ludivine. With the assistance of the Abbé Picot, they tried to carry the Baroness; but when they lifted her, her head fell back and her dress, which they had grabbed hold of, began to rip, such was the weight of her large person and so difficult was she to move. Horrified, Jeanne began to scream. They placed the enormous, limp body back on the ground.

They had to fetch an armchair from the drawing-room; and once they had seated her in it, they were at last able to move her. They climbed the steps one by one, and then the stairs; and when they finally reached her bedroom, they laid her down on the bed.

While the cook was removing an apparently endless number of clothes, the widow Dentu appeared opportunely, having turned up suddenly, like the priest, as if they had both 'smelt death', as the servants put it.

Joseph Couillard rode off at the gallop to inform the doctor; and the priest was about to depart to fetch the holy oil when the nurse whispered in his ear:

'No need, Father. She's gone, I can tell.'

Jeanne was panic-stricken and kept asking for assistance, not knowing what to do, what to try, what remedy to use. The priest pronounced absolution, just in case.

For two hours they waited beside the purple, lifeless body. Having now fallen to her knees, Jeanne was sobbing, wracked by anguish and grief.

When the door opened and the doctor appeared, it was as though she had seen a vision of salvation, of solace and hope; and she rushed towards him, stammering out everything she knew about what had happened:

'She was taking her walk, as she did every day... she was well, indeed very well... she had had some broth and two eggs for lunch... all of a sudden she fell... and then she turned quite black as you can see... and she hasn't moved since... we've tried everything to revive her... everything.'

She stopped, startled by the nurse's discreet signal to the doctor that it was all over. Then, not wishing to understand, she asked the doctor anxiously:

'Is it serious? Do you think it's serious?'

Eventually he said:

'I am very much afraid that... that it is... that it is all over. You must have courage, great courage.'

And Jeanne opened her arms wide and threw herself upon her mother.

Julien had returned. He stood there in astonishment, evidently put out, making no audible sound of grief or despair, taken too rapidly by surprise to be able to assume at once the required expression and demeanour.

'I was expecting it,' he muttered. 'I knew it wouldn't be long.'

Then he took out his handkerchief, wiped his eyes, knelt down, crossed himself, mumbled something or other, and on getting to his feet, tried to help his wife up. But she was clinging to the body and kissing it, almost prostrate on top of it. They had to drag her away. She seemed to have lost her reason.

An hour later they allowed her to return. All hope was gone. The room had now been arranged as a mortuary chamber. Julien and the priest were talking in low voices by the window. The widow Dentu was already beginning to doze off, comfortably ensconced in an armchair with the air of one who is accustomed to vigils and who feels quite at home from the moment death enters.

Night was falling. The priest came up to Jeanne, took her hands in his, and sought to comfort her, pouring upon this inconsolable heart the unctuous waters of ecclesiastical consolation. He spoke of the departed, singing her praises in churchy language; and, with that affected sadness of clerics for whom corpses are their stock-in-trade, he offered to spend the night in prayer beside the body.

But through her convulsive sobbing Jeanne refused his offer. She wanted to be alone, quite alone, during this night of farewell. Julien stepped forward:

'But you can't do that. We'll both stay with her.'

She said 'no' with a shake of her head, incapable of speech. Finally she managed to say:

'She's my mother, my mother. I want to be left alone to keep vigil over her.'

The doctor murmured:

'Let her do as she wishes. The nurse can be in the next room.'

The priest and Julien consented, thinking of their beds. Then the Abbé Picot knelt down in his turn, prayed, rose to his feet, and left the room saying: 'She was a saint,' in the same tone of voice as he was used to saying: 'Dominus vobiscum.'*

Then the Vicomte said in a normal voice:

'Are you going to have something to eat?'

Jeanne did not reply, unaware that he was speaking to her.

'Perhaps you ought to eat something,' he persisted, 'to keep your strength up.'

She replied absently:

'Send for Papa at once.'

And he left the room to dispatch a man on horseback to Rouen.

She remained plunged in a kind of frozen grief, as if she were waiting for the moment when she would be alone with her mother for the last time before yielding to the rising tide of despair and regret.

The shadows of evening had filled the room, veiling the dead woman in darkness. The widow Dentu began to move about quietly, fetching and arranging invisible objects with the noiseless movements of a nurse. Presently she lit two candles and placed them gently on the bedside table which stood at the head of the bed covered in a white cloth.

Jeanne seemed to see, feel, understand nothing. She was waiting to be alone. Julien came back. He had had dinner, and again he asked her:

'Are you sure you don't want anything?'

His wife shook her head.

He sat down, looking more resigned than sad, and stayed there without speaking.

The three of them remained like this, each sitting apart from the other, on their different chairs, not stirring.

Occasionally the nurse would snore a little and then wake up with a start.

Finally Julien got up and, coming over to Jeanne, enquired:

'Would you rather be on your own now?'

She took his hand in an involuntary gesture:

'Oh yes, leave me now.'

He kissed her on the forehead, and murmured:

'I'll come back and see you now and again.'

And he left the room with the widow Dentu, who rolled her armchair into the next room.

Jeanne closed the door, then went and opened the two windows wide. She was met in the face by the warm caress of night air at haymaking time. The grass on the lawn, scythed the day before, lay ungathered in the moonlight.

This sweet sensation grieved her, wounding her like an irony.

She walked back to the bed, grasped one of the cold, motionless hands, and began to study her mother.

She no longer looked as bloated as she had at the time of the attack, and seemed to be sleeping now more peacefully than she had ever slept; and in the pale light of the candles flickering in the draughts, the shadows cast on her face shifted this way and that, making her seem alive, as though she herself had moved.

Jeanne gazed at her avidly; and from the deep, distant recesses of her early childhood came a host of memories.

She recalled Mama's visits to the parlour at the convent, and the way she would hold out the paper bag full of cakes, and a whole multitude of small details, trivial incidents, little kindnesses, words, inflections of her voice, familiar gestures, the wrinkles round her eyes when she laughed, the great sigh she gave when she sat down out of breath.

She continued to stare at her, repeating to herself in a kind of daze: 'She's dead;' and the full horror of the word struck her.

This woman lying here—Mother, Mama, Madame Adélaïde— was dead? She would never move again, never speak again, never laugh again, never have dinner again sitting opposite Papa; she would never again say: 'Good morning, Jeannette.' She was dead!

They would nail her up in a box and bury her, and that would be that. They would never see her again. Was it possible? Really? She was no longer to have a mother? This dear face that was so familiar, beheld since the moment eyes could see, loved since the moment arms first opened wide, this supreme conduit of affection, this unique being that is a mother, more important to the heart than any other single being, was gone. She had only a few hours left in which to gaze at her face, this still face from which all thought had departed; and then nothing, nothing more, just a memory.

And she fell on her knees in a dreadful agony of despair. Clutching the sheet that covered the body and twisting it in her hands, her mouth pressed to the bed, she cried out in a heart-rending voice that was muffled by the bedclothes:

'Oh! Mother, my poor, poor Mother!'

Then, as she began to feel herself becoming overwrought, as overwrought as she had been that night when she ran off through the snow, she got up and rushed to the window to clear her head, to drink in the fresh air that was not the air around this bed, the air around this dead woman.

The cut grass, the trees, the heath, the sea in the distance, all lay in silent repose, slumbering beneath the tender spell of the moon. A measure of this gentle, soothing stillness communicated itself to Jeanne, and slow tears began to fall.

Then she came back to the bed and sat down, taking Mama's hand in hers again as though she were nursing her when she was ill.

A large insect flew in to the room, attracted by the candlelight. It bounced off the walls like a ball, flying from one end of the room to the other. Jeanne, distracted by its droning flight, looked up to see where it was; but she could only ever make out its shadow flitting haphazardly across the whiteness of the ceiling.

Presently she could hear it no longer. Then she noticed the
gentle tick-tock of the clock and another faint sound, or rather an
almost imperceptible whirring. It was Mama's watch, still going,
forgotten about in the pocket of her dress which was draped over
the chair at the foot of the bed. And suddenly a vague parallel
between the dead woman and this mechanical object which had
not stopped brought a new, sharp pang of grief to Jeanne's heart.

She looked at the time. It was barely half past ten; and she was
seized with terrible apprehension at the prospect of spending the
entire night there.

Other memories began to come back to her, memories of her
own life—Rosalie, Gilberte—the bitter disillusions of her heart.
So there was nothing, then, but sorrow, grief, misfortune, and
death. It was all just deceit and lies, things to make one suffer and
weep. Where was there a little respite and joy to be found? In
another life no doubt! When the soul had been delivered from its
ordeal upon earth! The soul! She began to reflect on this
unfathomable mystery, yielding readily to fanciful certainties only
for these to be replaced forthwith by no less flimsy hypotheses.
Where, then, was her mother's soul at this precise moment, the
soul that had gone from this motionless, ice-cold body? Far, far
away perhaps. Somewhere in space? But where? Evaporated like
the scent from a dried flower? Or wandering about like an invisible bird that has flown its cage?

Recalled to God? Or scattered, randomly assumed into the
process of new creation, mingling with the seeds that were about
to spring into life?

Or close by, perhaps? In this room, hovering around the lifeless
flesh from which it had just departed! And suddenly Jeanne
thought she felt a current of air brush over her, like the touch of a
spirit. She was afraid, desperately afraid, so violently afraid that
she did not dare move, or breathe, or turn round and look behind
her. Her heart was pounding as though she were in the throes of
some nightmare horror.

And all at once the invisible insect took off again and began to
bump into the walls as it whirled its way round the room. She
shivered from head to toe; then, having been reassured when she

recognized the droning of the winged insect, she rose to her feet and looked round. Her eyes fell on the desk with the sphinxes' heads, the place where Mama kept her 'relics'.

And a most singular and tender thought occurred to her: which was, during this final vigil, to read—as though from some pious work—these old letters that had been dear to her mother's heart. It seemed to her that she would be performing a delicate and sacred task, the act of a true daughter, which would bring pleasure to Mama in the other world.

They were old letters from her grandfather and grandmother, whom she had never known. She wanted to reach out to them over their daughter's body, to go towards them on this funereal night as if they too were suffering, to form a kind of mysterious chain of affection between those long dead, their daughter just departed, and herself left behind on earth.

She stood up, lowered the lid of the desk, and took from the bottom drawer ten or so little packets of yellowed paper, neatly tied together with string and stored side by side.

She placed them all on the bed, between the arms of the Baroness, out of a sort of sentimental courtesy, and began to read.

They were the sort of old letters one finds in ancient family desks, letters redolent of another age.

The first began: 'My darling.' Another with 'My beautiful grand-daughter,' then it was 'My dear little one,' 'My sweet,' 'My dearest daughter,' then 'My dear child,' 'My dear Adélaïde,' 'My dear daughter,' depending on whether they were addressed to the little girl, the older child, or later the young woman.

And they all contained warm, inconsequential expressions of affection, a thousand little intimate details, or the important but unexceptional events of family life that seem so paltry to those not directly concerned: 'Papa has flu; Hortense the maid has burnt her finger; Ratscov, the cat, is dead; they've cut down the fir-tree on the right of the front gate; Mother lost her missal on the way back from church, she thinks it's been stolen.'

There was mention, too, of people Jeanne did not know, but whose names she vaguely remembered cropping up in conversations, long ago, when she was a child.

These details moved her as though they had been revelations, as though she had suddenly entered Mama's secret past, her heart's history. She looked at the body lying there; and all at once she began to read aloud, to read to her dead mother, as though to amuse her, to bring her comfort.

And the motionless corpse seemed happy.

One by one she tossed the letters onto the foot of the bed; and it occurred to her that they ought to be placed in the coffin, as is the custom with flowers.

She untied another packet. The writing was different. It began:

'I can't live a moment longer without your caresses. I am mad with love for you.'

That was all; there was no name.

Puzzled, she turned the piece of paper over. Sure enough it was addressed to 'Madame la Baronne Le Perthuis des Vauds.'

Then she opened the next one:

'Come this evening, as soon as he's gone out. We shall be able to have an hour together. I adore you.'

In another one: 'I spent last night in a fever, wanting you desperately. I felt your body in my arms, your lips against mine, your eyes gazing into mine. And I could have thrown myself out of the window in frustration at the thought that you were lying by his side at that very moment, that he could have you as he pleased...'

Thoroughly perplexed, Jeanne still did not understand.

What did this all mean? To whom, for whom, from whom were these words of love addressed?

She went on reading, coming on yet further wild declarations of love, notes about assignations accompanied by the advice to be careful, and then always these five words at the end: 'Be sure to burn this.'

Finally she opened a harmless-looking note, a simple message accepting an invitation to dinner, but written in the same hand and signed: 'Paul d'Ennemare', the man the Baron still called 'my poor old Paul' whenever he referred to him, and whose wife had been the Baroness's best friend.

Suspicion dawned on Jeanne in an instant and became all at once a certainty. Her mother had taken him as her lover.

Distraught, she immediately flung these vile documents from her, as though she were casting off some poisonous creature that had attacked her, and she rushed to the window, weeping horribly as involuntary cries tore at her throat. Her whole inner being collapsed, and she slumped down at the foot of the wall; and as she hid her face in the curtain so that people would not hear her groans, she sobbed her heart out, plunged into fathomless despair.

She might have remained like this all night; but the sound of footsteps in the next room brought her to her feet in an instant. Perhaps it was her father? And all these letters lying on the bed and on the floor! He had only to open one of them! And then he would know! Him of all people!

She rushed forward, grabbed pieces of old, yellowing paper by the handful, the grandparents' letters and the lover's, and those she had not yet opened, and those that still lay in bundles in the drawers of the desk, and threw them into the fireplace in a great heap. Then she took one of the candles burning on the bedside table and set fire to the mound of letters. A tall flame sprang up and shone out across the room, over the bed and the corpse, a bright, dancing shaft of light that lit up the white curtain at the foot of the bed and there etched in black the quivering profile of the stiffened face and the contours of the enormous body lying beneath the sheet.

When all that was left in the grate was a pile of ash, she went and sat by the open window as if she no longer dared remain near the dead woman, and she began to cry once more, with her face in her hands, groaning in anguish, in a tone of desolate lament:

'Oh! my poor mother, oh! my poor mother!'

And an awful thought struck her:

What if by any chance Mama were not dead, if she were merely in some deep sleep, and if she were suddenly to get up, to start talking?—Wouldn't the knowledge of Mama's terrible secret diminish her daughterly love? Would she kiss her with the same respectful lips? Would she cherish her with the same, devout affection? No. That was now impossible! And it broke her heart to think so.

The night was fading, and the stars were turning pale; it was that chill hour which precedes the dawn. The moon, already low in the sky and about to sink into the sea, cast a pearly glow across its entire surface.

And Jeanne suddenly recalled that night she had spent standing at the window when they had first arrived at Les Peuples. How distant that was, how everything had changed, how different the future looked now!

With that the sky turned pink, a joyous, blushful, spellbinding pink. She watched this radiant birth of a new day, and with surprise on this occasion as though she were witnessing some strange natural phenomenon, wondering how it were possible for neither joy nor happiness to exist in this world when such dawns as these could break upon the Earth.

The sound of a door opening made her jump. It was Julien.

'Well, not too tired?' he enquired.

'No,' she mumbled, glad not to be alone any more.

'You go and get some rest now,' he said.

She kissed her mother slowly, with a long, sorrowful, heart-broken kiss; and then she returned to her bedroom.

The day was filled with all the sad business consequent upon a person's death. The Baron arrived towards evening. He cried a great deal.

The funeral took place the following day.

When she had pressed her lips to the ice-cold forehead for the last time and put the final touches to her mother's toilette and seen the coffin lid closed, Jeanne retired to her room. The guests would be soon be here.

Gilberte arrived first, and threw herself sobbing into the arms of her friend.

From the window the carriages could be seen turning in at the iron gate and arriving at a trot. And voices echoed down in the hall. Women dressed in black gradually began to appear in the room, women whom Jeanne did not know. The Marquise de Coutelier and the Vicomtesse de Briseville embraced her.

Suddenly she noticed Aunt Lison sidling up behind her. And she hugged her with warm affection, which almost caused the old maid to pass out.

Julien walked in, dressed in full mourning, elegant, looking busy and important, satisfied at the presence of all these people. He spoke in hushed tones to his wife, asking her advice on some matter, and then added in a confidential tone:

'The whole of the nobility has come. It will be very fine.'

And off he went, bowing gravely to the ladies.

Aunt Lison and the Comtesse Gilberte remained alone with Jeanne during the funeral service. The Comtesse kept kissing her all the time and saying:

'My poor darling, my poor darling!'

When the Comte de Fourville returned to fetch his wife, he was in tears as if he had lost his own mother.

X

The days that followed were particularly sad, those days of gloom when a house seems empty because of the absence of the familiar person who has gone for ever, days punctuated by grief at each chance encounter with all the objects the departed was wont to touch. At every turn some memory tugs at your heart and leaves its bruise. Here is her chair, her umbrella still in the hall, her glass that the maid forgot to put away! And in every room there are things still lying about: her scissors, a glove, the book with its pages worn by her swollen fingers, and a thousand other little things that assume poignant significance because they recall a thousand other little incidents.

And the person's voice pursues you; you think you can hear it; you want to escape somewhere, anywhere, to flee the haunting presence in the house. But you have to stay because there are other people there, and they, too, are staying and suffering.

On top of which, Jeanne continued to feel crushed by the memory of what she had just discovered. The thought of it weighed on her mind, and her wounded feelings refused to heal. The loneliness she now felt was increased by this horrible secret; her last vestige of trust in others had vanished with her last vestige of belief in another human being.

Some time later Papa departed: he needed to be doing something, to have a change of air and escape the black depression into which he was sinking further and further.

And the great house, which was used to its masters disappearing periodically in this way, resumed its calm, regular ways.

And then Paul fell ill. Jeanne was distraught, and went twelve days without sleep, without food almost.

He recovered; but she remained horrified at the idea that he might die. What would she do then? What would become of her? And very gradually her heart began to entertain the vague longing for another child. Soon she began to daydream about such a prospect, filled once more with her former desire to have two little creatures round her, a boy and a girl. And the dream became an obsession.

But ever since the business with Rosalie, she had lived apart from Julien. Any thought of a rapprochement indeed seemed impossible, given their respective situations. Julien loved elsewhere; she knew he did; and the mere idea of submitting once more to his caresses made her shudder with revulsion.

She would nevertheless have resigned herself to it, so driven was she by the desire to become a mother again; but she wondered just how their intimacy was to resume. She would have died of humiliation rather than let her intentions be known; and he did not appear to give her a thought.

She would have given up the idea perhaps; but now, each night, she began to dream of having a daughter; and she saw her playing with Paul beneath the plane-tree; and sometimes she felt almost an itching to get out of bed and, without uttering a word, to go to her husband in his room. Twice even she tiptoed to his door; but then she hurried back to her room, her heart pounding with shame.

The Baron had left; Mama was dead; Jeanne now had no one whom she could consult or in whom she could confide her innermost secrets.

So she resolved to go and see the Abbé Picot, and to tell him, within the secrecy of the confessional, of the difficult project which she had in mind.

When she arrived, he was reading his breviary in his little orchard garden.

Having chatted for a few minutes about this and that, she mumbled with a blush:

'I would like to say confession, Monsieur l'Abbé.'

He was astonished, and raised his glasses to observe her more closely. Then he began to laugh:

'But you can't have many terrible sins on your conscience.'

She lost her composure completely and replied:

'No, but I want to ask your advice, about something so... so delicate that I don't dare ask you just like that.'

Instantly he forsook his jovial manner and assumed his priestly air:

'Well then, my child, I shall listen to you in the confessional. Let us go.'

But she stopped him, hesitantly, given sudden pause by a sort of scruple at talking about these rather shameful matters in the peace and quiet of an empty church.

'Or else perhaps... Father... I could... I could... if you wished... tell you what I've come about out here. Look, we could go and sit over there under your little arbour.'

They walked slowly towards it. She cast around for how to express herself, how to begin. They sat down.

Then, as if she were saying confession, she began:

'Father...', then she hesitated.

'Father...', she said again, and fell silent, completely tongue-tied.

He waited, his hands crossed over his stomach. Seeing her embarrassment, he encouraged her:

'Well, my daughter, it would seem you cannot dare to speak. Come, don't be afraid.'

She made up her mind, like a coward steeling himself for the plunge:

'Father, I would like to have another child.'

He made no reply, not understanding the problem.

Then she tried to explain the position, panicking as the words failed to come.

'I am all alone now. My father and my husband barely get on. My mother is dead, and... and only the other day,' she whispered in a shaking voice, 'I nearly lost my son! What would have become of me then?'

She fell silent. The priest looked at her in bewilderment:

'Come now, to the point.'

She repeated:

'I would like another child.'

Then he smiled, accustomed to the coarse jokes of the farmworkers who were seldom inhibited by his presence, and he replied with a sly nod:

'Well, it seems to me that the matter lies entirely with you.'

She raised her candid eyes towards him and stuttered in embarrassment:

'But... but... you see... ever since that... that business...
you know... with the maid... my husband and I... we live... we live
quite separately.'

Accustomed to the promiscuous and undignified mores of the
countryside, he was quite taken aback by this revelation. Then
immediately he thought he could guess what the young woman
really wanted. He gave her a sideways look, full of benevolence
and sympathy towards her in her distress:

'Yes, I quite understand. I see that your... your widowhood is
a burden. You are young and healthy. And after all, it's natural,
only too natural.'

He began to smile again, carried away by the earthy humour of
a country priest, and he tapped Jeanne gently on the hand:

'It is permissible, thoroughly permissible even, in the context
of the commandments.—"Thou shalt seek carnal knowledge only
within marriage."—You are married, are you not? Well, you
didn't get married just to plant out the turnips, did you?'

She for her part had not quite understood his hidden meaning
at first; but as soon as she realized what he did mean, she turned
bright crimson, profoundly shocked, and her eyes filled with
tears.

'Oh, Father, what are you saying? What are you thinking of? I
swear to you... I swear to you...' And the sobs choked her into
silence.

He was surprised, and tried to console her:

'Come now, I didn't mean to upset you. It was just a little joke
really, and there's no harm in a joke between decent people. But
you can count on me, you can count on me. I shall speak to
Monsieur Julien.'

She did not know what to say any more. She wanted to prevent
this intervention which she feared might be dangerous and the
wrong way to go about things, but she did not dare; and she made
her escape with a stammered 'Thank you, Father'.

A week passed. She lived in a constant state of anxiety.

One evening, at dinner, Julien looked at her oddly, as a particular smile played across his lips that she associated with him
in his more puckish moments. He was almost, with just a hint

of irony, being amorous with her; and when they were walking subsequently in Mama's long avenue, he whispered in her ear:

'It would appear that we have patched things up.'

She made no reply. She was staring at the remains of a straight line running along the ground, almost invisible under the grass that had grown over it. It was the trail left by the Baroness's dragging foot, and now fading like a memory. Jeanne felt her heart contract, overwhelmed by sadness; she felt lost in the midst of life, so isolated from everyone.

Julien continued:

'Nothing would make me happier. I was afraid you might not want me.'

The sun was going down, and the air was mild. Jeanne felt like crying: it was one of those moments when a person needs to open her heart to a friendly soul, to hug someone and confide her troubles. A sob rose to her throat. She opened her arms wide and flung herself against Julien's chest.

And she wept. Surprised, he gazed into her hair, unable to see the face hidden under his chin. He thought that she still loved him, and he placed a condescending kiss on her chignon.

Then they went indoors in silence. He followed her to her room, and spent the night with her.

And so their former relations began anew. He undertook them as a duty which was not, nevertheless, unpleasurable; she underwent them as a distasteful and painful necessity, fully intending to bring them to a halt once and for all as soon as she was pregnant again.

But presently she noticed that her husband's caresses seemed different from before, more refined perhaps, but less complete. He treated her rather as would a circumspect lover, and no longer as a carefree husband.

She was surprised and then realized, having observed matters more closely, that all his embraces ceased before she could be made pregnant.

Then one night, her lips against his, she murmured:

'Why don't you give yourself to me completely the way you used to?'

He began to sneer:

'Good heavens, so as not to make you pregnant, of course.'

She gave a start:

'But why don't you want any more children?'

He was almost speechless with astonishment:

'What? What did you say? Are you mad? Another child? Honestly, what an idea! It's bad enough having one of them bawl- ing its head off, and having everybody running after it, and costing money. Another child? No thank you!'

She held him to her, kissed him, wrapped him in love, and whispered:

'Oh, please, I beg you, make me a mother just once more.'

But he became angry, as though she had insulted him:

'Really, you're out of your mind. Please, no more of such silliness.'

She fell silent but resolved to trick him into giving her the happiness of which she dreamed.

So she tried to prolong his embraces, pretending a wild passion, holding him tightly in her arms in simulated ecstasies. She tried every ruse, but he remained within the bounds of self-control. Not once did he forget himself.

In the end, tormented more and more by her desperate desire, driven to the limit and ready to face anything, to take every risk, she went back to see the Abbé Picot.

He was just finishing his lunch and looked very red in the face, for he always had palpitations after meals. When he saw her enter the room, he cried: 'Well?', anxious to know the result of his negotiations.

Filled now with resolve and no longer bashful and timid, she replied at once:

'My husband doesn't want any more children.'

The Abbé turned towards her, profoundly interested, ready to pry with priestly curiosity into these mysteries of the marriage bed that made the confessional such an agreeable place for him.

'How do you mean?' he asked.

Then, despite her determination, she found it difficult to explain:

'Well, because he... he refuses to make me a mother.'

The Abbé understood; he knew about these things; and he began to question her in precise and minute detail, with the avid relish of a man who has been fasting.

Then he reflected for a few moments, and calmly, as though he had been talking of a harvest safely gathered in, he outlined a cunning plan of action, arranging it in every particular:

'There's only one thing you can do, my dear child, which is to make him think that you are already pregnant. He will stop controlling himself; and then you really will be.'

She blushed to her eyeballs; but, being prepared for everything, she persisted:

'And... if he doesn't believe me?'

The priest knew what it took to have a hold on a man and make him do what was wanted:

'Tell everyone, wherever you are, that you're pregnant, and eventually he'll believe it himself.'

Then he added by way of exonerating himself for this stratagem:

'It is your right. The Church tolerates relations between men and women only for the purpose of procreation.'

She followed his astute advice, and a fortnight later she announced to Julien that she thought she was pregnant. He jumped:

'It's not possible! It can't be true!'

At once she specified the reason for her supposition. But he was reassured:

'Pah! Just wait a while. You'll see.'

Thereafter he enquired each morning: 'Well?' And each time she replied: 'No, not yet. I shall be very surprised if I'm proved wrong.'

He in his turn became anxious, at once furious and downcast, as well as thoroughly baffled. He kept saying:

'But I just don't understand it. If only I knew how it happened. It's quite beyond me.'

A month later she announced the fact to all and sundry, except for the Comtesse Gilberte, out of a complex and delicate reticence.

Ever since he had first become worried about the matter, Julien had stopped going to her room. But eventually he swallowed his anger and accepted the situation:

'Well, that's one we didn't ask for.'

And he began once more to visit his wife's bedroom.

What the priest had foreseen came to pass perfectly. She became pregnant.

Thereupon, filled with delirious joy, she locked her door each night, dedicating herself—in a fit of gratitude towards the ill-defined deity she worshipped—to eternal chastity.

She felt almost happy once again, and surprised at the speed with which the pain she had felt at her mother's death had eased. She had thought herself inconsolable; and now in barely two months the wound had healed. She was left with merely a sense of affectionate regret, like a veil of sorrow placed across her life. No new major event in her life now seemed possible. Her children would grow up adoring her, while she herself would grow old in peaceful contentment, not giving a thought to her husband.

Towards the end of September the Abbé Picot came to pay a formal visit, wearing a new cassock with only one week's stains on it; and he introduced his successor, the Abbé Tolbiac. This priest was very young, thin, and extremely short, with a portentous way of speaking, and his deep-set eyes surrounded by dark rings bespoke a violent soul.

The old priest had been appointed Dean of Goderville.

Jeanne felt real sadness at this departure. The good fellow's face was bound up with all her memories of early womanhood. He had married her, baptized Paul, and buried the Baroness. She could not imagine Étouvent without the Abbé's paunch passing along the line of farmyards; and she liked him because he was cheerful and unaffected.

Despite his preferment he did not seem to be in good spirits.

'It's not easy for me, Madame la Comtesse, it's not easy,' he kept saying. 'I've been here these eighteen years now. Oh, the parish doesn't bring in much, it doesn't have much. The men have no more religion than they need, and the women, well, the women are not exactly well-behaved. The girls only come to church to get married after they've made a pilgrimage to Our Lady of the Fat Stomach, and orange blossom comes cheaply in these parts. But, no matter, I've loved it here.'

The new priest was gesturing crossly and getting red in the face. He said sharply:

'Now I'm here, that will all have to change.'

He was like a child having a tantrum, all scrawny and frail-looking in his cassock that was already well-worn but clean nonetheless.

The Abbé cocked an eye at him, as he always did in moments of merriment, and continued:

'Oh, Monsieur l'Abbé, you know, to stop that kind of thing going on you'd have to chain your parishioners up. And even then it wouldn't help.'

The little priest replied curtly:

'We shall see.'

And the old priest smiled as he took a pinch of snuff:

'Age will calm you, Monsieur l'Abbé, and experience too. You'll only succeed in driving the rest of the faithful away. People round here believe all right, but after their own stubborn fashion. So beware. My goodness, when I see a girl coming to church who looks a bit fat, I tell myself—"Well, that's one more parishioner she's bringing me"—and I try and find her a husband. You won't stop them sinning, you see. But you can go and find the lad and prevent him from abandoning the mother. See them married, Monsieur l'Abbé, see them married, and don't worry about anything else.'

The new priest replied roughly:

'We think differently, that's all. There's no point in our discussing the matter further.' And the Abbé Picot resumed his expressions of regret at having to leave this village of his, and the sea which he could see from the windows of the presbytery, and the little funnel-shaped valleys where he would go and recite his breviary, as he watched the boats passing in the distance.

Then the two priests took their leave. The old one embraced Jeanne, who nearly burst into tears.

One week later the Abbé Tolbiac returned. He talked about the reforms he was introducing as though he were a prince taking possession of a kingdom. Then he requested the Vicomtesse always to attend Mass on Sundays and to take communion on every feast of the Church:

'You and I', he said, 'are the leading figures of the locality. We must rule over it and always set an example for others to follow. And we must act as one if we are to be powerful and respected. With the church and the chateau walking hand in hand, the cottage will fear us and obey.'

Jeanne's religious beliefs were entirely a matter of sentiment. She had that star-gazing faith that no woman ever loses; and if she observed almost all of her religious duties, it was largely out of habit following her convent upbringing, for the Baron's free-thinking philosophy had long since undermined all her beliefs.

The Abbé Picot had been satisfied with the little she could give him and never admonished her. But his successor, having noticed her absence from church the previous Sunday, had come rushing to see her, troubled and ready to rebuke.

She did not wish to sever relations with the presbytery and promised to do as he asked, privately intending to oblige him as a dutiful churchgoer for no more than a few weeks.

But gradually she became accustomed to going to church and fell under the influence of this frail Abbé and his righteous, domineering ways. Being of a mystical bent, he pleased her with his moments of exaltation and religious ardour. He struck the chord of religiosity which all women carry in their soul. His unbending austerity, his disdain for the things of this world and for the sensual, his disgust at normal human preoccupations, his love of God, his crude, youthful inexperience, his stern language, and his inflexible will all gave Jeanne an idea of what martyrs must have been like; and she allowed herself to be charmed—she who had suffered and was already so disillusioned—by the rigid fanaticism of this child, God's minister on earth.

He led her towards Christ the comforter, showing her how the pious joys of religion would assuage her suffering; and she knelt in the confessional, humbling herself, feeling small and weak before this priest who seemed to be no more than fifteen.

But he was soon hated by the whole district.

Unflinchingly severe on himself, he displayed implacable intolerance towards others. One thing in particular moved him to anger and indignation: love. He spoke of it in his sermons with vehemence and, in the usual ecclesiastical manner, always in black-and-white terms, raining down sonorous periods against concupiscence upon this audience of country-folk; and he would shake with fury, stamping his feet, his mind a prey to the images which he was wont to call forth in the course of his ranting.

The strapping lads and the country wenches swapped knowing glances across the aisle; and the old peasants, who like to joke about these matters, voiced their disapproval of the little priest's intolerance on the way back to their farms after the service, as they walked beside their sons in their blue smocks and the farming-women in their black cloaks. And the whole region was in an uproar.

People muttered to each other about how strict he was in the confessional, and about the harsh penances he imposed; and when he obstinately refused to grant absolution to girls whose chastity was no longer quite intact, the whole thing became a source of merriment. At High Mass on feast days people laughed to see some of the youngsters remain behind in their pews instead of going up to take communion with the others.

Soon he started spying on courting couples in an effort to prevent their trysts, like a gamekeeper pursuing poachers. On moonlit nights he would chase after them along the ditches, behind the barns, and between the mounds of gorse that grew on the low hillsides.

One time he caught a pair who refused to let go of each other; they were holding one another round the waist and went on kissing as they walked along a ravine strewn with rocks.

The Abbé shouted:

'That's enough of that, you filthy country swine.'

And the lad turned round and retorted:

'Mind yer own business, Father, for this ain't none of yours.'

Then the Abbé picked up some stones and started pelting them, as though they were dogs. The pair ran off laughing; and next Sunday he denounced them by name in front of the whole congregation.

All the lads in the district stopped going to church.

The priest came to dine at the chateau every Thursday, and often visited at other times during the week to talk with his penitent parishioner. She would enthuse as he did, and talk over matters of the spirit, and deploy the whole, complicated, centuries-old arsenal of religious controversies.

They would walk together in the Baroness's long avenue, talking of Christ and the Apostles, the Virgin and the early Fathers, as if they had known them personally. Sometimes they would stop and consider profound questions that propelled them into mystical surmise, with Jeanne losing herself in fanciful arguments that soared into the heavens like rockets, while he, being of a more precise turn of mind, argued away like some self-confessed crackpot trying to give a mathematical proof of the squaring of the circle.

Julien treated the new priest with great respect, and kept saying: 'I do like this new man, he doesn't fudge the issues.'

And he was forever going to confession and taking communion, setting an example most liberally.

By this time he was visiting the Fourvilles almost every day, out shooting with the husband who now found his company indispensable, and going riding with the Comtesse in all weathers.

'They're completely mad about their horses,' the Comte would observe, 'but it does my wife good.'

The Baron returned towards the middle of November. He was a changed man, older and much more subdued, filled with a dark melancholy that had taken over his mind. And it was immediately apparent that the love which bound him to his daughter had grown stronger, as if the few months of loneliness and gloom had increased his need for affection, for intimacy and loving tenderness.

Jeanne did not tell him of her new outlook on things, about her close bond with the Abbé Tolbiac and her religious fervour; but the first time he saw the priest he took an ardent dislike to him.

And when Jeanne enquired that evening: 'How do you find him?', he replied: 'That man's an inquisitor! I should say he's very dangerous.'

Subsequently, when he heard from the peasants with whom he was friendly about the young priest's strict ways, about his violent behaviour and what amounted to his campaign of persecution against the laws and instincts of nature, dislike turned to hatred in his heart.

For his own part he belonged with those thinkers of old who worshipped nature, and he was readily affected by the sight of two animals mating. The God to whom he prayed was of a more or less pantheist type, and he was fiercely hostile to the Catholic conception of a God characterized by bourgeois motives, jesuitical wrath, and despotic vengeance, a God who diminished the spectacle of Creation as he himself dimly perceived it, that is, of Creation as a fateful, limitless, all-powerful force; Creation as simultaneously life, light, earth, thought, plant, rock, man, air, beast, star, God, insect; which created precisely because it *was* Creation, stronger than any individual will, vaster than any capacity to reason, and productive for no purpose, without cause or temporal limit, in all directions and in all shapes and dimensions, across the infinite reaches of space, as chance and the proximity of world-warming suns dictated.

Creation contained all the seeds of existence, and thought and life developed within it like flowers and fruits upon the trees.

For him, therefore, reproduction was the great, general law, a sacred, divine act to be respected, which accomplishes the obscure and constant will of Universal Being. And so, from farm to farm, he embarked upon a fervent campaign against their intolerant priest, the persecutor of life.

Distressed by this, Jeanne prayed to the Lord, and begged her father to refrain; but he kept saying:

'Such people must be resisted, it is our right and duty to do so. They're inhuman.'

'They're inhuman,' he insisted, shaking his long white hair, 'they're inhuman, they understand nothing, nothing, nothing. They're labouring under a fatal illusion. They hate the physical!'

And he would shout 'They hate the physical!' as though he were uttering a curse. The priest was well aware of his enemy, but as he was keen to remain master of the chateau and its young mistress, he temporized, sure of the final victory.

Then a new obsession came to haunt him. He had discovered by chance what was going on between Julien and Gilberte, and he wanted at all costs to put a stop to it.

One day he came to see Jeanne, and after a long discussion over mystical matters, he asked her to join with him in combating, in extirpating, the evil within her own family, to save two souls in mortal danger.

She did not understand and asked him to explain.

'The hour is not yet come,' he replied. 'I shall return before long.'

And he departed abruptly.

Winter was now nearing its end, a rotting winter, as men of the soil put it, both damp and mild.

The Abbé returned some days later and spoke in oblique terms about one of those unworthy relationships between people who should be above reproach. It behoved those who had knowledge of the facts, he said, to put an end to the business by whatever means. Having first broached the subject of there being higher considerations, he then took Jeanne by the hand and beseeched her to open her eyes, to understand, to help him.

This time she had understood, but she remained silent, horri- fied at the thought of all the unpleasant consequences which might ensue in her now peaceful home; and she pretended not to understand what the Abbé meant. So he hesitated no further and spoke plainly:

'It is a painful duty which I have to perform, Madame la Comtesse, but there is no other way. My ministry obliges me not to allow you to remain in ignorance of that which you are in a position to prevent. Know then that your husband is engaged in a criminal friendship with Madame de Fourville.'

She lowered her eyes, in powerless resignation. The priest went on:

'What do you intend to do about it now that you know?'

Then she stammered:

'What do you *want* me to do about it, Father?'

He answered fiercely:

'Come between them and prevent this sinful passion.'

She began to cry and said, in an unhappy voice:

'But he's been unfaithful before, with a maid. And he doesn't listen to me. He has ceased to love me any more, and he mistreats me as soon as I show the slightest intention that doesn't suit him. What can I do?'

The priest did not anwer her but exclaimed:

'So you give in to it! You've resigned yourself to it! You consent in it! Adultery is here beneath your roof, and you tolerate it! The crime is taking place before your very eyes, and you look the other way? And you call yourself a wife? A Christian? A mother?'

She was sobbing:

'What do you want me to do?'

He replied:

'Anything rather than allow this infamous situation to continue. Anything, I tell you. Leave him. Leave this home that has been defiled!'

'But I have no money, Father,' she said, 'and indeed I haven't the courage, not in the present situation. And in any case, how can I leave him without there being proof? I do not even have the right to do so.'

The priest rose to his feet, quivering:

'Cowardice is your counsel, Madame, I had thought you were different than this. You are unworthy of God's mercy!'

She fell to her knees:

'Oh, I beg you, do not abandon me, tell me what to do!'

'Open Monsieur de Fourville's eyes to the truth,' he declared sharply. 'It is up to him to break this attachment.'

At this suggestion a horrible thought struck her:

'But he would kill them, Father! And I should be the accuser! Oh, no, not that, never!'

Then he raised his hand as though to curse her, beside himself with anger:

'Continue then in your shame and your crime, for your guilt is greater than theirs. You are the complaisant wife! There is nothing more I can do here!'

And he left, in such a fury that his whole body was trembling.

She went after him, distraught, ready to concede, beginning to promise him. But, still shaking with indignation, he walked briskly ahead, all the while furiously brandishing his large blue umbrella, which was almost as big as himself.

He caught sight of Julien standing by the gate overseeing the removal of some branches from the trees, and he turned left to walk through the Couillards' farm, continually repeating:

'Leave me, Madame, I have nothing further to say to you.'

In the middle of the farmyard, directly in his path, a bunch of children from the farm itself and from others nearby were gathered round the kennel that belonged to Mirza, the bitch, and they were staring intently at something or other, rapt in silent concentration. Standing in the midst of them, with his hands behind his back, was the Baron, who was also watching with interest. He looked like a schoolmaster. But when he saw the priest coming, he walked off so as to avoid meeting him and having to greet him and exchange words.

Jeanne said beseechingly:

'Give me a few days, Father, and then come back to the house. I shall tell you how far I have got and what I intend to do; and then we can decide.'

At that moment they were just reaching the group of children, and the priest went up to see what they were so interested in. The bitch was whelping a litter. In front of her kennel five pups were already squirming round their mother, who was licking them fondly, lying on her side and evidently in pain. Just as the priest leaned over, the animal tensed her body, stretched, and a sixth little puppy appeared. Then the young scamps, thrilled with joy, began to clap their hands and chant: 'And there's another one! And there's another one!' It was only a game to them, a perfectly natural, innocent game. They were watching the birth as they would have watched apples falling from a tree.

At first the Abbé Tolbiac stood in frozen astonishment; then, seized with uncontrollable fury, he lifted his large umbrella and began to lay about the bunch of children, hitting them on the head as hard as he could. Terrified, the little mites ran away as fast as their legs would carry them, so that all at once he found himself standing in front of the whelping bitch, who was making an effort to stand up. But he did not even let her get to her feet; rather, having now completely lost his temper, he began to beat her with his umbrella, holding it first in one hand and then in the other. Being chained up she could not escape, and she groaned wretchedly as she endeavoured to resist the blows. He broke his umbrella. Then, empty-handed, he stood on her, trampling on her in a frenzy, pounding her and crushing her into the ground. He caused her to give birth to one last pup, squeezed out under the pressure; and then, with a wild stamp of his heel he dispatched the blood-smeared body, which continued to quiver where it lay, surrounded by the other squealing, newborn pups, themselves blind and heavy-limbed and already searching for a teat to suck.

Jeanne had made her escape; but the priest suddenly felt someone grab him by the collar, and a slap across the face sent his hat flying. Furious, the Baron carried him over to the gate and threw him out onto the road.

When Monsieur Le Perthuis turned round, he saw his daughter on her knees, sobbing among the little puppies and gathering them up into her skirt. He strode over to her, gesticulating and shouting:

'See! See! A man of the cloth! Now do you see what he's like?'

The farm-tenants had come running up, and everyone was gazing at the murdered animal.

'It don't seem possible!' Mère Couillard declared: 'To think that anyone could be so cruel!'

Jeanne, however, had picked up the seven pups and said that she intended to raise them herself.

They tried to give them some milk; but three died the following day. Then Père Simon scoured the district for a bitch with a litter. He could not find one, but came back with a cat which he claimed would do just as well. So they put down three more of the litter and gave the remaining pup to this wet-nurse from another species. She adopted it immediately and lay down on her side, offering it her teat.

So that the puppy should not exhaust its adoptive mother, they weaned it a fortnight later, and Jeanne assumed responsibility for feeding it with a baby's bottle. She had called it Toto. The Baron, without asking, changed its name to 'Slaughter'.

The priest did not return, but the following Sunday, from his pulpit, he uttered a stream of oaths and curses and threats against the chateau, saying how it took a red-hot iron to treat a running sore, heaping anathemas upon the Baron—much to his amusement—and hinting, with a veiled and as yet tentative allusion, at Julien's latest amours. The Vicomte was infuriated, but the fear of a dreadful scandal cooled his anger.

Thereafter, in sermon after sermon, the priest continued to announce his forthcoming vengeance, prophesying that the hour of the Lord was at hand, that His enemies would be cast down, every one.

Julien wrote a respectful but firm letter to the Archbishop. The Abbé Tolbiac was threatened with public disgrace. He fell silent.

He could be seen now going for long solitary walks, striding along with an exalted look on his face. Gilberte and Julien kept seeing him in the course of their rides, sometimes in the distance as a black speck on the far side of a plain or by the edge of a cliff, sometimes reading his breviary in some narrow valley which they were about to enter. They would turn away so as not to have to pass near him.

Spring had arrived, stirring their love into new life and throwing them each day into one another's arms, in this place or that, in whatever sheltered spot their rides took them to.

As the leaves on the trees were as yet sparse, and the grass wet, and since they could not disappear into the undergrowth in the woods as they did in the middle of summer, they had mostly chosen to conceal their embraces in a shepherd's caravan, which had been left abandoned since the previous autumn on the top of the cliff at Vaucotte.

There it remained, out on its own, perched on its big wheels, some five hundred metres from the cliff-edge, just where the valley begins its rapid descent to the sea. They could not be surprised here, since they had a clear view right across the plain; and their horses would wait for them, tethered to the shafts of the caravan, until they had wearied of their embraces.

But it so happened one day, just as they were leaving this refuge, that they caught sight of the Abbé Tolbiac sitting almost hidden from view amidst the gorse growing on the cliff-top.

'In future we'd better leave our horses in the ravine', said Julien. 'They might be seen from the distance and give us away.' So they adopted the habit of tethering the horses in a fold in the valley where there were plenty of bushes.

Then, one evening as they were both returning to La Vrillette, where they were to join the Comte for dinner, they met the priest from Étouvent just leaving the chateau. He stood aside to let them pass, and bid them good-day but without looking them in the eye.

They were worried for a moment, but soon forgot all about it.

Now one afternoon, when there was a strong gale blowing (this was at the beginning of May), Jeanne was sitting reading by the fire when suddenly she caught sight of the Comte de Fourville arriving on foot and at such speed that she thought something dreadful must have happened.

She rushed downstairs to receive him, and on seeing him face to face she thought he had gone mad. He was wearing a thick fur cap which he only ever wore at home and the loose smock he usually went shooting in; and he was so pale that his red moustache, which did not normally stand out particularly against his ruddy complexion, looked like a streak of flame. And he had a wild look in his eyes, rolling his eyeballs as though his mind were completely blank.

'My wife is here, isn't she?' he stammered.

Jeanne, not thinking, replied:

'Well no, I haven't seen her at all today.'

He sat down, as if his legs had given way beneath him, and took off his cap, wiping his forehead with his handkerchief, several times, quite unaware of what he was doing. Then suddenly he leapt to his feet and came towards Jeanne, holding out his hands, his mouth open as though he were about to say something, to share some terrible sorrow with her. Then he stopped, stared at her, and said in a kind of trance:

'But it's your husband... You too...'

And he fled in the direction of the sea.

Jeanne ran to try and stop him, calling to him, pleading with him, her heart numb with terror, and thinking:

'He knows everything! What is he going to do? Oh! Just as long as he doesn't find them!'

But she couldn't catch up with him, and anyway he wasn't listening to her. He just kept on, not pausing for an instant, sure of his goal. He crossed the ditch and made towards the cliff, striding over the gorse-bushes with a giant's steps.

Jeanne stood on the woody bank for a long time and watched him go; and then, when she had lost sight of him, she returned indoors in a torment of apprehension.

He had turned to the right and broken into a run. The heavy sea churned; great black clouds came rolling in at vertiginous speed and passed overhead, only to be followed by others; and each one pelted the coastline with a furious burst of rain. The wind shrieked and moaned, skimming the grass and flattening the new crops, taking hold of large white birds, like flakes of spume, and sweeping them far away inland.

The squalls lashed against the Comte's face, one after another, drenching his cheeks and dripping off his moustache, bringing uproar to his ears and tumult to his heart.

Ahead of him lay the entrance to the deep gorge of the Vaucotte valley. So far he had seen nothing, only a shepherd's caravan beside an empty sheep-pen. Two horses were tethered to its shafts. (Why fear to be seen in such a storm?)

The moment he saw the horses, the Comte lay down on the ground and then dragged himself forward on hands and knees, looking like some monster with his long body all covered in mud and his cap of animal fur. He crawled up to the solitary caravan and hid underneath so as not to be seen through the cracks in the wooden sides.

The horses had seen him and were restive. Slowly he cut

through their reins with his knife, which he kept open in his hand; and when a sudden gust blew, the animals ran off, unnerved by the hail which was beating down on the sloping roof of the caravan, making it rock on its wheels.

Then the Comte knelt up, put his eye to the gap under the door, and looked inside.

He did not move; he seemed to be waiting. Quite a long time passed; and all at once he stood up, covered in mud from head to foot. With a violent shove he shot the bolt that fastened the penthouse on the outside, grabbed hold of the shafts, and began to shake the little love-nest as though he wanted to break it into tiny pieces. Then suddenly he placed himself between the shafts and bent his tall body forward, straining with a desperate effort, pulling on them like an ox, and panting for breath; and he dragged the caravan and those shut up within it towards the steep slope.

Inside they were screaming, banging their fists against the walls, not understanding what was happening to them.

When he reached the top of the slope, he let go of the flimsy dwelling, and it began to roll downhill.

Gradually it gathered pace, careering madly downwards, faster and faster, leaping and stumbling like some living animal, its shaft banging on the ground.

An old beggar huddling in a ditch saw it pass in one bound over his head; and he heard the dreadful screams coming from the wooden box.

Suddenly it lost a wheel, torn off by one particular jolt; then it toppled over on its side, and resumed its course, rolling down the slope like a ball, or like an uprooted house tumbling from a mountain summit. Then, on reaching the edge of the final gully, it bounced upwards, arcing through the air, and fell to the bottom, where it shattered like an egg.

As it lay broken on the stony ground, the old beggar who had seen it pass crept down through the brambles; and moved by peasant caution, not daring to approach the eviscerated box, he went to the nearby farm to report the accident.

People came running; some of the wreckage was pulled away;

two bodies were discovered. They were bruised, mangled, bleeding. The man's forehead was split open, and his whole face was smashed. The woman's jaw was hanging down, severed during the fall; and their broken limbs were limp as if there were no bones left beneath the flesh.

People recognized them nevertheless; and they began to argue at length about how this disaster could have happened.

'What was they up to, then, in that there van?' asked a woman.

Then the old tramp said that they seemed to have taken refuge in it to shelter from the gale, and the strong winds must have blown the caravan over and sent it tumbling down the slope. And he explained how he himself had thought of taking cover there, when he had seen the horses tethered to the shafts and realized that the place was already occupied.

'Otherwise it were me that was a goner!' he added with satisfaction.

'Might 'a been better so,' said another voice.

At which the fellow flew into a terrible rage:

'Why might it 'a been better so? Just coz I be poor and them's rich! Well, just look at 'em now!...'

And standing there shivering in his rags, soaked to the skin, filthy dirty, his beard matted and his long hair hanging down beneath his battered hat, he pointed to the two corpses with his crooked stick, and declared:

'We's are all equal when it come to this.'

But other peasants had arrived and stood watching shiftily, with a look in their eye that was at once uneasy, sly, horrified, selfish, and cowardly. Then they all discussed what to do; and it was decided that the bodies should be taken back to the two manors in the hope of a reward. So they hitched up two carts. But a new difficulty presented itself. Some wanted simply to put straw on the floor of the carts; others thought it more seemly to lay mattresses.

The woman who had already spoken shouted:

'But them mattresses'll get all covered in blood, and they'll 'ave to be washed in bleach.'

Then a stout farmer with a jovial face replied:

'But they'll pay for 'em. And the more it seems we've spent, the more they'll give us.' This argument carried the day.

And the two carts, perched high on springless wheels, set off at a trot, one to the right, the other to the left, jolting over the deep ruts in the road, shaking the remains of these two people who had once embraced and now would never meet again, and making them bounce up and down.

As soon as the Comte had seen the caravan rolling down the steep incline, he had fled the scene as fast as he could, tearing along through the wind and the rain. He ran like this for several hours, taking short cuts along the way, leaping over banks, pushing through gaps in the hedge, and he reached home at dusk without knowing quite how.

The servants were waiting for him, panic-stricken, with the news that the two horses had just returned riderless, Julien's having followed the other one.

On hearing this, Monsieur de Fourville staggered and said in a choked voice:

'They must have had some accident in this dreadful weather. Quick, everyone go and look for them.'

He set off again himself; but as soon as he was out of sight, he hid beneath some brambles, watching the road along which would return, dead or dying, perhaps crippled or disfigured for life, the woman he still loved with a savage passion.

And soon a cart passed by, bearing a strange-looking load.

It stopped outside the chateau, and then turned in. This was the one, yes, this was Her; but a terrible anguish rooted him to the spot, an awful dread of finding out, a horror of the truth; and he remained still, crouched like a hare, quivering at the slightest sound.

He waited for an hour, perhaps two. The cart did not come out again. He told himself how his wife was dying; and the thought of seeing her, of encountering her gaze, filled him with such horror that he was suddenly afraid of being discovered in his hiding-place and having to return home to witness this final agony; and so he raced off once more into the middle of the wood. Then all at once he reflected that perhaps she needed his help, that there was probably no one there to look after her; and he came running back, thoroughly distraught.

As he reached home, he met the gardener and shouted to him: 'Well?'

The man did not dare reply. So Monsieur de Fourville almost screamed:

'Is she dead?'

And the servant muttered:

'Yes, your lordship.'

He felt immense relief. A sudden calm flowed into his veins and through his aching muscles; and he walked resolutely up the grand flight of steps and into his house.

The other cart had reached Les Peuples. Jeanne caught sight of it in the distance, saw the mattress, guessed that a body was lying on it, and understood at once what had happened. The shock was so great that she collapsed unconscious.

When she came round, her father was holding her head and rubbing her temples with vinegar:

'Do you know...?' he asked hesitantly.

'Yes, father,' she murmured.

But when she tried to get up, she was unable to; she was in too much pain.

That same evening she gave birth to a stillborn child: a daughter.

She saw nothing of Julien's funeral; she knew nothing about it. She noticed only that one or two days later Aunt Lison had returned; and in the feverish nightmares which haunted her, she tried stubbornly to recall how long the old maid had been gone from Les Peuples, when she had left and in what circumstances. But she could not remember, even in her more lucid moments, and knew only that she had seen her after the death of Mama.

XI

She did not leave her bedroom for three months, and had become so weak and pale that people thought, indeed predicted, that her end was near. Then, little by little, her strength returned. Papa and Aunt Lison did not leave her again, having both taken up residence at Les Peuples. After the shock she had been left with some sort of nervous illness; the slightest noise made her feel faint, and she would lapse into long periods of unconsciousness from the most trivial of causes.

Never once had she asked for details of Julien's death. What did it matter to her? Didn't she know enough already? Everyone thought that it had been an accident, but she knew better; and though it tortured her, she kept the secret to herself: the fact of the adultery, and the vision of the Comte's sudden and terrible visit on the day of the tragedy.

And now her soul was filled with fond, bittersweet memories of the brief moments of joyful love her husband had once brought her. She was continually startled as things unexpectedly came back to her; and she saw Julien once more as he had been during the period of their engagement, and the Julien, too, whom she had loved during those few hours of sensual passion that had blossomed beneath the Corsican sun. Now, as they receded into the gathering distance of the sealed tomb, all his faults seemed less evident, all the cruelty vanished away, and even the infidelities became less stark. And Jeanne, overcome by a sort of posthumous gratitude for this man who had held her in his arms, forgave the past suffering so that she might remember only the moments of happiness. Then, with the passage of time, as month followed on month, the dust of oblivion gathered as in layers upon her recollections and her sorrows; and she devoted herself entirely to her son.

For the three persons now assembled round him he became an idol, the unique centre of their thoughts; and he ruled as a despot rules. A sort of jealousy began even to manifest itself between these three slaves of his, as Jeanne nervously observed the big kisses given to the Baron after the child had played at horse-riding on his knee. And Aunt Lison, neglected by him as she always had been by everyone else, and treated sometimes even like a maid by this young master who could as yet barely talk, would depart to her room to cry, as she compared the perfunctory kisses which she had to beg for and then very nearly did not receive with the hugs he reserved for his mother and grandfather.

Two peaceful, uneventful years elapsed, during which the child was the constant focus of attention. At the beginning of the third winter they decided to go and live in Rouen until the spring; and the whole family migrated. But on arriving in their former house, now damp and deserted, Paul contracted bronchitis so severely that it was thought it might develop into pleurisy; and his three distraught relatives decided that he evidently needed the air at Les Peuples. They took him back there as soon as he had recovered.

There then followed a succession of agreeable years, each one like the last.

Always gathered round the little one, whether in his bedroom or in the drawing-room or in the garden, they went into ecstasies at his first words, at the funny expressions on his face, at his gestures.

His mother affectionately called him Paulie, but he could not say the word properly and pronounced it 'Pullie', which caused endless laughter. The nickname 'Pullie' stuck.* He was never called anything else.

As he was growing rapidly, one of the favourite occupations of his three relatives (the Baron called them his 'three mothers') was to measure his height.

On the door-frame leading into the drawing-room they had cut a series of little notches with a penknife which recorded his growth month by month. This measuring device, christened the 'Pullie scale', assumed considerable importance in everyone's life.

Then a new individual began to play a significant role as a member of the family—namely Slaughter the dog, whom Jeanne had neglected in her exclusive devotion to her son. Ludivine fed him. He slept in an old barrel outside the stable, where he lived a lonely life forever tethered to a chain.

Paul noticed him one morning and began to scream and shout that he wanted to give him a hug. They led him over to the dog with great misgivings. But the dog was delighted to see the child, and barked when they tried to part them. So Slaughter was let off his chain and installed in the house.

He followed Paul everywhere, a companion for every moment of his life. They rolled about on the floor together and went to sleep side by side on the carpet. And soon Slaughter had made his friend's bed his own, since Paul now refused to leave him. From time to time Jeanne worried about the fleas; and Aunt Lison resented the fact that the dog had come to occupy such a large place in the child's affection, affection which the animal had stolen, she felt, and which she would so much have liked for herself.

Occasional visits were exchanged with the Brisevilles and the Courteliers. Only the mayor and the doctor regularly disturbed the solitude of the old house. Since the murder of the dog and the suspicions which Jeanne had entertained about the priest at the time of the dreadful deaths of Julien and the Comtesse, she had ceased going to church, vexed with a God who could have such ministers.

From time to time the Abbé Tolbiac would denounce the chateau in unambiguous terms as a place haunted by the Spirit of Evil, the Spirit of Eternal Revolt, the Spirit of Error and Falsehood, the Spirit of Iniquity, and the Spirit of Corruption and Impurity. He meant the Baron.

His church in any case was deserted; and when he walked along the edge of the fields where the ploughmen were pushing their plough, the peasants did not stop to speak to him or even turn round to say hello. Moreover he was considered a sorcerer, because he had exorcized a woman possessed by the devil. He knew mysterious words, it was said, that could break spells, which, according to him, were just Satan's little jokes. By means of a laying on of hands he treated cows who gave blue milk or had curly tails, and after a few unintelligible words from him lost objects would suddenly turn up again.

His narrow, fanatical mind was passionately interested in the study of religious books about the history of the Devil's apparitions on earth, the different manifestations of his power, his diverse occult influences, the various resources at his disposal, and the techniques he usually employed in the performance of his cunning tricks. And as he believed that his particular calling was to combat this mysterious and fateful Power, he had learned off by heart all the formulae for exorcism contained in the ecclesiastical manuals.

He was always imagining that he could sense the Evil One roaming abroad in the shadow of darkness; and the Latin phrase —'Sicut leo rugiens circuit quaerens quem devoret'*—was never far from his lips.

Whereupon fear began to spread through the district, terror at his hidden powers. And even his colleagues—ignorant country priests of the kind for whom Beelzebub is an article of faith and who are so troubled by the minutely prescribed rituals to be observed in the event of any manifestation of this power of evil that they end up mistaking religion for magic—they, too, considered the Abbé Tolbiac to be something of a sorcerer; and they respected him as much for the obscure power which they supposed him to possess as for the unimpeachable austerity with which he governed his life.

Whenever he met Jeanne, he refused to acknowledge her.

This situation worried and upset Aunt Lison, who, in her timid, old maid's soul, could not understand people not going to church. For presumably she was pious, and presumably she went to confession and took communion; though nobody knew for certain, or sought to know.

When she found herself on her own and all alone with Paul, she would talk to him, very quietly, about God. He would listen more or less in silence when she told him the miracle stories of the early days of creation; but when she told him that he had to love God very, very much, he would occasionally respond: 'But where is he, Auntie?' Then she would point towards the sky: 'Up there, Pullie, but you mustn't say anything.' She was afraid of the Baron.

But one day Pullie told her:

'God is everywhere but he's not in the church.'

He had spoken to his grandfather about his aunt's mysterious revelations.

The child was nearly ten; his mother looked forty. He was strong, boisterous, bold enough to climb trees, but he knew very little. His lessons bored him, and he would interrupt them at the drop of a hat. And every time the Baron kept him reading a book a little longer than usual, Jeanne would appear immediately and say:

'Do let him go and play now. You mustn't tire him out, he's still so young.'

In her eyes he was still no more than six months or a year old. She had scarcely taken in the fact that he could now walk, run, talk, just like a little person! And she lived in constant fear that he might fall, or that he was cold, or too hot from running around, that he was eating too much for the size of his stomach, or else not enough if he was to grow properly.

When he was twelve, a major difficulty arose: the question of his first communion.

Lise came to Jeanne one morning and pointed out that the boy could not continue for much longer without receiving instruction and carrying out his first duties. She presented her case from every angle and gave a thousand reasons in support of it, above all what the people they knew would say. Jeanne, at a loss and uncertain what to do, hesitated to say yes, maintaining that they could leave things a little longer.

But a month later, as she was returning one of the Vicomtesse de Briseville's visits, the lady happened to enquire:

'I suppose your Paul will be making his first communion this year, will he?'

And Jeanne, taken off guard, replied:

'Yes, Madame.'

This simple answer decided her, and without saying a word to her father, she asked Lise to take the child to catechism classes.

For a month all went well; but one evening Paul returned home with a sore throat. And next day he was coughing. His anxious mother questioned him, and she discovered that the priest had ordered him to go and wait in the draughty porch outside the church door until the lesson was over, because he had misbehaved.

So she stopped him going and taught him this alphabet of religion herself. But in spite of Lison's entreaties the Abbé Tolbiac refused to accept him as one of the communicants, on the ground that he had been inadequately prepared.

It was the same the following year. Then the Baron, infuriated, swore that the child had no need to believe all this nonsense, all this infantile symbolism of transsubstantiation, just to be a decent human being; and it was decided that he would be brought up as a Christian, but not as a practising Catholic, and that when he reached the age of majority he would be free to choose for himself.

And when Jeanne made a visit to the Brisevilles some time later, this visit was not returned. She was surprised, knowing how meticulously polite her neighbours were; but the Marquise haughtily informed her of the reason for their omission.

On account of her husband's position, which derived both from his well-established title and from his considerable fortune, the Marquise regarded herself as a sort of queen among the Norman nobility, and she reigned accordingly, expressing her opinions freely, gracious or cutting as the occasion demanded, admonishing, rebuking, or congratulating as she saw fit. Jeanne having therefore presented herself at her home, this lady began with a few icy remarks and then declared tersely:

'Society is divided into two classes: those who believe in God, and those who do not. The former, even the humblest among them, are our friends, our equals; as for the latter, they simply do not exist in our eyes.'

Jeanne, alive to the implied criticism, retorted:

'But can one not believe in God without going to church?'

The Marquise replied:

'No, Madame. The faithful go and pray to God in His church just as one goes to visit people in their houses.'

Conscious of the slight, Jeanne continued:

'God is everywhere, Madame. For my part, as one who believes in His goodness with all my heart, I no longer feel His presence when certain priests come between us.'

The Marquise rose to her feet:

'The priest carries the church's banner, Madame. Whoever chooses not to follow this banner is against him, and against us.'

Jeanne had risen in her turn, shaking:

'You believe in the God of one party, Madame. I believe in the God of decent human beings.'

She bowed and left the room.

The peasants, too, privately blamed her for not having had Pullie make his first communion. They were not regular church-goers, did not take the sacraments, or else received them only at Easter in deference to the strict rules of the Church; but it was a different matter for the little ones; and none of them would have had the audacity to bring up a child outside this common law, because Religion is Religion.

She was well aware of this disapproval, and in her soul she felt indignant at all these accommodations and squaring of con-sciences, this universal timidity, this great cowardice lurking deep down in everyone's heart and dressed in the mask of respect-ability whenever it showed itself to the light.

The Baron oversaw Paul's education, and started him off learning Latin. The child's mother had only one piece of advice: 'Whatever you do, don't tire him out;' and she would hover anx-iously outside the bedroom door during lesson times, Papa having forbidden her to enter because she kept interrupting his lessons with questions like: 'Are your feet warm enough, Pullie?', or 'Are you sure you haven't got a headache, Pullie?', or else, to stop the teacher: 'Don't make him talk so much, you'll strain his throat.'

As soon as the boy was free, he would come down to help his mother and aunt in the garden. They had developed a passion for gardening; and they would all three plant saplings in the spring, and sow seeds and eagerly watch them germinate and grow, and prune branches, and cut flowers to make bouquets.

The young lad was particularly interested in growing different varieties of salad leaf. He was in charge of four large squares in the kitchen garden where, with the utmost care, he grew cabbage-lettuce, cos lettuce, royal lettuce, chicory, endive, succory, in fact every known variety of edible leaf. He would dig, and water, and hoe, and prick out, assisted by his two 'mothers' whom he kept to the task as though they were hired hands. They were to be seen kneeling in the plant-beds for hours on end, getting dirt on their dresses, their hands busy inserting the roots of young plants into the holes they made by pushing a single finger straight down into the soil.

Pullie was growing tall, and had almost reached the age of fifteen; and the scale in the drawing-room showed one metre, fifty-eight; but mentally he was still a child, ignorant and foolish, smothered between these two petticoats and this kind old man who belonged to another era.

Eventually one evening the Baron talked of sending him to school; and immediately Jeanne burst into tears. Aunt Lison, aghast, sat quietly in a dark corner of the room.

The boy's mother replied:

'What does he want with all that knowledge? We'll make him a man of the soil, a country gentleman. He can cultivate his estates, the way lots of noblemen do. He can live and grow old happily here in this house where we have lived and where we shall die. What more could one want?'

But the Baron shook his head:

'What will you say when he comes to you at the age of twenty-five and says: "I'm nobody, I know nothing, and all because of you, because of your selfishness as a mother. I don't feel equipped to work, to become someone, and yet I wasn't meant for this thoroughly dreary life of humble obscurity to which your thoughtless affection has condemned me."'

She was still crying, and appealing to her son:

'Tell me, Pullie, tell me you won't ever reproach me for loving you too much. You won't, will you?'

And the tall lad looked surprised, and promised:

'No, Mother.'

'You swear?'

'Yes, Mother.'

'You do want to stay here, don't you?'

'Yes, Mother.'

Then the Baron said in a firm, loud voice:

'Jeanne, you have no right to decide his life for him. What you're doing is cowardly, almost criminal. You're sacrificing your child to your own personal happiness.'

She hid her face in her hands, her sobs coming in rapid succession, and she stammered through her tears:

'I've been so unhappy... so unhappy! And now that life is peaceful, here with him, he is to be taken away from me... What will become of me... all alone... from now on?'

Her father got up, came and sat beside her, and took her in his arms:

'And what about me, Jeanne?'

She suddenly flung her arms round his neck and embraced him wildly. Then, still choking with tears, she managed to say in a strangled voice:

'Yes, you're right... Perhaps you're right... Papa. It was silly of me, but I have suffered so much. Yes, of course, let him go to school.'

And Paul, not quite understanding what was going to happen to him, began to cry also.

Then his three 'mothers' embraced him, cajoling him and trying to cheer him up. And when they all went up to bed, they each had a heavy heart and cried into their pillows, even the Baron, who had been hiding his feelings.

It was decided to send the boy to the college in Le Havre at the beginning of the coming school year; and throughout the summer he was spoiled even more than he had been before.

His mother's heart sank repeatedly at the prospect of their separation. She assembled what he would need as if he were departing on a voyage that was to last ten years. Then one morning in October, after a sleepless night, the two women and the Baron boarded the carriage with him, and the two horses set off at the trot.

On a previous visit they had already chosen his place in the dormitory and where he would sit in the classroom. Jeanne, with

Aunt Lison's assistance, spent the whole day unpacking his clothes and arranging them in the small chest of drawers. Since it was not big enough to hold even a quarter of what they had brought, she went to find the headmaster to ask him for a second. The bursar was summoned; he pointed out that such a quantity of linen and personal effects would never all be used and would simply serve to get in the way; and he refused to allocate another chest of drawers on the grounds that it was against the rules. Mother was heartbroken, and decided thereupon to rent a room in a small hotel nearby, instructing the proprietor to take Pullie whatever he needed as soon as the child asked for it.

Then they went for a walk along the quayside to watch the ships passing in and out of the harbour.

This sad day was drawing to a close, and dusk fell on the town, which was gradually lighting up. They went to a restaurant for dinner. None of them was hungry; and they looked at each other with moist eyes as dish after dish was placed before them and went back almost untouched.

Then they set off slowly to return to the college. Children of all ages were arriving from every direction, brought by their families or by servants. Many were crying. The sound of weeping could be heard all over the dimly lit courtyard.

Jeanne and Pullie held each other in a long embrace. Aunt Lison stayed in the background, completely forgotten, her face buried in a handkerchief. But the Baron, who was becoming upset, cut short the farewells and dragged his daughter away. The carriage was waiting by the gate; the three of them climbed in and drove back through the night to Les Peuples.

From time to time a loud sob echoed in the darkness.

The following day Jeanne wept until evening. On the day after that she ordered the phaeton and set off for Le Havre. Pullie seemed to have got over their parting. For the first time in his life he had friends of his own age; and the desire to go and play made him fidget as he sat in the visitors' parlour.

Jeanne returned like this every other day, and on Sunday for the exeats. Not knowing what to do between break-times, during the lessons, she would remain sitting in the parlour, having neither the strength nor the courage to leave the school. The headmaster asked to see her and requested that she visit less frequently. She ignored the suggestion.

He then informed her that if she continued to prevent her son from playing during the recreation periods and from working without her constant interruptions, they would be forced to send him back home to her; and the Baron was informed accordingly in writing. So she remained at Les Peuples, under detention as though she were a prisoner.

She waited for the holidays even more anxiously than her son.

And her soul was filled with constant worry. She began to roam around the countryside, spending whole days on solitary walks with Slaughter the dog, absently dreaming. Sometimes she would remain sitting all afternoon gazing out to sea from the top of a cliff; sometimes she would go down to Yport through the wood, retracing the steps of former walks the memory of which still haunted her. What a long, long time ago that was, when as a young girl she used to wander round this same countryside, intoxicated by her dreams.

On each occasion that she saw her son again, it was as though they had not met for ten years. With each month that passed he was turning into a man; and with each month that passed she was becoming an old woman. Her father seemed more like her brother now; and Aunt Lison, who seemed not to age, having lost the bloom of youth when she was twenty-five, looked more like an elder sister.

Pullie hardly did any work; he had to stay down for a year in the third form. Somehow he got through the fourth form, but he had to do another year in the fifth; and he was still only in the lower sixth by the time he had reached the age of twenty.

He had grown into a tall, fair-haired boy, with sideburns that were already bushy and the beginnings of a moustache. It was now he who would make the journey to Les Peuples every Sunday. Since he had been taking riding lessons for some time, he simply hired a horse and rode home in two hours.

In the morning Jeanne would set out to meet him, accompanied by her aunt and the Baron, who was now becoming more and more stooped and walked along like a little old man, his hands clasped behind his back as though to prevent himself pitching forward onto his nose.

They would walk slowly along the road, occasionally sitting down by the roadside and peering into the distance to see if they could catch sight of the rider yet. As soon as he appeared like a black dot on the white line of the road, the three of them would wave their handkerchiefs; and he would put his horse to the gallop and arrive like a hurricane, which left Jeanne and Lison with their hearts in their mouths but delighted his grandfather, who would cry 'Bravo' with the enthusiasm of one whose riding days were over.

Although Paul was a head taller than his mother, she always treated him like a small boy and still asked him 'Are your feet warm enough, Pullie?'; and when he went for a walk at the bottom of the front steps after lunch, to smoke a cigarette, she would open the window and shout:

'Please, you really must not go out without something on your head. You'll catch your death of cold.'

And she worried terribly when he set off to ride back after dark:

'Whatever you do, don't go too fast, my dear little Pullie. You will be careful, won't you? Think of your poor mother, how miserable she would be if anything happened to you.'

But then, one Saturday morning, she received a letter from Paul announcing that he would not be coming home the next day because some friends had arranged an outing to which he was invited.

She was beside herself with anxiety throughout the whole of Sunday, as though some disaster threatened; and by Thursday she could bear it no longer, and set off for Le Havre.

He looked different to her, without her being able to explain quite why. He seemed excited, and spoke in a more manly voice. And all of a sudden he said to her, as if it were the most natural thing in the world:

'You know, Mother, since you've come to see me today, I think I shan't come home again next Sunday, because we're planning another outing.'

She was completely taken aback, dumbstruck, as though as he had announced that he was leaving for the New World. Then, when at last she could speak, she said:

'Oh, Pullie, what is it? Tell me, what's going on?'

He began to laugh and gave her a kiss:

'But absolutely nothing's going on, Mother. I'm just going to have fun with some friends. People of my age do that sort of thing.'

She could think of no reply, and when she was alone in the carriage once more, some singular thoughts occurred to her. She had not recognized her Pullie, her little Pullie of old. For the first time she realized that he was grown up, that he no longer belonged to her, that he was going to start living his own life without worrying about his elders. It seemed to her that he had changed overnight. Was this her son, the same dear little child who had once had her pricking out lettuces, this grown man with a beard and, increasingly it seemed, a life of his own?

And for the next three months Paul came home to see his family only on rare occasions; he was always clearly eager to be off again as soon as he could, and each evening he tried to leave an hour earlier. Jeanne was becoming alarmed, and the Baron kept endeavouring to comfort her:

'Let him be. The boy's twenty now.'

But one morning a rather shabbily dressed old man called and asked in German-sounding French for 'Matame la Vicomtesh.'

After much bowing and scraping he took a dirty wallet from his pocket and said: 'I hab a leetle beet of paper for you;' and he unfolded a sheet of greasy paper and handed it to her.

She read it once, read it twice, looked at the Jew, read it a third time, and then asked:

'What does this mean?'

The man explained obsequiously:

'I vill tell you. Your son is habing need of a leetle money, and since I am knowing zat you are a good movver to heem, I lend heem a leetle zumzing to help heem.'

She was shaking.

'But why did he not ask me himself?'

The Jew explained at length that it was a matter of a gambling debt which had to be paid by noon the next day; that since Paul had not yet reached the age of majority, no one else would have made him a loan; and that his 'honour vould hab been compromised' without the 'leetle favour' that he had done the young man.

Jeanne wanted to summon the Baron, but she was so numb with shock that she was unable to get up. Eventually she said to the moneylender:

'Would you be so kind as to ring the bell for me?'

He hesitated, fearing a trick, and mumbled:

'If I deesturb you, I komm back anover day.'

She shook her head. He rang the bell; and they waited, in silence, the one facing the other.

When the Baron arrived, he saw the situation at once. The note was for fifteen hundred francs. He paid him a thousand and said, looking him straight in the eye:

'And don't come back.'

The man thanked him, bid them good-day, and disappeared.

Mother and Grandfather set off at once for Le Havre; but on arriving at the school, they were told that Paul had not been there for the past month. The headmaster had received four letters signed by Jeanne saying that his pupil was ill and subsequently giving news of his progress. Each letter had been accompanied by a medical certificate—all forgeries, of course. They were flabbergasted, and sat there staring at each other.

The headmaster, having expressed his regrets, escorted them to the police station. They spent the night at a hotel.

The next day the young man was found lodging in the town with a kept woman. His mother and grandfather took him back to Les Peuples, and not one word was exchanged throughout the journey. Jeanne wept, her face hidden in her handkerchief; while Paul looked out of the window with an air of indifference.

During the following week it was discovered that over the past three months he had run up debts amounting to fifteen thousand francs. The creditors had not come forward at once, knowing that he would soon be of age.

There were no angry scenes. They wanted to win him over by kindness. They gave him special dishes to eat, they pampered him, they spoilt him. This was in the spring: they hired a boat at Yport, despite Jeanne's terrified misgivings, so that he could go sailing as he pleased.

They did not allow him to have a horse in case he should ride to Le Havre.

He lived an aimless existence, and was irritable, sometimes even rude. The Baron was concerned at his unfinished studies. Jeanne, appalled at the thought of a separation, did nevertheless wonder what they were to do with him.

One evening he failed to return home. They learnt that he had gone out in a boat with two sailors. His distraught mother rushed down to Yport in the dark, not even stopping to put her hat on.

A few men were waiting on the beach for the craft to return.

A small light appeared out at sea; it was coming nearer, swaying to and fro. Paul was no longer on board. He must have had himself taken to Le Havre.

The police searched for him, but in vain. The girl who had hidden him the first time had also disappeared, without trace, having sold her furniture and paid her rent. In Paul's room at Les Peuples they discovered two letters from this creature, who seemed to be madly in love with him. She talked about travelling to England, having raised the necessary funds.

And for the three inhabitants of the chateau life went on in sombre silence, a gloomy hell of mental torment. Jeanne's hair, already grey, had now turned white. She wondered innocently why fate continued to strike at her in this manner.

She received a letter from the Abbé Tolbiac:

'Madame, God has laid His hand upon you. You refused Him your son; now He has taken him from you and cast him into the arms of a prostitute. Will this lesson from on high not open your eyes? The Lord is infinite in His mercy. Perhaps He will pardon you if you return and kneel before Him. I am His humble servant: knock and it shall be opened unto you.'

She sat for a long time with this letter on her lap. Perhaps what the priest said was true. And every possible religious uncertainty began to gnaw at her conscience. Could God be vindictive and jealous like men? But if He didn't show Himself to be jealous, no one would fear Him, no one would worship Him any more. That we might know Him better, presumably, He chose to manifest himself to human beings in terms of human feelings. And her soul having filled with the craven doubt that sends the troubled in heart and those of little faith scurrying off to church, she hurried secretly to the presbytery one evening at dusk and knelt at the feet of the gaunt Abbé to beg for absolution.

He promised her half a pardon, God being unable to lavish all His grace upon a house which continued to harbour a man like the Baron.

'You will soon', he assured her, 'know the effects of His Divine Compassion.'

And indeed, two days later she received a letter from her son; and in her panic and distress she regarded it as the first stage in the relief which the Abbé had promised.

'My dear Mama, do not worry about me. I am in London, in good health, but I have great need of money. We haven't a penny left, and some days we have nothing to eat. My companion, whom I love with all my soul, has spent everything she had so as not to leave me: five thousand francs; and, as you will understand, I have given my word of honour that she shall first be reimbursed this sum. It would be very kind if you would advance me fifteen thousand francs of the money left to me by Papa, since I shall soon be of age. You would be assisting me out of a very difficult situation.

Adieu, my dear Mama, I embrace you with all my heart, as I do Grandfather and Aunt Lison. I hope to see you again soon.

Your son,
Viscount Paul de Lamare'

He had written to her! So he had not forgotten her. She did not give a thought to the fact that he was asking for money. If he had none, they would send him some. What did money matter! He had written to her!

And she rushed off in tears to show the letter to the Baron. Aunt Lison was summoned; and word by word they went over it again, discussing every syllable of this piece of paper that had brought them news of him.

Jeanne, having gone in an instant from being in a state of complete despair to being almost intoxicated with hope, defended Paul:

'He'll come back. He's written to us, and that means he'll come back.'

The Baron, more composed, declared:

'That's immaterial. He's left us for this creature. Clearly he loves her more than us, since he didn't hesitate to go.'

Jeanne felt a sudden, terrible pang in her heart, and all at once she was filled with burning hatred against this mistress who was stealing her son from her; a savage, unswerving hatred, the hatred of a jealous mother. Until then her thoughts had been only for Paul. It had scarcely occurred to her that some strange woman or other was the cause of his misdemeanours. But suddenly the Baron's remark had called this rival to mind and revealed her fatal power; and she sensed that a fierce struggle was now beginning between this woman and her, and felt too that she would rather lose her son than share him with this other person.

And all her joy vanished.

They sent the fifteen thousand francs and heard nothing further for five months.

Then one day a lawyer called to discuss the details of Julien's will. Jeanne and the Baron accepted his proposed figures without discussion, even forgoing the life interest in the estate which was due to the mother. And when he returned to Paris, Paul came into one hundred and twenty thousand francs. After that he wrote to them four times in six months, providing terse news of himself and ending in perfunctory protestations of affection: 'I'm working now,' he assured them; 'I have found a position on the Bourse. I hope, my dear family, to be able to come and see you some day at Les Peuples.'

He said not a word about his mistress; and this silence meant more than if he had written whole pages about her. In these cold letters Jeanne could sense the woman lying in ambush, implacably, the eternal enemy of mothers, the harlot.

The three lonely people debated what they could do to save Paul; and they could think of nothing. A journey to Paris? What for?

'We must let his passion burn itself out,' the Baron would say. 'He'll come back to us of his own accord.'

And life was wretched.

Jeanne and Lison went to church together, concealing the fact from the Baron.

A quite considerable time elapsed without further news, and then one morning a desperate letter struck terror into their hearts:

'My poor Mama, I am ruined. I may as well blow my brains out if you do not come to my rescue. An investment which had every chance of success has just failed; and I owe 85,000 francs. I shall be disgraced if I do not pay up, bankrupted, and barred from all further dealing. I am ruined. I tell you again, I shall blow my brains out rather than live with the shame of it. I should probably have done so already without the support of a woman of whom I never speak and yet who is my guardian angel.

I embrace you, my dear Mama, from the bottom of my heart; and perhaps for the last time. Farewell.

Paul'

Some bundles of paper enclosed with the letter gave detailed explanations of how the disaster had come about.

The Baron replied by return that they were considering how best to proceed. Then he left for Le Havre to see what could be done; and he mortgaged some land in order to realize the money, which was sent to Paul.

The young man replied with three letters of effusive gratitude and fondest affection, announcing that he would come immediately to embrace his dear family.

He did not come.

A whole year went by.

Jeanne and the Baron were on the point of leaving for Paris to try and find him and make one last effort to save him when he sent a brief message to say that he was once more in London,

setting up a steamship company called: 'Paul Delamare and Co.'
He wrote:

'I stand to make money out of this, perhaps a great deal of money. And
there is no risk attached. You will see at once what a wonderful
opportunity it is. When we meet again, I shall have a fine position in
the world. There is only one thing for it these days: business!'

Three months later the steamship company had gone into
receivership, and its managing director was being pursued for
irregularities in the accounts. Jeanne had an attack of nerves
which lasted several hours; then she took to her bed.

The Baron went back to Le Havre, sought information,
consulted barristers, solicitors, commercial lawyers, bailiffs, and
established that the Delamare Company owed two hundred and
thirty-five thousand francs; and once more he borrowed on his
estates. The chateau at Les Peuples and the two adjacent farms
were mortgaged for an enormous sum.

One evening, as he was sorting out the final formalities in a
lawyer's office, he collapsed on the floor in a fit of apoplexy.

Jeanne was informed by dispatch rider. When she arrived, he
was dead.

She brought the body back to Les Peuples, so numb with grief
that her sorrow was more like paralysis than despair.

The Abbé Tolbiac refused to allow the body into his church,
despite the desperate entreaties of the two women. The Baron
was buried at nightfall, with no ceremony whatsoever.

Paul heard of what had happened from one of the receivers. He
was still in hiding in England. He wrote to apologize for not
having come, having learnt too late of the unhappy event.
'Besides, now that you have got me out of my difficulties, my dear
Mama, I shall be returning to France, and soon I shall be there to
embrace you in person.'

Jeanne was now living in a state of such mental collapse that
she did not seem to take anything in any more.

And towards the end of the winter Aunt Lison, now sixty-eight,
developed bronchitis which turned into pneumonia; and she died
peacefully, murmuring:

'My poor little Jeanne. I shall ask God to have mercy on you.'

Jeanne followed her to the cemetery, saw the earth falling on her coffin, and was on the point of sinking to the ground, wishing in her heart that she, too, could die, could cease to suffer, could cease to think, when a robust peasant woman caught her in her arms and carried her home like a small child.

On her return to the chateau Jeanne, who had spent the previous five nights at the old maid's bedside, allowed herself to be put to bed by this unknown rustic who handled her with gentleness and authority; and she fell at once into a deep sleep, overcome by exhaustion and grief.

She woke up in the middle of the night. There was a night-light burning on the mantelpiece. A woman was asleep in the armchair. But who was this woman? She did not recognize her, and she leaned out of bed trying to study her face in the flickering light of the wick floating in oil in a kitchen glass.

She felt as though she had seen this face before. But when? And where? The woman was sleeping peacefully, her head to one side, her bonnet on the floor. She was perhaps forty, forty-five. She had a strong, powerful build, with square shoulders and a high complexion. Her large hands hung down on either side of the chair. Her hair was turning grey. Jeanne stared at her fixedly, her mind in that confused state which follows on waking from the feverish sleep induced by great misfortune.

Certainly she had seen this face before! Long ago? More recently? She could not tell, and her obstinate desire to find out began to make her agitated and cross. Quietly she got out of bed to take a closer look at the sleeping figure, and tiptoed over to her. It was the woman who had picked her up in the cemetery and subsequently put her to bed. That much she could vaguely remember.

But had she met her somewhere else, at some other period in her life? Or else did she think she recognized her simply because of her dim recollection of the previous day? And then how did she come to be here, in her bedroom? And why?

The woman opened an eye, saw Jeanne looking at her, and shot up out of the chair. They found themselves standing face to face, their chests lightly touching.

'What are you doing out of bed?' the stranger scolded. 'You'll catch your death at this time of night. You just get back into bed.'

'Who are you?' asked Jeanne.

But the woman threw her arms wide, seized hold of her, picked her up once again, and carried her back to the bed with the strength of a man. And as she laid her gently between the sheets, bending over her, almost lying on top of her, she burst into tears and began to kiss her wildly on the cheeks, on the hair, on the eyes, wetting her face with her tears and stammering:

'My poor mistress, mamz'elle Jeanne, my poor mistress, don't you even recognize me?' And Jeanne exclaimed: 'Rosalie! My maid!'; and throwing her arms round her neck, she hugged her and kissed her; and they were both sobbing, holding each other in a tight embrace, mingling their tears, unable to let go of each other.

Rosalie was the first to recover herself.

'Come now, you must be sensible,' she said, 'or you'll catch cold.'

And she picked up the blankets, remade the bed, and replaced the pillow under the head of her former mistress who was continuing to sob, stirred by all the old memories which had come flooding back.

Eventually she asked:

'But my poor Rosalie, what are you doing back here?'

'Bless me,' Rosalie replied, 'as if I was just going to leave you here, now that you're all on your own.'

'Light a candle,' Jeanne said, 'and let me get a proper look at you.'

And when the light had been brought to the bedside table, they looked at each other for a long time without saying a word. Then Jeanne stretched out a hand towards her former maid and said softly:

'I should never have recognized you, my dear. You have changed a lot, you know. But even so, not as much as I have.'

And Rosalie gazed at the gaunt, faded features of this white-haired woman whom she had last seen young, beautiful, and fresh-cheeked, and replied:

'Yes, it's true, Madame Jeanne, you have changed, and more than you ought. But you know, it's twenty-four years since we last saw each other.'

They fell silent, once more reflecting. Finally Jeanne muttered:

'Have you been happy at least?'

And Rosalie, hesitating for fear of stirring some memory that might be too painful, answered falteringly:

'Oh... yes, Madame... yes. I can't complain... I've been happier than you... that's for sure. But if there's one thing I've always regretted, it's not having stayed on here...'

Then she stopped abruptly, distressed at having made this unintentional allusion.

But Jeanne went on gently:

'But there you are, my dear, one can't always do as one wishes. You're widowed now, aren't you?'

Then, as her voice shook with anguish, she continued:

'Did you... have more children?'

'No, Madame.'

'And him, your... your son... How's he getting on? Are you pleased with the way he's turned out?'

'Yes, Madame, he's a good lad, and a hard worker. He got married six months ago, and he's going to take over my farm now, what with me being back here with you.'

Jeanne, trembling with emotion, murmured:

'Then you won't leave me again, Rosalie?'

And Rosalie replied brusquely:

'Certainly not, Madame, seeing as how I've made my arrangements so.'

Then they fell silent for a while.

Despite herself Jeanne began to compare their two lives, but without any bitterness in her heart, resigned now to the cruel injustice of fate. She said:

'And how did your husband treat you?'

'Oh, he was a good sort, Madame, and no idler neither, he did well for himself. He died of pneumonia.'

Then Jeanne sat up in bed, eager to hear it all, and said:

'Come, my dear, tell me everything, your whole life. It will do me good, now.' And Rosalie brought up a chair, sat down, and began to talk about herself, her home, the world she lived in, going into minute detail the way country folk like to, describing her farmyard, sometimes laughing at things long past which recalled happy moments, gradually raising her voice in the manner of a farmer's wife accustomed to giving orders. She ended by saying:

'Yes, I have my place in the sun today all right. I have no need to worry.'

Then she became embarrassed and continued more quietly:

'But I owe it all to you. So I don't want any wages, you know. Oh, no! Certainly not! And if you don't agree, I shall be on my way.'

'But you're not going to be my servant for nothing?' Jeanne objected.

'But of course I am, Madame! Money! You give me money?! But I've got almost as much as you. Have you any idea how much you've got left, after all your messing about with mortgages and loans, and all that unpaid interest piling up each time it's due? Have you? You haven't, have you? Well, I can promise you, you've got no more than ten thousand a year coming in now. Less than ten thousand, do you hear me? But I'll sort all that out for you, in no time at all.'

She had begun to raise her voice again, angry and indignant at the interest which had not been paid and the threat of ruin. And as the shadow of an affectionate smile passed across her mistress's face, she shouted crossly:

'It's no laughing matter, Madame, because without money we're all just ignorant country folk.'

Jeanne grasped her hands once more and held them in hers; and, still pursued by the thought that obsessed her, she said slowly:

'As for me, well, I just haven't had any luck. Everything's turned out badly. Fate has had it in for me.'

But Rosalie shook her head:

'You mustn't say that, Madame, you mustn't say that. You married badly, that's all. And that's no way to get married either, not even knowing what one's intended is like.'

And they both continued to talk about themselves in this way as if they were old friends.

The sun rose, and still they talked.

XII

Within the space of a week Rosalie had taken complete control of every thing and every person in the house. Jeanne obeyed in meek resignation. Frail and dragging her feet now as Mama used to, she went outside supported on the arm of her maid, who would take her for gentle walks, variously lecturing her or comforting her with rough, affectionate words, and treating her like a sick child.

They were always talking about the past, Jeanne with a catch in her voice, Rosalie in the even tone of the imperturbable peasant. The old servant returned several times to the matter of the unpaid interest. Then she insisted on seeing the papers which Jeanne, who was totally ignorant of business matters, kept hidden from her out of shame for her son.

After that Rosalie spent an entire week travelling to Fécamp each day to have things explained to her by a notary she knew.

Then one evening, having helped her mistress retire for the night, she sat down by the bedside, and said brusquely:

'Now that you're in bed, Madame, we must talk.'

And she outlined the present position.

When everything had been settled, there would be somewhere between seven and eight thousand a year in income. No more.

'But what of it, Rosalie?' Jeanne replied. 'I know I shan't live very long. I shall always have enough to get by.'

But Rosalie grew angry:

'In your case, Madame, quite possibly. But what about Monsieur Paul? Don't you want to leave him anything?'

Jeanne shuddered.

'I beg you, never mention his name to me. It's all too painful to think about.'

'On the contrary, I shall mention his name, Madame, because what you're doing is just not right, you know. Yes, he does some stupid things, but not all the things he does will be stupid; and then he'll be getting married one day, he'll have children of his own. He'll need money to bring them up. Listen to me now. You're going to sell Les Peuples!...'

Jeanne sat up in bed with a start:

'Sell Les Peuples! How can you think of such a thing? Oh, no, never!'

But Rosalie was unmoved:

'I tell you, you're going to sell Les Peuples. You have to.'

And she explained her calculations, her plans, how she saw things.

Once Les Peuples and the two dependent farms had been sold (she had found a buyer) they would retain four farms at Saint-Léonard, which, once unmortgaged, would bring in eight thousand three hundred francs a year. They would set aside thirteen hundred a year for repairs and the upkeep of the properties, which would leave seven thousand, of which they would spend five thousand on the year's expenses. They would put two thousand aside to build up a reserve for emergencies.

She added:

'Everything else has been squandered, it's all gone. And I shall have the key, you understand. As for Monsieur Paul, he shall have nothing, absolutely nothing. He would take it all if he could, down to your last penny.'

Jeanne, who was weeping in silence, muttered:

'But what if he hasn't even enough to feed himself?'

'Well, he can come and eat with us then, if he's hungry. There'll always be a bed and something cooking in the pot for him. Do you think he would have done all the stupid things he has done if you hadn't given him a penny at the beginning?'

'But he had debts, he would have been disgraced.'

'But when you've nothing left, will that stop him getting into further debt? You paid them, all well and good; but you won't pay any more. I mean it. And now, good night, Madame.'

And off she went.

Jeanne could not sleep, deeply upset at the thought of selling Les Peuples and going away, of leaving this house in which her whole life was bound up.

When she saw Rosalie enter her room the next morning, she told her:

'My poor Rosalie, I shall never bring myself to leave this house.' But the maid grew angry:

'But that's how it's got to be, Madame. The notary will be here shortly with the person who wants to buy it. If you don't do this, in four years you won't have a button to your name.'

Jeanne lay there in a daze and kept saying:

'I can't do it, I could never do it.'

An hour later the postman brought her a letter from Paul, who was asking for a further ten thousand francs. What should she do? At a loss, she consulted Rosalie, who threw up her arms:

'What did I tell you, Madame? Oh, you'd have been in a fine pickle, the pair of you, if I hadn't come back!'

So Jeanne, bowing to her maid's will, wrote back to the young man:

'My dear son, I can do nothing more for you. You have ruined me; I even find myself obliged to sell Les Peuples. But remember that I shall always provide you with shelter whenever you need to seek refuge with your old mother, to whom you have caused so much suffering.

Jeanne'

And when the notary arrived with Monsieur Jeoffrin, a former sugar refiner, she received them herself and invited them to inspect the house as they pleased.

A month later she signed the contract of sale, and at the same time bought a modest house situated outside Goderville, on the main road to Montivilliers, in the hamlet of Batteville.* Then she spent the rest of the day walking alone in Mama's avenue, with agony in her heart and turmoil in her mind, bidding a desperate, sobbing farewell to the view, and the trees, and the worm-eaten bench beneath the plane, to all these things she knew so well that they seemed to be inscribed on her eyes and in her soul, the copse, the bank overlooking the heath, where she had sat so often and from where she had seen the Comte de Fourville running towards the sea on the terrible day of Julien's death, an old, lopped elm she often used to lean against, the whole, familiar garden.

Rosalie came to take her by the arm and force her to return indoors.

A tall peasant lad of twenty-five was waiting by the door. He greeted her in a friendly tone as if he had known her for a long time.

'Hello, Madame Jeanne, how are you? Mother told me to come and help with the moving. I wanted to know what you'd be taking with you, seeing as I'll be doing it times when it don't interfere wi' me work on the land.'

It was her maid's son, Julien's son, Paul's brother.

She felt as though her heart had stopped; and yet she would like to have embraced the boy.

She looked at him to see if he resembled her husband, or her son. He was a strapping sort, with a ruddy complexion, and he had fair hair and blue eyes like his mother. And yet he looked like Julien. But how? What was it? She could not really say, but there was something of Julien in the general cast of his face.

The lad continued:

'If you could show me now, I'd be very obliged to you.'

But she did not yet know what she would decide to take with her, given that her new house was so small; and she asked him to come back at the end of the week.

From then on the move preoccupied her, bringing a sad distraction into her dismal, prospectless life.

She would go from room to room, seeking out pieces of furniture which recalled particular events, those pieces which, like friends, are part of a person's life, almost of a person's own self, known since childhood and to which attach memories of joy and sadness, dates in our lives, pieces which have been the mute companions of our sweet or sombre moments, which have grown old and worn alongside us, their material split in places, the lining torn, the joints loose, the colour faded.

She chose them one by one, frequently hesitating, troubled as though faced with some momentous decision, continually changing her mind, weighing the merits of two armchairs or some old desk against those of a work-table she used to use.

She would open the drawers, trying to remember things from the past. Then, when she had firmly said 'Yes, I'll take this,' they would carry the object in question down to the dining-room.

She wanted to keep all her bedroom furniture, her bed, her tapestries, her clock, everything.

She took a few chairs from the drawing-room, the ones with the patterns she had loved since her early childhood; the fox and the stork, the fox and the crow, the cicada and the ant, and the melancholy heron.*

Then one day, as she continued to prowl through every nook and cranny of this home that she was about to leave, she decided to go up to the attic.

She was astounded; it was a jumble of objects of every description, some broken, some simply dirty, and others taken up there for no apparent reason, either because nobody liked them any more or because they had been replaced. She noticed a whole host of ornaments that used to be familiar and which had suddenly disappeared without her having given them another thought, knick-knacks that she had once held in her hands, trivial little objects from the past which had lain about her for fifteen years, which she had seen each day without noticing them, and which suddenly—rediscovered here in this attic, among others still older, things about which she could remember where they went when she had first come to live in the house—assumed a new importance as forgotten witnesses, like friends encountered anew. They had the same effect on her as those people one has known for a long time but without their ever revealing their true selves and who suddenly, one evening, out of the blue, start talking compulsively and pouring out innermost secrets of which one had not the slightest suspicion.

She went from one to the other, with pangs of recognition, saying to herself.

'Oh yes, I was the one who cracked this china cup one evening shortly before I was married.—Ah, there's Mama's little lantern, and the stick Papa broke that day he tried to open the gate when the wood had swollen with the rain.'

There were also many things up there which she did not recognize and which held no memories for her, having been handed down from her grandparents, or great-grandparents, dusty objects of the kind that seem to have been exiled to an age not their own, to look sad at having been abandoned, things whose past history and adventures nobody knows, because nobody has met the people who chose them, bought them, owned them, loved them, and nobody has known the hands which once used them as familiar objects or known the eyes which once looked upon them with pleasure.

Jeanne held them and inspected them, leaving her fingermarks on the accumulated dust; and she remained standing there in the midst of all these old things, beneath the dim light coming in through a few small panes of glass let into the roof.

She examined some three-legged stools minutely to see what memories they might recall, a copper warming-pan, a battered foot-warmer which she thought she recognized, and a heap of kitchen utensils which were no longer used.

Then she made a pile of the things she wanted to take, and when she came downstairs, she sent Rosalie up to fetch them. The maid was indignant and refused to bring down 'that filthy rubbish'. But Jeanne, though she no longer had a will of her own, held firm this time; and her wish prevailed.

One morning the young farmer, Denis Lecoq, Julien's son, came with his cart to take the first load. Rosalie went with him in order to supervise the unloading and to put the furniture where it was to go.

Left on her own, Jeanne began to wander through the rooms of the house in sudden, awful despair, kissing all the things she could not take with her in surges of passionate affection, the great white birds on the drawing-room tapestries, some old candelabras, everything she came across. She went from room to room, distraught, her eyes streaming with tears; and then she went outside to 'say goodbye' to the sea.

This was towards the end of September, and a lowering grey sky seemed to weigh upon the world; the drab, yellowish-looking waves stretched away as far as the eye could see. She remained standing on the cliff for a long time, mulling over a series of anguished thoughts in her head. Then, as night was falling, she returned to the house, having suffered as much in this one day as during any of her previous periods of greatest sorrow.

Rosalie had returned and was waiting for her, delighted by the new house and declaring that it was considerably more cheerful than this great barracks of a building which wasn't even by a main road.

Jeanne spent the evening in tears.

Ever since they had heard about the chateau being sold, the farm tenants had treated her with the bare minimum of respect, calling her 'the madwoman' among themselves, without knowing exactly why but no doubt because they sensed, in their brute, instinctive way, her increasingly morbid sentimentality, the dreamy exaltations to which she was now given, the utter disarray to which her poor soul had been reduced by relentless misfortune.

On the eve of her departure she happened to walk into the stable. A growl made her jump. It was Slaughter, whom she had scarcely thought about for months. Blind and paralysed, having reached an age which dogs of his sort rarely attain, he clung to life lying on a bed of straw, and looked after by Ludivine, who never forgot him. Jeanne held him in her arms, kissed him, and took him into the house. Fat as a tun, he could scarcely drag himself along on his stiff, splayed legs, and he barked like those wooden dogs that are given to children.

The last day finally dawned. Jeanne had spent the night in Julien's old room, the furniture having been removed from her own.

She got out of bed, exhausted and gasping for breath, as though she had just been running a great distance. Down in the courtyard the cart carrying the trunks and the remainder of the furniture had already been loaded. Another cart, a two-wheeled trap, was standing harnessed behind it, which was to take the mistress and the maid.

Père Simon and Ludivine would remain behind on their own until the new owner arrived; then they were to retire to live with relatives, Jeanne having arranged for them to receive a small annuity. They had some savings also. They were now very old to be servants, at once talkative and not able to do very much. Marius, having taken a wife, had long since left the household.

Towards eight o'clock rain began to fall, a fine, icy rain blown in on a gentle sea-breeze. They had to spread covers over the cart. The leaves were already being blown off the trees.

On the kitchen table stood steaming cups of café au lait. Jeanne sat down at hers and drank it in little sips. Then she got up and said: 'Let us go.'

She put on her hat and shawl and, while Rosalie was helping her on with her rubber boots, remarked, with a lump in her throat:

'Do you remember, Rosalie, how it rained the day we left Rouen to come here...'

She had a sort of spasm, clutched both hands to her chest, and fell back unconscious onto the floor.

For more than an hour she lay there as though dead; then she opened her eyes again and began to heave convulsively as tears flowed from her eyes.

After she had calmed down a little, she felt so weak that she could not get up. But Rosalie, who was afraid that there might be further attacks of this kind if they delayed their departure any longer, went and fetched her son. Together they took hold of her, lifted her up, carried her out, and placed her in the two-wheeler, on the wooden bench covered in polished leather; and the old servant, having climbed up beside Jeanne, wrapped a rug round her legs and put a thick coat over her shoulders. Then, holding an umbrella over her head, she shouted:

'Quick, Denis, let's be off.'

The young man clambered up beside his mother and, perching with one thigh on the edge of the crowded bench, put his horse to a fast trot, and the two women began to bounce up and down to its jolting rhythm.

When they turned the corner in the village, they caught sight of someone pacing up and down the road; it was the Abbé Tolbiac, who seemed to have been waiting for their departure. He stopped to let the carriage go past. He was holding up his cassock with one hand to keep it out of the puddles lying on the road, and his spindly legs, clad in black stockings, disappeared into enormous muddy shoes.

Jeanne lowered her eyes so as not to have to meet his gaze; and Rosalie, who knew the full story, was filled with rage.

'Ignorant boor,' she muttered, and then, grabbing her son's hand, cried:

'Give him a flick of your whip.'

But just as he was passing the priest, the young fellow guided the wheel of his ramshackle conveyance smartly into a rut at full speed, sending up a sheet of mud which covered the ecclesiastical gentleman from head to toe.

And Rosalie turned, with a beaming smile on her face, and brandished her fist, as the priest took a large handkerchief and wiped himself down.

They had been under way some five minutes when Jeanne suddenly exclaimed:

'Slaughter! We've forgotten him!'

They had to stop, and Denis got down and ran back to fetch the dog, while Rosalie held the reins.

The young man eventually reappeared, carrying the large, flabby, mangy animal in his arms, and he placed it on the floor between the skirts of the two women.

XIII

The carriage drew up two hours later outside a small, brick-built house surrounded by an orchard of espaliered pear-trees and standing by the side of the main road.

Four trellised arbours covered in honeysuckle and clematis marked the four corners of the garden, which was laid out in small squares of vegetable beds divided by narrow paths bordered by fruit-trees.

A very tall hedge ran round the whole property, which was separated from the neighbouring farm by a field. There was a forge about a hundred metres up the road. The nearest houses after that were one kilometre away.

The surrounding view extended over the plain of the Pays de Caux, dotted all over with farmhouses, each of them hidden by the four double rows of tall trees that enclosed its apple-yard.

As soon as she arrived Jeanne wanted to rest, but Rosalie would not let her, fearing that her mind might start to wander again.

The carpenter from Goderville was on hand to help them move in; and they began at once to arrange the furniture which had already been delivered, while they waited for the final cart-load which would be arriving soon.

It was a major task, requiring long deliberation and extensive discussion.

An hour later the cart appeared at the gate, and they had to unload it in the rain.

When evening fell, the house was in total disorder, full of objects piled up higgledy-piggledy; and Jeanne, exhausted, fell fast asleep as soon as she got into bed.

During the days which followed she was so busy that she had no time for tears. She even took a certain pleasure in making her new home pretty, continually mindful of the fact that her son would one day return there. The tapestries from her former bed-room were hung in the dining-room, which served also as a sitting-room; and she took particular care in arranging one of the two rooms on the first floor, which she began to think of as 'Pullie's room.'

She took the other for herself, while Rosalie was to live above her, next to the attic.

Once furnished with care, it was a nice little house: and Jeanne liked it at first, although something was missing which she could not quite identify.

One morning the notary's clerk from Fécamp brought her thirty-six hundred francs, the value of the furniture left behind at Les Peuples and which had been estimated by an upholsterer. She felt a thrill of delight as she accepted this money; and as soon as the man had gone she quickly put on her hat, wanting to get to Goderville as soon as possible to send this unexpected sum to Paul.

But as she was hurrying along the main road, she met Rosalie on her way back from market. The maid suspected something without immediately guessing the truth; but when she found out—for by now Jeanne found it impossible to keep anything from her—Rosalie put her basket down on the ground the better to give full vent to her anger.

With fists clenched on her hips, she stood there shouting at her. Then she grabbed her mistress with her right arm, and her basket with her left, and set off back to the house, still furious.

As soon as they reached home, the maid demanded the money. Jeanne gave it to her, keeping back six hundred francs. But her subterfuge was soon discovered by the servant, who had now been put on her guard; and she had to hand over the whole sum.

Rosalie agreed nevertheless to this residue being sent to the young man.

He wrote a letter of thanks some days later:

'You have done me a great service, my dear Mama, for we were living in dire poverty.'

Jeanne, however, could not get used to living at Batteville; she felt constantly as though she were no longer able to breathe properly, that she was even more alone now, more abandoned, more lost. She would go out for a walk, as far as the little hamlet of Verneuil and back via the Trois-Mares; and no sooner was she home than she would be up on her feet again, wanting to be off as if she had forgotten to go where she had originally intended, where she really wanted to take her walk.

And she carried on like this every day without understanding the reason behind her strange urge. But one evening a chance remark revealed to her the secret cause of her restlessness. As she sat down to dinner, she said:

'Oh, how I long to see the sea.'

It was the sea that she had been missing so much, her great neighbour for twenty-five years, the sea with its salty air, its angry moods, its scolding voice, its powerful gales, the sea which she could glimpse every morning from her window at Les Peuples, whose air she breathed day and night, of whose presence nearby she was always conscious, and which she had come to love like a living person without realizing that she did.

Slaughter, too, was extremely restless. Since the evening of their arrival he had installed himself in the open space at the bottom of the kitchen dresser and refused to budge. He would lie there all day, hardly moving, merely turning round from time to time with a muffled growl.

But as soon as night came, he would get up and drag himself over to the door into the garden, bumping into the walls as he went. Then, when he had spent the few minutes he needed outside, he would come back in and squat on his haunches in front of the stove, which was still warm; and after his two mistresses had gone to bed, he would begin to howl.

He would howl like this all night long, in a plaintive, mournful tone, sometimes stopping for an hour only to start up again in an even more heart-rending manner. They tethered him in a barrel at the front of the house: he howled under the windows. Then, since he was sick and going to die soon, they put him back in the kitchen.

Sleep had become impossible for Jeanne, who could hear the old animal continually moaning and scratching, trying to find his bearings in this new house and quite aware that he was no longer in his own home.

Nothing could pacify him. Having dozed all day long, as if his failing sight and the awareness of his own infirmity prevented him from stirring when every other living thing is up and about, he would begin to prowl around ceaselessly as soon as dusk fell, as if he only dared to live and move about in the darkness, when all creatures are blind.

They found him dead one morning. It was a great relief.

Winter was coming on; and Jeanne felt a growing sense of overwhelming despair. This took the form not of an acute sorrow of the kind that seems to wring the soul, but rather of a dismal, mournful sadness.

No distraction could rouse her. No one paid her any attention. The main road stretched to right and left outside her front door, almost always deserted. From time to time a tilbury would trot by, driven by a red-faced man whose smock billowed as he sped along and looked like a blue balloon; sometimes a cart trundled past, or else it was two peasants approaching in the distance, a man and a woman, very tiny at first on the horizon, then getting bigger and bigger, and then, when they had gone past the house, getting smaller again, till once more they were no bigger than two insects, away in the distance, at the end of the white line that stretched as far as the eye could see, rising and falling over the gentle undulations of the ground.

When the grass started to grow again, a little girl in a short skirt would come by the gate every morning, leading two bony cows that grazed along the edge of the ditches beside the road. In the evening she would return, at the same sleepy pace, moving slowly forward every ten minutes as she followed her beasts.

Each night Jeanne dreamt that she was still living at Les Peuples.

She was back there with Papa and Mama, as in the old days, and sometimes even with Aunt Lison. She would do over again all the things that were now finished with and forgotten, imagine herself supporting Madame Adélaïde on her journeys up and down her avenue. And each waking was followed by tears.

She thought of Paul all the time, wondering 'What's he doing? How is he now? Does he think of me sometimes?'

As she strolled slowly along the sunken footpaths between the farms, she would ponder in her mind all the things which tormented her; but she suffered above all from uncompromising jealousy at the thought of the unknown woman who had robbed her of her son. It was this hatred alone which gave her pause and stopped her from doing something, from going to find him, from seeing where he lived. She could picture his mistress standing at the door and asking: 'And what brings you here, Madame?' Her maternal pride rebelled at the possibility of such an encounter; and the haughty pride of a woman still pure and unbesmirched, who had never lapsed, made her rage all the more at the cravenness of human beings, slaves to the foul procedures of carnal love that makes cowards of the heart as well as the body. Mankind seemed to her unclean when she thought of all the dirty secrets of the senses, the degrading caresses, and the dimly discerned mysteries of inseparable couplings.

Spring and summer came and went once more.

But when autumn returned with its long periods of rain, its grey skies and dark clouds, such a weariness of living seized hold of her that she decided to make one final effort to get her Pullie back.

The young man's passion must surely now be spent.

She wrote him a tearful letter:

'My dear child, I am writing to beseech you to come home to me. You must remember that I am old and ill, and all alone from one year's end to the next, with a maid for company. I am now living in a small house on the main road. It is very dismal. But if you were here, everything would be different for me. You're all I have in the world, and I haven't seen you for seven years! You will never know how unhappy I've been, and how much my heart depended on you. You were my life, my dreams, my one and only hope for the future, my one and only love, and I miss you, and you have deserted me!

Oh, do come back, my dear little Pullie, come back and kiss me, come back to your old mother who holds out her arms to you in despair.

Jeanne'

He replied a few days later.

'My dear Mother, There is nothing I should like better than to come and see you, but I haven't a farthing to my name. Send me some money and then I shall come. I had in any case intended to come and see you to talk about a plan I have which would allow me to do as you ask.

The selfless affection shown for me by the person who has been my constant companion throughout these bad times remains boundless. It is no longer possible for me to continue like this without acknowledging publicly such faithful love and devotion on her part. Moreover she is very refined in her ways, as you will be able to discover for yourself. Also, she is very well educated and reads a lot. And, lastly, you have simply no idea how much she has always meant to me. I would be a brute not to show her my gratitude. I am writing therefore to ask your permission to marry her. You would forgive me my various escapades, and we should all live together in your new house.

If you knew her, you would grant me your consent at once. I assure you that she is quite perfect, and very genteel. You would love her, I am certain. For my own part, I could not live without her.

I await your reply with impatience, my dear Mama, and we send you all our love.

Your son,
Vicomte Paul de Lamare'

Jeanne was aghast. She sat quite still, with the letter on her lap, and reflected on the cunning of this girl who had continually prevented her son from leaving, who had not once let him come and see her, all the while biding her time and waiting for the moment when the old mother, in desperation, and no longer able to resist the longing to embrace her own child, would weaken and consent to everything.

And the great sorrow of Paul's stubborn preference for this creature tore her heart asunder. She repeated over and over again:

'He doesn't love me, he doesn't love me.

Rosalie came in. Jeanne stammered:

'Now he wants to marry her.'

The maid started in surprise:

'Oh, Madame, you can't allow it. Monsieur Paul's not going to saddle himself with that slut.'

And Jeanne, heartbroken but unbowed, replied:

'No, never, Rosalie. And since he won't come to me, I shall go and find him, and then we'll see which of us shall prevail, she or I.'

And she wrote at once to Paul to tell him of her forthcoming visit, and asking to meet him somewhere other than in the house inhabited by this trollop.

Then, as she waited for a reply, she made ready for the journey. Rosalie began to pack her mistress's linen and personal effects into an old trunk. But as she was folding a dress, an old one of the type worn in the country, she exclaimed:

'You haven't a single thing to wear. I shan't let you go like this. Everyone would look down on you, and the ladies of Paris would think you were a servant.'

Jeanne let her have her way. So the two women went into Goderville together and chose a green check material, which was then entrusted to a local seamstress. Afterwards they went to see the notary, M. Roussel, who spent a fortnight in the capital every year, and asked him for information. For Jeanne had not been to Paris for twenty-eight years.

He gave them plentiful advice about how to avoid getting run over, and how not to be robbed, suggesting that they sew their money into the lining of their garments and that they keep an absolute minimum in their pocket. He talked at length about moderately priced restaurants, indicating two or three which were frequented by women; and he recommended the Hôtel de Normandie, where he had stayed himself, next to the railway station. They could mention his name.

For six years one of these railways that everyone talked about had been operating between Paris and Le Havre.* But Jeanne, full of her own woes, had not yet seen these steam engines that were revolutionizing the whole area.

Meanwhile Paul did not reply.

She waited a week, then a fortnight, each morning going out to meet the postman on the road and approaching him with trepidation:

'Anything for me this morning, Père Malandrain?'

And each time the man would reply in a voice made hoarse by the inclemency of the season:

'No, nothing again, my good lady.'

Clearly that woman was stopping Paul from replying!

Jeanne then resolved to leave at once. She wanted to take Rosalie with her, but the maid refused so as not to add to the cost of the journey.

Indeed, she would not let her mistress take more than three hundred francs with her:

'If you need more, you can write to me, and I'll go to the notary and have him send it to you. If I give you any more, Monsieur Paul will simply pocket it.'

So one December morning they climbed into Denis Lecoq's cart when he came to take them to the station, this being as far as Rosalie was to accompany her mistress.

First they enquired about the price of tickets; then, when everything had been paid for and the trunk registered, they waited by the railway line, trying to understand how it all worked and so preoccupied by its mystery that they forgot the sad reasons for the journey.

Eventually the distant sound of a whistle made them look round, and they caught sight of a black engine looming into view. It came past with a terrifying roar, pulling a long chain of wheeled vehicles behind it; and when a porter opened one of the doors, Jeanne embraced Rosalie tearfully and climbed into one of the compartments.

Rosalie, overcome with emotion, shouted:

'Goodbye, Madame. Have a good journey. We'll see each other again soon.'

'Goodbye, my dear.'

Another whistle went, and the whole rosary of carriages began to move forward, slowly at first, then faster, and finally at a terrifying speed.

In Jeanne's compartment two gentlemen were sitting in the corners, asleep.

She watched the countryside slip by, with its fields, its trees, its farms and villages, frightened by this speed and feeling as though she were caught up in some new way of life, being borne off into a new world that was no longer her own, no longer the world of her tranquil youth and her present monotonous existence.

Evening was falling when the train entered Paris.

A hotel doorman took Jeanne's trunk; and she followed him anxiously, bumping into people, unskilled at moving through the bustling crowd, almost running after the man for fear of losing him from sight.

When she reached the reception office at the hotel, she hurriedly announced:

'I have been recommended to you by Monsieur Roussel.'

'Monsieur Roussel? Who's he?' asked the Patronne, an enormous, unsmiling woman, sitting at her desk.

Taken aback, Jeanne replied:

'But he's the notary at Goderville. He stays here every year.'

'Perhaps he does. I don't know him,' the large lady declared. 'Do you want a room?'

'Yes, Madame.'

And a porter picked up her luggage and climbed the staircase ahead of her.

She felt very miserable. She sat down at a small table and asked them to send up some broth and a chicken wing. She had had nothing to eat since dawn.

She ate glumly by the light of a candle, thinking of a thousand different things, remembering her brief visit to this same city on her return from honeymoon, and how the first signs of Julien's character had manifested themselves during that stay in Paris. But she had been young then, and confident, and ready for anything. Now she felt old, awkward, timid even, and the slightest thing made her feel nervous and incapable. When she had finished her meal, she stood by the window and gazed down into the street, which was full of people. She wanted to go out, but did not dare. She would most assuredly get lost, she thought. She went to bed, and blew out the light.

But the noise, the sensation of being in a strange city, and the upheaval of the journey combined to keep her awake. The hours ticked by. The sounds from outside gradually subsided, but still she could not sleep, made restless by this semi-slumber of large cities. She was used to the deep, peaceful sleep of the fields, which exercises its soporific effect on everything, whether man, beast, or plant; whereas now she was aware of a whole mysterious stirring going on around her. The barely audible sound of voices reached her, as though they had secreted themselves in the hotel walls. From time to time a floorboard would creak, a door would shut, a bell would ring.

Suddenly, about two o'clock, just as she was beginning to doze off, a woman screamed in a room nearby. Jeanne sat up in bed with a start; then she thought she heard a man's laugh.

Later, as dawn approached, she began thinking about Paul; and she got dressed at the first sign of daybreak.

He lived in the rue du Sauvage, in the Cité. She intended to walk there, in order to save money as Rosalie had advised her. The weather was fine; the cold air pricked her skin; people in a hurry were rushing past along the pavements. She was walking as quickly as she could along a street which had been pointed out to her, at the end of which she was to turn right, then left; when she reached the square, she would need to ask the way again. She did not find any square and asked at a baker's, where she was given different directions. She set off again, got lost, wandered around, asked the way again several times, and in the end had not the faintest idea where she was.

In her panic she was now walking almost without direction. She was about to call a cab when she saw the Seine. Then she followed the river.

About an hour later she entered the rue du Sauvage, which was a sort of dark alleyway. She stopped outside the door, so over-come with emotion that she was unable to move another inch.

Pullie was here, in this house.

She could feel her hands and knees trembling. Finally she went in, followed a long corridor, saw the concierge in his lodge, and, giving him a coin, made her request:

'Could you go up and tell Monsieur Paul de Lamare that an old lady, a friend of his mother's, is waiting downstairs?'

'He doesn't live here any more, Madame,' the porter replied.

A great shudder ran through her. She stammered:

'Ah, where... where does he live now?'

'I don't know.'

She felt dazed as though she were about to fall, and she stood there for some time unable to speak. Eventually, with immense effort, she recovered her wits and murmured:

'How long has he been gone?'

The man informed her expansively:

'A fortnight now. They left just like that, one evening, and they haven't been back. They owed money everywhere around here. So, as you will appreciate, they didn't leave their address.'

Jeanne could see flashes of light, great jets of flame, as though someone were firing a gun right in front of her eyes. But her one ambition sustained her and enabled her to stand there, apparently calm and collected. She wanted information, she wanted to find Pullie.

'So he didn't say anything when he left?'

'Oh, no, not a word. They cleared off so they wouldn't have to pay, and that's the long and the short of it.'

'But he must send someone to fetch his letters.'

'More often than I'd give him any. And anyway they never got more than maybe ten in a year. I did take one up to them, though, two days before they left.

Her own letter, presumably. She said hurriedly:

'Look here, I am his mother, and I've come to find him. Here's ten francs for you. If you hear from him or have any information about him, bring it to me at the Hôtel de Normandie, in the rue du Havre, and I'll make it worth your while.'

He replied:

'You can count on me, Madame.'

And she made her escape.

She set off on foot once more, not caring where she went. She hurried along as though engaged upon some important errand, keeping close to the walls and continually jostled by people carrying parcels; she crossed the streets without looking to see if anything was coming, and coachmen swore at her; she stumbled over steps in the pavements, not looking where she was going. She just kept on going, her mind far away on other things.

Suddenly she found herself in a public garden, and felt so weary that she sat down on a bench. She remained there for what seemed a very long time, unaware of her tears until passers-by stopped and stared at her. Then she felt very cold, and stood up to leave; her legs could barely support her, so weak and exhausted was she.

She wanted to go and have some soup in a restaurant, but she lacked the courage to enter such an establishment, overcome by a sort of shame, or fear, a kind of modest desire to conceal her sorrow which she could sense was quite plain to see. She would stop for a moment outside the door, and look in, and see all the people sitting at tables and eating; and then she would walk away, intimidated, but telling herself:

'Next time I'll go in.'

And next time she did not venture in either.

In the end she bought a small crescent-shaped roll from a baker's, and began to nibble it as she walked. She was extremely thirsty, but she did not know where to find a drink, so she went without.

She walked through another archway and found herself in another garden, surrounded by arcades. She recognized the Palais-Royal.*

Since the sun and the walking had warmed her up again, she sat down for another hour or two. A crowd of people came past, an elegant crowd all chatting, and smiling, and greeting one another, the kind of happy crowd where the women are beautiful and the men are rich, people who live only for self-adornment and the pursuit of pleasure.

Jeanne, alarmed to find herself in the midst of this brilliant throng, stood up intending to beat a hasty retreat; but suddenly it occurred to her that she might meet Paul here; and she began to wander round studying the faces, continually walking up and down from one end of the garden to the other with her rapid, timorous steps.

People turned round to look, others laughed and pointed at her. She noticed and fled, thinking that no doubt they were amused by her appearance and by the green check dress for which Rosalie had chosen the material and which the seamstress at Goderville had made up according to Rosalie's specifications.

She was even loath now to ask other pedestrians the way. But she risked it nevertheless and eventually found her way back to the hotel.

She spent the rest of the day sitting on a chair, with her feet up on the bed, not stirring. Then she had dinner, which consisted as on the previous evening of soup and some meat. Then she went to bed, performing each action mechanically, out of habit.

The next day she went to the police station and asked them to find her son. They could promise nothing, but they would nevertheless see what they could do.

Then she roamed the streets, always hoping to bump into him. And she felt more entirely alone in this bustling crowd, more wretched and lost, than if she had been standing in the middle of an empty field.

When she returned to the hotel in the evening, she was told that someone had been asking for her on behalf of Monsieur Paul and that he would come back the next day. Her heart leapt at the news, and she did not sleep a wink that night. What if it were Paul himself? Yes, it must be, even though she had not recognized him from the details she had been given.

About nine o'clock there was a knock on her door, and she shouted: 'Come in!', ready to rush forward with open arms. A total stranger walked in. And while he was apologizing for disturbing her and explaining what business brought him, namely one of Paul's debts for which he had come to demand payment, she could feel herself crying but tried to conceal the fact, removing each tear with the tip of her finger as they welled up in the corners of her eyes.

The man had learnt of her arrival from the concierge in the rue du Sauvage, and being unable to find the young man, he was now turning to his mother. And he held out a piece of paper which she accepted automatically. She read the figure of ninety francs, took out her money, and paid.

That day she did not go out.

The following day other creditors presented themselves. She gave them all the money she had left, keeping back only twenty francs; and she wrote to Rosalie informing her of the situation.

She spent her days wandering about, waiting for her maid to

reply, not knowing what to do or where to while away the endless, dismal hours, with no one to exchange a kind word with, no one who knew of her sad plight. She walked in no particular direction, now filled with a longing to depart, to go back home, back to her little house beside the lonely road.

Only a few days earlier she could not have borne to live there any longer, so overwhelmed by sadness had she been; and now she felt that, on the contrary, she could not live anywhere else but there, in the place where her life of dull routine had taken root.

At last, one evening, she received a letter and two hundred francs. Rosalie wrote:

'Madame Jeanne, come back at once, because I shan't send you any more. As for Monsieur Paul, I shall go and look for him myself as soon as we hear news of him.

Greetings. Your servant,
Rosalie'

And one bitterly cold morning, with the snow falling, Jeanne set off on her return to Batteville.

XIV

Thenceforth she never went out, never stirred. She would get up each morning at the same time, look out of the window to see how the weather was, and then go downstairs and sit by the fire in the living-room.

She would spend whole days sitting there, not moving, her eyes fixed on the flames, letting her sorry thoughts wander where they pleased and observing the sad procession of her miseries. Darkness would gradually descend on the little room, and still she would not have moved, except to put more logs on the fire. Then Rosalie would bring in the lamp and exclaim:

'Come now, Madame Jeanne, it's time you were up and about, or you'll not be hungry again this evening.'

She was often pursued by obsessive notions which refused to go away, and tormented by trivial concerns, as the slightest matter came to assume the utmost importance in her ailing mind.

She lived above all in the past, in the distant past, haunted by memories of her early days and her honeymoon in far-off Corsica. The island's landscapes, long since forgotten, would suddenly appear before her among the blazing embers in the grate; and she would recall every detail, every little incident, every face she had met there. The features of Jean Ravoli, their guide, never left her; and sometimes she thought she could hear his voice.

Then she would think back to the tranquil years of Paul's childhood, when he used to make her prick out his lettuce seedlings and she knelt in the heavy soil beside Aunt Lison, each of them vying to please the child in the care and trouble they took, competing to see who could show the greatest skill in getting the young shoots to take and producing the greatest number of successful plants.

And softly her lips would murmur: 'Pullie, my little Pullie,' as if she were talking to him; and with her reverie now focused on this single word, she would sometimes spend hour after hour trying to spell out the letters of his name in the air with a single, outstretched finger. She would trace them slowly, in front of the fire, imagining that she could see them, and then, thinking that she had made a mistake, she would begin the P again, her arm trembling with the effort, desperately trying to spell out the name from beginning to end; and afterwards, when she had finished, she would start all over again.

Eventually she could manage no more; she would become confused and start sketching out other words until she was driven almost mad with frustration.

She acquired all the obsessive habits of people who live on their own. The tiniest object not in its right place irritated her.

Rosalie often insisted that she take exercise, and used to lead her out onto the road; but twenty minutes later Jeanne would say: 'I can go no further, my dear,' and sit down at the edge of the ditch.

Soon she came to hate all forms of movement, and would remain in bed for as long as possible.

Ever since childhood one particular, ineradicable habit had remained with her, that of getting up immediately after drinking her morning café au lait. Indeed she was excessively attached to this particular beverage, and to have been deprived of it would have meant more to her than any other such deprivation. So each morning she would await Rosalie's arrival with an almost physical longing; and as soon as the full bowl had been placed on the bedside table, she would sit up and quickly, almost greedily, drink it down. Then she would throw back the sheets and begin to dress.

But gradually she had begun to sit dreaming for a few moments after replacing the bowl on its plate. Subsequently she had taken to lying down again; and then with each succeeding day she extended this period of idleness, which lasted until Rosalie would return, furious, and dress her almost by force.

In fact she no longer seemed to have any will of her own, and each time her maid asked her advice, or put a question to her, or wanted her opinion on some matter, she replied:

'Just as you please, my dear.'

She believed herself to be so directly the target of unrelenting misfortune that she became as fatalistic as an Oriental; and the habitual experience of seeing all her hopes and dreams crumble and vanish meant that she shrank from all further endeavour, and she would spend whole days in hesitant deliberation before doing the simplest thing, persuaded that she was bound to choose the wrong course and that it would turn out badly.

She kept saying:

'I just haven't had any luck in life.'

Whereupon Rosalie expostulated:

'And what would you say if you had to earn your daily bread, if you had to get up at six o'clock every morning and go and do a full day's work! Yet lots of women have to, and when they get too old, they die of poverty.'

Jeanne would reply:

'But I'm all alone, my son has abandoned me.'

And then Rosalie became furiously angry:

'Oh dear, how dreadful! And so? What about the sons who have to go off for their military service? And the ones that emigrate to America?'

For her America represented some remote place where people went to make their fortune and never came back.

Then she would say:

'There always comes a time when you have to part,'coz old and young was never meant to live together.'

And finally, by way of fierce conclusion:

'And anyway, what if he were dead?'

To which Jeanne would offer no reply.

She recovered a little of her strength when the air turned milder at the beginning of spring, but she devoted this new energy merely to wallowing yet deeper in her sombre thoughts.

When she went up to the attic one morning to fetch something, she happened to open a box full of old calendars; they had kept them all, as some country folk do.

It seemed to her as though she were rediscovering the years of her own past, and she was filled with strange and conflicting emotions at the sight of this heap of cardboard squares.

She took them down to the living-room. There were calendars
of every shape and size, large and small. And she began to arrange
them by year on the table. Suddenly she came on the first one, the
one she had taken with her to Les Peuples.

She gazed at it for a long time, at the dates she had crossed out
on the morning of her departure from Rouen, the day after she
had left the convent. And she wept. She wept slow, dejected tears,
the pitiable tears of an old woman confronting the spectacle of
her unhappy life spread out before her on this table.

And an idea occurred to her which soon developed into a
terrible, ceaseless, unrelenting obsession. She decided to try and
piece together everything she had done, almost day by day.

One after another she pinned the bits of yellowing cardboard to
the tapestries on the wall, and she would spend hours in front of
one or other of them, thinking: 'Now what happened that month?'

She had underlined each of the particularly memorable dates
in her past, and sometimes she managed to recover an entire
month by recalling, one by one, all the minor incidents which had
preceded or followed an important event, then grouping and link-
ing them.

By virtue of dogged concentration, much searching of her
memory, and a concerted will to succeed, she managed to
reconstruct her first two years at Les Peuples almost in their
entirety: the recollections of her distant past flooded back with
remarkable clarity, as though etched in relief.

But the following years seemed lost in a fog, each one merging
and overlapping with the other; and sometimes she would spend
endless hours peering at one particular calendar, as her mind
reached out to yesteryear but failed even to remember if it was in
that particular piece of cardboard that such and such a memory
were to be found.

She would move from one to the other, circling this living-
room that was surrounded by these registers of bygone days as
though it had been hung with prints depicting the Stations of the
Cross. Suddenly she would pull up her chair in front of one of
them, and remain staring at it, stock-still, till nightfall, rapt in her
investigations.

Then all at once, as the sap began to rise in the warmth from the sun, and the crops began to shoot in the fields, and the trees turned green, and the apple trees blossomed in the apple-yards like pink balls and filled the plain with their perfume, she was seized with a restless excitement.

Now she could not sit still. She was constantly on the move, going out and coming home twenty times a day; and sometimes she would wander off in the distance, from farm to farm, exalting in a kind of frenzy of regrets.

The sight of a daisy huddled in a tuft of grass, or a ray of sunlight slanting through the leaves, or the blue of the sky reflected in a puddle-filled rut, moved and warmed her heart, and unsettled her by recalling distant sensations, like the echoes of those emotions she had felt when, as a young girl, she had wandered dreamily round the countryside.

Then she had quivered with the same sudden stirrings, had savoured this sweet tenderness, this head-turning intoxication of warm days, as she awaited her future. And here she was now reliving it all, now that the future was closed to her. She could still feel the pleasure of it in her heart; but it pained her too, as if the eternal joy of the world's revival could exert only a scant and poignant charm as it entered her withered flesh, her thinned blood, her prostrate soul.

It seemed to her too that, all around her, things were somehow not quite the same. The sun was surely just a little less warm than in her youth, the sky a little less blue, the grass a little less green; and the flowers, less brightly coloured now and less strongly scented, were no longer quite as intoxicating as once they had been.

Some days, nevertheless, it felt so good to be alive that she began once more to dream, to hope, to anticipate; for, despite the relentless cruelty of fate, is there not always hope when the weather is fine?

She would walk on and on, for hours and hours, as though spurred by the excitement in her soul. And sometimes she would stop suddenly and sit down at the edge of the road to think sad thoughts. Why had she not been loved like other women? Why had she not known even the simple happiness of a peaceful existence?

And sometimes she could still forget that she was old, with nothing to look forward to but a few dismal years of loneliness, that she had reached journey's end; and she would make fond plans, just as she had when she was sixteen, a charming patchwork of tiny hopes for the future. Then the harsh awareness of reality would descend upon her; she would struggle to her feet once more, stiff and aching, as though some heavy weight had fallen and crushed her spine; and she would set off home again, walking more slowly this time and muttering to herself: 'You stupid old woman, you stupid old woman!'

And now Rosalie was forever saying to her: 'Calm yourself, Madame, calm yourself. Why must you always be in such a pother?'

And Jeanne answered sadly:

'I can't help it. I'm like Slaughter was at the end.'

One morning the maid came into her room earlier than usual and, putting the bowl of café au lait down on her bedside table, said:

'Come along, drink up. Denis is waiting for us at the gate. We're off to Les Peuples, I've a matter to attend to there.'

Jeanne was so affected by this news that she thought she was going to faint; and as she dressed, she trembled with excitement and nervous trepidation at the prospect of seeing her dear home again.

A brilliant, sunny morning shone across the land; and the trap-pony was full of such cheer that it would periodically break into a gallop. When they entered the village of Étouvent, Jeanne's heart was beating so wildly that she felt as though she could scarcely breathe; and when she saw the brick pillars of the front gate, she muttered two or three times, in spite of herself: 'Oh, oh, oh,' as one does at moments of particular emotional consequence.

They unhitched the trap at the Couillards'. Then, while Rosalie and her son went about their business, the farm-tenants suggested that Jeanne might like to look round the chateau, since the owners were away, and they gave her the keys.

She set off on her own, and when she had reached the side of the old manor-house which faced the sea, she stopped to gaze at it. Nothing had changed on the outside. And that day the weathered façades of the huge grey house were wreathed in smiles of sunlight. All the shutters were closed.

A twig from a dead branch fell on her dress, and she looked up; it had come from the plane-tree. She walked up to the thick tree-trunk, with its smooth, pale bark, and stroked it like an animal. Her foot trod on a piece of rotten wood lying in the grass; it was the last remains of the bench on which she had sat so often with her family, the bench they had installed the very day Julien first came to call.

Then she reached the double doors at the front and found great difficulty in opening them, as the heavy, rusty key refused to turn. Eventually the lock gave with a harsh grinding of springs; and one of the doors, itself a little stiff, yielded to a shove.

At once, and almost running, Jeanne went upstairs to her bedroom. She did not recognize it with its bright wallpaper; but when she opened the window, her heart stopped at the sight of the view she had loved so much, the copse, the elms, the heath, the sea dotted with brown sails which at this distance seemed not to move.

Then she began to wander all over the big, empty house. She noticed familiar-looking marks on the walls. She stopped by a small hole which the Baron had made in the plaster when, in memory of younger days, he frequently delighted in poking his stick into the wall as he went past, as if he were fencing.

In Mama's bedroom, stuck into the back of a door in a dark corner over by the bed, she found a fine gold-topped pin which she had put there once (as she now remembered) and which she had looked for for years afterwards. No one had ever found it. She took in her hand as though it were some priceless relic and kissed it.

She went everywhere, seeking and finding almost invisible marks in the drapery of the rooms which had not been redecorated, seeing once more the strange shapes which the imagination is given to perceiving in the pattern of material or marble, or in the shadows on the ceilings blackened with age.

She moved about noiselessly, all alone in the vast, silent chateau, as though she were walking through a graveyard. Her whole life lay buried there.

She went down to the drawing-room. It lay in darkness behind closed shutters, and it took her some time to make things out. Then, as her eyes got used to the gloom, she gradually recognized the tall tapestries with their strutting birds. Two armchairs still stood by the fireplace as though they had just been vacated; and the very smell of the room—a smell which it had always possessed, just as people have their own, a faint but easily recognizable smell, the sweet, indeterminate aroma of old apartments—took possession of Jeanne, surrounding her with memories and making her head spin in giddy recollection. She stood there gasping, breathing in this exhalation of the past, and staring at the two chairs. And all at once, in a sudden hallucination born of her one, single, overriding memory, she thought she saw, in fact she did see, as she had so often seen them in the past, her father and mother warming their feet by the fire.

She stepped back in terror, colliding with the edge of the open door, and grabbed on to it to prevent herself from falling, still staring at the two armchairs.

The vision had gone.

She remained in a daze for a few minutes. Then gradually she returned to her senses, and was about to flee the room, afraid that she might be losing her mind, when her eyes fell by chance on the door-jamb against which she was leaning; and she saw Pullie's scale.

The sequence of faint marks ran up the paintwork at uneven intervals, together with the numbers which had been scratched with a penknife to indicate the month and year and her son's height. Sometimes they were in the Baron's handwriting, which was bigger, and sometimes in her own, smaller, hand, and sometimes in Aunt Lison's, which was rather shaky. And at once it was as though the child of old was standing there in front of her, with his blond hair, pressing his little forehead to the wall so that they could measure his height.

'Jeanne,' the Baron would shout, ' he's grown a centimetre in six weeks.'

She began to kiss the door-frame in a frenzy of affection.

But someone was calling for her outside. It was Rosalie's voice:

'Madame Jeanne, Madame Jeanne, it's lunchtime, we're waiting for you.'

She went outside, her mind elsewhere, no longer capable of taking in whatever anyone said to her. She ate what was put in front of her, she heard people talking but had no idea what they were talking about, she conversed with the farmers' wives presumably, since they asked after her health, and she allowed herself to be kissed, and herself kissed various cheeks that were proffered, before climbing back onto the trap.

When she lost sight of the high roof of the chateau through the trees, she felt as though her breast were being rent asunder. She knew in her heart that she had just said goodbye to her house for the last time.

They returned to Batteville.

Just as she was about to enter her new home once more, she caught sight of something white beneath the door; it was a letter that the postman had slipped underneath while she was out. She saw at once that it was from Paul, and she opened it, trembling with anxiety. It said:

'My dear Mama, I have not written sooner because I did not wish to cause you an unnecessary journey to Paris, seeing that I would be coming to visit you soon myself. A great misfortune has befallen me at the present time, and I am faced with a great difficulty. My wife is dying, having given birth to a little girl three days ago; and I have not a penny in the world. I don't know what to do with the baby; my concierge is feeding her with a bottle as best she can, but I fear I may lose the child. Could you not look after her? I really do not know what to do, and I have no money to pay a wet-nurse. Reply by return.

Your loving son, Paul'

Jeanne collapsed onto a chair, hardly able to summon Rosalie. When the maid arrived, they read the letter again together, and then they just sat in silence, opposite each other, for a long time.

Finally Rosalie spoke:

'I'll go and fetch the little girl myself, Madame. We just can't leave her there like that.'

Jeanne replied:

'Go, my dear.'

After a further period of silence, the maid continued:

'Put your hat on, Madame, and we'll go to Goderville and see the notary. If that woman's going to die, Monsieur Paul's got to marry her, for the little one's sake, later on.'

And without a word Jeanne put her hat on. A great and un-avowable joy filled her heart, a perfidious joy that she sought to conceal at all cost, joy of that abominable kind which makes a person blush and yet which is fervently savoured in the inner-most secrecy of the soul: her son's mistress was going to die.

The notary gave the maid detailed instructions which she asked him to repeat several times. Then, when she was confident that she would know precisely what to do, she declared:

'Have no fear. I shall see to the matter now.'

She departed for Paris that night.

Jeanne spent two days in such a state of perturbation that she was incapable of any serious reflection. On the third morning she received a brief message from Rosalie announcing her return by the evening train. Nothing else.

Towards three o'clock she asked a neighbour to harness his trap and drive her to the station at Beuzeville to wait for her maid.

She stood on the platform, with her eyes fixed on the straight line of the rails stretching away into the distance and merging on the far, far horizon. From time to time she looked at the clock.— Ten minutes to go.—Five minutes to go.—Two minutes.—Now it's time.—Nothing appeared on the distant track. All at once she saw a white blotch, a trail of steam, and then, beneath it, a black dot getting bigger and bigger and racing towards them. Eventu-ally the great locomotive slowed down and began to thunder past Jeanne, who was eagerly scanning the carriage doors. Several opened, and people got out: workmen in smocks, farmers' wives with baskets, tradesmen in soft felt hats. At last she caught sight of Rosalie, carrying what looked like a bundle of clothing in her arms.

She wanted to walk towards her, but her legs had turned to water and she was afraid she might fall. The maid saw her, approached with her usual calm air, and said:

'Good evening, Madame. Here I am, I'm back. But it's not been easy, I can tell you.'

'Well?' Jeanne stammered.

'Well, she died last night,' replied Rosalie. 'They did get married. Here's the little one.'

And she held out the child, which was invisible wrapped in all its blankets.

Jeanne took her automatically, and they left the station and climbed into the trap.

Rosalie continued:

'Monsieur Paul will be coming as soon as the funeral's over. Tomorrow at the same time, I expect.'

Jeanne murmured 'Paul...', but did not finish.

The sun was sinking towards the horizon, pouring brilliant light down onto the greening plains blotched with golden rape and blood-red poppy. An infinite peace lay upon the tranquil earth and the seed that lay germinating within. Meanwhile the trap sped along, its driver busy clicking his tongue to urge his horse forward.

Jeanne was looking straight ahead of her into the distance, where the arcing flights of swallows criss-crossed the sky like rocket trails. And suddenly, through her skirts, a feeling of soft, gentle warmth, the warmth of life, touched her legs and entered her flesh; it was the warmth of the little creature asleep on her lap.

An enormous wave of emotion swept over her. Quickly she uncovered the face of this child that she had not yet seen: her son's daughter. And as the tiny creature, disturbed by the bright light, opened her blue eyes and began to move her lips, Jeanne started to embrace it wildly, lifting it up in her arms and showering it with kisses.

But Rosalie, the happy curmudgeon, stopped her:

'Steady, steady, Madame Jeanne, that's enough. You'll make
her cry.'

Then she added, no doubt in response to her own thoughts:
'You see, life's never as good or as bad as we think.'

EXPLANATORY NOTES

2 *in memory of a departed friend*: *A Life* is dedicated to Mme Léonie
Brainne, née Rivoire. Daughter of a Rouen newspaper editor and widow
of the journalist Charles Brainne (d. 1864), she was a close friend of the
novelist Gustave Flaubert, who 'departed' on 8 May 1880. (See Introduction, pp. ix–xii.) Mme Brainne had sought to launch Maupassant in
Parisian society, and her son Henry was a regular companion of his. She
died not long after publication of *A Life*.

3 *as an enthusiastic disciple of Jean-Jacques Rousseau*: Jean-Jacques Rousseau
(1712–78), one of the principal thinkers of the French Enlightenment,
argued for the natural goodness of human beings and held 'civilization'
responsible for moral corruption. His Deist beliefs were founded on the
belief that God's hand is manifest in nature.

4 *what had happened in '93*: a reference to the execution of Louis XVI on 21
January 1793.

She resembled a portrait by Veronese: Veronese (1528–88) was a painter of
the Venetian school, and his portraits and paintings of religious subjects
are noted for their richness of colour and harmony of composition.

5 *on the cliffs near Yport*: Yport is a small fishing village on the coast of
Normandy between Étretat and Fécamp.

as the berline drew up at the door: the berline (or berlin) is a four-wheeled
covered carriage, with a seat behind protected by a hood.

6 *a Norman girl from the Pays de Caux*: the Pays de Caux is that region of
Normandy north of Rouen and the river Seine which consists of chalky
plateaus ending in steep cliffs by the English Channel and interspersed
with valleys leading down to the sea.

for her mother had suckled Jeanne: it was customary for the babies of the
well-to-do to be breast-fed not by their mothers but by 'wet-nurses'
employed for the purpose.

8 *that's all that's left of my farm at Életot*: Életot is a small village some four
miles north-east of Fécamp.

She counted out six thousand four hundred francs: assuming that
Maupassant has in mind the monetary values of 1819 and not 1883, one
can multiply the franc in the period 1819–48 by three to obtain the very
approximate current value in pounds sterling. I am indebted for this
calculation to Graham Robb, *Balzac* (Picador, 1994), p. 430.

10 *and depicted scenes from the fables of La Fontaine*: Jean de La Fontaine
(1621–95) is celebrated for his *Fables*, written in verse. In his fable about
the Fox and the Stork, the fox invites the stork to dinner but serves a

broth which only he is able to lap up. The stork gains her revenge by inviting the fox to dinner and serving delicious meat in a vase with a narrow opening, from which only she is able to eat.

11 *the sorry tale of Pyramus and Thisbe*: Maupassant has in mind Ovid's version of this Classical myth (*Metamorphoses*, iv). Pyramus and Thisbe, two young Babylonian lovers who are forbidden by their parents to marry, arrange a tryst by a stream where a mulberry tree grows. On arriving first, Thisbe encounters a lioness: she flees to safety but drops a scarf, which the lioness takes in her mouth that is bloody from devouring prey. When Pyramus arrives he finds the scarf smeared with blood, presumes that Thisbe has been killed by a wild animal, and runs himself through with his sword. Thisbe returns to find her lover dead and kills herself with his sword. The fruit of the mulberry, hitherto white, turns red on account of the spilled blood.

17 *the hamlet of Étouvent in which Les Peuples was located*: both the hamlet and the name of the house are imaginary.

22 *she had read 'Corinne'*: *Corinne* (1807), by Mme de Staël (1766–1817), tells the story of Lord Osward Nelvil, a reserved and melancholy Englishman, who visits Italy and meets Corinne, a beautiful poetess, in Rome. They fall in love, but his father's dying wish, other family considerations, and his English suspicion of Corinne's flamboyant artistic temperament conspire, after many pages, to make him marry not her but Corinne's half-sister Lucile Edgermond. Corinne dies of grief.

all those langorous romances about swallows and captive maidens: these clichés of romance literature were also commonplace in the English poetry of the Victorian era, for example in *The Princess* by Alfred, Lord Tennyson (1809–92) and *Itylus* by Algernon Swinburne (1837–1909).

some bawdy songs by Béranger: Pierre-Jean (de) Béranger (1780–1857) was a popular versifier and songwriter of great renown, considerable facility, and a certain gift for Gallic ribaldry. In Maupassant's story *La Maison Tellier* Rosa sings Béranger's song entitled 'Ma Grand-Mère', with the refrain 'Combien je regrette | Mon bras si dodu, | Ma jambe bien faite, | Et le temps perdu!' ('How much I miss | My arm so plump, | My well-turned ankle, | And the time I've wasted!'). One verse elegantly recalls how Grandmama discovered the soporific benefits of onanism at the age of 15.

the novels by Walter Scott: Sir Walter Scott (1771–1832) had written many famous romances in verse—for example, *The Lay of the Last Ministrel* (1805) and *The Lady of the Lake* (1810)—before turning to the novel with *Waverley* (1814), the first of over twenty historical romances which were immediately and immensely popular in both Britain and France (and elsewhere in Europe) during the nineteenth century. *The Lady of the Lake* was first published in a French translation in 1820, *Ivanhoe* in 1821.

23 *in the days of the Enlightenment thinkers*: not only Rousseau (see above,

note to p. 3) but also thinkers such as Voltaire (1694–1778), Denis Diderot (1713–84), and Jean D'Alembert (1717–83), all of them either Deist or atheist, and strongly anticlerical.

30 *the small Porte at Étretat*: there are two *Portes* or 'gateways' at Étretat, archways hollowed out of the chalk cliffs: the smaller is the Porte d'Amont (literally the Upstream Gateway), to the east; the larger is the Porte d'Aval (the Downstream Gateway), to the west.

37 *my dear companion before God*: in the French text the Vicomte addresses Jeanne as 'ma commère', which can mean either conjugal partner or godmother. Maupassant uses the ambiguity to heighten expectation in the reader that Jeanne may be about to be married off without her consent.

38 *the serpent-player*: the 'serpent' was 'a bass wind instrument of deep tone, about 8 feet long, made of wood covered with leather and formed with three U-shaped turns' (*OED*).

51 *The Marriage at Cannes*: in the French the priest refers to 'les noces de Ganache', when he means to say not 'the Marriage in Cana' (John 2) but 'les noces de Gamache', a reference to Cervantes's *Don Quixote* (Part II, chs. 21–2) and a proverbial expression for sumptuous wedding celebrations. 'Ganache', rather than 'Gamache', means 'dolt'. The joke, therefore, is on both the mayor and the Abbé Picot.

57 *that he now said 'tu' to her*: having consummated their marriage, Julien now addresses his wife in the more intimate 'tu' form. When he subsequently suggests that in front of Jeanne's parents they continue to address each by the more formal 'vous' until after their honeymoon, it is clear that he does not want them to know how rapidly he has achieved such intimacy.

61 *the great man, away over there on Saint Helena*: the Emperor Napoleon (1769–1821), a native of Corsica, was imprisoned on the island of Saint Helena in the Atlantic after the Battle of Waterloo (1815) and died in this British colony six years later

66 *along the edge of the gulf of Sagone*: Sagone is a port some twenty-five miles north of Ajaccio.

Towards evening they passed through Cargèse: Cargèse was founded in 1676 by Greek refugees from the southern Peloponnese, who were fleeing the Ottomans and had sought asylum in Corsica, which was then ruled by Genoa. The settlement was burned to the ground by native Corsicans in 1731 but rebuilt by the French, the island's new rulers.

90 *on the upper part of the beach*: in French 'le perret', which denotes the upper part of the beach covered in sand or large stones ('galets') rather than the shingle nearer the water's edge.

their bottle of trois-six: a bottle of spirits, probably so-called because the alcohol was 36 per cent proof

131 *a phaeton requiring only one horse*: a phaeton is a light four-wheeled car-
     riage with seats for two persons.

132 *She looked exactly like the Lady of the Lake*: see above, note to p. 22.

143 *it's like something out of La Fontaine*: La Fontaine (see above, note to
     p. 10), is noted not only for his *Fables* but also for the *Contes et nouvelles en
     ver*, collections of light verse tales, of which many are licentious.

145 *she spent whole days reading 'Corinne' or Lamartine's 'Méditations'*: for
     Corinne, see above, note to p. 22. Alphonse de Lamartine (1790–1869)
     published his *Méditations poétiques* in 1820. His first collection of lyric
     verse, it proved an instant success and is generally considered to mark the
     beginning of the Romantic period in French literature. The poems are
     characterized by a gentle, but deeply personal, elegiac tone. Among sev-
     eral anthology pieces 'L'Isolement' ('Isolation') includes the famous line
     'Un seul être vous manque, et tout est dépeuplé' (freely translated, 'You
     have only to miss one single person for the whole world to seem empty of
     people'); while 'Le Lac' ('The Lake') reflects on the transience of human
     experience and contains the often-quoted line: 'O temps, suspends ton
     vol!' ('O time, arrest your flight').

149 *Dominus vobiscum*: 'God be with you.'

183 *The nickname 'Pullie' stuck*: in French the nickname is 'Poulet' (literally,
     chicken). The English 'pullet' will not suffice as a translation (being
     somewhat removed from a plausible diminutive of 'Paul'), but 'Pullie' has
     the disadvantage of being marginally less ridiculous than 'Poulet'.

185 *the Latin phrase—'Sicut leo rugiens circuit quaerens quem devoret'*: '[Be
     sober, be vigilant; because your adversary the devil,] as a roaring lion,
     walketh about, seeking whom he may devour' (1 Peter 5: 8). The phrase
     was well-known less as a warning against the devil than as a paradigm of
     Latin grammar.

208 *in the hamlet of Batteville*: this place-name is imaginary.

210 *the fox and the stork, the fox and the crow, the cicada and the ant, and the
     melancholy heron*: for the first of these fables by La Fontaine, see above,
     note to p. 10. In the well-known tale of *Le Corbeau et le renard* (The Crow
     and the Fox), the fox flatters the crow into singing and thus dropping the
     piece of cheese which it had been holding in its beak. In *La Cigale et la
     fourmi* (The Cicada and the Ant) the cicada, having been singing all
     summer, has no provisions laid up for winter. But when she asks her
     neighbour the ant to make her a loan, the ant has no sympathy and tells
     her to dance instead. In *Le Héron* the bird refuses to eat the easy prey
     which presents itself in the river because it constantly wishes for some-
     thing yet more succulent, only to find, when at last it is truly hungry, that
     the only available food is a slug.

221 *had been operating between Paris and Le Havre*: the line from Paris to
Rouen opened in 1842 and from Paris to Le Havre in 1847. The line and
its two termini provide the setting for *La Bête humaine* (1890), Zola's
novel about the railways.

226 *She recognized the Palais-Royal*: built for Cardinal Richelieu in 1629, the
Palais-Royal later served as a royal residence. Situated just off the rue de
Rivoli and not far from the Louvre, it is noted for its formal garden and
elegant arcades.

The Oxford World's Classics Website

www.worldsclassics.co.uk

- Browse the full range of Oxford World's Classics online

- Sign up for our monthly e-alert to receive information on new titles

- Read extracts from the Introductions

- Listen to our editors and translators talk about the world's greatest literature with our Oxford World's Classics audio guides

- Join the conversation, follow us on Twitter at OWC_Oxford

- Teachers and lecturers can order inspection copies quickly and simply via our website

www.worldsclassics.co.uk

American Literature

British and Irish Literature

Children's Literature

Classics and Ancient Literature

Colonial Literature

Eastern Literature

European Literature

Gothic Literature

History

Medieval Literature

Oxford English Drama

Poetry

Philosophy

Politics

Religion

The Oxford Shakespeare

A complete list of Oxford World's Classics, including Authors in Context, Oxford English Drama, and the Oxford Shakespeare, is available in the UK from the Marketing Services Department, Oxford University Press, Great Clarendon Street, Oxford OX2 6DP, or visit the website at www.oup.com/uk/worldsclassics.

In the USA, visit www.oup.com/us/owc for a complete title list.

Oxford World's Classics are available from all good bookshops. In case of difficulty, customers in the UK should contact Oxford University Press Bookshop, 116 High Street, Oxford OX1 4BR.